A
Buddha
From
Byron

by

Sunion C. Matheson

About the author

Sunion Matheson settled in Byron Bay in the 1980s and raised his family there. For over a decade prior to that, he travelled alone all over Australia, bush and city, working in a wide variety of jobs, exploring new experiences, and encountering a breadth of people with a diverse catalogue of confusion and pain. He was always an ardent supporter of anyone seeking freedom and the courage to be themselves, and he expressed that in the lyrics of his music, in the plays he's written, and in this novel.

A Buddha From Byron draws together a tangle of main characters, each a damaged victim of circumstance and the discourtesies of others. Their interaction creates unexpected choices for each of them. Unexpected choices, with unexpected consequences. Some good, some bad.

What a Buddhist would call karma.

If you don't know what you want,
how would you know if you got it?

Contents

Chapter 1.   Chris

Last drop of the day, a store in Newtown, block after next. Chris looked upwards through the dusty windscreen of his small delivery truck. A hot sun up there was urging a detour to Bondi after this. He could swim in his work shorts; they needed a wash.

He found Triple J on the truck's radio and cranked it up because the weekend starts on a Friday arvo, so long as there's a decent soundtrack. Back to the windscreen, he saw the traffic up ahead had suddenly stopped. Some idiot was trying to reverse a trailer into a lane off the busy clearway.

Chris hit the brakes, but nothing happened. He didn't slow down. He pumped them again, and again. Nothing! He could see, if he didn't do something fast, he was going to slam into the back of the car in front.

He had only two seconds, and he used the first one to dismiss the crowded footpath to his left. He snatched his eyes to the right, across an oncoming bus. No one on that footpath on that side of the road, and there was a vacant demolition site with a pile of old bricks and roofing iron that might just slow his truck down.

It was just a chance. And he grabbed it.

He plunged the accelerator to the floor and swerved violently across the prow of the bus. With a jolting thud, his truck bounced over the kerb and onto the rubble-strewn lot, smashing straight through the pile of bricks and rusting iron. A cloud of demolition dust exploded across his windshield, and his engine stalled to a halt just two metres before he would have slammed into the solid brick wall at the back of the site.

He let out a grunt of relief and flopped back into his sheepskin seat cover. The self-absorbed prattle of the radio DJ, oblivious to the drama that had just happened, was irritatingly loud. Chris snapped it off.

Hero! he began his mental accolades in the quiet. *Lightning reflexes.*

'You lunatic!' a voice raged, through the settling dust cloud.

Chris looked out through his open side-window and saw a furious man with a blanched face running towards him from the footpath.

'Settle down, mate,' he shouted back, unclicking his seatbelt.

'You ran straight into it!' the man screamed.

Chris looked back at the crumpled iron behind his truck.

'Bloody oath, I did,' he chirped with a cheeky pride. 'Had to.'

'They were in there!' the man shrieked, as he ran towards the flattened stack.

'What was?' Chris said, casually opening the door and stepping down from his truck.

'It's their cubby. Oh, God, you ran right over them!'

The distance from hero to villain can sometimes be measured in fate. The exact same actions would have earned Chris such enthusiastic praise if there hadn't been three children playing in that pile of tin.

But there were three children playing in that pile of tin.

The charge sheet was read out to the hollow courtroom. Chris only caught odd phrases. "Recklessly driving... defective braking system... inappropriate speed... blah, blah, blah". He wasn't listening. He'd already condemned himself, these proceedings were a mere formality. He sat silent, numbed by a massive blend of guilt, regret, and sorrow. It wasn't what he'd done that he was ashamed of, it was the consequence of doing it, and the barrage of courtroom jargon so far made no mention of that. The next three words, however, did, and they slammed into him like an out of control truck.

"Criminally negligent manslaughter".

He glanced at his parents. They looked at the floor.

The judge took into consideration that Chris was only twenty-six, and had no previous convictions.

'I further accept that you were attempting to avoid a collision,' he said, 'but your defence that you were unaware there were children in

4

the vacant lot is invalid. Your deliberate and dangerous course of action resulted in the tragic loss of three young lives, and that can not be taken lightly.'

He was ready to make his determination, and he turned to the clerk of courts. 'Three thousand dollars,' he declared, 'and an eighteen-month custodial sentence with a set minimum period of three months.' He looked at Chris. 'The balance being subject to the usual condition that the defendant does not re-offend during the term of the parole.'

Chris had nothing to say.

'Driver's licence suspended for the full eighteen months,' the judge added.

Suspended. Guilt itself is suspended by a single Damoclean hair, and it can hang over a conscience for far longer than eighteen months.

His mother visited him twice the first week he was in jail, and then only three more times during his term. His girlfriend, Josie, only visited him once. His father never came at all, but Chris sent word to ask him to sell his car for him and use the money to pay the fine. Which he did.

Three months in prison is ninety days. Ninety days of not having to think about dodging left or right to avoid a line of inmates shuffling along the corridor. No piles of rubble to decide whether or not to drive into. Everything was directed by the guards, by the system. It was their responsibility; Chris was merely a passenger now.

But ninety days is also ninety nights. Ninety nights of staring at the corridor lightbulb glowing in through the small gap high up in his cell wall. He couldn't escape from what happened in Newtown. He re-ran that afternoon, and each time he steered his truck around the pile of roofing iron. Each time, the kids poked their heads out and giggled at the silly man in the truck. Each time.

And then he remembered that's not how it happened.

He was sitting eating his dinner in the food hall one day in his second week when a fellow prisoner walked over with his own meal tray and sat beside him. Chris didn't even notice he was there.

'Sausages,' the prisoner said. 'Two big, fat turds on a plate.'

5

Chris didn't respond.

'You're a freshie,' the prisoner went on. 'What you in for?'

The last thing Chris wanted was to relive his accident. He just shrugged and continued to eat.

'Hey, gronk,' the prisoner said, 'I asked you a fucking question.'

Chris paused eating. He sat very still before he slowly raised his face, numb with emptiness, and looked dispassionately, straight into his inquisitor's eyes.

And right through them.

'Yeah, all right, don't go the spinner on me,' the prisoner said nervously, mistaking melancholy for malevolence. 'We all done something, haven't we? That's why we're here. No offence.'

Without reply, Chris went back to chewing his food. His demeanour was interpreted by everyone as the confident cruelty of a hard man, which was just as well. Some prisoners need a victim to repay what they felt the world was doing to them. Many of them have kids back on the outside so they particularly seek out anyone who's been charged with hurting children, and they mete out a stern moral 'justice' on them.

Perhaps years of surfing and loading heavy boxes into the work truck had given Chris a body that looked more dangerous than he actually was. Perhaps his constant vacant gaze was taken to mean he was capable of anything since he seemed to register nothing. Whatever it was, he survived the three months without incident from anyone, and he used the time as though he'd been cloistered in a monastery.

And found peace.

When he got out, he realised that staying with his parents was unthinkable. For him as much as for them.

'How are you going to get a job if you can't drive for another year or more?' his father prodded. 'You've got less than four grand left from your car. That won't last long. You're going to have to buckle down now and see what the real world's about.'

His father thought Chris could have been so much more, that he was a disappointment who had settled for an easy life, that he didn't go to uni or find himself a career and now he'd even lost the one crummy job he did have.

Chris wasn't allowed to leave the state for the remainder of his parole but he could move home, so long as he informed the police of his new address.

Perhaps it was running away, or turning the page, but he needed to start again. Somewhere completely different. Somewhere no one knew anything about what had happened. And somewhere he could forget.

Byron Bay!

'Wanna come?' he asked Josie.

'Maybe next year,' she offered, neither expecting nor wanting to follow up on that. 'I've just been made section manager at work.'

He said he had to go now. That he couldn't wait.

And he went.

The bus pulled out of the bus station into the early morning, and the sharp sunlight squinting between the tall office blocks stabbed Chris's eyes. He pulled his beanie down over his forehead, he didn't want to see the city streets anyway. They were nothing to do with a beginning, they were merely the ruins of an ending.

Fumbling the iPod from his jacket pocket, he pushed the buds into his ears, selected the soundtrack for his escape, and cranked up the volume. The music drowned both the motor and the thoughts, and he drifted into dazing.

A couple of hours or so later he raised his beanie and sat up. He stared out of the bus window and watched the roadside unravelling like wool from a snagged jumper. It was just something to look at like there was something to look at.

A passenger in the row behind him pulled at his headrest as they got up to move seats and brought Chris's attention back inside the bus. A child coughed from somewhere up in the front section. *Was it a cough? Could be chucking.*

Chris looked forwards down the aisle and out through the windscreen as the North oozed towards him. He was now the furthest he'd ever been from Sydney, but he was still hours away from Byron.

Should've checked for a cheap flight, he thought. Though maybe it was better that he established the distance properly by road; flying cheats the scale.

There were hills to crawl up, where the driver shuffled the gears with a jerk. There were small towns to dissect and larger ones to bypass. A row of trees ended abruptly and fields of sugarcane monotonised the landscape.

The bus thrummed on until late in the afternoon when it pulled into a servo and the disrupted passengers were invited to use the toilets there, or to buy some hot brown liquid in a thin plastic cup and grab one of the pre-made sandwiches suffocating in cling film.

That done, twenty minutes later, there was the straggling back on-board and the erratic resettling into the seats. The driver hissed the door closed and walked up the aisle, counting heads before the bus rolled out of the parking area and back into the tedium of journeying once more. Chris watched the window again till the sun melted into the horizon, and then he pulled his beanie back over his eyes.

It was fully dark when the bus jerked to a stop in Byron's main street. A line of accommodation touts was standing at the rear of the footpath, mostly there to rendezvous with the pre-booked, but two of them were holding inviting pictures of the places they represented. Chris had heard that Byron accommodation was tricky to get in summer, but he'd ignored that. He didn't necessarily believe the information was wrong, it was just he couldn't allow himself any doubt that this was where he had to go.

His only bag was the one he had stashed under his seat onboard the bus, so there was no need for him to have to loiter with the other passengers waiting for the driver to open the side luggage compartments. He approached the tout closest to him before anyone else was ready to, and he ended up scoring the last available bunk at the Arts Factory Backpackers, just a short walk from the town centre.

He threw his bag onto his given bed and went to check out the backpackers' Buddha Bar. It was a large dim room with several statues of Buddha set into the walls and behind the bar. He bought a beer and sat in one of the little booths.

Suddenly, Sydney seemed a long way away. A long time ago.

Despite it being the busy season, with so many people looking for a summer job, he found work the first day he looked. It was a part-time job, collecting empty glasses from the tables at the Beach Hotel. The same week, he scored a traineeship at the Dive Centre, where he helped kit-up the tourists and scrub the boats in return for free dives and a discounted dive licence. Within a month, he had his own room in a share house with Liam, another glassie at the hotel, and called it "home".

One Sunday morning, before his afternoon shift at the hotel, he checked out the Byron Markets. It was a pageant of peddlers flogging bric-a-brac, colourful costumes, and a varied menu of food. He bought a spinach and ricotta crepe and a sugarcane juice, and sat on the grass for a few minutes, listening to some guy with an accordion singing 'Where do you go to, my lovely?'

Chris felt okay in Byron. It seemed something had changed for him ever since he'd found a place to stay at the Buddha Backpackers. Everything was suddenly good. It had all just gone so smoothly.

He leaned back, spread his hands across the grass, squinted his eyes closed, and felt the warm sun painting a smile on his face. Smile. He hadn't done that for months. Maybe even years.

His fingers ran over something intriguing. He turned his head, parted the grass and saw a small silver Buddha pendant. Abandoned, dropped, forgotten. Waiting for him to find. A Buddha like the statues where his new life began. This tiny token symbolised all that was right for him.

It was his good luck charm.

Chapter 2.   Gary

'Gary Baker is a dangerous bastard,' Andy MacManus said. 'I want you all to know he didn't come here to be nice to us. He's got a bloody great axe in that briefcase, and I wouldn't be surprised if he came here to use it on someone, so be very careful what you say. Do I make myself clear?'

'You're the boss, Andy-Man. Bring him in.'

'Right, here we go then.........' Andy opened the door. 'G'day, Gary,' he said, with as much charm as he could muster. 'Thank you for waiting. Please come in.'

Gary stood up, straightened his suit, and grabbed his famous briefcase. He was mid-forties, tall, pale, almost bald. His smile was nothing more than an acknowledgement he'd been spoken to, and it carried no warmth at all. He came into the office, went straight to the desk and portentously set his briefcase on it.

'So, team,' Andy said, 'this is our State Manager, Gary Baker. Driven up from Sydney, specially. Gary, let me introduce you to Peter Burrows, my sales team leader. You know Maurice Harvey, accounts. And this is Kate Harrison, our newest addition to marketing management.'

'Good morning, everyone,' Gary said. He moved his briefcase over a little and sat on the desk, looking around at each of them in turn. His smile dropped to serious when his eyes returned to Andy. 'Okay then, let's get straight to it, Andrew. What on earth is going on?'

'Well,' Andy said, with a nervous chuckle, 'not much, actually. You know how it is.'

'No,' said Gary, 'I don't. That's why I asked my regional manager. Actually.'

'It's been a slow couple of months, Gary, what with the elections coming up and stuff.'

'The elections?' Gary queried. 'The elections are nationwide, Andrew, and yet it's only slow up here in Newcastle, now why is that?' He turned to face the startled salesman on Andy's left. 'Peter, wasn't it? What happened to Ralphie Jackson?'

Andy interrupted, 'We lost Ralph to Linton Bailey.'

'I replaced him as team leader after he left,' said Peter. 'I was just a regular salesman last time you were here. We didn't meet.'

'No, we didn't,' said Gary. 'I would have remembered if we had. First rule in selling, isn't it?' He paused till he got a nod from Peter. 'So: this slowdown thing?'

'No, it's like Andy said,' Peter stumbled. 'It's a… it's a slow time. Not sure what we could have done better.'

'Mmm,' was all Gary said to the sales leader, but he reminded himself that selling and leading are two quite different skills.

He turned to the accountant, who was demonstrating how he felt he shouldn't even be there by cleaning his spectacles.

'I just process the numbers, Gary, you know that. I count what comes in and what it cost to get it, that's all. I don't really have any say in … you know.'

'Fair enough,' Gary nodded. He turned to the woman sitting slightly apart from the others.

She was in her mid-thirties, composed, competent even. She was an exercised slim. Beneath her black business jacket was a crisp white shirt, three buttons open, which he avoided by concentrating his eyes on hers.

'Another new face,' he said. 'What do you think over there in marketing, Kate?'

'What do I think?' she asked. She held his attention by brushing an imagined renegade lock of styled blonde hair from her forehead. 'Oh, I don't think you'd want to know what I think.'

'Then you'd be wrong,' Gary said. 'I do want to know. That's why I asked.'

'Well,' she said, testing his response, 'I think we've been resting on the top five lines that we sell instead of breaking new ground with a wider range of product, price, and quality.'

'Resting? Go on,' said Gary.

She glanced around the room at the faces staring at her, and then looked straight at Gary once again. 'The stores are only one window to our merchandise, aren't they? And they certainly aren't the main one. It's no secret that the real potential, both nationally and even locally, is online. The operative costs of the bricks and mortar stores should really be incorporated into the advertising budget, with just a minimum of staff since they're virtually showrooms.' She paused while the mutter of disagreement settled down. 'Sure, they provide the touchy-feely thing, but their real value to this company is that they present an established proof that it exists. Customers are more likely to trust a business they know they could find physically, and that gives us a whopping edge over our online-only competitors.'

Gary looked at her in silence for a moment. He wasn't waiting for her to say more, he just wanted her to recognise he was taking in what she had said.

'And this "minimum of staff" thing,' he said. 'Just how would you accomplish that?'

'You have a reputation for answering that yourself, Gary,' she said. 'But I imagine that you'd start by axing the people who think elections are an excuse for under-performing, and then you'd go on to appoint a new regional manager who sees that.' She owned the silence before adding, 'Wouldn't you?'

Gary was waiting in the hotel lobby when Kate pulled up outside at seven, as arranged. The office was no place to be discussing the details of her promotion. Besides, he hated eating alone.

Her small black BMW gleamed with newness. He opened the passenger door, bent down and greeted her. She was wearing a white dress and long, dangling earrings. She looked quite different from the office exec he'd met earlier. Softer. Warmer. And, certainly, more beautiful.

'Nice aftershave,' she said, as soon as he sat in her car. 'I don't recognise it, but I can tell it's expensive by the way it whispers.'

'And what does it say?' he challenged, as he closed the door and fussed the seatbelt over his shoulder.

'What did you think it would say, when you bought it?'

'I didn't buy it. It was a gift.'

She turned away from him to look for cars, and drove off. He clicked his seatbelt up as she checked her rear-view mirror to adjust to the flow of traffic.

'Your wife?'

'My wife?'

'Gave you the aftershave?' She was making a left turn and conversation.

'I'm not married,' he declared.

'I should've known,' she said with a playful derision. 'It's too sexy a fragrance for a wife to give.'

'Actually,' he confessed, 'it was part of a boxed set I got last year. From the company.'

'From the company? Top sales or something like that?'

'Something like that,' he said.

'Well done.' She changed lanes and sped up. 'I got a holiday in Fiji,' she matched. 'Last year. From the place I was working then.'

The restaurant wasn't busy, so a table was easy to find. Midweek, provincial town. She had obviously selected the best restaurant there was. The ambience was a little formal, and there was not enough background noise to create adequate privacy, but that failed to daunt either of them. They were sales people.

'Shall we agree to turn our mobiles off during dinner?' he said.

'Are you expecting a call?' Kate asked.

'I'm not expecting anything,' he said, suggestively, and switched his phone off. 'Are you?'

'Not a phone call,' she joked, and turned hers off too.

The wait-staff were attentive. The menu was varied. The wine list was sufficient. Filtered water was brought and poured. The candle was lit. The night's specials were explained. Orders were taken, and then the diners were left alone.

'They don't usually give me a candle, Gary. They must think it's your birthday.'

'That was last week. March the fifteenth.'

'March the fifteenth?' she said. 'The Ides of March.'

'Ah yes,' he said, 'those famous Ides.'

13

'Shakespeare said to beware the Ides of March,' she added, with a playful portent.

'Shakespeare also said "Odds bodkin"!'

She saluted his repartee with her water. 'Hail, Caesar,' she mocked.

The waiter brought their red wine and opened the bottle. He poured a taste for Gary.

'You selected it, Kate,' Gary said, pushing the glass across to her.

She smiled to the waiter and gave a tiny shake of the head to forgo the tasting, and he poured them each a drink. He stood the bottle in the centre of the table, and left.

Kate raised her wineglass. 'So then, birthday boy, you must be, what, thirty-six, thirty-eight?'

'Thank you very much!' he said, chinking his glass against hers. 'Forty-five.' He sipped the wine, and nodded. 'Decent drop,' he said, examining the label, 'for such a young wine.'

'Age doesn't matter,' she said. 'That's why I chose a Grenache. It's ready now.'

'Mmm,' he agreed, still tasting the flavours.

'You're a nice-looking guy,' she said, putting her glass down and looking straight at him. 'You've got a good career, you seem pleasant enough.'

'Okay,' he said. 'Where's this going?'

'How come you aren't married?'

'Oh, there.' His gaze fell into his glass like it was a cocktail of sham pain and sudden discomfort.

'So, what's the story?' she asked, even though she could guess. Salesmen and their salaries. No incentive to slow down. Just the whirligig world of pitches and presentations. Of spiels and scoring. Paddling in the emotional shallows, safe from the depths where commitment lurked like a Great White.

'You get straight to it, don't you?' he said.

'You have a problem with that?'

'No. No problem. It's just seems, I don't know...'

'Too fast for you?' she pushed.

14

'No, not too fast. But surprising. I always thought that women like to take their time,' he said. 'Lord knows, they've kept me waiting plenty of times.'

'Yeah, I must admit we do like a little foreplay. But even then, only sometimes.'

'Okay. Good to know.' He laughed, covering the jolt her comment gave him. 'But I was referring to the time women take to get dressed.'

'Either way, Gary, it's just how long it takes a girl to get ready.' She raised one eyebrow a fraction, and smiled.

The lift floor-indicator arrow rose like a phallus when Gary and Kate were whisked upstairs.

They didn't say a word to each other in the lift. Or along the corridor. Or when they tangoed into his room. Or onto his bed. Then there was a grasping, grunting, desperate urgency.

'Hoo-wee,' he panted, when they fell apart. 'Well, you certainly didn't need time to get ready for that. You must have been ready the minute we walked in the hotel!'

'I was ready the second you walked in the office, Mr Baker. I'm a pushover for a man who's at the top of his game.'

Gary didn't offer her the regional manager position in Newcastle that she'd hinted she deserved. Instead, he told her Head Office was looking for a marketing manager down in Sydney. Same building he worked in. Better money, better prospects. He said he'd be happy to recommend her, if she wanted to apply. She applied, was successful, and by the end of the month she had rented an apartment down there.

Andrew MacManus chose to resign as regional manager. He was enough of a salesman to pre-empt his being asked to anyway. Note was made of Kate's other suggestions. She saw little of Gary at work, but they made up for that at night. Within a month they spent less evenings going out to clubs, restaurants and shows, but were more comfortable at one of their homes. Watching a movie together. Sharing a good red and a tale from each other's life path.

His work involved overseeing the various sales teams in the whole state, which he mostly did by phone, and email memos. His physical presence was only required at the provincial centres when things went very wrong there. He still dealt personally with the larger customer accounts in Sydney.

'Catching and killing my own meat' he called it.

It wasn't necessary for the company so much – there were any number of excellent sales staff on his team that could handle those clients – but it was crucial for him. He needed to keep up to date with sales techniques, any emerging customer resistances, and simply to remind himself what it was like in the field.

Kate had her own office. She quickly focused the advertising dollars to a three-month TV campaign, and expanded their exposure on the Internet. She advised against lowering the price of their best-selling lines, instead recommending they be exclusively shared with a top-quality homeware chain, which would provide them with additional exposure and advertising that they wouldn't need to fund themselves. A recommendation many in her office were reluctant to apply, but she was marketing manager, and the figures would eventually show whether she had it or not.

She obviously "had it" all right, and the healthy pay rise she was awarded reflected that.

She managed to take a week off to coincide with Gary's holiday. He told her he had planned to go skiing in New Zealand before the season finished, but said she could pick a holiday anywhere in the world.

She chose to go skiing in New Zealand.

They sat at the window of their chalet, gazing out over Lake Wakatipu and up at the white peaks surrounding them.

'It's so beautiful, Gary. It's like a painting on one of those European Christmas cards.'

'I could paint it for you,' he said, 'so you could remember it forever. I used to be quite the artist when I was a kid at school.'

'I don't need a painting to remember it. I'll never forget this,' she said, and took another sip of hot chocolate punch. 'It's a wonderful place. You're a wonderful man.'

'I want us to get married, Kate.'

'Wow! That came straight out of left field!'

'Makes sense to me,' he said. 'What do you think?'

16

'I hadn't thought of that. But I will.'

'Too fast for you?' He covered his disappointment at her not leaping at a "yes".

'Maybe,' she said.

'That's the "women taking their time" thing I was on about.'

She looked away.

'Not sure I'm ready for marriage,' she said.

'You just need some more foreplay,' he teased, taking her glass from her and placing it on the window ledge.

It was snowing outside, and a cold mountain wind was flurrying the flakes, but inside the cabin it was as warm as the tropics. He stared at her, and she knew what that look was asking. She smiled her answer, and then they were groping each other to naked on the bed. His determination thrust hard in her, and she wrapped her legs around him and urged him to go deeper, harder, faster. They morphed into a wild beast with two snarling mouths. Two mouths that both froze in a silent grimace long enough for her to whisper, 'Yes, Gary. Married.'

Chapter 3.   Amaranth

'This is where it really starts,' Amaranth said out loud. She was alone, she'd always lived alone, but a pledge that is spoken is a pledge that is binding.

She went to her bedroom window and separated the heavy curtains a little. An early Sydney morning swiped cold sunlight towards her wardrobe. She turned and faced the mirror on its door to examine the thin, shabby girl looking back at her.

'Thirty,' she said, trying it on like a new dress in a foreign sizing. She stepped closer to the mirror and fixed her reflection with a serious and determined eye. 'As of this day,' she said, solemnly, 'it changes.'

To further commit to the resolution, she sat on her bed and reached under her mattress for the notebook that she always kept wedged there.

'It's a journal,' her mother had said, when she'd given it to her exactly fourteen years ago. 'Every birthday, write a little something on its own page – life goes quick if you don't watch it. You'll finish school next, get a job, move away, then what do you want?'

'Dunno,' Amaranth had answered back then, with typical mid-teen indifference.

'Yeah. Well, you're still young. At sixteen, you don't realise how little time you've got to work that out,' her mother had said, sucking a tinge of blue self-pity from a cigarette, and exhaling it into the familiar mingle of her disillusionments. 'There's only one thing worse than not knowing what you want, Amma, and that's knowing what you want – but knowing you'll never get it.'

Amaranth had written that sentence down, there, on that very first page of her journal. They were the last words her mother had said to her on that birthday morning, as she'd headed off to school.

18

They were the last words her mother had said to her.

Ever.

When she'd come home from school that afternoon, trudging under a hot North Queensland sun, past the tall sugarcane lining both sides of their road, the first thing she'd seen under their high-set house was her mother, like a whole bunch of wrapped and ripening bananas, hanging in the shade.

Muffling her mother's cautionary epilogue, Amaranth had made a tradition of writing her own complaints, page upon page for fourteen birthdays but, until this morning, she'd never considered what a dismal catalogue it was.

Leaving school, leaving home, leaving North Queensland, and then living with her father in his house down in Brisbane were all significant thresholds that she'd crossed during the first year after her mother had died but, on her second page, she had written only two observations. The first was: *"It was your life, Mum, but you took my mother."* The second one read: *"Dad was a stranger, who became stranger."*

Her father wasn't a widower, it was sadder than that, he was a divorcee. It wasn't death that had stolen his wife; she'd chosen to leave him years before, and he'd nurtured his pain like it was one of his precious racing pigeons. Amaranth had only lasted a few months at his house. He didn't like the music she put on, didn't like the TV shows she wanted to watch, thought she left a mess everywhere. Thought she looked like her mother.

She flicked to the third page in her journal.

Ah, yes, she mused, *then there was Mal!*

To get out of her dad's place, she'd taken a room in a cheap guesthouse close to the city centre, and found a job scrubbing a café kitchen and making coffees. That's how she'd met Mal, a thirty-five-year-old project manager who'd stopped in for a late lunch. He'd asked her if she'd come out for a drink with him when she knocked off, and she'd said she couldn't because she only had her dirty work outfit. She smiled as she remembered how he'd come back later with a large paper carrier bag.

'It looks new,' she'd said, pulling the little black dress out of the bag. 'Whose is it?'

'It *is* new, and it's yours,' Mal had said. 'You're a ten, yeah? I'm good at sizing a girl up.'

At a quiet cocktail lounge around two corners, Mal had gone to the bar to get drinks as she'd gone to the Ladies to change into the dress. She remembered feeling so grown up, but so out of place in a licensed bar.

'Don't you have to be like twenty-one or something to come in here?' she'd asked Mal, when she'd joined him at a table.

'Eighteen,' he'd replied, as he'd pushed a chair out for her with his foot. 'You *are* eighteen, aren't you?'

'Almost,' she'd said.

'That's old enough to keep a secret,' she remembered him saying, as he'd slid a glass of gin and tonic across to her.

She recalled the first night he'd come to see her at the flat that he'd given her bond money for. How she'd washed and dried her hair for him that night. How he'd said how nice she smelled as he pushed her onto the bed. How angry with her he'd seemed because she'd said it hurt when he thrust himself into her. How he'd finished and rolled off her, carelessly squashing Fudge, her childhood teddy bear. How he'd looked at his watch more than he'd looked at her as he'd dressed to leave afterwards. Married men do that. They have to get home to their wives, even if their wives don't speak to them when they do.

Thresholds.

He never told her his surname, but her birthday page that year contained three she'd given him. "*Mal Treatment, Mal Ignant, Mal Odorous.*" Under those doodles, she'd written: "*I'd tell you more about him, Mum, but I haven't a clue who he is.*"

Searching for a blank page for this year's sentence, she skipped past her twenty-first birthday entry – a nothing event which, as usual, she'd celebrated by herself. This was after Married Mal and his wife had had their second baby and he'd told Amaranth, yet again, that he owed it to his children to try to be a family. She knew he would come back once the new baby drank all the energy from the mother, and she knew she would open her door and let him inside again. So, because she would never end it she'd had to put herself someplace he couldn't restart it. She'd packed Fudge into a suitcase with her clothes and her journal, and moved down to Sydney. Officially an adult, another unnoticed threshold.

She looked up from the journal and ran her eyes around her bedroom.

I've been here ten years, she thought. *Ten years!*

Her eyes stopped at the mirror once again. *Thirty!*

Her father was right, she did look like her mother. The same mousey-brown hair framing her face, skin that was pale and dry, but what most resembled her mother was the disappointment drooping from her eyes.

Mum was only thirty-four, she reminded herself.

Amaranth had no real friends, even as a child. What chance did she ever have to make friends? She'd never lived in a street until she'd moved down to Brisbane when she was sixteen. Up in Mackay, her nearest next-door neighbour had been over a fifteen-minute walk away, and they had no children her age, just two dogs that shouted that they'd bite her if she came any nearer. The Tree Gang Girls at school thought her name was too weird to let her sit with them. Even when she had a flat and was working in Brisbane, Mal didn't want her to have other girls around. Other girls might bring other boys around.

Still aiming for the waiting blank page, she continued flicking hurriedly over the next few entries: words that clung like dust onto something long abandoned. They were the early Sydney years, after she'd done a secretarial course at night school and found a job in an insurance office. Tethered to a desk by telephone lines and computer cables, she was like a fawn in a tiger trap as, one by one, the men had pounced on the chance to flirt with her. Salesmen can't help that. They flirt with women, and joke with men. It's how they hone their skills – reading responses, and pushing their personality. She'd enjoyed their facile attention, she'd almost felt pretty and popular, and she had short affairs with several of them. It suited her that they liked to move on and sell themselves to someone else because it ensured she didn't end up in a situation like the one she'd escaped back in Brisbane. It had, however, created a reputation for her, which the girls in the machine room eagerly amplified with a mixture of contempt and concern, so that it had eventually reached the boss's ears. A reputation he had then explored for himself until the whispers were loud enough so that his wife had heard them too.

Amaranth was fired.

One of the older filing clerks, who had her own agenda of retaliation against the boss, had slipped her the number of a lawyer, Ms Howard, and told Amaranth to call her as she was looking for a secretary. At the interview, just as the filing clerk had expected, she'd had to explain why she'd been fired, and Ms Howard said there was a strong case for Unfair Dismissal. Amaranth didn't want to make a fuss but Ms Howard seemed to almost insist, and so her first task, when she was hired as a secretary, was to hire her new employer to sue her previous one.

Amaranth had read the deposition that Ms Howard prepared for her to sign, and she'd thought it was written about someone else. It was factual enough, but it portrayed her as some sort of powerless victim, while she'd always thought of herself as an easy-to-get-along-with, low-maintenance kind of a person. Clearly, there was a different take between how things were and how things could be.

The case was successful and, for the first time in her life, a glimmer of glee stirred in Amaranth. It had nothing to do with the congratulatory phone call from the sympathetic filing clerk at her old workplace, or the settlement payout, it was that now she knew what it felt like to push back at the great unfairness. And win.

After feeling all her Christmases had come at once, however, came the Boxing Day of back-to-the-norm. Celebration settled into contentment, and contentment settled into comfort – the most fraudulent refuge there is.

Amaranth glanced at that twenty-fifth birthday page, one short sentence bragging: *"Hey, Mum, I'm a legal secretary!"* It was such an obvious attempt to sound mature and stable, but being a legal secretary was pretty much all she had been doing up to this thirtieth birthday. Her last four entries had basically just been desperate complaints about the security she had wedged herself into.

She took her pen and pressed its point against the blank page for this year's sentence. Letters took shape, words appeared.

"I see it now. I may not know what I want, but I know what I don't want. You chose to end it, Mum," she wrote, *"but I choose to change it, and today is the Start."*

It was a Saturday, and the calendar had organised a weekend to commemorate that she had survived for that thirty years. She slipped her journal back under her mattress for another year, straightened the doona, settled Fudge in his usual position on her pillow, and sat staring at unrecognised potentials. It was one thing to decide to make a change, but what change and how to bring it about?

Sometimes, Life answers questions like that. Perhaps Life always answers questions like that, but is only sometimes heard. Amaranth must have been listening later that day as she sat in the laundromat waiting for her washing.

A large girl blustered in with two full garbage bags of laundry. She was younger than Amaranth, but she had a hardness about her that made her seem older. She sorted her washing into three machines and loaded the coins in. Then she tacked a note on the noticeboard and sat down with a magazine she had brought with her.

There were several other people sitting around waiting. Like at doctors' surgeries, everyone pretended there was no one else there. One of the dryers ended and a tall, skinny man stuffed his cooked clothing back into a duffle bag. Amaranth's washing machine clicked and blinked an orange punctuation to confirm it was finished. She stood up and pulled her washed clothes into one of the plastic baskets that were provided.

As the skinny man left with his laundry, a young guy walked in with a load of wet towels in a big, green bin liner, and threw them straight into the vacant dryer. The only vacant dryer. The one Amaranth was going to use.

The large girl looked at Amaranth, then at the dryer.

'Oi!' she shouted across the room to the young guy. 'That's hers.' She indicated Amaranth with a flick of her thumb.

'It was empty,' justified the guy.

'It's her dryer, mate,' the large girl said.

'It's a public laundry. She don't own the dryer.'

The large girl pointed to a notice on the wall and read it aloud. 'Customers doing their washing on these premises have priority use of the dryers.' She turned to the assembled loiterers who now suddenly had a floorshow to break their monotony.

'Yes, that's right. You have to wait if you're bringing wet stuff in,' someone heckled, with the passion of a pedant.

The young guy cursed and lifted his soggy towels back out, slopping them into a basket. He plonked himself into a chair like a petulant schoolboy, and waited for another machine. Amaranth avoided eye contact with him as she threw her clothes into the now empty dryer and then sat beside the large girl.

'Thanks,' she whispered.

'What for?' No whispers from this girl.

'For getting him to give me the dryer,' Amaranth said, softly.

'He didn't give you the dryer, love. It was already yours. You make it sound like he gave you a present or something. It's not your friggin' birthday, is it?'

'Well, actually…' Amaranth started.

'Oh, don't tell me! For real? Today's your actual birthday?'

Amaranth nodded guiltily.

'And you're in here? On your birthday?'

'Long story.'

'In't they always? Anyhow, Happy Birthday.'

'Thanks.'

'So, how old are you?'

'Thirty today.' Amaranth gave a little laugh. 'Sounds old, huh?'

'Yeah, but you hide it okay. So, you've just gone through your Saturn Return.' Kirsten inspected the birthday girl as though she expected to see her going through the process right then and there.

'Saturn Return?' Amaranth queried.

'Yeah. I was only just reading about it in here.' She prodded the magazine on her lap, arousing its authority. 'When you're born the planets and stars and stuff are all like in a certain pattern in the sky, and that's your pattern: makes you who you are, dunnit? Saturn's supposed to be the one that affects how you get what you want from life, and they reckon it takes about thirty years to come back round again to be in the same position like when you was born. Saturn Return they call it. So, you get a second chance to get what you want.'

24

'That's all very well,' Amaranth sighed, 'but I don't really know what I want.'

'Crikey, you better get on to it then, quick smart. If you don't know what you want, how will you know you got it if you get it?' Kirsten said, with a chuckle of condemnation that touched off a smoker's hack. 'Nah,' she wheezed, mid-cough, 'Saturn Return means you got some big changes coming this year, girl.'

'I hope so,' said Amaranth. 'I really want this year to be different.' She let her eyes fall to the floor like she was examining a stack of potentials.

Kirsten fossicked in a bag for some tissues. 'So, what's your name then?' she asked, wiping her mouth.

'Amma,' Amaranth said, as clearly but as quietly as she could.

'Amma? With an A? That's a new one,' was the best Kirsten could offer. 'I'm Kirsten.' She swept her eyes around the laundromat, looking for some other drama to entertain her. 'Boring places in't they?' she said, after ten seconds of silence was too much to bear.

'Yeah, you'd think they'd make them more comfortable.'

'Too right,' Kirsten agreed, 'they ought to have little tables and comfy chairs, and play music, and serve coffee, and free Wi-Fi in these places. You can tell they was invented by a bloke. If I was at home waiting for something, I'm damned sure I wouldn't be sitting on a plastic chair, staring at the walls or a tatty magazine that was years old. It'd send me crazy, that would. That's why I bring me own in.' She proudly held up her magazine like it was a diploma.

'What's your sign say?' said Amaranth.

'You're the birthday girl, I'll read yours,' Kirsten said, rummaging for the astrology page. 'Gemini, innit?'

'No, I mean your sign – the notice you put on the wall there.'

'Oh that: I'm looking for a flatmate.'

Chapter 4.   Kate

With only a month's notice, Kate's family came over from Perth for the wedding. Mother and father, two brothers, an aunt, and a cousin. Gary's parents were both dead, and his only sister was married to an American and living there. She had just had their second child and couldn't get away.

Kate kept her own surname. She thought changing it would interrupt the communication flow she had developed with clients, particularly the new ones she was gathering from overseas. She didn't tell Gary that she didn't like the name "Baker" because it sounded like a tradesman to her.

Kate's abundance of friends attending the wedding compensated for the meagre two workmates Gary provided. At the reception, however, he was surprised and flattered to see the General Manager and the entire Board of Directors turn up.

'You two make quite a force to be reckoned with,' said the GM, as he added his toast to the festivities. 'Sales and marketing pay all our salaries, Gary. Now, you just be careful with that thing of yours. We don't want half this team having to drop out to have a baby, do we?'

And the whole Board drank to that event not happening.

They took a three-day honeymoon at Hamilton Island, off the North Queensland coast. Not that they needed to, their lives were floating together like a honeymoon anyway. They sat on the terrace of the resort, sipping margaritas and watching the moon rise over the ocean. There were several yachts moored offshore, their silhouettes casting glittery reflections in the wide beam of moonlight.

'I might get us a yacht, Kate,' Gary said. 'I've sailed quite a bit in my time. I love it.'

'Not me,' Kate said. 'I get seasick on a waterbed. You'd never get me on a boat. Never.'

After they returned to Sydney and the mundanities that brought, Gary sold his house and together they bought a harbourside apartment as high as their double incomes. He forgot about buying a yacht, and bought himself a new car instead. An Audi convertible. Black. Just like her Beamer. She liked his new car, but said it was too ostentatious for him to present the company to clients. But she liked it. She liked it a lot. Gary ended up driving her BMW.

She was brilliant at her job. He knew she would be. She made hard decisions easily. She was inventive and assertive. It didn't take long for the figures to greatly improve, and Gary reminded everyone who ought to know that it was the changes she'd suggested that brought that success about. Of course, everyone who ought to know hadn't forgotten that fact. She was invited into the next board meeting, and there she presented her strategy for developing the export division to drive international sales.

Within four months, she was Gary's boss.

'Are you okay with this, Gary?' she asked, when she told him of her promotion.

'Of course I am. You deserve it. I would hate the job, myself. I need to get out of the office. I'm more the sea-faring captain in this company. Master of my ship, and all that. And it's great for me to know the port is in capable hands while I'm away conquering new lands.'

Her upward transition wasn't difficult for any of the staff to accept. In fact, they had all predicted it for weeks. Kate had been making most of the decisions, and all of those decisions had turned out to be right. She'd first streamlined her department, then Head Office, and now she was steering the whole company.

Gary's sales section generally had little to do with the top brass, so at the office Christmas party it was not surprising that he saw only a glimpse of Kate as they celebrated the best year the company had ever had.

Gary was ganged up with his team. All male. All drinking heavily. All uniformed in casual style: suit jackets off, top shirt button opened beneath a loosened tie. Yet they were all so different from each other in everything except confidence. There was Mike, who was only in his early twenties but looked much older than that. He carried a lot of body weight and resembled a typical nightclub bouncer. Nick was almost the exact opposite. He was late thirties, but looked ten years younger. He had a mane of thick black hair, which he constantly finger-combed and flicked away from his face. He was toned, tanned, and tireless. He never maintained eye contact when he spoke with someone, constantly looking around the room in case he missed something. And there was Steve, who looked like a geek, a psychology professor or a librarian, but was really an ambitious go-get-'em salesman. Probably why he consistently made 'top gun' each month – customers didn't see the sale coming.

'Next year, Gary, you gonna head exports?' asked Mike. 'I hear we're into Singapore.'

'China, Korea, and Japan next, old son,' Steve added.

Gary raised his beer. 'We'll see,' he toasted.

'Gary doesn't want to be away overseas, lads, leaving that lovely wife of his alone back here,' Nick butted in.

'What?' Steve said. 'You reckon someone might just slip in there?' He made a fist with his hand, and his arm imitated a porn star's livelihood.

'Never know,' Nick jeered. 'Some bastards will do anything to get ahead.'

Mike threw his arm around Nick. 'Well Mr Jones, I'm quite partial to getting a head, myself.'

'Is that an offer?' Nick said, trying to lick the fingers on his shoulder.

Mike jerked his hand away as quickly as if a cigarette had burnt it. They all laughed. Except Gary. The best he could muster was a smile.

The city was packed with last-minute shoppers, just like Gary. It was Christmas Eve, and he hadn't bought Kate's present. He hadn't bought a Christmas present for years.

He read the billboards and the sides of buses, desperate for a suggestion. Photographs of half-naked women in slippery satin underclothing insisted that the respectable thing for a man to buy his wife would be lingerie.

He found a suitable store and went inside. Lingerie shopping scared him. He was afraid of the choices. Frilly and sexy, or sensibly supportive? And then there was the whole size thing: selecting either too big or too small was laced with a critical implication. How did those other guys do it? No, no, he couldn't buy lingerie. Besides, he felt the shop assistants were keeping their eyes on him, thinking he was some lonely desperado looking for titillation, as he slunk between the rows of silky underwear.

He ended up in a music shop, but a CD was too much of a cop-out. Then he saw a poster advertising the K D Lang concert on 18th January. Kate loved K D. She had two of her CDs. He bought the tickets, found a card, and felt very pleased with his day.

She got him an artist's set: blank canvas, an easel, oil paints and brushes.

Like many businesses, the company closed for the ten days of Christmas. At least the sales office did. The admin section remained open. It was the middle of the financial year and an ideal time to catch up on accounts. Stocktake the warehouse. Change the office around.

Kate went in each day to supervise some things and prepare for the usual monthly board meeting. Nothing got in the way of that.

Gary hated being home alone. He paced the apartment like a kid on a rainy weekend. There was nothing to fix, everything was new. He'd read the books he had. He'd read her magazines. The TV was crap. He tried relaxing, but that reminded him she was not there beside him.

He invented errands for himself and walked to the shops. Couples everywhere. He went to a bar. Lonely men in love with horses racing on overhead monitors, or else lurking in a shady side booth, their hands gripping the erect handle of a poker machine. The park was kindergarten. The beach was teeny. The mall was geriatric. He checked his phone, frequently, in case she'd texted him.

She hadn't.

All Gary had was his career and his marriage. Now they'd combined, and this week he was exiled from them both.

They had a quiet New Year's Eve. They didn't go out: too crowded everywhere. They were done celebrating, anyway. They were ten floors up, and they could see the Bridge, the Opera House, and the tall buildings round Circular Quay. They saw the kiddies' fireworks display at nine o'clock. They could have easily skipped the midnight and gone to bed, but they rarely went to bed that early. They were sitting on their balcony, catching the cool night breeze when the TV in their lounge room chimed through the flyscreen that another year was gone, as another year arrived. More fireworks, including further round, over Darling Point, this time. A longer show. Massive cloudbursts and sparkling showers. Cars and ferries tooting.

'Happy New Year, darling,' he said.

'Happy New Year.'

Her phone rang.

'Who the hell could that be?' Gary fumed, mildly.

She looked at her phone screen. 'I'll take it inside,' she said, rising.

She opened the flyscreen and went inside, closing the glass door behind her. Gary relaxed into the night. The ferries were still ploughing their way across the satin water. Lights illuminated all signs of life in the cityscape. A ginger cloud of gunpowder lingered in the sky over the harbour. He drained his wine glass and reached for the bottle. It was empty. He stood up and slid the door open, bumping the empty bottle against the glass pane.

Kate spun around when she heard the cool night coming inside.

'Gary! Hi!' she said, as though she were meeting him after years apart. 'It's Bob. He's rung to wish us Happy New Year.'

'Bob?'

'Bob Meyers.'

'Oh!' Gary said, as he sauntered off to the toilet. 'Say Happy New Year from me too.'

She had made a hot drink for them when he came back into the lounge.

'Five years I've been with the company,' Gary muttered to himself, but loud enough for her to hear, 'and that's the first time Robert Meyers has rung me on New Year's Eve.'

'Probably the first time you've been home.'

She was right. As usual. But that wasn't it.

'No. They never ring staff up.'

'I'm not exactly "staff", Gary.'

'Yes, you are. Management is staff. Management staff. Same as me.' The whine in his voice slurred by the wine in his voice. 'I'm State Manager. You're National Manager. Management staff.'

'Whatever.'

'That all he said? "Happy New Year"?'

'Pretty much. He doesn't say much. You know Bob.'

'Not really,' said Gary. 'Never had much to do with him.'

'He wants me to fly to Singapore next week.'

'Singapore? Why?'

'Kickstart the new office.'

'And what did you say?'

'I said of course, Gary. This is what I've been waiting for: start a business right from scratch, have full responsibility. Total control.'

'Next week? Shit, he didn't give you much time to prepare. Rings you at midnight on New Year's Eve to tell you...'

'I've known for some time it was coming. I thought I'd told you.'

'No, you didn't tell me. We hardly see each other these days.' He sat down. 'How long will you be away?'

'Two weeks should do it. I just want to make sure it happens exactly how I want it to.'

'Who'd we get to run it? A local bloke?'

'No. I got Nick Jones. I think he's the right man for it.'

31

Chapter 5.   Scott

Amaranth's room at Kirsten's third-floor flat in Chester Hill had a large window that looked out across the street and over the houses on the other side. She could see the tall city buildings in the distance, jutting into the sky like a tiara on the headland. Amaranth liked windows. She liked knowing there was somewhere else, with something else going on there.

Kirsten, though younger, was like the older sister Amaranth used to wish she had, but they were very different from each other. Almost exact opposites, in fact. Kirsten had just left her boyfriend. They had a little boy, aged two, and it had taken her those two years to work out she really wasn't the mothering sort. Not of a toddler, anyway. Maybe a teenager. She could thump a teenager, shout at a teenager, get a teenager to go to the shops for her, maybe bum a ciggy off occasionally, but two-year-olds wet beds, cry if you don't give them things, and generally don't let you have a life of your own. She'd left her child too.

On weekdays, Kirsten came home from work and slobbed in front of the TV, cigarettes rapidly overtaking the fragrance of factory that she brought in with her. On the weekends, her little boy came to stay with her, even when she started going out with some bloke called Rob. Amaranth was a great babysitter.

Quite soon, Amaranth saw that though she hadn't exactly made a mistake, she hadn't exactly made a friend. But she had made a move.

One Friday night, Kirsten asked Amaranth to come out with her. 'It's a twenty-first for a girl at work, but there's going to be some older people there so you'll be right,' Kirsten said.

When Amaranth saw that the 'older people' was just one person – the birthday-girl's father – she felt she should have been wearing a little gift tag saying *"Dear Reg, thanks for having Tracey twenty-one years ago, love from Kirsten"*.

Everyone else pretty much ignored her for the entire night. She saw Kirsten's bag and jacket, so she knew she was still at the party. Somewhere. Probably paired off with some guy, like all the other girls. Except Amaranth. She was sitting on an old Chrysler Valiant rear seat that was propped against the Hills Hoist on the back lawn. Tracey's father had toppled face down beside her.

'He's gone!' a slurry voice announced.

She looked up and saw a blue-checked shirt with what looked like a head-sized ball of black wool sticking out from the top of it, a hairy tangle of Afro and mullet. He was a visual collaboration of several decades, none of which included the current one. A rocker, a surfer, a punk, a feral. Tight denim jeans that were torn from neglect, not fashion. Cigarette hanging from his mouth, key chain hanging from his plastic belt, and drunken opportunism hanging from his horniness. And it was talking to her.

'I'm Scott. You here with Tracey's old man, then?'

'No, we were just talking.'

'So, what's your name?'

'Amma.'

'Hello, Emma. I'm Scott, or did I tell you already?'

'Hi, Scott. I'm Am-ma,' she repeated, emphasising the "Am" part.

'Yeah, yeah. I memembra. Nice name. So, d'you live round here or what?'

'No, I live over in Chester Hill. Do you know Kirsten?'

'Kirsten? S'nice name, that. I've never known a Kirsten before. Knew a Kristy once. More than once, if you get my drift.'

He raised his stubby cooler to toast his imagined prowess and saw she had no drink.

'Wanna beer, Krispy? I've got some by me bike.' He pointed over to the garage where a shabby red motorbike was guarding a small esky with a helmet on top. 'No one touches beer beside a bike. Could be a fucking Hell's Angel's, innit?'

Amaranth looked around for Kirsten but everyone else was in the house. The back garden was the sad shambles of a party. All she saw was the deserted barbie, the ripped beer cartons overflowing with empties and used paper plates, the pathetic string of coloured party lights with its several blown bulbs, and the dead-to-the-world dad.

'Come on, you look like you need a beer,' Scott said, hauling her to her feet and pulling her over to his bike.

He opened his esky and rescued a floating survivor from the Arctic waters. It was a twist-top but he used the flash bottle opener he had on his chain. It didn't impress her, but it impressed him, and that was all that really mattered.

She took a sip. The first beer she had ever tasted. That taste would forever remind her of this moment. He pulled her to him and kissed her, his tongue sponging the beer froth from her teeth, his free hand groping for her breast. She could feel his expectant arousal poking at her hip.

'I haven't got a franger. You on the pill or anything?' he asked.

'Yes,' she said, and she was. It seemed it was going to have to do more than regulate her periods this night.

Scott pushed her backwards and into the garage and kicked the door shut behind them.

It was dark inside and she turned and grasped for something solid, finding a pile of crates. Scott pressed up behind her and pushed her into a bending position over them, then he fumbled her skirt up and her panties down. She wished Kirsten would walk in now and tell her she had to go home this instant. That would have been perfect. Then Kirsten would know that Amaranth had boys after her too. And Scott would have to stop doing what he was going to do.

But Kirsten didn't come into the garage. And Amaranth didn't have to go home. And Scott didn't stop doing what he was going to do. And it was as awful as she expected. And she never, ever took a sip of beer again.

When he finished, he zipped his pants back up, crept over to the door and peeked out at the party, then he went back to the pile of boxes that she was still bent over.

'Listen, err, give us your mobile number,' he whispered. 'I have to get back inside.'

'I don't have a mobile,' she said, hauling her underwear back up and feeling politely irritable.

'Didja lose it here?'

'No,' she said. 'I've never had one.'

'You never had a mobile? Christ, you must be the only person on the whole fucking planet who doesn't. How come you don't have a mobile?'

'Never needed one,' she said.

'You got a landline at home or what?'

'Yes.'

'Well, give us that. Hurry up, I have to get back inside.'

In the thin beam of party light spilling through the slightly opened door, she opened her bag and tore a piece of paper from her little notepad.

Maybe the phone will ring just once for me, she thought, as she wrote her number for him. She surrendered the piece of paper to him and he examined it.

'And write your name on it,' he said, handing it back.

She wrote her name in four large capital letters for him.

He looked at it. 'How d'yer say that?'

'Amm-ahh,' she said, slowly. 'Like: I AM-A person. Amm-ahh, Amma.'

'Yeah, all right, I'll *amm-ahh* that fuckin' in,' he said, thumping his forehead. 'Oops, pardon the language. No, seriously, but s'nice name that.' He carefully put the piece of paper in his wallet. Like he hoped to never lose it, or hoped to never have someone find it.

She didn't see Kirsten all day Saturday, but on Sunday afternoon, when Amaranth came home from the supermarket, Kirsten was in the lounge room.

'Did you get bread?' she asked, as she turned the TV off and followed Amaranth into the kitchen.

'Yes. I got everything, I think.'

'Thank God. I'm starving.'

Over a scrambled eggs lunch, Kirsten asked how Amaranth had got home from the party.

'Taxi.'

'I looked for you, Amma. Thought you must've gone with Tracey's dad. You two seemed to hit it off okay.'

'Gone where? He was unconscious on the back lawn.'

35

'Poor Reg. You going to see him again?'

'No way.'

'No need to say it like that, Amma. What's wrong with Tracey's old man?'

'He's an old man, for starters.'

'He's not old. Not real old. He was still in his forties only last year.'

'No, I met someone else.'

'What, at the party? You met a bloke there?'

'Yes.'

'Who?'

'Just someone. I don't want to say anything more till he rings.'

'Rings? He's going to ring? When's he going to ring?' Kirsten asked, getting noticeably excited.

'I don't know. I expect he'll want to wait a few days. They don't like to look desperate.'

'You sly old dog, you. Didya get a bit?'

Amaranth giggled.

'You did, didn't you?'

'Yes,' Amaranth eagerly admitted.

'You didn't bring him back here, didya? I don't like strange guys coming here when I'm not home. Not till I've met them and sussed them out.'

'No, we didn't come here.'

'Went back to his place, didya?'

'No.'

'So, where'd you do it?'

'In the garage at the party.'

'In the garage! Didn't know you had it in you, girl. But now I know you've had it in you.'

They both laughed, and Amaranth almost felt they were friends. *This year is already so different!*

The following Saturday, Amaranth heard Kirsten's mobile three times, but the home phone stood idle. And silent. On Sunday it rang once. A homeowner-seeking telemarketer who hung up when Amaranth said they were just renting.

The next weekend it was the same, and Amaranth went back to ignoring the phone that wasn't asking for attention anyway. However, as she returned from work the following Friday, before Kirsten got home, the home phone was ringing.

'Is that Amma?'

'Yes.'

'Hi, this is Scott. I think we met at Tracey's twenty-first.'

He lived in a small flat above a shop. Just one room with a kitchenette and a shared bathroom on the landing outside. He couldn't have the music up too loud because the neighbours could hear it, and he told Amaranth not to scream or anything when they got it on.

She didn't scream or anything when they got it on, but that had nothing to do with the neighbours hearing.

After sex, he switched on the TV and flicked channels till he found something he liked. An American cops-and-robbers series. It was halfway through an episode, but he knew the characters well enough to enjoy it. Amaranth tried to watch the show, but TV seemed too harsh, too alien, too cold. She snuggled closer to him, but he pulled his arm free of her and reached for his ashtray and cigarettes. She wondered how someone who seemed so into her a few moments ago could be so distant so quickly. It was a wonder, not a worry, however, because she knew that was simply what guys did. She settled herself on the pillows and optioned to look at his hunched and naked back. His thin, white frame heaved in some cigarette smoke and then breathed a blue haze into the beams of light from the TV. She saw his shoulders relax, and noticed a freckle on his right shoulder blade. Then another.

Lots of freckles. Or moles. Or pimples. Blemishes, anyway. Lots of them. One there, and there, and there, and there – that's how many? Four. One there: five. Six. She yawned. *Seven. Eight. Nine. Ten. Elev... ... ...*

'Hey, hey, don't go to sleep,' he said, nudging her eyes open. 'I only have one helmet, so I can't give you a lift home and the last bus goes at ten past twelve.'

Amaranth sat on the bus, looking at the raindrops on the window, and the traffic splashing puddles into tiny crescendos of wetness. The rain was so fine she could only see it actually falling in the headlights of passing vehicles, but when she got off at the Chester Hill shops it was raining much harder. She ran into a shop doorway to shelter till it stopped. It didn't stop.

She was cold. The night was an unfriendly, sodden greyness.

'Count your blessings,' Mum used to say. So, let's see: I have a job. A place to live. Boys after me. Well, a boy. Two, if I count Tracey's father. I have my health. Both my legs and both my arms. I have good teeth. My body is okay, not much up top – no, that's thinking about what I don't have, mustn't go there. I have a flat tummy. I've got some good savings still put away from the settlement. I am very organised. Methodical. Tidy. God, I sound like an old maid!

A taxi pulled up and tooted. She ran to it and got in. The driver was an Indian guy who spoke with a heavy accent. He was perhaps the kindest person she had ever met.

'You looked like you are needing a cab,' he said. 'On rainy nights, they are always very much in demand. Not a nice place for a pretty girl like you to be standing around unescorted.'

It wasn't far to her street, she paid him and thanked him again. She opened the door and dashed into her block of flats, and the taxi dissolved into the oblivion.

Kirsten was up when she got in.

'Is it raining that hard?' she asked, looking at the drowned rat at her door.

Amaranth went in to her room to change. Kirsten had the kettle on when she came back out.

'So, where is he, Amma?'

'Back home.'

'You could've brought him up. I wouldn't bite him, you know.'

'No, I caught a cab. He wasn't with me.'

'So, he lives round here then? When will I get to meet this mystery man?'

'I don't know. Why do you want to meet him so much?'

'Just want to know he's good enough for my flatmate, that's all, Amma. Don't worry, I'm not going to steal him from you.'

Amaranth laughed. 'Yeah, I know there's no chance of that.'

'What do you mean?' said Kirsten, defensively.

'I mean you just wouldn't do that to me.'

Kirsten settled her feathers. 'That's right. I wouldn't. So you don't have to go on keeping him such a secret.'

'I'm not.'

'So, what's his name then?'

'Scott.'

'Scott who?'

'I don't know his last name.'

Kirsten gave her a look of disbelief.

'I don't,' insisted Amaranth.

'So, tell me about him. Where's he work? What kind of car he's got? How old is he? What's his star sign?'

'He doesn't have a car.' It was the only question Amaranth could answer. 'He has a motorbike. Don't know what kind, it's an old red one with an eagle on the tank.'

'Scotty Metcalfe?' gasped Kirsten. 'You're bonking Tracey's boyfriend?'

Chapter 6.   Nick the Flick

Gary drove Kate to the airport in the Audi. He hauled her two suitcases from the boot, and they trundled one each from the car park into the departure hall, right up to the counter.

'Both flying today?'

'No, just me.' Kate smiled perfunctorily.

While the check-in agent tore a page from the tickets and attached a destination tag to each bag, Gary looked at his wife. She looked lovelier today than he could remember. He wondered if that was because she was possessed of a sparkle of excitement. And that sparkle: was that because she was going away? Or going away alone? Either way, he was already missing her.

'There you are, Ms Harrison. You're departing from Gate 24. Boarding time is sixteen-ten. I hope you have a pleasant flight, and thank you for choosing Emirates Airlines.'

A few more steps. A kiss. The kiss families use. A wave goodbye. One person turns a corner. One person turns away. Airport terminal. Terminal indeed.

Gary didn't want to go home straight from the airport. He had taken the afternoon off work, and he thought he'd go back there and catch up on some things.

He pulled into the car lot and was surprised to see several other vehicles.

He walked into the building. Somehow the office seemed different. Hollow. Synthetic. And even though he generally didn't see Kate at work, it felt utterly Kate-less.

Nick was downloading some files at his computer as Gary passed by.

'Still here, Nick? Everyone working late tonight?'

'Yeah. Got a stack of stuff to get ready for tomorrow.'

'Tomorrow?'

'Singapore.'

'You're flying there tomorrow?'

'It was all very much last minute. They couldn't get me on Katie's flight. I wanted us to fly together to save her having to come back to collect me from the airport.'

'I doubt she'll have time to be running around taxiing people from the airport, Nick.'

'I asked her to meet me,' Nick explained, characteristically combing and flicking his hair. 'I'm fucking hopeless trying to grope around the uncharted territory. I don't like foreign places.'

'Oh. Yeah. Well, I can't say I'm too fussed on them, either.'

'That why they didn't offer it to you?'

'No,' Gary said. 'I expect it was because I was married.'

'So's your wife.'

'Yeah. Well, I'd pretty much told them I didn't want to take it.'

'A tad ironic, isn't it?'

'Mmm?'

'Well, you didn't want the posting because you'd have to leave Katie behind, and she's going to be over there at least a fortnight every month anyway.'

'What do you mean?'

'She didn't tell you?' Nick asked, exaggerating his scoop. 'We've got to be happening in Korea by April. Japan by the end of the financial year. She told me she'll be pretty much fifty-fifty here and there for the next six months.'

Gary was as weirdly silent as the eye of a cyclone.

'I guess that's the downside of marrying the boss, Gary. They're always so damned busy. Every bastard wants them.'

'I didn't marry the boss. She got the promotion after we were married.'

'Either way. She's the boss. You married her.'

Gary walked off towards his office.

'Hey,' Nick called, 'I don't suppose there's any chance of a lift to the airport tomorrow?'

'I'm flat out tomorrow, Nick. Catch the shuttle.'

'Where do they go from?'

'Fucked if I know. Ring a travel agent, for Christ's sake.'

'What time does it get into Singapore, Gary, did Katie say?'

'Eleven. Their time.'

'Oh yeah,' Nick said. 'They're three hours behind, aren't they? Our body clocks will still be on Aussie time, though. I'll be so ready for bed.'

Gary had trouble getting to sleep that night. He remembered all the nights she'd been beside him and he hadn't noticed, and now she wasn't, it was all he was aware of. His bed was uncomfortably large. His bedroom, too quiet. His mind, too desperate. Just as he exhausted his torture and fell into the salvation of slumber, his phone rang.

She'd arrived safely. The flight was good. The weather was hot. Hotter than the day in Sydney, and it was the middle of the night there.

'Middle of the night plus three hours here,' he reminded her.

'Oh, I'm sorry, darling. I just wanted to let you know I'd arrived. I had my mobile switched off on the flight, so I just got your sweet message now. I thought you'd want me to call.'

'Yeah, yeah, of course I did.' He rubbed his eyes and took a rousing breath of oxygen. 'They were saying you're going to be going over there every month.'

'Who was?'

'Nick Jones.'

'He doesn't know anything. That was just something we discussed as a possibility. In case he can't manage things.'

'What about Japan?'

'That's all a long way off, Gary. Anyway, I'd better go, I'm at the airport and my driver is waiting. I'll call you tomorrow at work. Okay?'

'I guess.'

'Okay. Bye.' Click.

Gary listened to the silence. He continued to just sit there, holding the phone against his face. Thinking.

#

Gary hadn't realised how many incoming calls the company took each day. Every time the phone rang in at the main switchboard, he waited for his office phone to buzz. And even when it did, it was just some stupid customer. He rang her mobile twice, but only got message bank. It was after four when she finally called back.

'So busy, Gary. You wouldn't believe the mess this place is in. I haven't stopped for a minute all morning. It's lunchtime here. They brought me some tiny little sandwiches with the crusts cut off. The bread doesn't taste like bread, it's like edible polystyrene. Supposedly edible. I've got a ton of work on this afternoon. I tell you, I am so looking forward to a long Singapore sling or two this evening.'

That night was even harder for him to get to sleep. Her phone still went to message bank, and she didn't call back. He imagined Nick the Flick plying her with yet another Singapore sling at two am in a tropical garden that was as hot as a Sydney summer.

Top Gun Steve was sitting on Gary's desk, waiting to ambush him with the announcement he'd also accepted a job with Linton Bailey.

'Nature is always hungry,' Steve said, justifying his ambition.

The day got worse and worse for Gary. The mainframe crashed and they couldn't access any customer files in the computers and then there was a problem in production.

And Kate didn't ring.

'What happened yesterday?' were his first words to her the following night.

'Jesus, Gary! You sound like my mother. I'm not on holiday here, you know. I'm having really full-on days.'

'And nights.'

'What the hell is that supposed to mean?'

'You could ring after work.'

'And then you complain I'm ringing in the middle of the night. I can't win with you.'

'How's Nick Jones working out?'

'Nick?' she said.

A muffled voice somewhere in her background said something, but he couldn't hear what.

'Who's that there with you?'

'No one.'

'I heard a voice. Is Nick there?' Gary shouted.

'No-Nick-is-not-here.' Gary wondered if the clear placing of each word was for him, or for the person who was in the room with her.

'So, whose voice was that?'

'Room service. I have to eat this late, Gary, because my days are so hectic. I'd better get it while it's hot.'

She didn't ring again that week. Not even a text. He missed her terribly. On the weekend, he missed her even more. He wanted to get on a plane and fly over himself, but he knew she would react badly to that.

The following Monday, she called him at work, but only discussed work-related things. She left the journal of her trip to just one sentence. 'It's not so bad here, once you're used to it.'

'And how's the office going? Is Nick handling things?'

'He's great, Gary, absolutely at the top of his game here. He's got a real flair for this, but even so, I can see I *will* have to come back over again. That's something you and I will need to discuss when I get back.'

On the weekend before she came home, Gary changed the bed sheets, and rounded up his strewn clothes. He dragged the laundry basket out from his wardrobe, and there, where he'd stashed them, were the canvas and easel she'd given him for Christmas. They were out of their gift wrapping, but the easel was still bound with the clear plastic shop wrapping.

He put a load of washing on and returned to the wardrobe. It was a good present, he thought as he opened it completely. He was impressed that she'd remembered he used to paint at school, and wondered if she'd guessed or known that he'd often wished he'd painted since.

He carried them out onto the balcony and set them up. The harbour adopted her usual pose for him. It was a perfect day and, as he waited for the spin cycle to end, he gazed into the view and then back to the blank canvas.

The harbour was like a postcard. But it was too tame. Loveliness was good to look at, but he didn't feel lovely. And he realised why he hadn't painted anything since school. A view, a person, a thing: a camera can catch them all. But a painting: a painting can catch the artist too. Not merely what the artist sees, but how the artist feels.

He disciplined himself with house chores, clearing his mind of clutter as he cleared the apartment. It was late afternoon by the time he stopped for lunch and, after he had eaten, he felt ready. He mixed up some colours, his mind overflowing with thoughts of her. He painted a sailing ship, its sails billowed to bursting by storm winds, and its hull smashing against an enormous, angry sea. He finished it at nine o'clock.

About the same time K D Lang would have been walking onto the stage.

They had been married six months exactly to the day when she flew back into Sydney, but she was too tired from the flight to go out and celebrate. He didn't mind. She was home.

An evening snack. A bath while he cleared the kitchen. A kiss. The kiss married couples exchange when they are about to go to sleep. After fifteen agonising nights of re-learning to be in bed alone, he now lay awake beside her, trying not to display how exciting that was for him.

And she slept.

The following morning, Sunday, she woke and slipped out of bed. He thought she was heading to the bathroom, and she'd come back to bed. But when too long had gone, he looked around the room, half-expecting, half-hoping she would be there, sitting, watching him. But she wasn't. She was out on the lounge room balcony.

He wrapped a towel around his waist and went out to her. He kissed her forehead and told her how good it was to have her home. How much he'd missed her. How he didn't think he could stand her going away again.

'Gary! Jesus, you're like a little kid. I have a career you know, with huge responsibilities. Don't you dare try to guilt me out with

45

your pathetic insecurities. I have two offices to run, and two more to open, and I need the freedom to do that job to the best of my ability.'

'So, you're going to Japan and Korea as well?'

'Is this what it's going to be like from now on?'

'That's up to you, Kate.'

'It's not up to me. It's my job. I don't think you give a shit about that.'

'I don't,' he said. 'All I care about is you – who you *are*. I don't give a rat's about what you do.'

'You don't get it, Gary, do you? I love my job. It's more than what I *do* – it's what I am.'

She stood up and went inside. He wanted to follow her, but he was afraid he would seem even more like the child following mummy around. He sat there, staring at the blank canvas that his view had suddenly become.

The sun passed behind a cloud, and he felt the chill on his bare back. His kidneys reminded him that he had come straight to the balcony from bed. He slid the screen door open and, bypassing the bedroom where he could hear her sorting through her wardrobe, he went in to the bathroom.

When he came out again, she was gone.

All the following week, she tolerated him. And he tolerated her tolerating him. The weekend, she avoided him. And he avoided confronting her about that. By mid-week she had told him she was going back to Singapore on Friday. And she did.

They didn't phone each other at night, and when he spoke to her on the office phone, she concentrated only on business. He had a feeling like their relationship was over. Not for him, but certainly for her. It was just a feeling. He had no real evidence of that.

Until she told him.

When she came home, he saw she was still overseas. She was a stranger who was visiting him. She announced she was going to be away in Korea for a month. She was only back for three days. She was taking Monday off work to buy some things she needed for her next trip.

On Monday, he was seated at his desk. He just couldn't close this deal. There was something she needed that he simply didn't have to offer her. But he had no idea what it was. He, however, needed to talk. Maybe they could sort it out. There was still time. He picked up his mobile from where he'd placed it on his desk, but he stopped before he called her. He knew he needed to be face-to-face with her. He gathered his jacket from the back of his chair and walked out of the office, ignoring the voice calling out that there was a client waiting to see him in reception.

He opened the apartment door and walked towards the bedroom. The door was slightly open and he could see her lying there, naked, like she was waiting. He recognised the look on her face. He hadn't seen it for some time, but he recognised it. It was the same mischievous look of readiness he'd seen that first night they had dinner together. But her look changed when she saw him standing there. It fell through surprise and into shame.

It worsened into cruelty when Nick came in from the bathroom.

Chapter 7.   Daniel

Daniel looked at the car in the driveway. It was less than five years old. A sporty maroon-coloured Honda Prelude hatchback. With personalised number plates – DAN 21.

'Here comes Dan the Man,' Daniel's father shouted.

Daniel was not at all "the man" yet. He was still quite boyish-looking, the fact he was a little short amplified that. He kept his curly, black hair long and messy, which also suggested the careless youth thing.

'Thanks, Dad,' he said.

'It was only traded in last week. Perfect timing. I'd had my eye out for the right car for your twenty-first. Low kms, straight chassis, no rust, one careful owner.'

'Yeah okay, Dad. You don't need to sell it to me.'

'Old habits, son.'

The blonde on his father's arm spoke.

'Your father just wants you to know he found you a good car,' she said. 'The one he sold me when we first met is the best car I've ever had.'

Daniel looked at her. Stella. She would have still been able to model twenty years ago, but now her face showed that cameras are as cruel as clients. Just over a year ago, she'd come into his father's car saleyard looking for a new car and left with a new boyfriend, if you can really call a sixty-three-year-old man a *boy*friend.

'And your brother has something for you, haven't you, Joshua?' his father said.

'Yes, I do.' Joshua pulled a folded sheet of paper from the inside pocket of his suit jacket.

'What's this?' said Daniel, moving closer to read it.

'It's the plans for my new house. And this area here, over the garage and laundry, this whole section here — bedroom, verandah, en suite — is yours. I built it for you. It'll be finished in three weeks.'

There was ten years between the brothers and, quite suddenly, Daniel felt that twenty-one wasn't the prelude of his adulthood, it was the epilogue of his pubescence. 'I don't want to appear rude or anything, Josh,' he said, 'but I don't want to move. I like it here. This house. Where I've always lived.'

'Dan, Dan, Dan,' his father said. 'I'm selling this place.'

'What are you on about? This is our home, Dad.'

'It hasn't been our home since your mother passed away, Dan. You know that. Besides, you're a man now.'

'Key to the door,' chimed Joshua, waving the plans.

'I don't get it. If you sell this house, where are you going to live, Dad?'

'Dad and Stella are moving. Tell him, Dad.'

'Stella wants to spend some time with her family,' his father said, pulling his trophy closer to his side. 'It snows at Christmas in New York, and I've never seen snow, so that's where we're going. We leave in nine months.'

'And where will you be living when you get back?' Daniel tried to get to grips with it.

'No,' his father said with a chuckle. '*Moving* there.'

Daniel looked at his brother, begging for his disapproval, but all Josh offered was a smile.

Daniel used the silence they left him to catch up.

'When did you decide this?' he asked his father.

'Only this week. And...' he paused to make sure Daniel was attentive, '...we're getting married before we go – I wanna make an honest woman of this girl before I meet her folks.'

Daniel shook his head. 'Moving? It's so fast, Dad. What's the rush?'

'Just one of those spontaneous things, Dan. You know.'

'No, I don't know.'

'Well maybe you should, son.'

Spontaneous. Sudden. Unexpected. That was how they described his father's heart attack. Perhaps it was deep vein thrombosis from the long flight to the States. Perhaps his heart had only been beating to the rhythm of the tappets in the cars he sold, and as soon as he stopped, it stopped too. Perhaps he knew it was coming, and that's why he'd grabbed at that last tiny snowflake of joy, hoping his palm was chilled enough by the cold sweat of panic to be able to hold on to it for long enough to appreciate it.

The house had sold surprisingly quickly and Stella received the bulk of the will. They sold the car yard. Joshua had his own business, and he gave Daniel a job there. So now they worked together. And lived together.

For Daniel, Joshua's house was an orphanage, and they lived apart. Daniel's area was like a separate flat that used a communal front door. The only room where they crossed paths was the kitchen, but even then, only occasionally. Daniel liked to cook. Joshua liked to eat out.

In his room, Daniel had a wide-screen TV, his computer, stereo, CDs, an electric kettle for coffees, his large bed, and his precious window. Josh got that right. It looked out over a park, and he spent hours sometimes, just looking out at the parade of people who wandered along the park paths.

It was two years since he'd dated one of the office girls. It hadn't worked out. Like the girl before that. He was only in his twenties and already resigned to being single for the rest of his life. If Josh had let him, he would have got a dog.

Dogs are cool, he thought. *They don't judge you, or want you to be something other than what you are. What you were when you met them.*

Joshua was the exact opposite. He had many girlfriends. Often at the same time. And never the same girl for more than a couple of dates. Until he brought Rebecca home.

'Bec's going to be staying for a while, Dan.'

She smiled at Daniel. 'I hope that's okay with you,' she said, through a smirk.

'It's his house,' Daniel said, and went off to his room.

50

Joshua owned a fashion warehouse. He had a factory that made some exclusive lines, and he imported several other ranges from China and Indonesia. Daniel's job was to maintain those overseas purchases and keep a steady supply up to their local customer chains. It had its harder days, but usually he had plenty of free time at work. He wrote poems. Pages and pages of poems. Dark pieces of misery and despondency, which he kept stashed in a bottom drawer at his desk.

No one came into his cloisters. Even the cleaners only gave it a quick sweep out once a week. He kept to himself, and everyone at work was okay with that.

But at home, someone wasn't.

It irritated Rebecca that she was sharing the home space with someone who shared nothing with her. Living with two guys was like she was flatting. If it was just Joshua, it would be like they were married.

Saturday lunchtime, Daniel woke up to the sound of a yapping dog echoing in the hallway. He got up and went into the lounge room.

'Isn't he gorgeous!' cried Rebecca. 'His name is Spritzer. Here, Spritzer! Here, Spritzer! He doesn't know his name yet. I called him that because he knocked over my drink.'

Daniel stared down at the barking mophead.

'Does Joshua know you have a dog?'

'Joshua gave him to me, silly. It's my birthday on Monday. Spritzer the Shih Tzu. Isn't he so cute? Yes, you are. You're such a cute, cute, cute little doggie, aren't you?'

'Where's Josh?'

'Aren't you going to wish me Happy Birthday?'

Spritzer ran past Daniel and into his room.

'Where's Josh?' Daniel repeated.

'Where do you think? Back at work, where he always is. Come on, Spritzer, come out of there!'

She moved towards Daniel's sanctuary, but he blocked her.

'It's all right,' he said, 'I'll get him.'

The dog yelped when Daniel scooped him up and bowled him down the hallway. He slammed his door shut and strode across to his bed, stepping in the soggy stain on his rug.

That night, Joshua knocked on his door.

'Are you in there, Dan?'

Rather than calling out for his brother to enter, Daniel opened the door, and filled the space he created between it and the wall. The polite way of telling someone to go away. He didn't want to discuss anything, because he knew what someone wanted to discuss.

'Can I come in for a sec, Dan?'

'Can it wait till tomorrow?'

'It'll only take a few minutes.'

'I was just going to bed. Can't it wait?'

'Fuck! What is your fucking problem, man? Let me in your fucking room for a minute.'

'Josh...'

'You're creeping us out, Dan, all your secrecy shit, and you've left dishes in the sink again...'

'What dishes? They're not mine.'

'That's not the point, you do leave dishes. Often. I've told you many times. And we hear you moving around the kitchen at night after we've gone to bed. You're like a fucking rodent.'

'Oh, thank you very much, Josh. A fucking rodent.'

'Every time me and Becky are getting it on, we have to stop because she can hear you out there. What are you doing?'

'Washing up my dishes, probably, Josh.'

'And hurting the puppy: what the fuck is that about? You've gone weird on us. We can't handle it, man. I want you out of here this weekend.'

'Why, what's happening this weekend?'

'You're out of here, that's what. Find some other sucker to sponge off. You're gone, Dan. I mean it. Got that?'

'Settle down!' Daniel said, stepping back into his room, inviting his brother in. 'Can't we at least talk about this?'

But Joshua stormed off down the hallway.

#

Gary would have resigned anyway. It was as difficult for him at work as it would have been for Kate, had she been there. She'd had a word with Bob Meyers, and he had a word with Gary. The word was 'sacked', but he hid it in sentences about Gary being distracted the past few weeks and needing a bit of a break to sort his personal life out. The company had already lost Steven Chatt, the sales area needed new blood. And spilled blood.

Gary and Kate met only once more, at the signing of the divorce settlement. They were alone for just thirty-seven seconds.

'What was it that I did, Kate?' he whispered.

'Nothing.' She looked away and sighed. Then she looked back. 'I told you I wasn't ready to get married. There are still things I want to do with my life. Things you don't give me.'

'I gave you everything I had.'

'So, what was there left for me to want?'

'Isn't marriage all about keeping what you have? Wanting what you have?'

'Not when it's not enough,' she said, as the solicitor came back in with the papers.

Gary lost the apartment. He had no fight in him because what he most wanted to keep wasn't on the inventory, except as her hurried initials of acceptance. He was, however, awarded the value of the house he'd sold because it was his before they had married. His name was on the Audi registration so, much to her disappointment, he retained that. He kept his clothes and the painting he'd done. She pretty much got the rest.

He bought a small house in Potts Hill, a nondescript part of Sydney's outer suburbs, far from the cafés and shops where he might just bump into her. He sold the Audi the first weekend he advertised it, bought a Ford and, in a fit of self-therapy, he also bought his yacht. A twelve-year-old, twenty-six-footer named *Deep Desire*, which he promptly re-named *Away* so he could sail away whenever he wanted.

He had no verve for the sales position that he'd taken in a suburban real estate office. Showing young couples their potential homes, knowing the houses were for sale often because of someone's misfortune. It only further soured his cynicism. Good salespeople succeed because they are successful, and Gary felt a failure. He'd lost his wife, his apartment, his career, and his lifestyle. He had no family, no friends, and no future.

He attempted the game that is played at night. In places where fake is flaunted. Where strangers meet and remain strangers. The smile. The look. The laughter. The questions. The invitation. The act. As potent as hope. As impotent as disappointment. He couldn't participate. No one matched the legend he created of his wife. He knew it was illogical, but when some attractive woman let her glance linger just that crucial extra two seconds, he would feel like he was cheating on Kate, and he'd turn away.

He met other men, so many other men, eager to share their stories of suffering. Damaged people seem to find each other. They pile in the corners of public bars like wheelless car bodies at the wreckers. Losers telling their stories of loss like soldiers showing photographs of their girls back home. The entrenched and ditched war-weary describing the ones they love. 'Cunts, mate. That's what they are.'

He'd been married six months, but the weeks that passed after his divorce seemed longer than the lifetime his marriage seemed to have been.

Time, however, eventually dulls even the sharpest pain, and crusts up the deepest cut. Gary saw evidence of that when he bumped into Bob Meyers.

'Good to see you, Gary,' Bob faked. 'How's everything?'

'Fine, Bob. You?'

'Oh, we're flying along. Kate has established a very strong presence for us in South East Asia. She got us Tokyo, Seoul and Manila, as you know.'

'No, I didn't know,' Gary said, trying to emphasise how out-of-the-loop he felt.

'Well anyway, she did, and now she's in Beijing. The Big One!'

Gary didn't feel bitter. He didn't feel anything other than that salesman-twinge, like a spur digging at his pride, rousing him to not walk away a loser.

'Good on her,' he said flatly, devoid of any sincere praise. 'And good on you and the whole blooming company, but I'm sorry, I have

54

a client waiting to buy another huge slice of Sydney from me, so I have to dash.'

Gary sailed on the weekend if there was a decent wind, but one Sunday afternoon, as he sat becalmed in his backyard, a stubby in one hand, a chicken sandwich in the other, he watched the ants colliding with the crumbs he dropped. He recalled Top Gun Steve's parting words about Nature being always hungry.

Ants never stop moving, he thought. *The constant, desperate forage for a chance encounter with something worthwhile. They survive on hope.*

That night he hurled the folded men's magazine across the room. He didn't want to see a naked woman. He wanted to feel one. To hold one. To smell one. To have one. No trips. No pretence. No bullshit about getting to know each other first. But always there was that rigmarole of role-play with women who were not content with faking orgasm; they had to fake foreplay too.

The following lunchtime Gary walked back into the real estate office with his coffee and sausage roll. There was a message for him to call someone back about a house in Regents Park that he had listed. He finished lunch first, and then rang her number.

He arrived at the house at four, as arranged, and she was waiting outside.

He greeted her and they shook hands. Her name was Julie Marsden. In business by herself. Some sort of personnel business. She liked working with people, she said. She looked like she was in her sixties, but she might have been younger and just carrying the ravage of her excesses. She was confident and direct. Just the kind of person he liked dealing with. He knew where he was with her. What she was looking for. How much she had to spend. She spoke of her business and how the house would be ideal for it. When he pointed out this particular street hadn't yet fulfilled its potential as a good business area, she smiled.

'It's the right area for my business,' she said.

She bought the place, and Gary banked a healthy commission, but he still had plenty left from the sale of his house and car so it didn't inspire him to push hard to earn more. Instead, he went sailing for three days in a row. He grinned like he'd done as a boy on the family yacht, when his father first handed him the tiller, or like when his regional manager gave him his first major company account. First sail, first sale. The thrill was discovering he had the skill, but whereas selling had shrivelled to merely sustaining him, sailing continued to nourish him. He loved setting a course, reading the winds, judging the swells. To be blown where you want to go, and trick the wind to blow you back the opposite direction. In control, answering to no one. Out there: away from land, houses, people, traffic, work.

Work! He decided he'd go back to the office the next day and resign. That's how good he felt. And how bad.

The next day, of course, he didn't resign. He did use his work computer to have a quick look at an online employment agency, but he abandoned searching after only reading two job descriptions.

I'm comfortable enough working here, he reasoned, closing his laptop with a slam. To clinch the sale of that idea, he leaned back in his chair, with his arms behind his head, and threw his feet up onto his desk. *It's just a job,* he reminded himself, *something to do, and pay the bills.*

That's all he wanted.

So that's all he got.

Chapter 8.   Cinnamon

Amaranth reached out and switched her alarm clock off before it sounded. As if it had set *her.* Seven twenty-nine am on the dot, the first of her daily rituals began.

Shuffling out of bed, she straightened her doona and settled Fudge in his usual position at the base of her abandoned pillow. Another typical weekday. Getting up and going to work in the legal office wasn't what she wanted to do. It was simply what she did.

She finished showering, dried herself thoroughly, and hung her bath towel along the full length of the lower chrome rail. Then, wrapping her dressing gown about her like it was a great overcoat and she was stepping out into a storm, she traipsed back up the hallway. Just when she reached her bedroom door, the phone rang in the kitchen. It was only a further five paces, but she knew it wouldn't be for her. Scott hadn't rung for nine weeks now, and no one else had her number.

As she closed her door, she heard Kirsten's bedroom door snatch open. Grouchy footsteps flumped up the hallway, the muffled voice delivering expletives to the phone for ringing, to Amaranth for not answering it, and ultimately to the caller.

Amaranth clipped up her comfortable bra, buttoned up her crisp blouse, hauled up her twill skirt, laced up her sensible shoes. Neat. Like she'd looked for all the years she'd been at school. And most of the years since. Disguised as clothing, it was uniform all the same.

She returned to the bathroom and stared at herself in the mirror, seeing only the base-face upon which she painted an office girl. Cheeks that lacked foundation. Lips that lacked colour. Eyes that lacked the ability to see that they lacked, so she decorated their frames with mascara and shadow.

Kirsten bustled in and, pushing in front, proceeded to brush her teeth.

'Thank God I don't have to stuff around with make-up for my job!' she said, through a mouthful of toothpaste.

Amaranth knew that Kirsten judged all that time at the mirror just made her a dowdy girl in disguise.

'Oh, listen…' Kirsten spat the toothpaste froth into the sink with a practiced hoick that cleared the remnant tobacco tar from her adenoids as well, '…can you pay the rent on your way to work? I've left mine on the kitchen table.' She wiped her mouth on Amaranth's bath towel. 'I'm a bit short: can you put it in for me? I'll fix you up Monday.' She didn't wait for a reply, she knew it would be "yes" anyway. 'Oh, and I really need you to babysit Jesse tonight. That was that bastard ex of mine on the phone and he just sprung it on me. Knows I go out Fridays. Rob'll be picking me up at ten. Probably going to that new club on Dennis Street. You know, the flash one with them big pillars in front. You don't have to stay up till we go out or anything, just need to know you're home for Jess, okay?'

Amaranth didn't move. Didn't speak. She just stared into the empty mirror, until she heard the front door slam.

'Bye,' she murmured sarcastically, and continued with her illusion.

The walk sign said wait, so Amaranth waited. The only thing actually on the road at the intersection was another pedestrian who was hurrying across against the lights. But Amaranth waited. It was safer to wait. *You never know what will just come zooming around the corner.* She checked her watch, and tried to estimate how long she'd need to pay the rent on the way to the station. But she waited.

She checked her watch again as she entered the real estate office. The receptionist was on the phone, but a young salesman noticed she was agitated and approached her.

'Can I help you?' he asked.

'Just want to pay some rent,' hurried Amaranth.

'For which property?'

'Three, nineteen Bright Street.'

She counted out the money, and looked up to catch him inspecting her blouse.

'Flat?' he enquired.

I know what he's implying, she thought. She'd hated her small breasts when she was younger. Now, she was just grateful men didn't generally ogle them.

'Unit? Apartment?' he continued.

She didn't know if there was a difference between a unit, an apartment and a flat.

'Apartment number?' he elaborated, agitated at her hesitancy.

'Oh,' she panted a little laugh of fake politeness. 'Three. Apartment three.' She checked her watch again.

'Apartment three, at three-nineteen Bright Street,' he said, typing the keyboard.

'No, no,' Amaranth said. 'Apartment three, at nineteen Bright Street.'

'Right. I'll start again.' He huffed and edited the screen on his computer. 'Nineteen Bright Street, apartment three. Much clearer when you say it like that.'

Emerging from the real estate office, she was focused on the street up ahead when a hand grabbed her upper arm and held it firmly. She dropped her handbag, spilling her chattels onto the footpath.

'Amma!'

'Oh hi, Scott,' she replied, devoid of as much emotion and response without actually seeming rude.

The chronic cigarette, key chain, and opportunism all still hung off him. He released her and held his arms open for an embrace.

She escaped that ordeal by ducking down to collect her purse, *make up, breath-mints, hairbrush, pack of tampons, tube of cold-sore cream, god-everything-had-to-fall-out ...*

'Would you believe it?' he faked, making no attempt to help her. 'I was just thinking about you only last night!'

She stood up and faced him. 'I'm so late. I really have to...'

'I've missed you, you know, baby,' he said, oblivious to the fact that she was already a block up the street in her mind. 'Lots of nights I wished things had worked out different between Tracey and me.

Always had a bit of a soft spot for you. Quite the reverse, actually!'
He stepped back and raised his eyebrows twice as he adjusted the
front of his jeans.

'Scott, I've got to...'

'How about a drink sometime?'

'Maybe.' She thought it more expedient than to try to decline.

'How about tonight?'

'Tonight? Can't: I'm babysitting,' she said, grateful she had a
genuine excuse.

'You still at the same place?' he sleazed. She wanted to deny that,
but she stalled. He didn't notice, instead fumbling with his mental
appointment list. 'Oh no, shit, hang on! I can't tonight. Look, give us
your mobile again, Amma. I'll give you a ring.'

'I don't have a mobile. Remember?'

'Oh, yeah, S'right. You got the home phone, but?'

'Yes.'

'Well, give us that one again,' he said, beckoning with two
agitated fingers. 'And bung your address on there, an all.'

She reached obediently into her bag and found paper and pen,
jotting down her address and number. Remembering to add her name,
she slapped it into his palm and dashed on to work.

'I'll call you, baby. I promise.'

Yeah, whatever, she thought. *Sure you will.* And she hoped he
wouldn't.

With almost circus-skilled accuracy, Amaranth plonked herself into
her desk chair as the clock on the office wall twitched to nine o'clock.
She could feel the perspiration on her forehead from running all the
way from Wynyard Station. Second drawer down, box of tissues.
Dab, dab. Bin. She reached into her desk tray, and started to prepare
some paperwork.

Ms Howard arrived. A stiff woman in her mid-fifties. Smart
appearance. Expensive apricot suit that advertised her success, and
indicated her fee. Fulvous chiffon scarf, which she routinely removed
upon entering the office, viciously flicking it from her shoulders like
she was cracking an ineffectual whip. Hair that was brittle with spray.
Make-up smeared thickly over years of other people's quarrels.

'Good morning, Ms Howard,' chirped Amaranth.

'Was that you running ahead of me?' came the curt rejoinder.

'Yes, I just made it on time.'

'You were not "on time", Amaranth, if you had to run.' She took her briefcase into her inner office and continued calling out from there, her raised voice only adding to the chiding. 'I do not like my staff running in the streets, and I'm quite sure my clients wouldn't like it either. And look at you now. Go and fix yourself up. And I'll have my coffee straight away, thank you.'

The day dragged typically. Ms Howard made frequent references to the fact Amaranth had been "late" and proffered them as the reason the workload seemed excessive.

At ten to five, Amaranth's intercom buzzed. She never liked the sound it made. So impolite. So imperative. So impersonal. But at ten to five, it was so impossible: this was the time to finish things off, shut things down, straighten things up, get away home because she was babysitting that night. She filed her frustration away in the cabinet and walked over to the intercom but even before she reached it, it buzzed another bullying bray for attention.

'Just pop in, Amaranth, would you?'

Amaranth 'popped in' to where Ms Howard was seated behind the dark mahogany ramparts of her imposing desk, studying a document. She seemed less a lawyer, more a magistrate. Her forehead creased with comprehension. Her lips crimped with cruelty. She didn't look up to acknowledge her secretary's entrance. Or existence.

Amaranth shuffled awkwardly from foot to foot. A charade for Ms Howard to select between someone busting to go to the toilet, and someone really having to be somewhere when someone else was holding them up unnecessarily.

'I need you to work back tonight,' Ms Howard proclaimed casually.

Amaranth began to explain about babysitting for Kirsten that night.

'I've never heard mention of a child before,' Ms Howard cross-examined. Which was true, both because she rarely enquired in any real depth about Amaranth's life, and also because Kirsten generally only had her son every second weekend. Jesse's father ceremoniously dropped him off with the sound of a car horn. The same trumpeting he used to collect the three-year-old the following evening. Less a fanfare, more an edit for unexpressed expletives.

'And why is she going out this evening if she's agreed to receive delivery of the child?' pursued the inflexible matriarch.

'Jesse will be asleep when Kirsten goes out at ten,' Amaranth elaborated.

'She goes *out* at ten?' Ms Howard huffed judgementally, with a display of bewilderment that exaggerated her condemnation. 'Well, you'll be done by seven or half past at the latest, so you've plenty of time to get home.'

Decision sustained, objections overruled.

'You can use the office phone to call her,' Ms Howard generously allowed. 'It's a sort of business call.'

Amaranth made no appeal. Her eyes surrendered to the carpet, her lips winced into a quarter of a smile of compliance, and she obediently escorted herself to the door.

'And if there's any problems, Amaranth… put her through to me.'

#

Gary was over in Regents Park looking at a block of four flats that had just come on the market. Walking back to where he'd parked, he saw Julie Marsden, the woman he'd sold to a few months back. They greeted each other, and he asked her how business was. She told him it was booming.

'Perhaps you're ready to look at buying another place then. If not for expansion, then investment.' It was meant as a joke, but she said she was thinking the same thing.

'Let me give you my card,' she said. 'Call me if you find anything similar, either in Crofton Road or the top end of Albert Street.'

He took the card and read it aloud. 'Cinnamon — Select. Sensual. Sublime.' He glanced at her. 'Subtle,' he added playfully.

She frisked a pen from her bag. 'Actually, I'd better put my home number on there. I have a machine, you can always leave a message. And anyway, you wouldn't want to call the work number.'

'So you don't live here then?' he asked, handing the card back for her to write on.

'Of course not. Cinnamon is just one of my businesses. I own Peppers in the City, and Mustard Seeds on the North Shore.'

'Quite the original Spice Girl, aren't you?'

'I'm more Sporty than Scary,' she sang her usual response to that, and finished writing her number down.

'And your new place? What are you going to call that: Cumin?'

She laughed as she handed him her card. 'Very good! Perhaps you should consider a career in naming businesses rather than selling them. No, my next place will be especially for gentlemen who have a penchant for something more adventurous. I'll be calling it The Spice Rack.'

That night Gary was leaving work a little later than usual. He fossicked in his jacket pockets for his car keys and found Cinnamon.

'*Sometimes Life deals you a winning card*,' he almost said aloud.

It was after eight when he approached the front door. This was the property he'd sold to Julie. It looked like any other house in the street from the outside, except the front door had been removed and a vestibule constructed to allow a more discreet entry. No lurking out front. Just slip in, do your business, and slip out.

Gary slipped in.

He had never been in a brothel before, and he wondered why. It seemed both logical and natural.

The place had been completely redone inside; he didn't recognise it at all. Polished wood floors, red painted walls, nice art work in heavy frames. Julie obviously went for the 'classy' look.

The first room on the right was exposed to the hallway by having half its wall-to-ceiling removed. It was transformed into a generous alcove, lit like a cocktail bar. A girl, twenty years old at the most, was on a barstool. Her skirt did not get any longer when she stood up to greet him. Her breasts introduced themselves first. Then her eyes. Then her lips. Plump, wet, and so, so red.

'Hi. I'm Maxine.'

'Maxine. I'm Geoff,' he matched pseudonyms.

'Hi, Geoff.' She sounded like she was in a B grade porn movie doing an impersonation of Marilyn Monroe. So used to fantasy, she couldn't imagine speaking any other way when she was working there. Or maybe, that was how she survived. *She* didn't work there. That was Maxine.

She sat down at the bar and patted the stool beside her. 'Wanna drink something, Geoff?'

'Sure.'

'Wanna buy me a drink too?'

He opened his wallet. There was only a twenty and a five in there.

'We take all the major credit cards,' she said.

He didn't want to use his card. He didn't want a trace of his visit – neither for prying eyes, nor his own recollection. First timers are often like that, until habit overcomes the pseudo-shame.

'I don't have a credit card,' he lied. 'Is there an ATM close?'

'We have EFTPOS here.'

'I prefer to use cash. If that's okay?'

'Yes, of course. There's a teller machine just round the corner at the top of this street. Why don't you pop up there, while I mix us a cocktail?'

'Yes,' said Gary, already imagining her doing exactly that.

It was as far to walk up to the corner as it was to walk down to his car, so he left it parked where it was. The pavement echoed with his eager footsteps. He turned the corner, and saw the familiar neon bank symbol on a wall. It was beside a closed shop that had a small stack of bread delivery crates waiting for the early morning bakery run.

He hurried to the ATM and stood before it. He was so turned on that even this seemed like a lewd thing to be doing. He slid his bankcard into the slit. His frantic fingers prodded the keys with his secret code. The screen flashed responsively, asking him exactly what it was that he wanted. The stimulated machine surrendered to him and six golden notes poked out like a rigid tongue from cold metal lips that begged 'Take Me'.

He stuffed his card back into its compartment in the front part of his wallet, and wedged the notes into the back part. His mind already back at Cinnamon, he turned to leave when suddenly, out of nowhere, a kid on a pushbike zipped passed him, and snatched the wallet right out of his hands. Startled, it took Gary three vital seconds to process what had just happened.

'Hey, you little fuck! Get back here!' he yelled, but the kid was halfway to the bottom of the street, and disappearing into the night.

Furious, Gary kicked the stack of plastic bakery trays that were just standing there and doing nothing to help him, and they slithered in several different directions across the pavement.

'Shit! Shit! Shit! Fucking typical! FUCK!!!!!'

Chapter 9.   The Boy on the Bike

Amaranth felt urgent as she approached Wynyard Station around seven-forty. She didn't know the times of these later trains, but she had convinced herself there was one leaving in just a few moments. She arrived on the platform as the rear of the last carriage snaked into the hole that led west. The announcement board spun like a poker machine and settled to say she had forty-two minutes to wait for the next train.

She looked around her. The platform was almost empty. Everyone else had hurried just that little bit more than she had. Or else they were sauntering at leisure, and would arrive fresh and relaxed in half an hour. She wondered what Kirsten would be thinking right now. What she would be saying later. *One of those moments a mobile phone would be good,* she thought.

Amaranth sat because there was nothing else to do except let the disturbed flurry of dirty, grey dust settle on her. The first fine layer that life-like, yet life-less, statues are made of.

Forty-two minutes to wait.

Waiting was just more wasting in her endless day to day, and she ought to be comfortable with it. All her life she'd waited. Waited for something to happen. What became of that Birthday Promise she'd made? That this year was the Start?

She read the billboards. She noticed how dirty the walls were, and how tidy the track was, and she calculated that the trains must be like some huge leaf blower, only less annoying. She wondered how long the tunnels took to dig. Whether the drivers liked their job. What kind of fellow passengers she would encounter, and why they were out at this time. She imagined her desk at the office and mentally checked to see if she had put everything away. She glanced at the announcement board again to see how many of the forty-two minutes were left to

66

wait. Her conscious thoughts exhausted, she still had thirty-nine minutes to go.

She stared into the eternal night of the tunnel, whose purpose was emptiness. Slowly the sombre space enveloped her like a cathedral, freeing her from the thoughts that she created and controlled.

Odd phrases from the self-assertion course she'd dropped two years ago echoed in the blear. Ideas she hadn't fully understood at the time, and had refused to challenge. Prompts such as: *what stops you doing the things you want to?* Hard to answer if there was nothing she wanted to do. They called it fear on the course. They told her that everything she denied displayed her fear. That her fear was not a protection, it was an obstruction. That she lay beyond its barrier, past the prison she'd constructed around herself. Fear is a door, they told her, but it's an unlocked door, and always worth going through.

The train smashed out of the blackness like a bullet bursting a balloon and clattered to a halt in front of her. It collected her thoughts and bustled them into a carriage, leaving any realisations where they fell on the cold concrete platform behind her.

She took a seat in the carriage and checked her watch. She should arrive home less than half an hour before Kirsten was due to go out.

The train jerked and began to move slowly at first, then quite quickly picked up speed as the yellow lights of the platform dodged the blackness inside the tunnel. The train emerged into a broad inner suburb. She looked out of the window. A mottled vein of street-lit houses poured passed, plunging into oblivion as the train punched into another tunnel and all she could see was her own reflection in the glass.

She turned away and looked at the mixture of people in her carriage. Two over-excited children playing with a mummy who wasn't playing with them. A young guy in carelessly tattered jeans picking at a pimple on his cheek. A sour and sombre businessman worrying some wondering. All being rushed, like her, from somewhere to somewhere else.

She idly examined the window frame. Something small, attached to the upper corner, caught her eye. It was the chrysalis of a vagrant caterpillar. *How did it get in here?* she wondered. *This is no place for a butterfly.* She reached up and plucked the tiny case carefully from its silky tether. She placed it in her left palm and gently closed her fingers about it, turning her hand over to check her watch. It was eight fifty-five; she was making better time than she imagined.

Twenty-five minutes later, the train stopped at Regents Park.

Regents Park? Amaranth thought, with a small panic. *Regents Park isn't on this line.*

She caught up to the exiting passengers as they traipsed along the platform.

'Excuse me,' she asked the old man ahead of her, 'I don't know how I ended up in Regents Park. Do you know what time the next train to Chester Hill is?'

'Chester Hill? You should have got off at Birrong. The Bankstown Line splits back at there, love,' he chuckled, surprised she didn't know that. 'This arm heads up to Lidcombe. You wanted the Liverpool arm.'

She realised waiting for a train heading back to Birrong, and then waiting for another train going down the Liverpool arm to Chester Hill was going to take far too long. She thought about how angry Kirsten would be if she was late.

'Or you might get a bus on Amy Street,' he offered, to calm her obvious worry. 'I think the Chester Hill bus goes right along Amy Street.'

'Where's Amy Street?' she asked.

'Main road on the other side of Guilfoyle Park out behind the station.'

Amaranth left the station and headed past the Community Centre on the path that led to the park. She stopped at the entrance, the streetlight behind her accentuating the darkness beyond its reach. No trees at this end, it was more like a field with a cricket pitch and a tarred tennis court. An unfriendly cold breeze found the sweat around her neck and chilled her.

She could see the traffic way across on the other side, but it was quite a long way. The path wasn't lit and it disappeared into a lonely darkness. She looked at her watch, angling it to catch the spray from the streetlight behind her. Nine thirty-four: Kirsten was going out at ten. She looked again at the park. Not *that* dark. Not *that* far.

Fear is an unlocked door, she reminded herself. If she was strong enough to take whatever life threw at her, she was strong enough to change it. This test, this long dark walk through a strange deserted park, this was the initiation, this was the real threshold of her Start! *Besides,* she thought in the more familiar areas of her brain, *Kirsten will really spew if I get home late!*

She had only gone forty paces when she heard a rattly noise behind her. She spun around to face a shivering dazzle that was racing towards her. Right at her. She froze as a pushbike clattered past. The light suddenly went out but a faint wisp of streetlight, stretching from way back where the path began, glowed into the bloodshot reflector just a few metres ahead of her, and she realised that the bike had stopped.

'Shit, sorry!' a young male voice called out. 'I didn't see you till I was almost on top of you.'

'Yes, well I'm okay, thank you,' she shouted back, hearing a shake in her voice. 'You can go on.'

He didn't go on. Instead, he turned his little bike around with a practised spin, and cycled slowly to her. She didn't move. The darkness soaked up enough of the residue of streetlight for her to see he was in his late teens, with a wild mop of blond curly hair. *I bet the schoolgirls love those locks,* she thought. He seemed too big for such a small bike, which contradictorily exaggerated both his youth and his maturity. Despite the surprise of his arrival, she realised she didn't feel threatened by him at all.

This is the new me in action, she reassured herself.

'I freaked you out a bit. I'm sorry,' he said. 'I'd be pretty freaked out myself if someone came hooning up behind me at night. Are you okay?'

'No, I'm fine,' she asserted, 'I'm just going to Amy Street there. Do you know where the bus stop to Chester Hill is?'

'Amy Street?' He pulled an exaggerated puzzled face. 'That's Regent Street. Amy Street is over that way!' He pointed to the road across the park, but at right angles to the path she was on. She could see car lights winking in the orange glow over there, but it was a lot further to get to. And darker.

'You want me to come with you?' he asked.

'No, no, I'm good,' she said.

'Look, if you're worried about me, I'll show you some I.D.' he reassured, as he fished a wallet out from his waistband. He rummaged through several cards, selecting one. 'See?' He switched his bike light on and read the card with her. 'That's me. And that's my address, 26 what's it say? Barton Street, Potts Hill.'

'You've got a long ride home,' she said with a laugh.

'Yeah, bit of a way, but I'm not in a hurry,' he said, switching the light off again and stuffing the wallet back in his waistband. 'Come on, I'll walk you over.'

Yielding to his presentation, she set off with him towards the road he had indicated. She felt like she was a teacher walking with a student, or he was a boy scout escorting a not-too-old lady across a street. A nice boy, who asked all the usual questions that strangers feel obliged to ask. And answer. What did she do for a job? Did she live in Chester Hill? How long for? Who did she live with? Then somehow, in keeping with the darker part of the journey, his questions became just that little bit more intentional. Like: did she have a boyfriend? How come someone as nice looking as her didn't? Did she feel lonely at nights? Wasn't she scared, walking alone in a dark and deserted place?

She offered a happy little laugh of counterfeit coyness. He was flirting with her. This boy was actually flirting with her. And, perhaps for the first time in her life, she felt that it was she who had control of the conversation and therefore the outcome. They were passing a rock wall that surrounded a flowerbed, and she bent down to ease her palm against some folded petals.

'A chrysalis,' she explained. 'I found it on the train.'

She looked up at the boy. A laurel of frangipani framed his face. Even in this darkness she could see his eagerness, and she realised she would have to put things straight now or this would become embarrassing.

'Listen,' she began, 'you're a very sweet...'

Amaranth's words were shattered, as though she'd been watching TV and the station had suddenly dropped out. Sound became a rushing static, and images were a confusion of pixels dashing in their madness. Her mind grabbed for reason. Something to stop this and make sense of what was happening. There was a shadow raging against them. She heard primal grunts of combat and the muffled crunches of fist against skin. There were cries of pain and then the youth was hunched and fallen. His bike was kicked aside and it crashed into the rocks. She heard her own voice shouting for the shadowy man to stop but he turned on her, gripping her tightly by her upper arms, and shook her roughly, demanding she 'shut the fuck up!' Again her voice, but somehow not her voice: it was an animal voice she didn't recognise, and it was shouting for him to let her go. That he was hurting her. He slapped her face hard, and she fell down, losing her voice on the way to the abrasive pathway.

The shadowy man leaped on the youth, who was rousing. He scuffled with him, the lad's legs clawing at the night like a spider climbing an invisible web.

'Where is it, clever boy?' the man spat through bared teeth. He began frisking the crumpled teen. 'Where is it? Where's my fucking wallet?'

He found the wallet in the boy's waistband, opened it and checked that his money was still there. Then he glanced at Amaranth, who was lying where she'd fallen. His eyes smeared over her body. Her skirt was crumpled up from the fall, and her upper legs were clearly exposed. He slithered his gaze back to her face.

She stared back at him through the grey-brown night. She could feel her heartbeat: a strong, regular accompaniment to the aftermath. The storm had passed. This lunatic had found what he had wanted. It was over now. He had no argument with her. She was innocent.

'Don't give me that butter-wouldn't-melt-in-my-mouth look, you're a part of this,' he accused.

'No. No, I'm not. He said it was his wallet.'

'His?' He turned back to the youth. 'So you think it's okay to take whatever you want from someone, do you? You need to know what it's like to have something taken from *you*, pal.'

He left the dazed youth where he lay, and strode back over to Amaranth, snatching her hair and holding her down by it. 'This is probably what she's up to the minute your back's turned anyway,' he justified.

Dropping his wallet beside her head, he thrust his now free hand up under her skirt and grabbed at her panties, which scrunched into a cotton cord that tore into her legs.

She wanted to scream but she was too afraid he would hit her again. She turned her head away, like she did when she was getting a needle at the doctor's, as if not seeing the action would diminish the severity. *Just get it over with*, she thought. She'd wished that same thing with other men before. She felt the attacker's intrusive fingers feverishly ripping her panties down over her thighs. She clenched her teeth, and readied herself for the stab of his wanting.

But he stopped.

The youth had rallied himself and jabbed the bike pump across the assailant's throat, holding each end tightly. He pushed his knee against the madman's back as he pulled on the pump with all his strength, but he was no match for the other's rampant rage.

The older man wrenched away from Amaranth, and, like a baited bull shaking off a hunting dog, he broke free of the chokehold. He struck wildly at the boy, sending him crashing into the rock wall face first. There was an ugly crunch as the youth's skull smashed into a rock, and blood oozed through the crack in his forehead into the tangle of surf-blond hair. His body flopped unnaturally, and lay still.

The horror of realisation sucked the air from the scene and the man's anger was suspended in a reverend silence. These two would hardly have reported his punishing them for stealing his wallet, but it had become way more serious now: he had killed the thief, and the girl he had sexually violated was the only witness.

He breathed out hard, and claimed a moment to calculate the consequences. His disgust turned to defence, and he turned to her.

'What am I going to do with you?' he said, genuinely scrambling for an answer.

'Nothing,' she suggested, recognising the danger she was now in. 'That was just an accident.' She glanced where the boy lay.

He followed her glance at the crumpled youth, and then slowly looked back at her.

'You've seen my face,' he pronounced, his voice laden with portent.

'Yeah. It's a nice face,' she attempted.

'You know who I am.'

'No, I don't. I've never seen you before in my life.'

He fumbled with the logic. 'You'll be able to identify me. Right?'

'Wrong. I can hardly see you. It's too dark.'

He saddened. '"Nice face", huh?'

She almost forgot the whole situation, and began to debate with him. 'What I can see of your face it seems like a nice one, but I don't think I could draw it or describe it very well.'

'But you've seen enough of it to know that you don't know me, so you must have an idea what I look like. I could remember you.'

'But I won't tell any…'

He burst into incredulity. 'Your fucking boyfriend is dead!'

'He wasn't my boyfriend. I don't know him. I only just met him a few minutes ago.'

'In the park in the middle of the night?'

'I had to get to my bus over there. He nearly knocked me over. He came flying out of nowhere.'

He looked over at the fallen youth. 'Little bastard grabbed my wallet at the ATM on Auburn Road.'

'He told me it was his,' she said. 'He showed me some I.D. so I'd let him walk with me.'

'Did he just? So you know my name then?' Gary asked.

She knew what his insinuation meant. She could identify him as the killer. She could ruin his life.

If she lived to tell.

'I won't turn you in,' she insisted. 'He attacked you with the pump. He was a thief who lied to me about who he was and why he wanted to walk with me. Who knows what you saved me from? I owe you. I won't turn you in.'

'Bullshit!'

'I won't!' she asserted firmly. 'I promise,' she accentuated softly.

He wanted to accept this, but he shook his head slowly, his voice shrinking to a whisper that echoed his prior pain. 'You're a fucking woman. You all lie.'

So that was his demon. There, in the midst of his chaos, she saw his two sides. His threatening dominance, his suffering deficiency. Her escape hatch.

'I must be the exception then,' she said, with a steady, determined voice. 'I…never…lie.'

His lips curled to a sneer. 'Exactly what a liar would say.'

'Or a truthful person,' she insisted.

'They'd say that too.'

'I'm not a liar,' she said, 'and you're not a murderer.'

'A bit late for that,' he muttered, his voice stumbling as he stared at the boy.

She sat up straight to counsel his contrition. 'That was an accident, that's not murder. Okay, you want to make sure I don't give you up? Take me with you, and I will owe you my life.'

It was a pivotal moment, and it reached him.

'Here it is,' she said. 'Take it.'

Their eyes remained locked. Searching for the intent within the other's gaze. Each hoping that, just maybe, this trade of desperation would take place.

Gary moved to her, and she flinched instinctively as he reached down and grabbed her arm, pulling her to her feet. He glanced once more at the crumpled boy, then around into the darkness of the park. They were alone and unseen.

'Come on then. Let's go! My car's over there,' he urged.

'Wait!' she exclaimed.

His brain flooded with doubt.

'Your wallet.' She pointed to it on the ground behind him. 'They could trace you with that!'

Chapter 10.   Fudge

Amaranth stared out of the passenger window of Gary's car as he sped along the expressway. It seemed like only a blink since she was staring out of the train window, and yet that seemed like almost a whole lifetime ago. In truth, it was a lifetime ago. It's just that lifetimes can pass in a blink.

Suddenly, there was a thumping and the steering wheel wobbled uncontrollably. With a curse, Gary pulled over. She remained sitting as he got out to inspect the front tyre on her side of the car. Another curse. Then he returned to retrieve his keys from the ignition, and went to the boot to get the spare. Amaranth opened the door to help, but he snapped at her to close it and stay put.

As he changed the wheel, he constantly glanced up at her to see she hadn't taken off into the night. She, however, sat motionless, staring forwards through the windscreen.

Headlights flashed under his vehicle, and he looked up to see a police car pull in behind him. No sense him running, he glared at Amaranth.

There were two cops. One stood by the patrol car doing a rego check, the other put his cap on and strode over.

'You going to be long?' he demanded.

'Just a flat. Nearly done.'

The cop checked the tyre tread, and then he looked at the windshield. He saw Amaranth. Her hair was dishevelled and the red slap on her face was worsening into a bruise. He tapped her window and motioned for her to open it.

'She's okay!' Gary assured.

The cop ignored him, and repeated the gesture for her to open the window. It was electric and Gary still had the key, so she opened the door.

'What have you been up to, then?' the cop enquired.

'Nothing,' she mumbled, like a naughty schoolgirl.

'You all right, love?' he asked more compassionately.

'She's fine. I told you,' Gary shouted.

'I wasn't talking to you!' the cop snarled. 'Come on, back up over there!' He motioned for the other cop to watch Gary, and turned back to Amaranth. 'What's up? Someone's obviously been knocking you around. What's been happening?'

She looked over her shoulder at Gary who was practically in the custody of the burly policeman at the rear of the car. Then back to the cop beside her. She was quite obviously safe, but somehow that was no longer the issue. As she saw it, Gary had rescued her. No matter that he had been the threat, he was now the saviour, and she had given her word to protect him. Beyond that, however, she had some sense that things were going to be very different for her now. And she needed him in order to hold on to that.

'His ex,' she explained, recalling his "all women lie" comment. 'I got caught up in some stuff from his past. He sorted it out.'

'And exactly how did he do that?'

'Just got between us.'

The cop looked approvingly at Gary. 'You're a bit of a hero,' he praised. He turned to his mate. 'Getting in the middle of a catfight would've been pretty hair-raising.'

'Raise more than my hair, if I'd seen it,' the other cop muttered sleazily.

'You've got to keep this lane clear,' the first cop reverted to formality. 'This is an expressway, so hurry along with it.'

He walked back to his patrol car, muttering: 'Not his night, is it? His ex showing up, a flat tyre.'

'Seen worse,' his partner added.

They drove off and Gary walked over to the woman in his car.

'You could have turned me in.' His mystified tone appealed for an explanation.

'My life's yours,' she said matter-of-factly, as though it ought to be as obvious to him as it was to her. 'I gave you my word.'

He just stared at her. Amazed.

'The tyre,' she urged, breaking the moment. 'Before they come past again.'

They didn't speak whilst he finished changing the tyre. They didn't speak when he climbed in behind the steering wheel. They didn't speak as he pulled back onto the expressway. They were each staring at the road before them. Seeing where they were. Where they were going.

Discounting the horror of the evening, Amaranth was almost excited. She had set the terms, and Gary had accepted them. Accepted her. She was his now, but she had initiated the proposition so she didn't feel like his prisoner. She felt like his partner.

He broke the silence. 'What's your name, anyway?'

'Amaranth Vaughan. Amma, for short. Yours?'

'Gary Baker.'

'Oh yeah. You look like a "Gary". That guy on the bike didn't.'

'He was up to no good, that one. Lucky I came along when I did,' Gary said, missing the irony.

'He was a delinquent,' legal secretary Amaranth said, without inflection, so that her voice sounded like she was reading from a script she had not yet learnt. 'He had lured me into the darkest part of the park to do God knows what.'

'He got what he deserved,' Gary added, checking his rear-view mirror for traffic as he changed lanes. 'Let's never talk about him again.'

She asked him where they were going. He told her Potts Hill, about fifteen minutes' drive. She looked at her watch. 'It's nearly eleven,' she worried. 'I should call home.'

'Boyfriend?' he queried, feigning a confidence.

She explained about Kirsten, and about her being supposed to be home at nine-thirty.

'You got a mobile?' he asked.

'No.'

He rummaged in his jacket pocket and pulled his out. 'Shit, that'd be right!' he cursed. 'Battery's flat.'

'I just hope they aren't worried,' she explained. 'Wouldn't want them to report me missing or anything.'

The caution was implanted. 'Where do you live?' he asked.

77

'Chester Hill,' she said.

'Right,' he said, 'you've got ten minutes to pack up your stuff. You're shifting in with me.'

He turned off at the next exit into the warren of the suburb. 'Okay, this is where you start giving me directions, Amaranth Vaughan.'

Neither Kirsten nor her boyfriend, Robert, looked up when Amaranth opened the front door. He was watching footy on the telly, sprawled with one leg on the couch, the other on the coffee table beside the empty pizza box and collection of drained tinnies. His large round belly was a clear indication this was a very familiar situation. Kirsten was drowned in her lounge chair, a magazine on her lap, an ashtray on that, a pile of stubs on that, and the sourest of looks on her face.

'I'm sorry I'm late,' Amaranth stated, with only a trace of apology. 'I hope it didn't stuff things up too much.'

'Two frigging hours late, Amma?' said Kirsten, without taking her eyes from her magazine. 'Oh, no, we've had a lovely meal and watched some riveting games.' She flicked the page like she was slapping a face. 'Just exactly the night we had planned.'

Gary closed the door behind him. Kirsten and Robert both looked up.

'This is Gary,' announced Amaranth.

Robert did the 'How-do?' blokey-nod. Kirsten offered a fake smile, and then dropped it as she smacked her eyes back onto her flatmate.

'I didn't plan being late either,' explained Amaranth. 'Something sort of just happened.'

'See,' Kirsten said, angrily, 'this is exactly why I told you to get a mobile fucking phone like normal people, Amma, then we could have called you to find out what the hell was going on.'

'I hope you weren't worried,' Amaranth said.

'Of course we were worried,' snapped Kirsten. 'It's impossible to get a cab after ten, and Rob's already over the limit. By ten-thirty I knew you weren't coming. Yeah? Our night was wrecked. Then Jesse woke the fuck up, saw we were dressed to go out, and chucked a tizz. It's been one of *them* nights!' She turned to Robert, who was stuck into the telly. 'You still want to go out, Rob?'

'Yeah, all right,' Robert said, through a yawny stretch. 'TJ's doesn't get going till after midnight anyway.'

Amaranth glanced at Gary, and then she took a deep breath. 'I can't babysit,' she declared. 'I'm sorry.' She marched off to her bedroom.

Kirsten got up and followed her.

Robert's yawn was frozen into a gesture of surrender. With a long out-breath, he let his hands fall onto his head and he massaged comprehension into his brain through the ginger bristles that passed as a haircut.

'There's a beer in the fridge, mate,' he said to Gary, his eyes re-absorbing the game. 'We might be here a while!'

Amaranth grabbed a suitcase from the top of the wardrobe in her bedroom and began packing as her flatmate stormed in.

'What are you doing?' demanded Kirsten with a mixture of chastisement and panic.

'I'm moving in with Gary.'

'Who the fuck is Gary? You've never mentioned a Gary before. How come you're moving in with him?'

Amaranth avoided response by going to the bathroom to gather her things.

Kirsten followed her again. 'Like for the weekend, you mean?' she prodded. 'Or are you leaving the flat? Amma! If you're thinking of leaving the flat, you've got to give me at least two weeks' notice. Where am I going to find a flatmate? No, that's my conditioner. And what about your share of the phone bill? And the electric? I'm not giving you your bond back till it's all paid for, Amma.'

Amaranth glimpsed herself in the bathroom mirror. She was quite used to not replying to Kirsten's babble, but she had never actually ignored her before.

Back to her bedroom, she grabbed her teddy bear and packed it on top of the things in her suitcase. Then, collecting her pillow, she turned to Kirsten, who had fallen silent spectator of this evacuation.

'You can have the sheets if you're prepared to wash them, Kirsten. You can have the doona too. And the pot plants. I paid a fortnight's rent this morning, including an extra fifty for you. Keep the bond for the bills and whatever. I'm sorry if it mucks you up, but it's just how things are, that's all.'

Kirsten's little boy came in, rubbing his eyes and grizzling.

'Great!' spat Kirsten, as she took the child angrily by his shoulder. 'It mucks us all up, Amma, now Mummy will have to spend the next ten minutes stroking his friggin' back till he settles down.'

Amaranth opened her suitcase and took out her teddy bear. 'Here you go, Jess, you can have Fudge. He's terrific at getting his friends to sleep. You can keep him.'

The little boy looked at Fudge, then at Amaranth.

'Don't you want him anymore?' he asked.

'He wants to live with you now. He told me.'

'Why doesn't he want to live with you anymore?'

Amaranth zipped up her case and looked around her room. Then she smiled at Jesse. 'It's just time for us to live in different places. We both know that, him and me. Look after him, hey? He loves to be loved.'

And then she left.

Kirsten stood for a few seconds and stared at the front door after it had closed behind Amaranth and Gary. It seemed to her that *two* strangers had just left through it. The TV disturbed her thoughts, and she zapped it with the remote.

'Hey!' shouted Robert. 'I was watching that…'

'What did he say, that Gary bloke?'

'About what?'

She became irritated. 'About anything. About him and that weird bitch. I thought she didn't like the older men. He must've been what: forty, forty-five? She'd been crying, I could see that. And they both looked like they'd copped a smack in the face.'

'He didn't say nothing,' attempted Robert, as his mind imagined the goal that he'd just missed.

Kirsten was suspicious. 'There's something fishy going on,' she said. 'People don't just suddenly up-and-off like that.'

'She might have had it planned for weeks,' Robert suggested.

'Nah, she's just not herself.'

'How do you know she was being herself before?'

'I've been living with her for the best part of a year, Rob. I think I know her by now. People don't just fucking change.'

'Maybe not, but they don't always let on who they are.'

'Oh yeah, and why would she be doing that?'

'I don't know,' he squirmed, trying to climb out of the conversation, 'I'm not a fucking psychologist.'

'Well,' said Kirsten, 'she's certainly given herself away now.' She scooped her child up from where he'd been standing by the kitchen bench and headed for the bedroom.

Jesse had loads of questions himself, but he was waiting until Mummy wasn't around, and he could ask Fudge.

Robert flicked the TV back on, and caught the ads that announced he'd missed the final score. He took solace in another coldie from the fridge, flicking the metal ring-pull carelessly into the sink, without thought of how it would eventually progress from there to the rubbish bin.

Kirsten came back, and immediately started on about how was she going to manage paying the rent on her own now that Amma was gone. She suggested he move in with her, arguing that her flat was a better one than his anyway.

Robert wouldn't have a bar of it.

'Who'd Davo find to share with if I moved out?' he reasoned.

'Fuck Davo! Who am I going to find? How come you're so worried about him?'

'We're mates, Kirsty.'

The mate thing! She hated the mate thing.

'We go back a long way, him and me,' Rob continued.

'And just where do we go, Rob?'

Robert looked awkwardly to the window.

She reverted to comparing the actual premises, stressing that her flat was closer to his work.

'But I've got undercover parking!' he moaned.

That did it. All the frustration she felt for Amaranth, she now hurled at her partner.

'It was bad enough it was your mate – but your fucking car?'

'Hey, hey, hey!' he threatened, attempting to calm her. 'Watch your language. There's a kid here tonight!'

'There's two here tonight,' she shouted, as she stormed out. 'I'm going to bed.'

Yeah, thought Robert as he skulled the last of his tinny, *that's where we'll sort this.*

Chapter 11.   Away

Amaranth stepped out of the shower in Gary's bathroom and began drying herself. She looked around this stranger's wash-space. It wasn't dirty, but it had no sparkle. It was a man's bathroom: a practical place to get clean. No bath crystals, no indulgent beauty products, no pretty exfoliating nylon scourers, no fragrance but the one disappearing down the drain.

Gary knocked. 'Everything okay in there?' he called.

She wrapped the towel tightly around herself and opened the door.

He smiled at her. It was the first time she had seen him smile. It was the first time she had really looked at the details of his face. His pale blue-grey eyes like chilled sadness, their corners pendent with despair. His fragile smile, though genuine, was more hopeful than happy. She wasn't afraid, she was curious, wondering where this was going, and how it would get there. She wasn't his prisoner; she'd accepted this situation willingly despite the threat, but now they had to define it. There was congealed blood around his mouth and, wetting the corner of a towel, she carefully wiped his lips. It was an intimacy he interpreted as like a woman with her lover. She thought it was like a mother with a small child.

#

The man with the dog waved urgently to the ambulance when it pulled up at the park in Amy Street.

'Where is he?' one of the ambulance men shouted, as they grabbed their medical bags, torches and a stretcher.

'Over this way,' the man called back, and they hurried after him into the park.

83

They reached the flowerbeds, and the man shortened his dog's leash.

'Looks to me like he rode straight into the rock wall in the dark,' he said, catching his breath.

The driver knelt beside the boy and checked his neck for a pulse. Then he examined the gory head wound with his torchlight.

'He's a fair way from his bike, he must've been really shifting, poor kid,' the other ambulance man muttered, as he helped the driver lift the youth onto the stretcher.

'Yeah, he's copped a nasty bang on the head,' confirmed the driver. 'He's lucky he didn't kill himself!'

#

At seven twenty-nine, Amaranth awoke. Even though it was Saturday, she reached out to where she usually had the alarm, and instead touched Gary, lying beside her. They had talked till they were falling asleep, and had lain on the bed without either expectation or excitement the night before. She snatched her eyes open.

'Good morning,' he said softly.

She was startled but not frightened. She looked around her in the dimness of the day's first light. It was a room where somebody slept, but not a room that somebody liked to sleep in. Same as the bathroom; there was no trace of luxury, everything was adequate at best. The curtains hung carelessly. The light bulb in the bedside lamp stood shamelessly shade-less. Open drawers formed a miniature staircase leading nowhere but up and down the dull oak cabinet. Clothes were left where they fell, on the floor, over a chair. A desk, cluttered with books, laptop, phone, near-empty whiskey bottle, and a used mug, was smothered by an abandoned open newspaper, like a layer of frost on a council rubbish tip. A large oil painting of a sailing ship was propped against the wall. Her open suitcase, with her towel draped over its upright lid, declared her inclusion.

'You look really nice,' he continued, easing her towards him. She felt the stubble on his face. It announced his gender as his hand slid down over her stomach to hers.

'Can we wait?' she said softly. 'A couple of days or so? Just till we get to know each other.'

Stung by guilt, he immediately withdrew his hand to her hip. 'Yeah. Yeah, sure,' he obliged. Her nightie was tight against this contour, and he played with its smoothness, letting the weight of his arm glide his palm over the precipice of her hip again and again. 'I forgot about all that. I'm so sorry,' he whispered, then he rolled onto his back and sighed, like he was expelling an out-breath of cigarette smoke filled with his memories of the night, as much as his imaginings of the morning.

By midday, they had showered, dressed, had breakfast, and walked to the corner shop to get her bearings, some fruit, and the weekend papers. Later, Gary made a stir-fry while Amaranth tried to not feel like a visitor, or a captive, by walking outside into the back garden. Alone. She returned inside just as he was serving the food. Once they had finished eating, Gary took her plate and stacked it on top of his.

'That was delicious. I'll get the dishes,' she rhymed.

She washed, he dried and put away. It was all very domesticated.

'Can you cook anything else?' she enquired.

'Course I can. I've been looking after myself for over a year now. Any rate, I always liked to do a bit of cooking.'

Amaranth nodded and continued with the chore.

'So who looked after you last year then?'

'Who looked after me? I'm not a kid. I've always looked after myself.'

'I mean, you said you'd been looking after yourself for over a year. "Always" is not "over a year", is it?'

'Yes. It is actually,' he said, slipping beneath her cross-examination.

'Don't you want to tell me?'

'No.'

'Well then,' she said kindly but firmly, 'that's all you have to say. We don't ever have to pretend with each other.'

He put the plate he was drying back on the dish rack. Looping the tea towel over the back of her neck, he gently drew her to him. 'You are so different,' he said.

85

'From?'

'From other women.'

'Oh,' she said, slipping from under the tea towel and returning to the dishes in the sink. 'That old line.'

'No, you are,' he said. 'Even your name is different. Where's it from?'

'My mother was sort of a hippy,' she said with an apologetic little laugh. 'Amaranth is a kind of grain you can get in health food stores these days, but it wasn't around when I was born. Mum got the name from an old Greek legend. It's supposed to be an invisible flower that never fades. I always wondered: if it's invisible, how would you know if it had faded or not?'

'Ah, the old Schrödinger's Cat thing,' he said with a laugh. 'And why is the flower invisible? Surely the whole thing about being a flower is to be seen? It'd be pretty dismal if they didn't get noticed, wouldn't it?'

'It explains a lot,' she said, recalling how unseen she felt. 'Maybe the legend shaped me.'

'So, you're a bit of a legend then?' he said with a boyish grin.

'Legends are stories of lives that didn't really happen,' she said, stacking the dish rack with the last of the plates. 'It's quite suitable, actually.'

'You're being a tad harsh on yourself there,' he said.

'Oh, I'm good at that,' she said. 'But then if you don't know your failings I don't suppose you're going to improve, are you?'

He smiled.

'What about you?' she shuffled the focus back to him. 'Have you got any failings?'

'Failings? Oh, yeah, I've got plenty of failings.'

'What's the worst one?' she asked, fishing for the knives and forks in the water.

'Well, obviously I've got anger issues,' he said. 'That's definitely my big one.'

'And what is it makes you so angry?' she asked.

He took her hands out of the dish water, and dried them with the tea towel. Then he led her into the lounge room. They sat side-by-side on the couch, and he told her about finding Kate in bed with Nick Jones.

'I can hardly believe it,' he said, 'but I just stood there. Silent. I just stood there and watched as they got up, got dressed, and got out of there.'

'There wasn't much else you could have done, Gary.'

'I could've beaten the crap out of him,' he seethed.

'And what would that have done for you?'

'For a start, I wouldn't have had to carry all this anger around with me for over a year.'

'Anger?' Amaranth queried. 'Don't you mean hurt?'

He changed the focus back to her.

'So,' he said freshly, 'tell me about *your* last.'

'My *last*? Hah, that's a joke. I haven't had much luck with guys.' She was attempting to flippantly brush this confession off even though it was draped on her like a wet blanket. 'I always seemed to pick the wrong ones, or they picked me, more like, and I just went along with it,' she continued, without shame. 'I seem to attract guys that just want a couple of nights here and there.'

'And you? What do you want?'

'Something,' she enthused. 'I haven't done anything with my life, there's so much catching up to do. Maybe climb mountains and swim rivers and…'

'Want to go sailing?' he interjected. 'I've got a little boat in the harbour.'

Gary's twenty-six-footer, *Away*, sliced through the afternoon. Amaranth, as exhilarated as the spray, sat bolt upright, holding on to the side rail. She had never done this before. Saturday afternoons usually dragged like a Sunday, only with added housework and shopping. A weekend for her was usually just recovery time. Time to prepare for the reality of her job. But here, in this boat, in this water, in this day, in this world, suddenly, she felt she was actually living.

They headed towards the shore, and she saw a large sign saying *Lifesavers* painted on the side of the pavilion building. *Yes*, she thought. *Yes!*

That awful thing in the park seemed so long ago; her life was filling now. The slap on the face was like a ritual re-birthing for her. All birth is a painful ugliness described as a beautiful miracle because the consequence was welcomed.

Gary beamed his boyish grin as he leaned on the tiller and looked at her. He loved sailing, but he loved seeing Amaranth so happy to be playing with him even more. She looked good in her bathers. Her pale skin declaring her inexperience, the life-vest somehow enhancing her innocence. But her smile: her smile was abandoned. Her hair: wild. Her cheeks: flushed. She was just so naturally beautiful.

He shouted for her to duck her head as he brought the boat around, and the boom swung recklessly across the deck. Engaging the less rigorous long tack, he gestured the tiller to her.

'You wanna take over?' he said.

That evening, Gary stepped out of the hot bath that Amaranth had insisted he would enjoy. He wrapped a towel around his waist and, steam still rising from him, he emerged into the lounge room where she was standing looking out of the window.

He walked over and stood close behind her.

'What you looking at?' he enquired, putting his arms around her.

'Out there, that's all. I like looking out of windows. It's good to know there's something else.'

'You don't like it here?'

'It's not that,' she answered thoughtfully. 'I suppose I just want to know a little about where I'm not. I guess it's like I want to know what's on the whole menu, even if I know what I'm having.'

'Are you still hungry? Do you want to go out someplace?'

'No,' she said, with a little laugh and turning towards him. 'I'm fine.'

He reached behind his head with one hand and pinched the top of his spine.

'Is your neck sore?' she asked.

'Yeah. I carry tension there. It's okay.'

'Should I give it a rub?'

Amaranth woke first the following morning. She could tell it was a Sunday. Sundays sound different.

Gary roused as she slid out of bed and headed for the toilet. When she returned, she felt a little cool so she rummaged in her suitcase for a sweatshirt to throw over her nightie. She looked at Gary as she put it on, and saw that he had fallen back into a deep sleep. Her eyes stumbled on the drawers, some of which were still open, and wondered if there were any empty where she could put her things. She saw one crammed with socks and underpants. Another had just a few business envelopes and letters in it. She lifted them out and placed them on top of the drawers, but she noticed one hand-written envelope addressed to 'Kate Harrison, 12 Langtree Close, Cedar Waters.' It was unopened and stamped 'Return To Sender'. She turned it over, and just under where Gary had written his address was the one word, "*Please*".

Gary stirred and sat up.

'What are you doing?' he challenged sleepily.

'Looking for an empty drawer,' she said, hurriedly slipping the envelope into the pile she'd made on top of the drawers. 'I don't want to keep living out of a suitcase, Gary. I'm not just here for the weekend.'

He cleared two drawers out for her, and then went to the bathroom as she unpacked her case.

'I need some more furniture, don't I?' he said when he came back in.

'Yes,' she chuckled. 'I reckon we do.'

Sunday became shopping-for-stuff-for-the-house day. She exerted the taste she had acquired from all the magazines she'd bought for the train rides to and from work. Mostly Balinese style items – dresser, coffee table, large lounge room cushions, small, interesting knick-knacks.

Over dinner that night, he asked her if she was from Sydney.

'No, I'm a Queensland girl. Mackay. Do you know where that is?'

'Up north someplace,' he said through a mouthful of pasta.

'That's it exactly,' she reflected. 'Up north some place.'

'What did your old man do for a crust?'

'That's such a male question,' she said, her voice tinged with a mixture of curiosity and ridicule. 'I lived with my mum there. My dad moved out when I was four. I only met him two or three times after that, till Mum died, so I didn't really know him. Then I moved in with him for a bit, but we didn't get along. He tried to be nice, but it wasn't real. You can't get to know someone when they're being "nice" to you.'

Chapter 12.   Ms Howard

Monday morning, Gary was sitting at the breakfast table. He was still unshaven, as he usually started work around eleven, but Amaranth was dressed for her office.

'I don't know about this,' he said. 'I don't really like you going to work.'

'Why not?'

'Who d'you work with?'

She stopped picking the lint from her skirt and looked at her inquisitor.

'Why?'

'Just wondered,' he said. 'Nice people?'

Amaranth looked towards the door, then at her watch. She plonked her bag on the vacant chair beside him and leaned her hip against the table.

'I work with just one person. A lawyer. My boss. She's not very nice.'

'Right. I see.' He held up the coffee percolator to her but she shook her head. He poured himself another cup. 'I suppose you get a lot of businessmen coming in?'

'A few,' she said.

'I'd have thought there'd be a lot.'

'Why?'

'Business. Law. I just thought there would be.'

'No,' she affirmed, 'not really.'

He took a sip of comfort, and she took the opportunity to check the weather outside.

'So,' she said, standing up straight, 'I turn left after the shops, first right, and the station is halfway down?'

'Young hotshots with too much money and no time to read their contracts. There must be a lot of that sort.'

She shunted her train of thoughts back for him.

'A lot, a few, what's the difference? Too many I say!'

Gary placed his cup back carefully in the middle of the saucer and stared into it like he was doing a reading.

'You shouldn't have to work.'

'Everyone has to work, Gary.' She gathered her bag to demonstrate she was ready to go.

'You don't need to,' Gary said, looking up at her. 'I've got a bit put aside.'

'I'd go crazy if I just sat around here all day,' she said, checking she had the office keys.

'You don't even like the job. It doesn't make you happy,' he threw in with desperation.

She stopped fussing and looked at him, processing his interrogation for motive.

'Do you want me to quit?' she asked him.

He nodded.

She stood silent, considering this. Well, he was right: she didn't like her job. It didn't make her happy. Somehow, that had never been enough justification for her to leave, but if *he* wanted her to? Suddenly here was someone else telling her what she ought to do. Telling her what she wanted to do.

'I can't just not turn up, Gary. I'd have to go in and do it personally.'

'Why?'

'Give her the keys back. Empty my drawers. See the look on her face.'

Amaranth sat on the train heading into the city and played out the scene with her boss. There was devilment in her head. She hadn't acknowledged how resentful she felt for the way Ms Howard had treated her with such contempt all the years she'd worked there. She wondered if what had attracted the lawyer to her was that she recognised a girl who was easily bullied. *Well not anymore.* Gary wanted her to resign, so resign she must, and there could be no question of her backing down. This was something she had long wanted to do, but hadn't realised, and now she had to do it.

She bought a large bunch of flowers from the vendor at the station. It wasn't a gift to thank her boss, nor was it to soften her announcement. It was simply to do something she had never done before. That, and arriving ten minutes late.

Ms Howard emerged from the interior office, her arms folded fiercely across her chest.

'Is someone sick?' she demanded of her employee.

'These?' said Amaranth, smelling the bouquet. 'I couldn't resist them.'

'I hope you have a good excuse.'

'For buying flowers for the office, Ms Howard?'

'For being late,' she snapped, ignoring the gift. 'The phone rang and there was no one here to answer it.'

'Well, if you heard it, you must have been here,' Amaranth said, amazed at her own attitude.

Ms Howard was furious. She shouted about how she didn't employ a girl for the office, and then answer her own phones. She went on about how flowers were hardly appropriate for a legal office and since she had not requested someone to buy them it was therefore no excuse for someone to be late. Case closed. Verdict: guilty. Sentence: she would be deducting an hour's pay from Amaranth's wages this week.

'An hour? I'm less than fifteen minutes late.'

'You are paid by the hour, I don't deal in fractions,' her boss stated.

The phone rang and Ms Howard stepped back to allow her secretary access to it. Amaranth walked over to her desk, but instead of attending to the phone, she bent down and collected her plastic rubbish bin. She walked to the rest room with it.

'The phone, girl!' screamed her boss.

'I'm not working till ten,' Amaranth sang out, as she ran some water into the bin.

'Excuse me?' Ms Howard shouted over the amplified splashing. 'You're working the minute you walk in that door.'

'Fractions of an hour, Ms Howard,' came her secretary's rejoinder over the persistent ringing of the phone. 'You're not paying me till ten, I don't work till ten.'

This is so much easier than I thought it would be, Amaranth decided. *And fun!* All the encouraging directives from those self-help courses she'd done suddenly made sense to her. Like getting a joke, getting that ah-hah moment, understanding what it's about.

Ms Howard felt her neck tighten. Her upper lip quiver. Her forehead scrunch. Her hands jitter. She snatched up the phone and slammed it straight back down.

Amaranth turned off the tap and came back in to arrange the flowers.

'I don't know what's got into you this morning, Amaranth, and I haven't time to be bothered with it right now.' She squeezed the words through clenched teeth. 'Very well, you have a point: I shan't deduct any pay from you provided you get straight back to work.'

The phone rang again.

'And you can start with *that*!' Ms Howard stood like the Statue of Justice. One hand balancing the scales of her sanity, the other pointing to the nagging phone. 'Just give me your assurance that you will not be late for work again, flowers or no flowers.'

Amaranth picked up the phone, and then hung up straight away, as her employer had done. 'You have my assurance, Ms Howard. I won't be late for work in future as I won't be coming to work in future.'

And then she chucked the office keys on her desk. And left.

Amaranth caught the train to Chester Hill. She'd remembered she had left a bundle of photographs in her bottom drawer at Kirsten's. Souvenirs of a past she could barely recall, but thought she might want to someday. The Tree Gang Girls' giant fig tree. Her cat, Misha. Their house stuck in the middle of that lonely sugarcane nowhere. Her mother. The group shot of the family who came to the funeral with more condemnation than compassion. They were all strangers, except for 'Uncle' Warren, who used to like helping Amaranth tuck her top into her skirt whenever her mum wasn't home, and whose face she had cut out from the group photos, and burned. There was no one to blame for her mother's suicide so the family said she'd been unwell for a long time. They animated the explanation to each other with an accusative forefinger drawing tiny, rapid circles beside their temples.

Amaranth arrived at Kirsten's door and almost knocked. She already felt like a visitor there, but she recalled that Kirsten would be at work so, finding her keys at the bottom of her bag, she opened the door.

As she stepped from the hollowness of the hallway into the muted apartment, she heard a scuffling in her old room. Then a drawer shut, and another one opened. *The place is being robbed!* She armed herself with the heavy African woodcarving that Kirsten had bought from the op shop and displayed on the hall table so it was the first thing anyone would see when they entered. Amaranth-the-new crept towards the bedroom door to confront the intruder, something unthinkable for Amaranth-of-old to do.

Looking in, she saw the profile of a stranger. A guy in his twenties, with dishevelled jeans, T-shirt, and a thick mop of straggly dark hair. He spun around, clearly startled to see her there.

'What's going on?' she demanded.

'Holy shit!' he yelped.

'What are you doing here?' she clarified.

'You gave me a shock. I'm moving in. Are you err, Amma, that used to live here?'

She could see he was delivering, not stealing, because there were shirts and books and all manner of new things strewn around the room. She relaxed her shoulders.

'Yes. That's me.' She laughed at, and to, herself. 'Nice stereo.'

He glanced at the carving in her hands. 'I've put some other stuff of yours in a bag there,' he said, indicating a large plastic garbage bag in the corner. 'I hope that's okay. I'm sorry. I needed the drawer space. I didn't know you were coming today.'

'Neither did I. Just wanted to check. I left in a bit of a rush.'

'So Kirsten was saying,' he said. 'She works for a friend of my brother. That's how I got onto this place so quickly.'

She walked across to the bag and looked inside. It was nearly full, and she glimpsed her slippers, some antiquated Michael Jackson CDs, copies of old telephone bills with her calls marked. Nothing she wanted to see. She delved further down and found her bundle of photos.

'Ah, these I want, but it'll take me a while to sort through the rest of this lot. Most of it I wanted to dump to be honest,' she said, abandoning the rummage.

'That's what I felt when I left where I was living,' he agreed. 'It was my brother's place – till he virtually gave it to his girlfriend and Spritzer the Shih Tzu, their surrogate son. Anyway, most of the housie-stuff belonged to Josh, so I hardly brought a thing. Clean break. Fresh start.'

'Totally,' she agreed. 'What's your name?'

'Daniel. Daniel Epstein.'

'Jewish, yeah?' she startled herself by asking.

'Sometimes. Whenever I'm at a family do and I want to feel the same as everyone else. Why d'you ask?'

'My mother was Jewish. When she wanted to feel different from everyone else,' Amaranth said.

'Your mother was Jewish? What's your last name?'

'Vaughan. It's Welsh, Mum married out. She was a Feigenbaum: you can see why she kept her married name even after she divorced.'

'Yeah, I guess,' he agreed. 'I suppose you'd always have to spell that.'

'Usually have to spell Vaughan anyway.' She shrugged a gesture of surrendering to the name fate. 'But at least it doesn't sound as bad as Feigenbaum.'

'Baum is a tree,' he said. 'Feigen probably means fig, so: Figtree.'

'Oh,' she said, 'yeah, probably. Very biblical. Fig leaves were quite the fashion in Eden or someplace.'

They both smiled.

'It's a good room,' she said, breaking the awkward realisation that they had finished smiling and were now simply staring at each other.

'Yeah,' he agreed. 'Great window.' He walked over to it, moved the curtain aside and looked out. 'I like windows,' he elaborated wistfully. 'I like knowing there's something else. Out there.'

'Mmm,' was all she could say, but she felt she was hearing her own secret thoughts out loud. And they had his voice.

96

'The good thing about my brother's place was that it looked onto a park. It was always busy. Kids, old people, couples, the lonely, they were all there.' Daniel let the curtain fall back across his window.

#

Gary let the curtain fall back across his window. He had been looking out of his lounge room, waiting for Amaranth to come walking down the street. He had decided, two hours before, not to go to work that day, and to be waiting at home when she came back. He checked his watch. Midday. *She should have been back by now,* he thought. *What's keeping her? Got to get her a mobile. Maybe her boss had insisted that she work the day out. Then why hadn't she phoned me from there to tell me? I should've decided to take the day off sooner, and driven her in. Maybe she's changed her mind about the whole thing. Maybe she isn't coming back.*

He switched on the TV. Distraction. That's what he needed. There was an American chat show on. The host was in amongst the audience, soliciting questions from them for her guest, a model called Sandi Sorrento. Someone wanted to know what happened when Donald Trump had rung Sandi for a date ten years ago, and the model explained that he had seen her in a fashion show and then got his male secretary to ring her. At first, she thought it was her boyfriend playing a trick on her, but eventually she believed it was indeed the wealthy man's personal secretary.

'He sent this huge limo for me,' the model gushed.

'And where did Donald Trump take you on your date, Sandi, and what happened?' asked another audience member.

'I can't really talk about that,' she stated firmly. 'There's a lawsuit in progress.'

Gary fumed. He assassinated the TV with the remote.

'What about your fucking boyfriend?' he vented at the blackened screen. 'How did he feel knowing you were out with some bloke who had to pay a pimp to date you for him? Jesus!' He was palpable as he went to the window again.

#

Daniel poured Amaranth a coffee from the percolator on the kitchen bench. 'Kirsten was saying you've moved in with your boyfriend.'

'He's not my boyfriend. He's, he's just someone who's working through some issues, and he needs…looking after.'

He brought the coffees to the kitchen table and settled a cup in front of her. She smiled a 'thank you' as he straddled the other chair.

'So, he's an old friend, is he? I don't mean geriatric.' He laughed.

'No. We only met recently.'

'Oh, so you must really like him.'

'Why?'

'You moved in with him,' he said, trying the coffee's temperature.

'Hadn't really thought about whether I like him or not. He needs me, that's all. And I owe him.'

'Owe him?'

She became uncomfortable and glanced at her watch.

'Wow, is that the time? I really must get going.' She took a sip of coffee, apologised for leaving the cup unfinished and unwashed, and headed for the front door.

'What about your stuff?' Daniel asked, holding up the plastic bag he'd dragged into the kitchen for her.

'Can't take it all on a train, not with this stuff I took from work. Can I pop back another day and sort it all out?'

'Sure. Make it Thursday. I'm taking Thursday off too this week. I could help you.'

'I'll be fine. I only want a few things anyway.'

'Whatever. But Thursday if you need me. Okay?'

She smiled a 'goodbye', and slipped out of the door, closing it behind herself. Waiting for the lift, she looked at the familiar light-brown hallway walls and saw that they were actually painted yellow.

Daniel walked straight to the bedroom. He lifted the mattress and picked up Amaranth's notebook, which he knew was hidden there. He sat on the bed and held the book for a moment, like it was a treasured artefact. He knew the page he wanted, the twelfth one, the one that read: '*All my life I've been giving. Giving in, giving up. I'm trapped in myself, and I long to be rescued.*'

Amaranth arrived home and slipped past Gary's car in the driveway. She wondered why he hadn't taken it to work. Perhaps he was home for a late lunch, he didn't start till eleven. Or maybe he was sick or something.

'So? What happened?' he probed as soon as she walked in through his front door.

She couldn't read his mood. He was trying to smile, stretching his unshaven cheeks, baring the tips of his upper teeth, but that gave him more of a snarl. He seemed edgy, as though he was displeased with her for something, but she had no idea what.

'What do you mean, "What happened"?' she asked.

'I mean what happened?' he repeated, exaggerating confusion at her response.

'At work?'

'Of course at work. Where else?'

She was surprised to realise she had almost forgotten about going in to work. She dropped guilt, and collected nonchalance.

'I just told her I was leaving. She flipped out, and I left. I think it's the first time she's ever given me a second thought, though. Or maybe even a first one. I bought her a lovely bunch of flowers, I should have kept them for myself, they were so beautiful. Mmm. What's cooking?'

She walked to the kitchen and he followed.

'I did a sort of casserole. You want some?' he asked.

She set the plates and cutlery on the table whilst he opened the oven. Grabbing a tea towel, he seized the dish with one hand, but it was way too hot for this inadequate insulation.

'Quick,' he shouted, 'get the chopping board!'

'Put it down if it's burning you,' she chastised, as she abandoned the plates and looked for the board, jerking her head around the kitchen like a chicken checking for grains.

'Quickly! Bottom drawer.' he urged.

She found it and slammed it on the table. He slid the dish onto the board and then ran to the sink and held his hand under the cold running water. Amaranth just stood by the table, shaking her head.

After they had eaten and cleared up, they were sitting in the back yard. Mugs of tea and warm sunshine.

'The grass could do with a cut,' he announced. 'I'll get on to it today.'

She didn't respond. She hadn't noticed the tall grass; the yard was only as much in need of attention as the rest of the house, but her gaze was inward.

'You quitting your job has inspired me to do the same,' he continued with his proclamations. 'I'm not going in again. Thought I might start looking for my own business. Maybe something we could do together.'

'Like what?'

'I don't know yet. But you've got secretarial skills, and I've got sales skills. Should be plenty of things we could do.'

Ignoring his dream, she asked, 'So, if you're not going to work tomorrow, can we take *Away* out for a sail again?'

'If the tide's right and there's a good wind.'

'Can't we go anyway?' she enthused.

'No good trying to sail against the tide, Amaranth, and we can't just sit in the boat, waiting for a wind.'

'Why not?' she retorted. 'That's what I'd do.'

Chapter 13.   Sparks

That night, Amaranth let Gary enter her. She recognised his expectation, and aligned it with her contractual obligations. She had agreed to give herself to him, and she knew that would involve this. After receiving him, she lay patiently witnessing his satisfaction, her mind free to wander where it would. She thought of some of the times she'd been in this exact position with different guys. She opened her mental filing cabinet and dragged their files out, flicking through their images, recalling their faces…till she recognised Daniel's.

Oh, what's he doing in there? she thought.

The next day, Tuesday, they did go sailing again, and there was just enough wind to thrill her. After hauling his dinghy up at the Yacht Club, Gary took Amaranth upstairs to the verandah bar. She looked out over the harbour. It really was a lovely day. Duck egg blue sky. Lemon rind sunshine. Green broccoli trees. Raw sugary sand. Lightly salted ocean breeze. She was hungry.

They ate a good meal there, and yet she felt a discontent as pressing as her hunger had been. His yester-dream of binding them together in a business tightened around her.

'Have you thought of looking for a business interstate?' she asked.

'No. Why?'

'I just wondered if you've ever thought of living somewhere else.'

'Yeah, I thought of it,' he said. 'But what's someplace else got you can't find right here?'

'It's someplace else, for a start off,' she answered quickly.

'Why, where would you like to go?'

'Away,' she said with a wistful gaze over his shoulder. 'See a bit of the world. Meet different people.'

'Are you bored with me?' Gary asked nervously, feigning playfulness.

She smiled. 'How could I be bored with you?' He relaxed. 'I hardly know you.' That didn't help. 'I meant I'd like *us* to meet more people.'

He reached over the table and held her hands like he was about to propose.

'Why?' he said, staring into her eyes. 'I could sail off to an island with you, stay there forever, and never see another person. I don't like people much. Except you. I like you. A lot.'

He stood up and came around to her side of the table. He squatted beside her and went to kiss her. She turned away. She cared for Gary, her agreement aside. She could see the healing she was promoting in him too. It was a trade that balanced the strengthening that he provided her. A trade that included servicing his sexuality, but she felt nothing romantically for him.

'What's the matter?' he asked.

'I don't like to be a public display, Gary.'

'No one's looking. And so what if they were? You see why I'd like that island?'

He moved to kiss her again, and this time she let him. Partly, because she thought a scene *about* kissing would be worse than a scene *of* kissing. Mostly, because she would do anything to deflect his thoughts of hermitising them. The kiss, however, was one-way. She accepted it, but she gave nothing.

#

Daniel was flicking through Kirsten's CD collection when Robert came in from the kitchen.

'What's the story with the coldies, mate?' Rob said.

'What coldies?' said Daniel.

'Exactly. There's none in the fridge. Did you polish 'em off?'

Daniel looked up. 'Beer?' he asked rhetorically. 'No. I cleaned the fridge yesterday and there weren't any in there then.'

'Shit, eh!' Robert said, as he chucked himself into a chair. 'Must've drunk the bastards meself! Don't you drink then?'

'Not big on beer. I like the occasional red. With a meal,' said Daniel, as he turned back to the CDs.

Robert pulled a face imitating a hoity-toit drag queen.

'So, what do you do for a quid?' he asked, expecting confirmation.

'I work in a fashion warehouse.'

Yep, there it is, right there, thought Robert.

'What about you?' returned Daniel casually.

'Sparks,' said Robert, as macho as he could, then clarified it for the hapless lad. 'Electrician. Work for a mob on the north side. Mainly rewiring old places and that. Bit dull but the coin's good. Couple of years and I'll strike out on me own.'

He was struggling to continue the conversation. Daniel at least had the CDs to fidget with.

Robert didn't like his girlfriend living with another man. Especially one he didn't understand. It was hard to know what was going on. Whether there was any threat. This bloke was on a completely different page. What were the ground rules now?

He spoke to Daniel's back, over by the stereo, and began to list the power points that he'd put in around the flat. That accomplished two things for him. It established his ability. And it marked his territory.

'And then there's that configuration in Kirsty's room,' Robert said with a tradesman's pride. 'Had to modify the power point and install the dimmer, timer, and master power board next to her bed. Have you seen that thing?'

'No, I've never even seen inside Kirsten's room, to be honest.'

'No,' said Robert, 'you wouldn't have.' He called out for Kirsten to hurry up before turning back to Daniel. 'All this time to put some make-up on. We're going to a movie, for God's sake. It's as dark as fuck in there. Who's going to notice what she looks like?'

'Ta-dah!' Kirsten entered, ready to go.

'Thank fucking Christ. Let's go,' said Robert, heading for the door. 'See you...err...'

'Dan,' said Daniel.

All the way down in the lift, Robert called Daniel a weirdo, a poofter, dodgy, shifty, up-himself, and a total drop kick. Kirsten said she thought Daniel seemed like a nice bloke, and any rate he paid the rent on the room. Who else could she get?

All that night, Gary held Amaranth closely. He fell asleep quickly and deeply. She lay awake for a long time. His arm was heavy on her. Restrictive. Assumptive. However, she didn't move it away in case it woke him. She thought back over the past few days. It seemed to her that clocks and calendars were poor methods of measuring time. Time couldn't really be fixed. A moment observed slows down. An hour of headaches lasted longer than an hour of happiness. Her empty days had dragged slowly by, but once gone they became a fleeting past. These full days flitted by, but formed a past so bursting with experiences and growth that it seemed as if it had been going on for decades.

Wednesday, Gary and Amaranth busied themselves with the house. Neither of them noticed how they just fell into the traditional male and female roles of the typical suburban couple. She was "adding the feminine touch", dowsing herself with the girly fragrance of furniture polish, Spray 'n' Wipe, and Windex. He was "doing the outside", dusting himself with the manly talcum of lawn clippings and earthy dust, which clung to the cologne of two-stroke and sweat.

In bed that night he made love to her again. He was thrusting hard on top of her. She was a blow-up doll. Her hands over her head, gripping the bedrails like she was tied there. Taking it.

'I can't hold on much longer,' Gary gasped.

'Don't then. I told you I never get there.'

He burst from his passion like a breaching whale, and flopped back to float on the settling bliss.

She lay there and waited, like a surfer's chick on a beach blanket.

'You've never come?' he asked.

'There was this boy, oh God, a long, long time ago. I'd get a sort of tingle when he used to touch me there. Then, after a few minutes, I couldn't bear it anymore. It was too intense. Too sensitive. Nothing like I'd read in the magazines.'

Nothing she particularly wanted to feel again.

'I'm happy just seeing you happy,' she continued softly. 'I really get off on seeing you get off.' And she meant that. It had become her pleasure with men. To give them what they wanted without demand. It gave her a glimpse of power. The power of being desperately needed, and to be appreciated in those after-moments. Praised, even.

He told her she was beautiful and gently stroked her. She took one of his hands and studied it in the half-light.

'You've got nice hands,' she said. 'Big. Strong hands. You have a deep love line here.'

'This from your mother being a bit of a gypsy, is it?'

She giggled. 'This is your fate line. This is your heart line. And this is your life line.'

'Does it say I'm going to have a long and happy life?'

She laughed. 'I'd better look at your other palm. Your life line pales out on this one.' She took his other hand. 'Mmm.'

'What's this one say?' he posed.

She examined the blister he received from the hot casserole dish. 'This one says that even when you know something is hurting you, you stubbornly hold onto it.'

He pulled his hand slowly from her.

'I reckon I've finally put that down on the chopping board too,' he said sincerely. 'My wife. My ex-wife. Kate. I can even say her name. Kate. I was so caught up with her – it seemed I lost everything when she left. And it wasn't just the divorce. It was the way she did it. She'd been on with that bloke for weeks. That's what got me. They were on during times I'd talked to her. Told her things. Felt things. Then… seeing them like that.'

He was on the verge of his sorrow, but he didn't plunge into it. Not because he held back, but because it had withered into a shrivelling scab ready to fall away from new skin.

'I trust you, Amaranth. That thing in the park, it was meant to happen, just so's I'd find you.'

She lifted his arm and placed it around her. Just the way he liked to fall asleep.

In the morning, Amaranth came into the kitchen straight from the shower, with her towel around her. Gary was dressed and at the table with a coffee, the newspaper and his phone.

'There's a couple of businesses I'm looking at this morning,' he announced. 'A shop over at Auburn, and an import-export thing. I'll check them both out and let you know. I probably won't be home till after one, I'd say.'

'It's Thursday today, isn't it?' she asked almost casually.

'Yeah, sure is. Why? What's Thursday?'

'I just want to know where I am. Off you go.'

And he went.

Amaranth hesitated at Kirsten's door and thought for a few more moments. She knew she hadn't just come to collect her things. This was Thursday; Daniel said he'd be home today. She didn't fully understand her feelings, but she knew that this was an important encounter for her. Something she had to explore. There was some danger in it too, and that seemed to spur her on.

It was Daniel's space now, and out of respect for that, she knocked. Of course, if he wasn't home, she still had her key.

He tore the door open and smiled a huge welcome.

She followed him inside and made comment about his improvements to the place. Things gone, things moved. He liked where he lived, she could see that. Her things were laid out on his bed, a consideration she appreciated. He had two empty bags set aside for her. One for the op shop, one for her to take away. The heavy African wood carving that he thought was hers was on top. That made her smile. In fifteen minutes she had it all sorted, and they were seated in two chairs by the famous bedroom window.

'I feel so comfortable here,' said Amaranth.

'Is it the room, the view, or the company?'

'All three. The room and the view because I know them so well. You...?'

'Me?' He leaned forward.

'I feel like I know you too.'

'I feel like that with you,' he said, and leaned back. 'But I've cheated. I've done the worst thing I've ever done in my life.'

'What?'

'I don't know how you'll feel about me when I tell you. I'm scared you'll despise me.' His voice was genuinely wavering.

'What? Shit, it can't be any worse than what I've done.'

'No, no. I *have* to tell you. It would be like living with a lie or something if I didn't.'

She looked at his frightened face.

'What then? What have you done that's so terrible?'

He drew a deep breath for courage, and confessed, 'I read the poems you wrote to your mum!'

'Poems?'

Daniel stood up and went to the bed. He reached under the mattress and retrieved her notebook. He sat down on the bed, maintaining the distance he imagined his action had created.

She recognised her book.

'Oh that! Wouldn't have thought that collection of grumbles was of much interest to anyone but me.'

He fingered the gilded writing on the cover.

'So Amma is short for Amaranth?' he asked.

'Yeah.'

'It's a nice name.' He smiled.

'It's too long, and it sounds like health food,' she said.

He told her that he found the journal when he'd flipped the mattress over. At first, he'd just glanced at the pages to see what it was and whether it was important, but once he started reading it he just couldn't stop, and he felt that he had got to know her quite well through the pages. He had got to like her.

She rose and walked to the bed. She held out her hand for the book. He surrendered it to her and she sat beside him, flicking through her familiar writings.

'Oh dear,' she said, 'it goes on a bit, doesn't it? I sound like such a loser.'

'It says a lot of things I feel too.' His voice was as soft as his pillow.

They recognised their attraction, yet each of them neither moved towards nor away from the other. Amaranth's thoughts stumbled into Gary and nudged her awake. She realised she could not proceed in the direction her feelings were urging her to go.

'I'm sorry,' she breathed. 'I can't do this. It's too complicated right now. I can't get involved with you.' She jumped up and looked around for her bag and stuffed her journal into it.

'Yeah,' he sighed, and lay back on the futon, studying the ceiling as though the paint was a painting. 'It's too quick. I know. I know.' He sat up again and stared into her face. 'But that's what's so brilliant about it!'

'I'm caught up with someone else right now,' she attempted to explain.

'The guy you're living with?'

She nodded.

'I thought you said he wasn't your boyfriend. Why are you using him as an excuse? Or is there someone else?'

She shook her head.

'So, what do you want?' he challenged.

'It's not about what I want. It's about what is right. It's about commitment. Trust. Betrayal. Having someone depend on you...'

He interrupted her. 'Jesus, you make it sound like he owns you. You're a free per...'

'I'm not free, that's just it, Daniel. I can't do this. I can't.'

'You can,' he said, grabbing her hands and gently persuading her towards him.

She pulled free from him and held her hands behind her back, as though he wouldn't find them there. As though they were cuffed.

He moved close to her. He reached around her and held her clasped hands. Slowly, he stepped back towards the bed, taking his anxious captive with him.

She fell onto the bed, leaving her resistance gawking at them from where it stood in the room, and the vacancy it left in her filled up with a reckless yes. They kissed. They rolled on top of each other. Each a virgin to these feelings. They pulled clothes off in a desperate race against reason, and before they had a moment to reflect and reject them, they were making love. It was beautiful. It was passionate and powerful. Amaranth was abandoned to it like she had never been before. She called out, like she was in pain, like she was in heaven, like she was dying, like she was being born. She climaxed for the first time in her life, and was amazed not only with the sensation, but also its occurrence. Daniel thrust a few more times and went to pull out, but she held him in her, whispering reassurance about being on the pill, and he came too. They fell away from each other, feeling closer than either of them had ever felt with anyone before.

She turned to him with exhausted bedazzlement, attempting a smile. They remained locked in each other's gaze for some time. She felt wonderful.

Till she remembered Gary.

Chapter 14.   Rapunzel

Amaranth saw Gary's car parked in his driveway. She had hoped to be home before him. She opened the front door, rehearsing her entry, and stepped in.

There were four large bunches of flowers placed in saucepans on the lounge room table.

'Finally!' he called to her. 'Wait till I tell you!'

He seemed in a really good mood, and she was grateful for that.

'Tell me what?' she asked as she entered the room.

'About the business I just bought!'

He was so excited. It was like Christmas, and he was a boy. It was like the day Kate had agreed to marry him. It was like that time, on holiday in Noosa, that he won the jackpot on a pokie. It was the day he bought a business that he and Amaranth could run together. He threw his arms wide apart, inviting applause.

She showed little interest, and no enthusiasm. His hands sank with the invisible weight of concern and disappointment.

'What's the matter?' he asked.

'Sorry, Gary, I'm just tired. You know what the city is like.'

'The city?'

'Yeah, you know. Buses, trains, shopping, people. What business did you buy?'

'Wait a minute. Wait a minute. What were you doing in the city? You see, we need to get you a mobile so I can contact you when this sort of thing happens.'

'I've told you what I was doing, Gary. I was shopping,' she replied, as irritated as she was defensive.

'What did you buy then?' he said, glancing at the plastic garbage bag she was holding.

'No, this is just some old junk. I couldn't find what I was really looking for,' she answered, all the time staying away from actually telling a lie. She recalled Daniel and spoke softly, almost to herself. 'Or rather, I did find something, but I couldn't afford it.'

'How much was it?'

'Too much.'

'What was it?' His suspicions rose on the emotional seesaw as his joy plummeted. 'Tell me.'

'I can't,' she said. 'It's a secret.'

'I don't like secrets,' he said ominously.

Still determined not to lie, she conjured with the truth.

'It was a surprise. I don't want to give it away just yet.'

He moved to her and embraced her.

'You don't have to go getting me expensive presents, Amaranth. Just be here for me, that's all I need.' He stroked her hair in a gesture that comforted each of them. 'How come your hair is wet?' he questioned. 'Wasn't raining in town, was it?'

'I dropped by my old flat. I wanted to see if I'd left anything important there.'

'Had you?'

'I'm not sure. I only found this junk. Someone else has moved into my room, and lots of my stuff has been put away someplace.'

'So how did your hair get wet then?'

'I had a quick shower to cool off. It was so stuffy today, wasn't it? I think it's going to storm, don't you?'

He ignored this further ploy of distraction.

'What's wrong with the shower here?'

'Nothing,' she replied, laughing. That laugh she did when she wanted to stay friends with someone who was asking her questions she didn't want to answer.

He paused and considered the whole situation.

'Was anyone else there?'

'Kirsten works during the day, Gary. Everyone does, except us. Now, tell me about this business. Come on. No more distractions.'

Somehow, that worked. She had managed to turn it all around, and he relaxed.

He gestured towards the table.

'Okay, so I thought what do we both know about?' he said. 'Offices. And offices need stationery, folders, ink cartridges, staples, pens, even greetings cards and all that. They're always running out of incidentals and they generally only restock once every month or so from their supplier, so there's a ready market for catch-up sales, and catch-up sales will lead to bigger orders once they get to know the local guy. So I bought an office-supply shop right in the heart of the Auburn business district. It's perfect territory.'

The following day, Gary took Amaranth to see his shop. First, however, he stopped at the Optus store and bought her a mobile phone. He tapped his number into her contacts list; it was the only one in there, making the phone another form of exclusive tethering.

They spent the afternoon in a café, talking about what he reckoned he could do with the shop, how he could extend the range and so on.

'I'm thinking a newsagency,' he said. 'There isn't one in the whole of Auburn, can you believe that? The closest is Regents Park. And, get this, I was thinking as I was buying the flowers, why not fresh flowers in offices? You bought your old boss flowers, you'd know which ones sell. You could work the counter and I could work the territory to rustle up new business clients for the stationery stuff,' he said. 'It's perfect!'

She didn't like that idea, but she didn't want to interrupt his enthusiasm so she just smiled.

#

That night, being Friday, Kirsten was going out with Robert. Once again, her ex had dropped Jesse off a day early, and so she enlisted Daniel to babysit.

'Here's Jess,' she said, coming into the kitchen carrying her pyjama-clad son. 'He's all ready for bed. Now, you'll be a good boy for your Uncle Dan, won't you, Jess? Straight to bed.' She set the boy down on the floor like he was a clockwork soldier.

'Story first!' squealed the toddler.

'I haven't time, Jess,' his mum explained, 'and I don't know if Daniel wants to be reading stories.'

'No, that's okay,' assured Daniel. 'Have you got one in mind, Jesse, my man?'

Jesse ran out of the room to get his favourite storybook. Kirsten called out for him to hop into bed with it, and that Daniel would be there in a minute. She finished getting her bag, checking her purse for money, mobile, and make-up, a quick glance in the bathroom mirror, and then Robert arrived. Wouldn't want to keep him waiting again, she thought, recalling the last fiasco and ensuing debacle. She shouted a goodbye as Daniel went in to Jesse.

Outside, in the hallway, waiting for the lift, Robert whispered, 'Did he just go into your room?'

'Daniel? Yeah.'

'I don't like him going in there.'

'He's reading to Jesse, Rob. Is that a bit of jealousy I detect?' she teased.

'Get real!' he snapped back. 'I just don't like him in there with your personal things, that's all.'

'What, he's going to use my deodorant? Try on my panties? Play with my vibrator?' she giggled.

'He could nick something,' Robert continued.

'Shit, Rob, if I can leave him with my fucking kid, I can leave him with my stereo!'

'He's a fucking weirdo!'

'Déjà vu,' she said, as the lift arrived.

'Me?' he coughed, faking flabbergast.

They got into the empty lift, pressed the down button, and the door closed.

'I didn't say you, Rob. I said "déjà vu". It's French.'

'Oh, excuse me!' he babbled. 'I thought we spoke Australian in Australia.'

'English actually,' she corrected.

'Whatever. I'd better learn Froggy talk. Do you even know what you're saying?'

'Yes. "We've done this before",' she stated, flatly.

'Course we have. It's fucking Friday, birdbrain. We always go out of a Friday.'

The lift reached the ground floor, and the door opened on the night. They walked through the foyer and out into the street.

'Hey,' Robert whispered, taking her arm, 'do you really have a vibrator?'

Daniel sat on the child's little mattress, leaning with his back against Kirsten's bed. He was reading to Jesse and Fudge, who were propped up by the pile of pillows that included Mummy's two big fat ones.

The book Jesse had chosen was a collection of fairytales, and Daniel opened it at random and read the first story that began after that point. Midway through it, he got to the part that read: *'And he called out to her, "Rapunzel, Rapunzel. Let down your hair!" And the prince climbed up to the lonely tower where she was imprisoned. As soon as she saw him in her room, she fell in love with him.'*

Daniel remembered how Amaranth had first seen him in her room. He continued with the story. *'But she was so afraid that he would be caught by the wicked magician that she told the prince to leave.'* Daniel lowered the book and considered the parallels.

'Go on!' urged Jesse. 'What happened next?'

'Next?' Daniel roused. 'Well, let's see.' He began to read again: *'But the prince had a plan.'*

#

Gary and Amaranth were in bed together. She was comfortable. He was not. The nearness of her body only added to his discomfort. He reached out and drew her closer. She said she was hot. He threw the doona off. She grabbed it back. Said she was cold. He tried to initiate lovemaking. She resisted him.

'Gary, come on. We've both had a really full-on day. I don't feel like…'

'What's up?'

She sighed a resignation. 'Where's the baby oil? I'll just do you.'

'No. No. I don't want it like that,' he said firmly.

'Okay,' she acquiesced, rolling over away from him, and going to sleep.

When she awoke the following morning, there was still a chasm between them. She slid quickly out of bed in order to escape having to explain further rejection. When she emerged from the shower, the bed was empty.

She got dressed, dumping her towel into the laundry basket on her way to the kitchen, where she expected him to be. The room was as empty as her insides. Convincing herself that the feeling was just hunger, she cut a tomato and laid two slices on a large rice cracker spread with mayonnaise. As she was juicing two plump oranges for herself, she looked out of the kitchen window and saw Gary in the driveway, loading the car up with boating gear, preparing for a day on the water. Another pleasure she suddenly realised she felt hypocritical about sharing with him. She skulled the juice and then went outside to him.

'I'm not sure I'm up to sailing today,' she said.

He looked up at her. His face dropped like a small child who'd just been grounded. 'I thought you wanted to take her out,' he sulked.

'I just don't feel good. That's all.'

'You should've said. I'm not doing this to make you suffer.' He grabbed a box of gear from the car, and marched it back to the garage.

She stood and watched for a while, then she tired of her guilt, turned, and headed back inside.

'The wind that you'd have waited for will just have to wait for you, Amaranth,' he called out.

Gary gave her the space she was clearly needing. He recognised there was no alternative, except confronting her about why she needed it. The remainder of that day, and all of Sunday, he busied himself 'tinkering' with the lawnmower blades, the car's engine oil, the storage of the boat gear. Then there was that loose paling on the back fence, the letterbox door, the jammed coffee grinder burrs. All in all, despite the fact it rained Sunday, it was a productive weekend for him.

Amaranth spent most of Sunday in bed. Rainy days are always good for hibernation. Midday movie. Tinned tomato soup and thick toast. A magazine. More hand washing. Toenails to manicure. A baked meal to prepare and cook.

Robert left without saying 'hoo-roo' to Daniel, who was cooking dinner on Sunday night. Kirsten came into the kitchen and asked if he needed a hand. He declined, told her to watch a bit of telly. Dinner would be another half hour or so. She hovered in the kitchen. Awkward. Superfluous. Nervous about something. She took a breath before she began her sentence.

'The thing is, Daniel,' she finally got around to saying, 'we need the spare room for Jesse.'

Daniel stopped stirring. He kept his back to her. 'When do you want me out by?' he said, cutting to the proverbial.

'Well, Rob wants to move in next weekend. It'd be pretty crowded with three of us and Jesse.'

'That's what we had this weekend,' Daniel said, rummaging along the spice rack. He clattered the jars together as if finding paprika was the most pressing problem he had.

She explained that Robert would need somewhere for all his gym equipment, and that three adults every day of the week would be simply too much for the one-bathroom flat to handle. 'It still gives you five days, Daniel. You're bound to find a nice place by then.'

Monday morning, Amaranth stayed in bed again when Gary got up. He came back into the room about half an hour later, dressed and ready for an early business day.

'You going to be all right, love?' he asked.

'I'll be fine. I'm just feeling a bit off colour.'

'Do you need a bucket or something? Do you feel like you're going to chuck up?' He suddenly alarmed himself. 'You're not pregnant?'

She placated his dread by reminding him she was on the pill.

'I'm just run down, Gary. Another day in bed will do wonders.'

He smiled and nodded. 'I should be done by four. Need anything before I go?'

'I'll be right.'

She released him from her gaze, and he left. She listened for the car driving off, and then checked her watch. Daniel wouldn't have left for work yet. She leaped out of bed, grabbed her handbag and found her mobile.

Chapter 15.   The Knight in Shining Armour

Amaranth ran up the stairs to Daniel's door. The lift was too slow for her excitement. She controlled the urge to knock.

Her key, his lock, their place.

She guided the tiny brass handsaw into the medallion above the handle, but he snatched the door open before she had a chance to turn it. He flung his arms around her and whirled her inside. She felt like she was home. More than when she had lived there. Way more than where she had moved to.

He kissed her, and without breaking lips from lips, they stumbled to the bedroom. The contortions continued as they undressed each other, still joined by lips spluttering with a laughter that acknowledged how ridiculous they must look. It was as if they were playing Twister and the prize was to share what lay behind the door of their longing.

His key, her lock, their place.

They languished in bed all morning.

The same time Gary went home to see how she was.

Amaranth went into the kitchen after first wrapping a sheet around herself. She sat on one of the bar stools majestically awaiting her servant, Daniel, who was clad in a towel loincloth, preparing a banquet of baked beans.

'Rob's moving in with Kirsten this weekend,' said Daniel, after they had finished eating and cleaning up. 'Apparently, he needs my room for his gym gear so she wants me out by then.'

He handed her a coffee and sat beside her at the table.

'Where are you going to go?'

'Dunno.'

'How will I know where you are?'

'That's why they invented mobiles, Amma,' he said. 'Which reminds me, I don't have your number.'

That startled her. If he rang her and Gary found out...

He put his cup down and grabbed her hand.

'Why don't you come with me?'

She snatched a breath of restraint, letting it out with despair.

'I can't,' she declared.

'Why can't you?'

'I just can't. Don't ask me why. I just can't, that's all.'

Daniel guessed why she couldn't.

'What's this "friend" of yours got over you?'

'Please don't. It's bad enough that I'm here with you, but I don't want to talk about it anymore. I won't betray him.'

'How can talking be betraying him after you just slept with me?'

'It just is,' she said. 'It just is.'

Her mobile vibrated. She looked at the screen and her face visibly blanched.

Suddenly, there was a loud banging on the front door of the flat. Daniel stood up to answer it and decided to put a pair of pants on first. He nipped up to the bedroom. The door banged again.

A muffled voice split through the timber barricade.

'Amaranth! Amaranth! Are you in there?'

Gary! She leapt to her feet and caught Daniel as he came back in and headed towards the front door.

'Don't answer it!' she whispered frantically. 'Please to God, Daniel, don't answer it!'

The fear she invested was contagious.

'If you promise to tell me why,' Daniel whispered back.

She nodded an agreement, her finger pressed hard over his lips.

'Amaranth!' Gary shouted, and gave the door a frustrated thump.

There was silence for a moment or two, then stifled voices and a door slamming somewhere down the corridor. They heard footsteps leaving. She was shaking. Daniel put his arm around her and led her into the bedroom.

'So?' he asked softly.

She just shook her head.

'You promised to tell me,' he pressed.

'I was afraid he would kill you,' she stated.

'Not why you didn't let him in. What he has over you. Why can't you tell me?'

'Same reason.'

He threw his hands up in the air, as close to anger as he could get with her.

'I made him a promise that I wouldn't tell anyone. And I won't break my word,' she pleaded.

He wanted to say something like "what about breaking your heart" but it would have sounded too soppy and melodramatic.

She grabbed her clothes from where they littered the floor.

'I've got to go. We can't keep doing this.' She dressed without further connection with him. Not even eye contact. Not even 'goodbye' as she walked out of his room.

He was full of emotion, yet motionless till he heard the front door close behind her. Then he went in to Kirsten's room where the window was directly above the front of the flats. He looked down and waited. He saw Amaranth come out of the building and start walking up the street. He wrenched at the window to open it, but then he saw a car pull up beside her. Gary jumped out of it, talked with her for a few moments, and then they both got in the car and drove off.

Jesse's fairytale book was the nearest paper Daniel could find. 'DPY 287, DPY 287,' he said, as he rummaged around for a pencil, something he could easily erase. He jotted the number in the top margin of the opened page. Just above the words '*but the prince had a plan.*'

He sprinted back into the lounge room, grabbed his phone and madly scrolled his contact numbers.

'Come on! Come on!' he shouted to the ring tone. 'Ah, yes, good afternoon. Vehicle registrations please.' There was a pause as he was transferred. 'G'day. May I speak with David Carlton? Just tell him it's Josh Epstein's brother, Daniel.'

Inside Gary's car, Amaranth was back to her familiar habit of looking out of the side window.

'What's going on?' he demanded.

'Nothing's going on.'

'Don't give me that crap! How come you didn't answer the frigging door?'

'I didn't hear you knocking.' She persuaded herself that his angry banging did not constitute 'knocking'.

'So how do you know I knocked?'

'I assumed you knocked, Gary. You were wondering why I didn't answer the door, remember?'

'How do you know I didn't ring the bell?'

'Because there isn't a bell,' she said curtly.

He sifted through the logic. 'You must've heard me. I banged so loud the neighbours came out.'

'Why wouldn't I have let you in if I'd heard you knocking?'

'Nice try! Now *you*'re asking me the same fucking question I'm asking *you*! How come you didn't answer your phone then?'

'My phone didn't ring.'

'I rang you as I was banging on the door,' he said.

'It must have been when I was in the stairwell. There's no reception there.'

His driving was erratic and pugnacious. The traffic conspired against him to block his lane changes.

The lights changed to red as he neared them.

'Oh, great!' He slammed his palms against the steering wheel. He had a moment to focus better on what she was saying.

'How come you didn't use the lift?' he asked.

'It was stuck on the top floor when I arrived so I used the stairs. You must've arrived after me. Maybe I was still on the stairs when you knocked.'

'The lift was on the ground floor when I arrived,' contradicted Gary.

'There you are then,' she said, hijacking his evidence. 'I was probably on the stairs.'

His attention had reverted to the traffic, and he realised he was sounding obsessed with the apartment so he abandoned trying to calculate how long it would take to walk up the three flights of stairs compared with taking a lift up, knocking on a door, and then taking the lift back down again. But he was still unsettled.

'I'm sorry, Amaranth. It's... I don't know. Something about that flat. I just don't know why you keep going there.'

'You're being silly, and anyway I'm not going there again,' she said. She opened her bag, pressed her window down, and threw the key out of the car.

He relaxed.

'Okay then,' she said, dolefully. 'Now there's nothing to worry about.'

Daniel waited on line till he heard David Carlton's voice at the Motor Registry, and then cut across the pleasantries of catch-up. 'Big favour time, mate. I really need the street address of a rego number.'

After they had been home for a while, Gary looked out of the lounge room window at the day outside.

'What do you want to do with the rest of the day, then? Considering you're feeling so much better,' he asked her, his voice struggling to find normality.

She shrugged.

'Do you want to go and wait for a wind?' His little joke was wearing very thin.

'I don't know what I want to do.'

'You can't not know what you want to do.'

'Yes, I can,' she said resolutely. 'I've been practising that forever.'

'Well, you can't do nothing, Amaranth. It's a fucking impossibility to do nothing.'

'Not if you're dead.'

'Oh, and you're dead, are you?'

'Aren't I?' she said, staring right into his anger with hers. 'You took my life, remember?'

'You gave it to me, remember?'

'And why was that?' she said.

'Because you wanted to. What were you doing with it when *you* had it? Legend!'

He was right. She saw that. 'Okay, thank you very much, Mr Knight-In-Shining-Armour,' she conceded. 'You saved me from my dragon.'

'Why the sarcasm?'

'Because you only saved me from *my* dragon to feed me to *yours*,' she replied without a trace of malice. 'I need to get away to find myself.'

'You want to get away? Away where?' he said.

'It doesn't matter where,' she muttered.

He went to his desk drawer and shuffled some papers till he found the one he wanted, took a pen, and hurriedly wrote something on it. 'There,' he said, slapping the paper on her lap.

'What's this?' she asked.

'*Away*. You now own the boat. Signed and delivered. You've got *Away*.'

'I don't want your boat, Gary.'

'Your boat,' he insisted. 'And same as with anything, just having it doesn't mean a thing. It's what you do with it, Amaranth, that counts.'

The energy changed, and they each calmed down.

She stood up and handed the paper back to him.

'I don't know a thing about boats – I'm only just learning about myself. I have no idea what I want from life.'

'Well, may I suggest you get some guidance? I mean, if you want to learn to sail, then you go with a sailor and let him show you the ropes. Same for life.'

'With life,' she said, 'I kind of want to just let the ocean teach me.'

'The ocean doesn't teach, Amaranth. It tests what you've learned, that's all. Your instinct to give yourself to me told me you knew that. I only took you on board because I believed you.'

'Well that's precisely what I've done, in case you haven't noticed,' she said, refreshing her tone with resent.

'Your body's here. But *you* aren't. I want you to want to be here.'

'Gary, when I met you I hadn't met myself yet. I'm just starting to get to know who I am. Who I *really* am. Me!'

'Exactly. And who's that thanks to?' he asked.

She knew it was Gary who had insisted she move out, stand up to Kirsten, quit her job. Following his orders had empowered her to speak out. Ironically, she knew she wouldn't even have met Daniel if it weren't for Gary. She owed him a lot. Maybe even as much as denying what she was feeling for another man.

'Let's forget about what I want,' she said. 'I said I'd do what you told me to do. 'Well, here I am. What do you want?'

'I want you to love me,' he croaked. He was the homeless man propped in a cold shop doorway on a deserted street. An open palm exhausted on his lap. Empty.

She didn't know how to answer his plea, and it showed on her face, with her silence, and in the hopelessness that draped itself around their situation.

'We can make this work,' he whispered. If we both try, there's no reason it won't work.'

Outside, at that very moment, Daniel was cruising slowly down Barton Street, counting the house numbers.

Twenty-two, twenty-four, yep, there we are!

He slowed right down. *And DPY 287 in the driveway. Got you!*

He sped off.

But he'd be back.

Chapter 16.   The Anniversary Cake

Daniel was cooking again when Kirsten and Robert arrived at the flat together. It was rare for Robert to come round on a Monday night, let alone pick Kirsten up from work. She'd got him to stop at the bottle shop on their way home, and had rewarded him with the carton she was lugging.

She sniffed the aromatic air like a lioness locating prey.

'Mmm. Smells good! I'm going to miss having a man around the house who can cook,' she said, more to Robert than to Daniel.

'I can cook,' Robert growled. 'I can't help it if you live on the third floor.'

'What's that got to do with it?' she asked, as she put his beer in the fridge.

Robert moved to the lounge area. 'I'm not running up and down three flights of stairs to the barbie. Oi!' he shouted, pointing to the beer. 'Leave one out. Whack it in a stubby holder, she'll be cold enough.'

Kirsten dutifully served him the beer in his cooler, then checking Daniel was okay in the kitchen, went to have a shower and wash away the factory.

'You hungry, Rob?' Daniel asked, as he finely chopped a leafy bunch of kale.

'Nah, looks a bit fancy for me. I'll grab something later.' He took a long swig of beer, exhaling a victorious gasp when the last of the mouthful was past his windpipe. 'So, did you find a place?'

'Not yet.'

'Cutting it a bit fine, aren't you?' Robert asked, oblivious to the fact he had made an allusion to the vegetable chopping.

'Actually,' Daniel said carefully, 'I could be gone this weekend, if you give me a hand.'

'Well, I dunno. I got to shift me own stuff in,' Robert protested. 'Heavy gym gear and the like.' He looked around the flat. 'You got bugger all anyways. So, what do you reckon you need a hand with?' he asked.

'I've got to get Amma away from the bloke she's living with.'

'Amma? That used to live here?' said Robert, putting down his beer so he could concentrate on this. 'Where do you know her from?'

'I met her the other day when she came round to collect some of her things,' Daniel explained.

Robert shouted to the bathroom. 'Hey, Kirsty! Did you know that Amma came round?'

'When?' came the remote response.

'When?' Robert translated for Daniel.

'Last week. Thursday,' he replied.

Robert shouted to Kirsten again. 'Last Thursday. To collect some stuff.'

Kirsten was in the shower now and barely heard.

'Did she leave her key?' she yelled.

Daniel told Robert that he'd forgotten to ask her for it, and he'd get it next time he saw her.

'You on with her or something?' Robert nosed.

'Something like that.'

'So... what, you met her last Thursday and you want her to bust up with her boyfriend?'

'He's not her boyfriend,' Daniel clarified sharply.

'And I suppose you are?'

Daniel shrugged.

'And,' continued Robert with a mocking tone, 'you want me to piss him off for you, is that it?'

'I'd just like to have company when I go round there, that's all. He's a big bloke, and pretty mean by the sounds of it.'

'Too right he's a big bloke,' Robert said, collecting his beer and drinking to that observation. 'And of course he'd be pretty mean if you showed up to pinch his fucking woman. What are you?'

'Desperate,' admitted Daniel, stripped of pride.

126

'You're not wrong there, mate! Nah, fuck it! You can do your own fronting-up on his doorstep, if you're game. The only doorstep I want to see you on is this one when you leave here!'

Kirsten returned in her bathrobe, rubbing her hair with a towel.

'Amma came round?' she repeated.

'And this little Romeo cracked onto her,' dobbed Robert. 'Now he wants me to bounce her old boyfriend for him. Too gutless to do it himself.'

'I didn't say anything about bouncing anyone, Rob.'

'Ahh! Stick to cooking. You suit women's work!' Robert said, with disgust. 'Grab us another beer, Kirsty, then go and get dressed. We'll eat down the road.'

The following day Kirsten went to the factory and told all the girls how her boyfriend had virtually proposed to her. And that she had virtually accepted.

The same day, Robert told Davo he was shifting in with Kirsten, insisting it wouldn't stop him going to the game. It wouldn't get in the way of anything. In fact, it would be easier living closer to work; Davo could stay over and they could go to that little pub on Fisher Street at five o'clock on Friday. Neither of them would have to risk driving. For Rob, living with Kirsten meant he was man enough to have a woman, not like that weedy little wanna-be who was moving out.

Amaranth yielded to her contract with Gary, but her eagerness was replaced with regret. Paramount to her, however, was protecting Daniel.

Gary busied himself with the office supplier, learning more about the business: who to get what from, when to order it. At night, he came home tired and went straight to bed. His mind, however, was too tortured to allow him to sleep, and he lay there listening to the sounds she made disturbing the dust in his dreams.

Daniel had Tuesday and Wednesday in bed but, unusually, went to work on Thursday. He spent most of the day ringing rental ads for spare rooms or small apartments, but he was using the weekend paper so those numbers that did answer told him the room had already gone. Late in the afternoon, Josh strode into Daniel's office.

'Daniel. I've been trying to ring through to you all day. Is there a problem with your phone line?'

'No, I've been calling out.'

'Who to?'

'I've been trying to find a place to live, Josh.'

'Did you just come in today to use the phone? All day?'

'Well...'

'Anyway, what happened to the place we found you?'

'Long story,' Daniel said, avoiding explaining what he barely understood himself.

'And you definitely haven't got time to tell me that story; look at all these orders. You haven't even touched the Adelaide stuff from last week. What the fuck do you do all day?'

'I need a place to live, Josh. You evicted me, remember?'

'You'll need a place to work if you keep this shit up.'

#

On Friday Gary got the keys to his new business. By lunchtime, all the paper transfers were signed and exchanged, and the previous owners had completely left the premises.

Gary walked around his new domain. Moved a few items here. Fussed a few there. Picked up a dead cockroach from behind a display stand. Straightened the pile of brochures. Sold a printer to a couple who wanted to print over a hundred of their holiday pictures at home. Sold three packets of coloured pencils for a kid's party. A stainless-steel commemorative pen-and-pencil set for someone who was leaving work. A packet of staples to a guy from the real estate's, two doors down. And a greetings card for someone's anniversary.

An anniversary! That's what we need, thought Gary. *We need to celebrate our relationship.*

He closed the shop right then and there, an hour early. He couldn't wait even that extra sixty minutes to reconnect with Amaranth. Any minute apart could be the one when they became a loveless couple, where the only interactions were snide comments and disappointments. No, he wasn't going to let them become one of *those* couples. Again.

128

He stopped at a cake shop as he walked to the car park, telling the young girl serving that he wanted a sort of wedding cake.

'Big day, today!' he announced, hopeful of a response.

'Is someone getting married?

'It's sort of a wedding, and sort of an anniversary.'

She looked puzzled, and asked if he meant a wedding anniversary. He explained that it was an anniversary and the beginning of a sort of marriage too.

'How romantic!' she gushed. The way he hoped Amaranth would.

He nodded, and she selected a suitable cake for his approval. As she slid it into a cake box, she asked, 'So you've been together for some time, and now you're going to get married?'

'We've been together for some time, and now we realise we sort of *are* married.'

'Lovely!' she enthused, handing the box to him and taking his money. 'So how long have you been together?'

'Exactly two weeks today,' he proclaimed with pride.

As Gary stepped from the cake shop, Robert looked up from the van that he was coiling electrical cable into. He called out a g'day, but Gary had no idea who it was.

'Rob,' Robert clarified. 'We met at Kirsten's. Where Amma used to live.'

Gary avoided even the pretence of enthusiasm.

'Oh, okay.'

'Yeah, I'm ripping into it. Got to rewire that shop there.' He indicated the old butcher's, next door to the cake shop. 'Then I'm shooting off to do a house over west end. So, you still together?'

'With Amaranth? Amma? Yes. Just bought us an anniversary cake.'

'Nice one,' Robert said automatically, without processing what an anniversary cake was all about. 'Listen, mate, probably none of my beeswax, but I reckon you should watch out for that Daniel weirdo.'

'Which Daniel weirdo?'

'Well, how many do you know?'

'I don't know any,' said Gary.

'Daniel. That took Amma's room at the flat. He reckons he's pretty sweet on your little lady. Watch out for him, mate, he's a fucking weirdo!'

Gary banged on the front door of Amaranth's old flat. No one answered. Like last time. He stood there, thinking. Long enough for the lift to return to the third floor. Their metal doors clunked open behind him.

Scott checked the crumpled piece of paper Amaranth had scrawled her address on, and stepped out of the lift.

'Is Amma home?' he asked Gary, as he approached the flat.

Gary glared at him.

'You her dad?' Scott asked.

'No, I'm not her fucking dad!' snarled Gary. 'I'm her fucking boyfriend! And if I ever see you... If she ever comes here again...' He didn't know how to put it.

Scott was confused. 'Yeah, all right. Settle down. She has to come here but. This is where she lives, innit?'

'Not any more, she doesn't,' Gary snarled.

'She never told me.'

Words rushed to the back of Gary's brain, and he lashed out one instinctive push that slammed Scott against the wall.

'Well I'm telling you, Loverboy,' he said.

Scott crossed his arms and hid behind them.

'What the fuck is your problem, man?' he shouted.

'You are,' Gary snapped back. 'Though what the fuck she sees in you is beside me.'

'Is that what she said?' Scott asked, suddenly flattered. He lowered his arms. 'Man, it was nothing. We only... I gotta girlfriend, Amma was just, you know...'

Wrong thing to say. Gary punched the mouth that was sullying her name.

'Is she in the flat now?' he screamed at Scott. 'Is she?'

'Thath what I wath athking you,' Scott said, blood sliding from his swelling lips. 'I don't know where the fuck thee ith.'

'But you came to meet her here?' Gary demanded.

'Hey, I bumped into her latht week. Only time I'd theen her for about a year. Gave me her number and addreth. Thaid to cath up. Thath all. I thwear.'

'Last week?'

'Or the week before. Fuck, I don't know.'

Gary stared at him.

'Hey,' Scott tried to further convince him, 'Theeth an old friend, thath all. I told you. Ain't nothing going on between me and her.'

'There better not be,' Gary said. 'Because if I find out you...' He made a tight fist to threaten the bewildered and bleeding Scott, cowering against the wall.

#

Daniel had a list of things to do on Friday.

He had to find somewhere to live.

He hadn't.

He had to finish compiling the Adelaide orders at work.

He hadn't.

He had to get Amaranth away from Gary.

Josh caught him as he was leaving early that afternoon, the orders still not done. And all the days he'd been taking off lately.

'Where's your responsibility, Daniel? Your loyalty? It's a two-way street, you know. If you don't display it, you don't receive it either. Dad wouldn't have put up with all this crap. I gave you fair warning.'

Josh sacked him.

Kirsten and Robert were waiting for Daniel when he got home. Said he'd had a week to find someplace else, and that was it. Robert demanded the flat key. Told him if he had any stuff that didn't fit into his car, he could leave it in a corner of the 'workout room'.

And then he could piss off.

Chapter 17.   The Visitor

Daniel sat in his car. All the signposts pointed to Gary's house and the imaginary freeway that spread away from there, blazoned with joy. If he could get Amaranth away – climb her tower and rescue her from that wicked magician – they could run off together. Make a fresh start somewhere else. He wouldn't need to have found a place to live, or finish work orders. He'd have her. And a whole future ahead of them.

He grabbed a pub meal. Pub meals are cheap, and they can include a couple of rum and cokes.

It was still light when he pulled up and parked a few houses up from Gary's. He had rehearsed the confrontation several times, and he always triumphed. Researched all the possible angles he could imagine. He felt confident and primed.

He got out of his car, observing himself as he did so. As if he were watching a character based on his life. The hero who looked like Daniel, but stood somehow taller, straighter. He walked more definitely. He was a guy to be reckoned with. He was a guy who knew what he wanted. He knew how to get it. He was unstoppable.

He stopped.

He saw Gary getting out of his car in the driveway. The cake box didn't soften the image. He watched Gary kick the car door closed, the way tough guys do. Stride to his door, the way thugs do. Stand on his doorstep and look back over his shoulder, the way gangsters do.

Daniel realised Gary was looking straight at him, as he stood there, just two doors up the street. He spun around on his heels, walked the eight paces back to his car, and got into it.

Gary noticed that sudden about-face, but he dismissed any significance, and opened his front door.

Amaranth came into the kitchen as he placed the box on the table.

'Hey,' she greeted him.

'Know what this is?' he asked her, opening the box out flat. 'It's our anniversary cake!' He went to the drawer and took out the cook's knife. 'Will you help me cut it?' he said.

'Gary,' she said, hoping her tone delivered how fraudulent she was feeling in this sham.

He ignored her hesitancy. He did not want to yield to it. He could beat this mood she had. He could win her over to happiness, and she would be his reward for that accomplishment. He could earn what she had previously offered.

Her.

She lingered as far from him as she could without actually taking a step away.

'It's traditional for us both to hold the knife when we put the first cut in.' He paused. 'Please,' he said.

She shook her head.

'It's symbolic, Amaranth, that's all.'

'Of what?'

'Of us,' he said, maintaining his intent. 'Our love for each other.'

Time for her to unlock her mental filing cabinet, lift out the Forget File and read it out loud.

'Gary,' she said, aware of her accusative tone, 'you smashed a boy's head in with a rock.' And with those words she brandished the justification for not loving him.

'I didn't smash his head in,' Gary exploded, stabbing the knife destructively into the cake. 'He did! He stole my wallet. I hit him. He hit his fucking head. What are you saying?'

'You hit him because he was trying to stop you raping me,' she whispered in contrast to his shouting. Was she now discovering another justification for not loving this man: that in fact, she despised him?

'I wasn't going to...' he cut himself off, unable to voice the word.

'Yes, you were.'

'No, I was just looking like I was, to piss him off,' Gary insisted.

'You were physically aroused, Gary. You can't just call up an erection to piss some guy off, can you? You were getting off on it.'

'I was doing it to punish him.'

133

'Him?' she demanded. 'How was it punishing *him*?'

'By taking from him the most sacred and precious thing any man has. His woman. And believe me, I know how that can fuck someone over.'

She had no argument for that. Just a crushing realisation that she was his last chance at salvation. The responsibility for another person's life was laid across her own.

'Don't hate me for that,' he implored.

'I don't hate you.' It was much, much worse. She pitied him.

'So,' he began again, 'are you on board or what?'

'What does that mean?' she asked.

'It means "on board" as in you want us to be crew together. Like we're married. Till death do us part, and all that.'

'And "not on board" meaning?' she posed.

He didn't want to answer that. There was no out that he had considered. There was only the illusion of choice. Exasperated, he turned to the window, as though he would find an answer out there.

And he did.

It was in a car a few doors up the street. Just sitting there. Waiting.

He stormed from the window, tore open his front door, and marched up the street to the car.

'Excuse me.' Gary faked politeness as he contained his desperation. 'Are you Daniel?'

'Yes,' was the placated response.

'Amaranth would like to see you. Will you come in, please?'

Amaranth was totally stunned when Gary returned with Daniel.

'We have a visitor, Amaranth. I believe you've already met.'

She ignored the invitation for formality.

'What are you doing here?' she asked Daniel.

'What are *you* doing here?' he replied.

'She lives here,' Gary interrupted, coiling around them like a taipan. 'The question is: what are you doing here? There, now we've all said it.'

Daniel looked at Amaranth, but replied to Gary.

'I came to see Amma.'

'How nice. Our first visitor. Shall we have a cup of tea? Mmm? And a little chat?'

Gary was playing. He put the kettle on, and got cups and teabags ready. He was enjoying the awkwardness that spellbound the other two. They just stood staring at each other, like roos in the headlights.

Amaranth and Daniel both felt they ought to be holding each other to give, and get, courage, but they remained where they were, separated by the width of the kitchen.

Gary continued making tea.

'Does your friend take sugar?' he asked Amaranth.

Daniel answered. 'Two,' he said, adding 'thanks.'

'I was asking your hostess, Danny-boy. I'm sure she knows.'

She was annoyed with his game, but accepted the insinuation.

'He takes two sugars. And milk. We've had a coffee together.'

'And what else, I wonder?' Gary smirked. 'Well, Daniel, you're just in time. We were about to cut our anniversary cake. Weren't we, darling?'

'Do you want me to go?' Daniel asked her.

'Of course I do,' she replied. 'I didn't want you to come here. How did you find us?'

'Well,' Gary interrupted, pouring hot water on their teabags, 'I, for one, do not want him to leave. Not just yet, anyway. I'd like to get more acquainted with this young gentleman.'

'Please go, Daniel,' urged Amaranth.

'Why are you so keen to have our guest leave? Is it, perhaps, you are afraid he might let it slip what you've told him about us?'

'She hasn't told me anything about you.'

Daniel took a step towards Amaranth. Only one step, but it placed him between her and Gary.

Gary didn't look up. 'Or is it,' he continued, removing the teabags as he spoke, 'that you're afraid he might let it slip what you haven't told me about the two of you?'

He walked over to Daniel and handed him a steaming cup.

Daniel was intimidated by the proximity of his nemesis, but he stood his ground.

'There's no need for any of us to get angry about this,' he said.

Gary stepped past him and handed a cup of tea to Amaranth. Although he continued to talk to Daniel, he fixed his gaze on her, searching her eyes for the secrets she guarded, and wondering were they his, or hers?

'I'm not angry, Danny. Why would you think I'd get angry?'

'You sounded pretty angry at the flat last week,' Daniel blurted.

'Ah, there it is!' Gary exclaimed calmly, still staring at Amaranth. 'The first slip, Danny-boy. So you were at the flat when I was knocking.'

'She was just collecting some of her things that she'd left in my room.' Daniel immediately realised there was an innuendo in that explanation. 'From when she used to live there, I mean,' he corrected.

'How very clarifying, Daniel. Thank you,' Gary went on. 'Alas: the second slip. She was also in the flat when I was knocking. Not on the stairs. In the flat.' He was glaring at her, quite coldly now. 'And heard me knocking.'

She looked away. 'I only said that because you'd jump to conclusions.'

'Conclusions which have delivered themselves at my doorstep anyway. The trouble with one lie, Amaranth, is that it casts doubt over everything else you say.'

Gary strode across his kingdom to the kitchen bench where he collected his own cup of tea. He took a sip and, in the quiet moment that created, all three of them considered his reaction to this discovery.

Daniel's urge changed from protecting himself to protecting her.

'You don't have to take this, you know.'

'Yes, she does. Don't you?' Gary glared at her.

She nodded slowly.

'What does he have over you?' Daniel asked, bewildered.

'I have something over her?' Gary said, neglecting to answer the question himself.

'That's why she's here, isn't it?' Daniel dared.

Gary's tone lowered to an even more sinister calm.

'She's here because she wants to be.' He put his cup down on the bench and went to her. 'True, Amaranth?'

She raised her head and looked at him.

'Please Gary.'

'Kindly tell this upstart about us,' he demanded.

'I promised I wouldn't tell anyone about that, and I haven't,' she said.

'Promises? I remember a certain promise of love that you made,' he accused.

'I never promised to love you, Gary.'

Gary turned back to glaring at Daniel. 'And I suppose she loves you, then? Is that right?'

There was silence. Gary slowly swept his gaze over to her.

'Well? Do you love this bloke then?'

'I don't think I know what love is,' she admitted.

'No, you don't,' Gary affirmed.

'But I feel something with Daniel that I've never felt before,' she said. 'Not with anyone. Not with you.'

There was another long pause as they allowed him to take that in.

And, he did.

Gary sniffed sense in through his nostrils and let out a long, deep breath. He relaxed his shoulders, and spoke softly.

'It's pretty hopeless then, isn't it?'

It was rhetorical, and the other two made no answer.

Gary turned back to Daniel, saying, 'You see, this is what they're all like.' His past begged him to let it back, like the old wound it was. 'They dump you like a used condom. Take up with someone younger. Sexier.' Now anger churned in his bitterness. He slowly moved closer to Daniel, his voice louder with each step. 'You're pretty sexy then, are you?' Closer and louder. 'You give it to her good, do you?' Closer, louder, and faster now. 'She likes it with you?'

He slammed into Daniel, his fury spurred by the hot tea that scalded his arm.

Amaranth dropped her own cup and tried to tear the two men apart, but she was no match for this desperate anger. Gary wrestled Daniel to the floor, and straddled him, pinning his arms with his knees and grabbing at his throat. Amaranth's pushes were just an annoyance. He flung her away, and she crashed into the table, instinctively breaking her fall by grabbing the handle of the cook's knife that was still standing stabbed into the cake.

Gary knew this fight was futile, and that he was the loser regardless of the outcome, but his tantrum cared nothing for that.

137

Amaranth didn't realise she still had hold of the knife as she ran back at him and wrenched at his shoulder with her free hand, pushing him off Daniel, who was left coughing and gasping for the precious air.

She stood between the two fallen men.

Gary looked up at the large knife still in her hand. The symbol of unrequited desire. He lifted himself to his knees, but only to his knees, and she defensively raised her fists like a boxer's, which made the blade point menacingly at him like a dagger.

He made no attempt to stand. He seemed almost relaxed. Kneeling on the floor. Waiting. Smiling an acceptance of his fate. The king at the execution block. The patriot before the firing squad. Maybe even Jesus pinned on the cross of his persecution. Their eyes locked, and each of them recognised that she was possessed of that same clarity she'd discovered two weeks before on a dark path through a flower bed, when *he* had hovered over *her*.

'Go on,' he breathed, through teeth clenched for the impact. 'Do it.' And he meant it. Surviving wasn't worth the suffering it if it delivered him back to further desolation.

She understood him. She knew the breadth of his misery. She gazed into his martyrdom, raised the ceremonial dagger high over her head, and with all her strength... she hurled it away. It smashed a small hole in the upper pane of the kitchen window and clattered back into the acoustic metal sink: a cymbalic crescendo that brought them all to their senses.

'Uh-uh, Gary,' she said, with a voice husky from exertion. 'The only life I'm taking is mine. I want it back, and I'm giving you yours as a trade. I-spare-you. We're even, now. Okay?'

She stood up, walked across to Daniel, and helped him to his feet.

'You got a car here?' she asked, and he nodded. 'Come on then, let's go.'

She turned and looked at the ruin that was once her master. She recognised how burdened he'd been, maintaining that role.

'I'm setting *you* free too, Gary,' she said solemnly. 'I hope you see that.'

Chapter 18.   Glassy-eyed

Amaranth woke to the sounds of the motel manager hosing the courtyard outside the room she and Daniel had taken for the night. Pulling her wrist from under a pillow that smelled of mildew and detergent, she focused on her watch. Ten past nine. Ten past *nine*! The excitement that she had actually slept-in roused her remnant drowsiness.

Daniel stirred beside her. He still wanted to stay sleeping, but the thought of Gary just down the road – a mere six hours' drive away – encouraged him to rise. They had to vacate the room by ten anyway, so they each took turns at a brief stint in the bathroom. All she had brought from Gary's was her handbag, so she borrowed a pair of jeans and a T-shirt from Daniel, who had all his belongings in the back of his car. He smiled when she came out in them. Symbolic to him of their closeness and sharing, for Amaranth, it was simply a clean reprieve in the wrong size, colour, and style.

On the stroke of ten they checked out, dropping their key onto the pile of gaudy tourist brochures that pleaded from the laminated counter, and drove off. When they pulled in for petrol later, Amaranth bought a toothbrush.

They were hardly speaking to each other, just as it had been during the previous night's drive. The car's motor droned like a monk in meditation for Amaranth as she focused in and out of random images from the past few days.

Daniel didn't like their silence. Her silence. He knew he had failed her. He had found the magician's lair and climbed the tower, but *she* had rescued *him*, and it was supposed to be the other way round.

#

Gary opened his shop late. He only went in because it was a distraction from his house, which was Amaranth-less and riddled with regrets. His first customer was a stringy young man who came in to find a "make-up" card for his girlfriend. He examined several options that might do the job, eventually settling on one.

'Words,' Gary said, as he slipped the chosen card and envelope into a small paper bag, 'they're the messengers of love, aren't they? With invisible meanings, like the perfume of invisible flowers.'

'Right,' the customer said, pushing some coins across the counter and checking beside himself to see if there was a more comfortable subject coming.

Gary scooped the coins up and clattered them into his till.

'You know what?' he said. 'I'm going to change the name of my shop to "Amaranth". Do you know what Amaranth means?'

'I've heard the word someplace,' the stringy man said.

'Amaranth is an invisible flower that never fades,' Gary said eagerly. 'Can you imagine that?'

The young fellow shook his head.

'Wrong,' Gary said. 'You can ONLY imagine that. They're invisible, but we still see them…' he tapped the temple on the right side of his head, '…in here! Where they never fade.'

'So, they're imaginary flowers, not invisible ones,' the young man said, preferring to debate semantics and philosophy rather than discuss romanticism.

'Same thing,' Gary said.

'Not at all,' the young guy insisted. 'Imaginary means they only exist in the mind. If they're invisible they actually exist, but you can't see them.'

'What about love, then? Is love imaginary?' Gary challenged.

'Nah, love actually exists,' the guy said. 'It's invisible, but it exists.'

'Only if you believe it does,' Gary asserted, handing the bag with the card to his customer. 'Belief is all that keeps it real. That's what stops the flower fading.'

#

'Let's stop for lunch,' Amaranth said, her drowse wakened by her hunger.

They ate sandwiches that they bought from a highway servo, and sat at an outside picnic table giggling together as Daniel made a list of comedic characters. The girl behind the counter who couldn't understand why Amaranth didn't want any butter on her bread. The man who was fatter than Santa and had to try three times to get out of his Ford Laser. Daniel's squeaky impersonation of Rebecca's voice, and how he had nearly used Spritzer as a mop. Robert and Kirsten. How lucky Daniel was to have moved into that flat. How amazing life was: the way something happens, that at the time seems bad, and then somehow it turns out to be so good.

By evening they arrived in Byron Bay. Obscure enough to be remote. Active enough to hide in. By the end of their third day there, they had rented a small, but expensive, furnished apartment one block past the shops and just one street back from the beach. Finally, they felt like they'd stopped running.

That night they made love for the first time since Sydney. He had been timid to initiate anything but she grabbed him as he came out of the shower. She pushed him to the bed and yanked off his towel. He was ready for her and she toyed with his enthusiasm till he was almost bursting. Then she straddled him, lowering herself over him till he was deep inside her. She squirmed slowly forwards and backwards. Forwards and backwards. Forwards and... stopped.

'I'm sorry, Daniel. I thought I wanted to. My head's all over the place. Maybe tomorrow, huh?'

He hovered in the purgatory position, jolting his senses back to his brain. She rolled off him.

He apologised.

That almost annoyed her, but she said he had nothing to apologise for. It was just her mood. She thanked him for understanding.

But he didn't understand. He was sure it was because he had failed her in the rescue. That he would always be the little guy she had saved. And luckily that thought destroyed the arousal that would have been so hard for him to deny.

After work, Gary drove all the way to the boat harbour. He parked and looked out over the calm waters. It was a perfect evening for sitting and looking. The tide had just started coming in and there was no wind. His boat, *Away,* was out there. *Away* is always waiting out there.

We should have just sailed right out of the harbour and never stopped, he thought. *She'd have loved that. She'd have really loved that.*

Then the storm: she'd told him she had never loved him, *would* never love him, because she *could* never love him.

Kate was the exact opposite, he remembered. *You'd have never got her on board that boat; all she ever thought about was her career. She used me till I was no further use. Our whole marriage was a lie.* He calmed himself. *Amaranth didn't lie. She told me, right from the start, that she didn't lie, and it was true. She never lied. That's what I loved most about her. She never said she loved me.*

He was holding on to the memory of what *he* had loved to avoid calling it by its proper name: loss.

When Gary pulled into his driveway, it was just getting dark. He glanced up at his kitchen window, still broken from when Amaranth had thrown the cake knife.

Glad it hasn't rained, he thought, *and it's an open invitation to thieves. Got to get around to fixing that. This weekend. Time to fix everything broken.*

Amaranth restocked a small wardrobe of clothes including a couple of light summer dresses that were free and bright. Nothing that resembled an office girl at work. Or even an office girl on holiday.

She had years of savings on top of the old Unfair Dismissal payout. She was in no hurry to find a job because, despite the perfect autumn weather, she saw that these were the rainy days she had been saving for.

Women didn't wear much make-up in Byron, and Amaranth became one of them. The emphasis was on taking things easy, and that's just what she did.

On Saturday, she got her hair cut and styled. Shorter. Younger. Stronger. The girl who washed her hair told her that there was a good band playing at the beachside hotel that night, and she coerced Daniel into going.

They arrived a little before seven-thirty. Daylight Saving was in its final week so it wasn't yet dark as they sat in the beer garden across from the beach, sipping supposedly fresh orange juice from schooner glasses, watching the world tilt into sunset. The band wasn't due to start till nine, so they sat there, taking in the excited chatter of lorikeets telling tales of their day to each other in the trees opposite. Below them, the straggle of beach-walkers traipsed into town, trading sand for cement, and cars of hungry diners circled for a parking spot like a flock of seagulls hovering over a picnic blanket.

At the table beside them, a large group of senior travellers suddenly rose as if the National Anthem had just struck up, and they all wobbled away to their accommodation before the "young people's hurdy-gurdy music started". Vigilant backpackers immediately grabbed the seats that had become so rare as the night progressed. At the hotel entrance, the security guy checked a young girl's I.D. as she came in, and she giggled to her boyfriend while she received the stamp of approval on the underside of her wrist.

Through the first hour and the second juice, they continued to examine the human zoo around them. Tourists and locals. Younger and older. Trendy and daggy. A speckled sampling that seemed to interact surprisingly well, and then, with a soft suddenness, the milieu reached out to include Amaranth and Daniel.

'Excuse me,' a voice beside them said. Amaranth looked up at the young guy with his hand on the back of one of the empty chairs at their table. 'Anyone sitting here?' he asked.

Daniel glanced at the vacant chair, as though he needed to confirm for himself that there was, in fact, nobody sitting there, then he released it with a wave of his hand. Instead of taking the chair away, as Daniel had expected, the guy beckoned to his friend carrying two beers, and then both of them sat down at the table.

'Thanks,' the guy's friend said. 'Hi, how're you going? I'm Liam, this is Chris.'

'Daniel, and this is Amma.'

'We're very lucky to find a seat tonight,' said Chris, rubbing his little Buddha necklace, a habit he'd created for himself since finding it at the markets. Each time he had good luck, he registered it into the charm, building a balance he could withdraw from when he needed it. 'You'd think we'd have had enough of this place. We both work here. This is our night off but the band tonight is going to be wicked.'

'Yeah, so we heard,' said Daniel. 'What do you do here? You behind the bar?'

'No, nothing so flash. We're both glassies. We pick up the empties and mop the spills, that's all,' Chris said with a chuckle. 'But it's an okay job.'

'You guys on holiday?' Liam asked.

'No,' Daniel said. 'I think we've sort of moved here. From Sydney.'

'Me too,' Chris said, raising his schooner. 'Last year.'

'Melbourne here,' Liam added.

The two boys seemed so easy to talk with, and this was exactly how Amaranth imagined travelling would be. New places. New habits. New clothes. New company.

'Band starts at nine, better get a round in before the crush,' exclaimed Chris, sculling his beer. 'It's going to get manic here soon.' He stood up. 'What are you guys drinking?'

'Oh no,' Daniel replied, covering his nearly empty glass, 'we're okay, thanks.'

Amaranth reached into her purse. 'I'd like a glass of white wine, thanks, Chris,' she said, offering him a ten-dollar note.

'You're all right, love,' he sang, 'I'll get them. Chards or sav blanc?'

'The second one, please,' she said.

'Good choice,' Chris reassured.

'You sure you don't want one, Daniel?'

'Err, yeah, okay then. Just an OJ for me, thanks.'

144

And so it began. A friendship was launched with a ceremonial toasting. Each team asked the other what they thought of Byron, what they thought of where they were from. The newly-arrived said how lucky the already-settled were to live in such a place. Amaranth bought the next round. Liam the one after that. Daniel still had a full glass of OJ when he got his round in. His thirst had long been quenched, even the salty chips couldn't revive it enough for a fourth orange juice plus the two he'd had with Amaranth. He thought he was being very noble, buying a round even though he was finished drinking, buying beer and wine when he was only on a cheap soft drink. No one noticed. Except him.

Their table was far enough from the dance floor so that even after the band had started playing, they were still able to talk. Liam asked if Daniel was going to look for work in Byron, and what job he usually did. Quite soon he and Daniel were deep in a conversation about how China was dominating the world's textile marketplace, leaving Amaranth to find something to chat to Chris about. She drummed her fingers to the band.

'Yeah,' Chris shouted to her. 'It's a killer song, hey?'

She turned to Daniel. 'I love this one! Come on, let's get up!'

She stood and pulled at Daniel's arm, but he shook it free from her and refused to move.

'I'll dance with you, Amma,' Chris offered, 'if you like.'

'Absolutely,' she said, finishing her fourth glass as though it were a refreshing first that surely would have gone sour by the time she returned.

Chris stood up and rubbed Daniel's shoulders. 'Okay with you, buddy?'

Daniel agreed as though it meant nothing to him. But he forgot what he was saying to Liam.

The band was getting towards the end of their first set, and the dance floor was fairly full. Enough people to make it feel like it was happening. Enough room to happen. The music was a compulsive rhythm that refused to let dancers just stand there and wobble. There was a swirl of bodies, and everyone was happy to smile with whoever their eyes fell on, as though they instinctively knew if you're dancing to this and dancing like that, then you must be okay and I like you.

145

Chris danced facing Amaranth, then he spun around and faced away. She did the same, and was dancing with someone behind her for a few seconds, then back around to face Chris again. The reckless twirling, aided by her four wines, lifted her into a rampage of exuberance – the carousel of carousal. And she laughed, and laughed, and laughed, and...

She held her hand tightly against her mouth as she panicked to the front of the short queue at the toilets, making it just in time. She threw up into the bowl, steadying herself on the cistern.

'Oh God, oh God, oh God, oh God!' she muttered rapidly, hoping that repeating the desperate mantra of the dizzy would somehow focus her mind and stop it spinning. She dragged a dank straggle of hair from her mouth, and it clung to her cheek like its stench would cling to her memory.

Daniel escorted the wreckage of Amaranth through the crowded bar, patrons parting like the Red Sea, as they raised their precious liquids away from her chaos. Behind her back, the girls giggled 'poor thing' and the guys smirked 'sure thing'.

Outside, passers-by excused her in much the same way as they would tolerate the very elderly and the severely disabled. Observed, but politely ignored.

It was only two blocks to their flat and Daniel kept her walking even though her body was pleading to just flump down and sleep right where they were. Her brain thought it agreed, and suggested that she was probably only dreaming that she was awake anyway, but Daniel steered and encouraged her till they were home, where all her realities converged onto the bed.

When she awoke next morning, her crumpled dress all twirled into the top sheet, panda-eyed from rubbed mascara, the inside of her head stacked like a dirty dishwasher, she traipsed to the bathroom for the detergent tablet of paracetamol. Daniel came in as she was swallowing the pills with a hand-scoop of tap water. She looked at him in the mirror, expecting sympathy, but seeing irritation. She splashed some refreshment onto her face and attempted to clean off the black smudges with her towel as she turned to face him.

'Are you finished in here?' he coldly asked her.

'Hey,' she said softly – partly to protect her headache, partly to elicit his compassion. 'I'm sorry about last night. The wine and...'

'Yeah, I want to use the toilet. Do you mind?'

His hand showcased the bathroom door like it was a prize on a TV game show, but she stood still, trying to comprehend his mood.

'A little bit of privacy!' he demanded.

Exiled, she set off on a pilgrimage to the kitchen. She needed perked coffee, the real deal. It was such a penance getting it happening, but finally she was sitting at the table, her lips on the communion cup. Caffeine. Ahh: born again!

Daniel came in. 'So, we're getting up now, are we?' he asked.

'I made coffee. Or did you want to go back to bed?'

'I'm awake now. Shit sleep. You were sprawled out right across the bed.' He grabbed a cup and poured himself a coffee from the jug. 'And you stunk of vomit.'

'I'm sorry,' she confessed, continuing the Sunday theme. 'I'm not used to drinking.'

'You made a complete idiot of me last night,' he said, condemning some sugar to a cruel scalding. 'Prancing around with that show-off on the dance floor. You looked like a right tart.'

She gave a quiet laugh of incredulity.

'A right tart?' she spluttered. 'Who uses words like "right tart"?'

'That's what the bloke you were gyrating with was thinking. You were a tart and I was a wuss.'

'No, he didn't! Why would he think anything like that?'

'Because you were slutting up to him and I just sat there and allowed it.'

'*Allowed* it?' she yelled, waking her headache. 'What do you mean, "allowed it"? I don't need your permission to dance, Daniel. That's what people do.'

'Some people,' he sulked.

'But not you.'

'Oh yeah, you really wanted me to come and dance with you, didn't you?'

She paused and thought about that.

Rather than acknowledge the silence, he chose to break it.

'Yeah, well I don't like making a spectacle of myself.'

'Dancing isn't making a spectacle of yourself. It's having fun,' she said, surly. Then she added a muttering: 'Something you seem to know very little about.'

He heard her just fine and steadied himself to aim his next sentence.

'Oh yeah, that's right, you think it's "fun" to be taken by men. I forgot.'

'What a heap of shit!'

'You don't see it, do you? That guy *took* you onto the dance floor. Just like how I *took* you away from that psycho, Gary. And he *took* you away from whoever it was before him.'

'Nobody took me – I went!'

'Christ, you were practically Gary's prisoner. Pretty sick fun.'

She dismissed his diagnosis, rolling her eyes and huffing an exaggerated weary breath.

'We were talking about dancing, Daniel. Last night. No one took me anywhere.'

'How did you get home, then?' he countered snidely.

'You helped me. Please don't tell me you fantasised that you *took* me.' She forced a mocking laugh. 'Even in the state I was in, I can't somehow see you *taking* me.'

Amaranth's hangover wasn't severe enough to demand that she spend the whole day in bed, but that's exactly what she did. Bed was a refuge from Daniel's rebuke. Her own, however, pestered her like a hyperactive child bouncing on the bed beside her. She was angry with herself for drinking too much in too short a time the previous night. Not her action – only her reaction. And she was angry with him. His jealous, possessive insecurity. His harsh, condemning judgement. His being too weak to comfort her with an apology, and when he did finally apologise that evening, she saw that as just further evidence of his weakness.

Romance is a wild flower, picked for its beauty, held on display, and then discarded when it wilts. She felt as though she was watching her own story unfold on a stage before her, and from this vantage point, she found much that she disapproved of in Daniel. How he had no stories to tell, except the one whinging tale about his brother and

Rebecca. How he never suggested doing anything. How he left all those little hairs in the bathroom sink after shaving. The way he tried to initiate lovemaking. The way he accepted that she didn't want to. He was an island she'd swum to when she was thrown overboard in the storm, and now she was bundling sticks together into a huge beacon on the shore, watching for a passing ship.

Chapter 19. Lightning Cracks

On Monday, whilst Daniel concentrated on finding a job, Amaranth went to the Woolworths supermarket to do a weekly shop. She didn't regard herself as a tourist; Byron had already become her home now, she lived there. In the mishmash of people on the street, she could already easily discern between those who measured their time there in years, those who measured it in months, and those in days. The rate-payers, the rent-payers, and the room-payers.

She had managed to dodge the campers and backpackers that thronged the supermarket aisles, hunting for instant noodles, tinned soups, and white breads. Different brands in different packaging, but all so much the same. Shopping done, she pushed her laden trolley to the boot of Daniel's car, when Chris bounced up to her.

'You look a lot better than the last time I saw you,' he said with a laugh.

'Oh, hi! Yeah, look, I'm so sorry about getting so totally dizzy.'

'My bad,' said Chris. 'All that spinning you around.'

'No, I loved the dancing.'

Chris smiled at her. 'Your fella, Dan is it? He seemed a little uptight. I don't think he liked me dancing with you.'

'It was how I handled the wines. He thinks I made a bit of a scene.'

'Nah, pub's always a scene, that's what we love about it. Pity it upset your tummy. Had you eaten that night?'

'No,' she grabbed at the excuse, 'that was the problem. Not that I'm a big drinker. You guys seemed very used to it.'

'Yeah, we put it away. Single man's girlfriend: alcohol.' He smiled again.

'And working at a pub wouldn't help much either,' she suggested.

'True that,' he said.

'Not working today?' she asked, as he helped to unload her trolley into the boot.

'No. Gotta fill in the final forms at the Dive Centre for my Master's this arvo. If I get that I can teach diving. I'm thinking of heading to Thailand. Liam worked on an island there last year, taking touros diving.'

'Wow,' she said. 'What a dream!'

'Yeah, should be good. I've never been out of Australia before. You?'

'No. But I really want to. One day.'

'How's young master Dan?'

'He's fine. I've got to go and tell him I'm done here. He's checking the job-search sites at the Internet place around the corner. Maybe he could have your old job at the pub when you go to Thailand.'

He laughed. 'It'll be a few weeks yet before I hear about that, and anyway the season here is finishing after Easter. Work will be hard to find in Byron.'

'Oh well,' she said, putting the last bag into the boot. 'There's always Plan B.'

'What's that then?'

'I don't know yet,' she said, 'but there always is one.' She slammed the boot closed. 'Now I'd better go find Dan and tell him I'm done shopping.'

They both lingered in a hesitant moment.

'It's going to get crazy here this week,' he said, trying to keep the conversation going.

'Why, what's on this week?' she asked, eager to help.

'Bluesfest. There'll be thousands coming for the weekend, down from Brisbane, up from Sydney. They'll mostly be at the festival site, I suppose, so maybe the pubs won't be that bad.'

A motorbike braked suddenly right beside them to allow a reversing car to complete its manoeuvre. The rider had a full-face helmet on so they couldn't see his expression, but his agitated body language and angry revving engine was evidence he was not obliging the reversing driver out of courtesy. The offending car drove off, but the bike rider lingered for a moment and looked at Amaranth. She

151

didn't notice him as he rode a short distance and parked. He sat, straddled on his mount, waiting.

The shopping loaded, Amaranth shunted the trolley into the requisite bay.

'Fridge stuff will start to melt if I don't get Dan,' she said.

'Okay. Say hi to him. Maybe catch you guys at the Beachie again this Saturday?'

'Yeah, that'd be nice.'

'After dinner, this time,' he laughed. 'Then, if there's room on the dance floor, maybe we could get some serious dancing in.'

'I'm up for it,' she said, sounding as modern as she could. With that, she hurried away to find Daniel.

As Chris turned to go into the supermarket, the motorcyclist swung his leg over the bike's red tank with an eagle painted on it. He uncorked his head from the helmet.

Scott.

'G'day,' he called to Chris, who looked at him like he suspected there was a candid camera filming this. Scott's hair was sculpted by sweat and the shape of the helmet. He looked a little like a cross between Marge Simpson and a Buckingham Palace guard. 'Was that Amma from down in Sydney you were just gabbing to?'

'Amma? Yes.'

'She here with her boyfriend?'

'He's round the corner.'

'This your car?'

'No,' Chris said, wondering what was the interest in the car.

'She don't drive, so it's her boyfriend's then?'

'Yes, she's gone to get him. If you hang around, they should be back in a minute or two.'

'Nah, don't get along with her new bloke. He got a bit stroppy with me last time we met.'

'Doesn't seem like the stroppy sort,' Chris doubted.

'Oh, he's stroppy. I used to have a little thing going on with Amma. Ended long before he come along, but. Jealous cunt. Knocked the crap out of me at her place last week. Only went round to say hello. I wouldn't want to be Amma with him for a boyfriend. I reckon he gives her a hard time.'

'Well I wouldn't know about that. Anyway, look, I better go.'
Chris headed into the supermarket.

'Yeah, right-oh.' Scott walked back over to his bike, crowned the side mirror with his helmet, and found a pen in one of his saddlebags. He tore off a piece of a cigarette packet and scrawled on the inside of it:

"Payback time, buddy. I'll see you in Sydney, but you won't see me."

Collecting his helmet, he walked over to Daniel's car and placed the note under the windscreen wipers. He furtively checked around the car park to make sure no one was watching him then, using his helmet as a club, he bashed the windscreen, which cracked like a bolt of lightning.

He looked around again and saw that his vandalism had gone unnoticed, so he sauntered back over to his bike and rode away.

Scott free.

Less than five minutes later, Daniel and Amaranth returned to the car and found both the damage and the note.

'Gary's a psycho,' screamed Daniel. 'He's followed us. We have to get out of here.'

'I'm not going anywhere.'

'Then we have to go to the police.'

'No!' Amaranth declared. 'No police. I'll pay for the damage to your windscreen.'

'And what about the damage he's going to do to me? Who pays for that? Me.'

Amaranth took the note from him and read it again. 'He's gone back,' she stated.

'Oh, sure he has!'

'It says "see you in Sydney", Daniel. So clearly, if you don't go to Sydney, you won't have to see him.'

'He says I won't see him! He says that in the note. He's just going to jump out on me one night in a dark alley.'

'And which dark alley is this, exactly?' she asked sarcastically.

'I don't intend to live my life always looking over my shoulder for some crazy madman.'

'So, stay away from Sydney,' she said. 'There's plenty of other places.'

'He knows we're here. He's here. He wrote it here. He's probably watching us right now.' He looked around the car park.

'So, stay away from here too.'

Daniel nodded. 'Where will we go?'

She looked at the ground. 'I'm not going anywhere,' she repeated, but this time with the ominous implication that she didn't include him in her defiance.

'Oh,' he said, emphasising a dropped penny. 'So that's it. I'm not the caveman-sort you go for, the kind of guy who bosses you around and bashes doors down.'

'Don't start that. You're only in danger if you're with me.'

'And what if there was no danger?'

'But there is,' was all she could offer. Even if it wasn't the whole reason, it was enough.

#

The next morning, the small square of grass where Scott's tent had been gulped a breath of sky and stretched towards the sun.

Scott picked up his helmet, and examined the scratch it had taken when he'd cracked Daniel's windscreen, as if it were a worthy battle scar.

His motorbike was packed like a mule, parked at the café while he ate a filling meal with a watchful eye on his saddlebags.

He finished eating and swilled down the rest of a Coke, then he walked across the footpath to his bike and threw his leg over the seat, like it was a thoroughbred and he was riding off into a prairie sunset.

He readied himself for the long and arduous trip home.

Tracey would be pretty impressed, he thought, *knowing I just up and went to the Bluesfest like that. Teach her to not nag on at me, saying I never did nothing. Too bad it had been sold out and I couldn't get in, but.*

#

Around the same time, Daniel threw the last of his things onto the back seat of his car.

'I seem to spend a great deal of my time getting kicked out of places since I met you,' he said, as he unwound the apartment key from his key ring.

'You're not getting "kicked out",' Amaranth reassured.

'So, remind me why I'm going.'

'It's just time,' she said softly.

And it was. A look, an embrace, a ripping away. He sat down in the driver's seat, feeling more like a passenger. He left his door open while he fiddled with his key ring, removing the flat key and handing it, ceremoniously, to her. Then he closed the car door, waited for the first break in traffic, and drove away as she turned to walk back inside. One door shut, and someone felt dumped. One door opened, and someone felt free.

She grabbed her sunglasses and wide-brimmed straw hat, her instinct ushering her out so she wouldn't be there if he weakened and returned. She headed to the beach, the best place for being alone, and sauntered along the cool, damp shoreline between those people being lazy on the sand and those being lively in the water. She was alone, but not lonely. She was still unsure of what she wanted but she knew now she had removed the clutter of the unwanted and that space felt good.

#

Panic frisked Scott's courage when he glimpsed the familiar lightning bolt cracked windscreen pulling in behind him at the highway service station just outside Coffs Harbour. But he stumbled into curiosity when he saw it wasn't Gary driving.

'G'day,' he offered Daniel. 'A bird hit your windscreen?' he asked, desperate to establish his ignorance and innocence.

'Nah,' Daniel replied casually. 'Girlfriend's ex.'

Shit, Scott thought. *Is he playing? Does he know it was me?* Ex-some guy was still an ex.

'She just broke up with him,' Daniel elaborated, and Scott relaxed. 'Followed us up the coast. The psycho.'

'So how did you get his car, then?'

'No, no, it's my car. My dad traded it in his car yard,' Daniel said, thinking it was an odd question.

'But it was him smashed your windscreen?' Scott continued.

'Yep,' Daniel said, pushing a petrol pump into his tank and watching the dial. 'Left a note under the wipers. Said he'd see me back in Sydney.'

'You got issues with him, then?' Scott prodded.

'He's got issues with me more like.'

'That 'cause you got his girl, is it? That why he smashed your windscreen?'

'Something like that.' Daniel finished topping his tank up and hung the pump back on the bowser.

'I'm off to Sydney too,' Scott proudly announced.

'On the bike?'

'Sure. I rode up on it. Bit sore-arsed, but bikes are cool. Wouldn't want to have a head-on or anything, but,' Scott said. 'What about you?'

Daniel thought about that question. 'Yeah,' he said seriously, 'I think maybe I want a head-on.'

Scott laughed. 'Nah, serious but, how far are you going?'

'I'm off to Sydney too,' Daniel replied decisively. 'Just as soon as I've had a coffee.'

Scott wanted to know more. 'I'll join you,' he said, as casually as he could fake. 'I need something to keep me awake on that thing. Gets a bit boring just sitting there, hanging on and listening to the motor.'

As they sat in the cafeteria, waiting for their cardboard coffees to lose some stinging heat, Scott asked where the windscreen smasher lived.

'Potts Hill. Why?'

'Just wondered,' Scott lied, continuing to evoke as much blasé as he could muster. 'I used to live in Potts Hill. What street?'

'Barton Street.'

'Oh yeah, I know that street well. Know lots of people living there. What number?'

'Err. Twenty-six.'

'Twenty-six. What's his name?'

'Gary Baker. Know him?'

'Gary Baker, Twenty-six Barton Street, Potts Hill,' Scott memorised. 'Nah, never heard of him. Anyhow, so you got the girl then?'

'Not even,' Daniel said, circling his finger around the curled rim of his cup. 'She dumped me too.'

'She's so different,' Scott said, unable to conceal his amazement at the change in her.

'Other girls don't dump guys?'

'None of the girls I've been with!' Scott said, and Daniel laughed, assuming it was a joke. It was a joke that Scott didn't quite get.

'To women,' Daniel raised his cup, 'who know what they want, and then throw it away when they get it.'

'Treat 'em mean, keep 'em keen,' Scott quoted.

'Nice guys finish last,' matched Daniel.

'Too right! Chicks like a man to be a man. Unless they're a lezzo.'

Daniel took a toasting sip of coffee and inhaled the rush of flavour. But coffee is bitter. He put his cup down and stared at the froth like it was an old sepia photograph.

'She was all "I love you because you're so caring and sensitive", and all along she was living with a gorilla.'

'This the Gary bloke from Barton Street then, is it?'

'Yeah. Then she dumped him when he got all needy and "I want you to love me"-ish.'

Scott raised his eyebrows with a cheeky confidence. 'He's not so tough then, is he?'

#

That Saturday morning, Robert let his face drop deliberately when he answered Kirsten's door and saw Daniel standing there in the hallway. Reluctantly, he admitted the previous flatmate who had come for the last of his things, but he avoided conversation by settling back into a lounge chair and lifting a copy of *The Telegraph* up in front of his face.

Daniel made several trips, lugging boxes and bags to his car, before announcing he had the last of it.

'This is Amma's address up north,' he said, placing a piece of paper on the kitchen bench, 'in case there's any mail or anything.'

'She still with that Gary bloke?' asked Robert, as he changed pages.

'No, he's history now.'

'What, you reckon you sorted him, did you?'

'We had a little "discussion", yeah,' Daniel said flatly. 'It got a bit physical, a bit nasty, but he was the loser.'

Robert shook his head, dismissing both the concept and the person as Daniel left.

Kirsten came up the hall from her bedroom.

'Was that Daniel's voice?'

'Yep,' said Robert, continuing with his newspaper. 'Just gone.'

'How's he getting along?'

'Same-oh: weird.' He changed pages like an agitated frill-neck lizard. 'Left you Amma's address – she's up north he said.'

'Did he say anything about...' but she was interrupted as Robert sat bolt upright.

'Shit! Fuck me!' he shouted, stabbing an article with a rigid digit. 'That Gary-bloke Amma was with: he lived at Potts Hill, didn't he?'

Chapter 20.   Wategos

On Sunday afternoon, Amaranth was standing near the dance floor at the Beach Hotel, sipping a Bacardi Breezer, as the band set up. Several pairs of male eyes around the room began the reconnaissance routine: *Nice body. All-right face. Is she waiting for someone? Boyfriend? Only holding one drink. Is she with the band? Is that guy over there checking her out? Should I make a move now? Oh shit, he got in there, the sleazy dog. I didn't fancy her anyway. Tits were too small.*

'Hi,' Chris said with a smile.

And Amaranth smiled back.

'Didn't see you here last night,' he said.

'No, I didn't make it.'

'Pity,' Chris said. 'There was a good band on, but it was fully packed out.'

'Daniel left Byron yesterday,' she said.

'Yeah? Where's he gone?'

'Dunno,' she shrugged.

Chris sensed what had happened.

'How long's he gone for?' he asked, to make sure he was right.

'For good, I think,' she said. 'Well, definitely for the better.'

'And you didn't come out last night because...?' He invited her to answer.

'I didn't want to come out by myself.'

'You wouldn't have been by yourself, I was here.'

'Yes, but you'd have been with your friends and I...'

'Anyway,' he said, 'I'm done for the day. I need to dive in the ocean and freshen up. You wanna come for a swim?'

'Maybe a walk,' she said. 'I don't have my bathers.'

'If you're up for a long walk, maybe we could find a spot you won't need bathers,' Chris said. He gave her a look that dared her to accept.

And she did.

They walked along Main Beach, past the crowds of swimmers and sunbathers. They walked past Clarkes Beach and all the surfers at The Pass. Over the headland and then across the tiny, perfect beach at Wategos. They climbed up the stairs at the far end and walked along the path. They climbed through a wire fence and ran down a grassy hillside that led them to a secluded little beach at the foot of the lighthouse where petrified lava splayed into the frothing sea. Between two of these stone 'toes' was a large natural basin that was filled by the incoming waves, and self-drained immediately after they had broken onto the shore. For a few seconds the water in the basin was two metres deep, but seconds later it was an almost empty, rough channel.

They stood on the rocky edge of the basin. The waves thundered in, filling it, swelling towards the rear, and then gushed back out. Similar to how it feels standing at the edge of a platform as a train rushes in, there's an illogical urge to jump.

'I reckon,' Chris said, 'if you timed it exactly right and leapt in on the crest of the wave, you'd be washed up onto the rocks at the back there, and then, if you held on, the wave would go out and you'd be left high and dry and you could scramble up from there to the top of the rocks.'

'Probably,' said Amaranth, not actually considering the probability.

'Wanna try?' he said, as he put one hand on her shoulders to steady himself and pulled off his shoes with the other.

She looked at him. Was he serious? "Try" always includes the possibility of failure. Jump too soon and the water would be too shallow and they'd smash onto the jagged rocks and then the wave would surge in and pummel them. Jump too late and they'd be caught in the outgoing maelstrom and swept back over the rocky entrance and out to sea. Even if they timed it right, and the crest carried them, they'd only have a few seconds to scamble up the slippery rocks before the next incoming wave grabbed them.

'Are you up for it?' he shouted. He had mischief in his eye as he crossed his arms and pinched the hem of his T-shirt, and with one swift manoeuvre he swept it over his head. He was now wearing only his shorts. 'I'll take these off if you take yours off,' he challenged.

She looked around. They were totally alone. This felt like yet another ceremonial action, that it would be an initiation, a baptism of a beginning for her. Without allowing herself a thought that might alter her decision, she dropped the little cotton bag from her shoulder and swept her dress up and over her head and laid it on top of his T-shirt on the rocks. Together, they took off their underwear. It was the first time in her life that she'd been naked outdoors, and the first time in her life a boy could see her. They were both so determined not to look at each other, they stared at the thrashing water below.

'I can't believe we're going to jump!' she shouted.

There's thinking and then there's doing. She had stopped thinking. It was a four-metre fall to the bottom of the basin but just a two-metre fall to the crest of the wave. The ride would last two seconds and sweep them eight metres to the back wall. They would have fourteen seconds to scramble up the rocks before the next wave crashed in. Of course, these were maths and measurements they had no control over once they jumped, and which would change drastically if they timed that jump incorrectly.

'Here it comes,' he shouted, grabbing her hand with one hand and his good luck Buddha with his other. 'Ready?'

She hadn't finished nodding when he leaped, pulling her with him into the plunge. She lost his grip as they struck the water. She went under and somersaulted, only to surface as she crashed into his body. Rocks, she felt rocks under her knees. She dug her nails into cracks and claimed the earth for all land dwellers. The surge changed direction, begging them to surrender and return with it into the wild, deep ocean, but they held on as the water drained away off them. Urgently, they clambered upwards with the triumphant laughter of survival.

Chris stood on the summit, the next wave slithering up the rocks just below them. He flung an arm into the air to claim the victory and he let out a celebratory cheer.

They sat, side by side, above the pleading tide line, and their breathing gradually slowed back to normal. Chris wiped his nose and laughed, but Amaranth was looking around them.

'Shit,' she shouted. 'How do we get off here and back to the beach?'

The back of the rock looked like it had been neatly sliced into a sheer drop of three metres onto the jagged rocks that penetrated the beach below. The front was the slippery scramble with a merciless incoming wave every fifteen seconds.

'We'll have to jump back into the basin and let the wave take us out to sea then try to swim back to shore.' She was desperate, but had no other solution.

'Hang on!' Chris said emphatically. 'The tide's coming in, isn't it? Look – each wave is a little higher. If we wait till the sea surrounds the rock, we could step off the back here into the water.'

'By then the shoreline will be way over there, Chris. We'll be out at sea! And the current is…'

'There's no other choice,' he said firmly. 'Is there?'

She saw he was right. They waited. Each new wave inched the waterline upwards towards them every fifteen seconds. The base behind them gradually dappled firstly with rock pools that slowly became one large pool, and then it was the ocean itself. Their rock was now a tiny, pinnacle island, and the basin, completely submerged, was soothed as the swell no longer had to squeeze through the narrow entry.

'Let's do it!' he shouted.

And, before they could think about rips, sharks, and submerged rocks, they jumped again.

'Wowee!' Amaranth shouted to him as he swam beside her. 'I've never been this far out before. You reckon we'll make it?'

'Yeah,' Chris shouted. But he wondered if they would. The ocean is really big when you are engulfed by it and you have nothing to keep you afloat but your determination.

They swam and swam and swam till they were aware they were being lifted towards the shoreline. The tide heaved them safely back onto the beach where they panted, realising the rock where they had left their clothes was now totally underwater.

Chris ran along the shallows, hoping to discover some of their sodden fabric washed up somewhere.

'Nothing,' he said. 'No sign of the clothes. Not even a bloody thong. Shit, my watch was in my pants.'

'Here and now.' Amaranth attempted philosophy.

'And how are we going to get home without any clothes, Amma?'

'We're just going to have to walk back like this,' she stated.

Chris hesitated.

'Come on,' she said. 'What's the problem? We can explain. Someone will help us out.'

Two naked lovers might be all very well in a lonely cove, but they had to get all the way back to town. A naked girl could probably get away with such a situation. Sure, there'd be whistles and leers, but soon enough a gallant person would interrupt the spectacle and offer assistance. But if it's a naked man it's called "indecent exposure", and Chris' parole still had a few days to go before it expired. He knew he wouldn't be allowed to leave the country if he got into any trouble with the law.

'Are you THAT shy?' she goaded. His reluctance seemed to embolden her. 'What's the matter?'

But he couldn't tell her. Three children. Criminally negligent manslaughter. He just shook his head.

'So, what: we're just going to spend the rest of our lives right here, Chris? Somebody will come along one day and find our two dead bodies. And we'll be naked anyway.' She laughed at her own little story.

'I can't get into trouble with the cops again, that's all,' he said.

'Again? Why, what happened?'

'Nothing. I... some traffic thing. Fuck! I don't want to go into it all, okay?' he said. 'Can we just leave it?'

She left it, but she wondered what she was leaving, and why she always seemed to end up with the bad boys.

'Well, I'm freezing so I'm going,' she said. 'I'll try to find someone with a towel they can lend us or something. There must be someone on the beach around the point there. Where will you be when I come back for you?'

'No. No, I'll come too,' he surrendered.

163

They walked briskly along the beach, but were dismayed to discover only a high cliff was lurking around the point. There was no option but to detour up beside it and climb the wooden rails back onto the lighthouse walking track. She giggled about what some poor exercising jogger would do when confronted with two naked hippies. But there were no joggers. It was almost dark by the time they walked down the steps onto Wategos Beach. Too dark now for swimming, the restaurant lights announced it was cocktail hour. The beach was empty.

They skulked along, staying close to the pandanus trees that defined the road running along the beach, and then climbed the long staircase that led to the track back to The Pass. Too late in the day for hikers, they saw no one on the track, but when they arrived at the southern end of Main Beach they could see some surfers busy pulling off their wet-suits near the rocks. Other than a self-engrossed couple ambling in an embrace along the shoreline, Chris and Amaranth were alone there too.

They kept to the base of the dunes, certain they could simply drop down and look like evening canoodlers should anyone appear. Thankfully, it was almost totally dark and the main beach was fairly deserted.

'I live just one street back,' Amaranth said.

'You reckon we could make it there without getting arrested?' Chris asked.

'Even if we did, we have a legitimate excuse, Chris. We lost our clothes.'

'Swimming naked?'

'What else can we do?' was all she could say. 'It's just right across the grass and down that little street, first turn left. Not far. Let's just run.'

They ran briskly down the side street, turned into her street and headed for her block of flats. It was as though they were wearing a cloak of invisibility – no one seemed to notice them except, inside a passing car, a man turned to his wife, raised his eyebrows and said, 'Welcome to Byron Bay, honey!'

Amaranth held open the main door to her block of flats for him because he was running with his hands cupped over his genitals in pretence of cover. They scurried along the brightly lit hallway to her door.

'Shit,' she said. 'My key was in my bag!' Her nudity panicking in the glaring light, she rattled the door knob as though there was even a chance she'd left it unlocked. 'I know: toilet window!'

Back out of the front doors, down the side of the block, through the gate that led to where the rubbish bins loitered, and up to her toilet window.

It was slightly open to provide a courteous ventilation. Chris reached up and took away the fitted flyscreen, then he pushed the window fully open. A small aperture gaped an invitation.

'I reckon I can get through there with a squeeze,' he said. 'Just need a bit of a leg-up.'

Amaranth crouched on all fours and he stood on her back, trying to make himself as light as he could. He pushed his arms into the open window and hunched his head and shoulders through, then he wriggled his torso in after them. When only his rear end was left outside, and he was frozen in a dive onto the toilet inside, he heard Amaranth laughing behind him.

'Don't look!' he shouted back at her.

'If only I had a camera,' she spluttered.

'Don't look! Don't look! Fuck!' He wriggled in a panic to end the show, and crumpled, headfirst, onto the hard tiled floor inside.

He stood up, switched the light on, and peered in the mirror over the sink to inspect the redness appearing over his left eyebrow and the window scrapes on his chest.

Noble injuries sustained whilst solving our dilemma, he thought. He peeled a towel from the rail and passed it out of the window for her to wrap around herself.

'Go to the front door and I'll let you in,' he shouted.

He grabbed a second towel, tied it around his naked waist, and headed for the front door. She was already tapping on it when he got there, but he left it closed.

'Chris? Chris? You there?'

'I'm not opening this till you erase that picture from your mental camera,' he shouted through the door.

'Hah, never!' she sang.

165

'I can wait all night if I have to.'

'So can I.'

'Yeah,' he tempted, 'but I've got a hot shower, food, and a bed.'

There was a short silence as she considered those comforts.

'But you don't have me,' she said.

And he opened the door.

Chapter 21.   Hanley

It was almost dawn by the time they fell asleep beside each other but, just as they slipped into dreams, there was a fierce, demanding knocking at the front door.

Chris whispered a groan to her. 'Oh, really? Please don't tell me that young Master Daniel has come back.'

'I hope not,' she whispered back, not fearful in the least but very reluctant to be dragged into explaining the situation to him. She checked the time on her phone. 'Five-forty!'

She wrapped a robe around the nakedness so celebrated moments before, and wrenched a slice of hall light between the door and the wall wide enough to see two men in suits.

'Good morning. I'm Senior Detective Hanley, this is Detective Tate. Are you Miss Amaranth Vaughan?'

Amaranth sat at the lounge room table across from Detective Hanley. Chris, wrapped in a sheet like a Roman toga, was standing behind her, rubbing reassurance into her shoulders. Tate sat close to the front door, a small notebook on his lap, his pencil poised like he was about to throw a dart into a bullseye.

'Are you the tenant, Miss?' Hanley asked.

'Yes. We can explain about the clothes.'

'That's all right, Miss. First thing's first, if you don't mind.' He turned to Chris. 'So, can I get your name, sir?'

'Chris Allen.'

'So that would be Christopher Allen? Allen is your surname?'

'Yes.'

'You have a middle name, sir?'

'James.'

'And can you spell Allen for me, please?'

'Two l's and an e. A-double l-e-n.'

167

'You have a driver's licence, sir?'

'I did, but it's suspended.'

'If I could just have a look at it, Mr Allen.'

Chris went to get his trousers from the bedroom, but he stopped.

'Yes, no, it was in my pants. They got washed away at the beach.'

'You have some other form of I.D in the home, sir?'

'Maybe, but this is not my home. It's Amma's place. I live in Marvel Street.'

Hanley looked at the other officer who raised his eyebrows and drew a line under the name he had written down.

'I see, thank you. Well, let's start with the young lady. Your name, Miss?'

'You said it at the door,' Amaranth said.

'I just need you to formally confirm it for me, Miss.' He looked at the other detective to be certain he was recording her words.

'Amaranth Vaughan,' she said peevishly. 'No middle name. A-m-a-r-a-n-t-h. Amaranth. V-a-u-g-h-a-n, Vaughan. I don't drive, and I lost my bankcard at the same beach, but I have a lease agreement on the bookcase there, and it's got my name on it.'

She stood up, grabbed the lease and handed it to Hanley, who read it carefully.

'I see that you signed this at three-fifteen on the afternoon of Friday, March thirty-first,' Hanley said, nodding to his partner to note that down. 'You don't have any other form of identity? One with a photograph perhaps?'

'It all got lost when we went for a swim,' Amaranth said to the interviewing detective. 'Our clothes got swept away by the sea and we didn't have any option but to run home naked. What else could we have done?'

'Perhaps you could have left some clothes on when you went for a swim. Underclothing, for example, passes satisfactorily for swimwear.'

'Amaranth?' Chris said quietly to her. 'That's what Amma is short for? That's a well pretty name.'

'Thanks,' she said.

'Okay,' Hanley said. 'We aren't here to discuss your swimming activities, Miss Vaughan. There is another, more serious matter.'

Her puzzled look invited him to explain.

'I believe you know a Gary Baker in Potts Hill, New South Wales?'

'Yes.'

'And when was the last time you saw him?' Hanley asked.

How would they know about me and Gary? she thought. *And what do they know about what he had done in Regents Park?*

'Last time I saw him was in Sydney about a fortnight ago,' she said. 'He was here in Byron last Monday, but I didn't see him.'

'And what makes you think he was here if you didn't see him, Miss?' Hanley researched.

'He left a note on our car. Oh, that's what this is about!'

Detective Tate asked if they could see the note.

'No, I don't still have it. Who keeps notes?' Her eyes fell to the book on the detective's lap.

'And what did this note say?' Tate asked.

Amaranth was reluctant to mention the threat the note contained because she might then have to explain all sorts of difficult things. 'It just said he was in Byron.'

Hanley continued his line of questioning.

'And this was last Monday? Are you quite sure it was Monday?'

Amaranth checked with Chris about when she was shopping, reminding him they had bumped into each other that day.

'Oh yes, that was definitely Monday,' Chris confirmed. 'I did my Dive Master's Certificate in the arvo. So that was Gary I met?'

'You met him?' Amaranth shrugged off his massaging hands and turned fully to face him.

'Yes. After you'd gone, he came up to me.' Chris looked up to Hanley. 'He asked me if it was Amma's car, and I guess he left the note after I went into Woolies.'

'And did he say anything else to you?' pushed Hanley.

'Not much. He just wanted to badmouth Daniel.'

'And Daniel is…?' probed Tate.

Amaranth took control of the explanation.

'Daniel is a friend of mine. He drove me up from Sydney in his car.'

'This would be Daniel…?' Tate elicited.

'Epstein,' she replied. 'I'm guessing that's who called you.'

'About?'

'About Gary smashing Daniel's windscreen on Monday. That's what this is about, isn't it?'

'Daniel Epstein?' Tate continued. 'Is he a resident in this flat?'

'He was,' Amaranth said. 'He left Byron.'

'In his car with a smashed windscreen?' Tate looked down at his notepad. 'Do you have the registration number of that vehicle?'

'DAN 21,' she said, choosing to explain that it had been a personalised twenty-first birthday present from his father. 'His father thought it was still a cool thing to do.'

'Make? Model?' Tate was as excited as a dog at a rabbit hole.

'Car, brown,' was her equivalent response. 'With a cracked windscreen.'

Hanley took over. 'And why do you think Mr Baker smashed the windscreen?'

'You'd have to ask Mr Baker that,' she snapped.

'So, there was tension between Mr Baker and Mr Epstein?' Tate asked.

'Yes.'

'And what was that about?'

Amaranth felt awkward and pressured.

'I don't know,' she snapped, 'Boy stuff. About me. What did Daniel say it was about?'

'I'm not aware of us having had any communication with someone called Daniel Epstein, Miss,' Hanley said.

'So why are you asking me about Gary?'

Detective Hanley cleared his throat and steadied his gaze at her pupils.

'Miss Vaughan,' he pronounced, 'a gentleman we believe to be Gary Baker was found dead in his home on Wednesday morning. He had sustained a blunt force trauma to the head.'

Amaranth's brain hollowed into a cavern of confusion where "found dead" echoed like a scatter of startled pigeons.

'Dead?' She tried to make sense of it. 'Oh my God. So... did he trip or did something fall on him, or what?' Amaranth asked.

'It would appear that Mr Baker was attacked from behind by an assailant who was inside his home. Possibly he surprised a burglar. There were signs of a forced entry via a broken window in the kitchen. Forensics are endeavouring to establish the exact time and date of the event. That's all the information we have. So far.'

'Gary,' Amaranth whispered, dazed. 'Oh no. Poor Gary.'

'Miss Vaughan? Miss Vaughan?' The detective's voice guided her back to comprehension. 'Certain persons, known to you, have made a statement that, until quite recently, you were living with Mr Baker. Is that correct?'

She nodded.

'I'll need you to accompany me to Sydney to identify the body and make a formal statement. Will that be convenient?'

She nodded again.

Tate checked his notes. 'Miss Vaughan, have you left Byron at any time since renting this flat?'

'No.'

'And can you confirm that, Mr Allen?'

'Sure,' Chris endorsed. 'Like she says, I saw Amma on Monday at the supermarket, and again yesterday. I was working at the Beach Hotel the days in-between.'

'But you can't confirm her whereabouts for the days in-between? Just Monday the third, and Sunday the ninth?' Tate asked, writing as he spoke.

'If today's the tenth,' replied Chris, clearly getting a little annoyed with the pedantry.

Hanley dropped his tone to that of a magistrate.

'So you're unable to corroborate Miss Vaughan's claim she was here for the entire week?'

Forgetting the caution about his traffic offence, Chris erupted.

'You surely don't think that she flew down to Sydney, bashed this Gary bloke, and then scarpered back here, do you?'

'I don't think anything at this present moment, sir,' Hanley quoted from the Elementary Text Book for Detectives.

Tate flicked back a page in his notes.

'And do you know where we can find your friend, Daniel Epstein?'

171

'No, I don't. Why do you want Daniel?'

'For a start-off, he'd be able to confirm your whereabouts last week.'

'No, he couldn't,' she confessed. 'He left town last Tuesday.'

'What time on Tuesday would that have been?'

'Just before lunchtime.'

Hanley turned to her. 'To drive back to Sydney?'

'Daniel's anywhere but Sydney,' she chortled.

'And what makes you think that?' Hanley asked.

'Because he was afraid of going there. Gary's note was...' she fished for the appropriate word, '...threatening.'

Both police officers became noticeably excited.

'So you believe there might have been an altercation, had these two encountered each other?'

'Daniel is not in Sydney,' she repeated.

'We still need to speak with him,' Hanley stated.

'Daniel wouldn't have hurt Gary,' she implored.

'Perhaps not, but someone did, Miss Vaughan, someone did.'

#

Scott rode his motorbike down Barton Street. He saw the blue-chequered tape wound across Gary's driveway, warning: 'Police – Do Not Cross'. He didn't stop. He didn't slow down. He just rode past, trying to look like he wasn't looking.

#

Kirsten had done four loads of washing on Saturday, and had got it all dry. She woke on Sunday morning in a fresh nightie, on fresh sheets, as Robert waddled back in from the bathroom. He had only his underpants on. He preferred two sizes too small, hopeful they would exaggerate the bulge they contained, but they merely exaggerated the bulge that spilled over the waistband like the froth from a shaken beer can.

'Did you put the deadlock on last night?' she quizzed him.

172

'Yes, I put the deadlock on. And I snibbed the bolt. Then I put the key in the bowl on top of the fridge, unlike Friday night when I left it in the lock on the outside of the door all night. Happy?'

Kirsten heard little if any of that. She was still coming to terms with the imagined fact that she had flatted with a murderess for all those months.

'She could have killed us in our sleep. I told the cops she wasn't right in the head.'

'And him,' affirmed Robert. 'That weedy little weirdo. A right pair they was. You seem to attract weirdos, Kirsty.'

Then he climbed in beside her, farting on the way.

'Robert!' she snapped.

'Oh, I just stepped on Jesse's duck,' he said. 'Sorry.'

And they both burst out giggling.

#

The two detectives sat in the front seat of their car, the running motor hinting at their tight schedule. They stared directly forward, providing the semblance of privacy for Amaranth as she said goodbye to Chris outside her flat.

'You going to be all right?' he asked softly.

She wasn't sure about that. She rehearsed her reaction to seeing Gary. To seeing Gary's body. His dead, damaged face.

'You want me to come down with you?' Chris continued.

'No. I'll be fine. But thank you.' She smiled at him. And he smiled back. 'If I leave you the spare key, Chris, could you be here when I get back?'

'Sure. How long are you going for?'

'Just the day. I'm not going to stay down there, I'll fly back tonight, if not to Ballina then I'll get a flight to the Gold Coast or Brissy, if I have to.'

'The last flight to Ballina is in the late afternoon,' Tate chipped in, helpfully, 'but a Jetstar to the Gold Coast gets in at ten pm.'

'There you go,' Chris said. 'My shift tonight ends at eleven so that works out perfect. It'll take you that long to get to Byron.'

Hanley leaned out of his window.

'We ought to be moving, Miss. We have a plane to catch.'

Chris pulled her close to him.

'They seem very interested in Daniel. You sure he wasn't involved?'

'You've met Daniel. Could you imagine him doing anything like that?'

'Not really,' said Chris, 'but Gary said Danny beat the crap out of him. They were his exact words.'

'No,' she insisted, 'it was the other way round. Gary got stuck into Danny.'

Chris lowered his voice conspiratorially.

'So he owed him one, then?'

Chapter 22. The Crowbar

Daniel pulled out of Joshua's driveway. He'd dropped the last of his boxes and bags in the garage. He needed the space in his hatchback if he was going to spend any more nights sleeping in there.

He turned down the main drag and headed for the shops. A coffee and the share accommodation pages would keep him busy.

He glanced in his rear-vision mirror. The patrol car behind him was flashing its lights, signalling him to pull over.

#

It was five pm. Amaranth hadn't eaten all day. The sight of Gary's mouth had disturbed her most of all. Gaping. Frozen in the shape of his last utterance. Pain.

Detective Hanley had taken her back to an interview room in the Sydney Police Station, and left her alone for a few minutes. He came back in with two mugs of tea, one of which he placed on the desk before her.

'There you go. Never an easy thing to do, Amaranth. Thank you.'

'I've done it before,' she said. 'I found my mother under our house when I was sixteen.'

'I'm sorry,' he said kindly. He felt oddly awkward but snapped back to his more usual comfort by reaching for the desk drawer and slipping it open. He took out a tape recorder and placed it on the desk between them, positioning the microphone towards her. He switched it on.

'My name is Senior Detective Hanley,' he said, sounding as policemanly as he could. 'Taking the statement of my witness Amaranth Vaughan in the matter of the demise of Gary Baker. I still

175

need to ask you a few questions, Miss Vaughan. Do you object to my recording this interview?'

She shook her head.

'I'm sorry, you'll need to make verbal responses.' He gestured to the tape recorder.

'I don't mind,' she obliged.

He spoke quickly into the machine, nominating the date and time, then reverted to his normal pace as he opened a manila folder he'd brought in with him.

'I just read a copy of an interview that Daniel Epstein gave to Sydney police officers this afternoon.'

'He's here?' She looked back towards the door as though she expected he would surprise her.

'He was here earlier. I passed the rego you provided us with to the officers here, and that assisted in locating him fairly promptly.' He examined the folder. 'We appear to have some confusion about exactly who cracked Mr Epstein's windscreen.'

'It was Gary. He left a note,' Amaranth said.

'On Monday, the third of April?'

'Yes.'

'I very much doubt it was Gary Baker,' Hanley said. 'Autopsy has set the time of his death as the evening of Friday the thirty-first of March.' He paused deliberately. 'That's the Friday *before* you say he was in Byron Bay.'

'What?' was all she could offer.

'So, I don't know who cracked the windscreen, or indeed who Mr Allen was talking with, but I'm quite certain it wasn't Gary Baker. However, it appears that both you and Mr Epstein had been signing the rental agreement in Byron Bay only a few hours prior to Mr Baker's death. There are no connection flights around that time, either from the Gold Coast, Ballina, or even Brisbane, and certainly not long enough to drive down.' He read further down the report. 'Now, Mr Epstein seemed to think this Gary Baker fellow was holding you captive for a time. Is that correct?'

'No,' she denied. 'Yes,' she confirmed. 'No,' she decided.

'You seem unsure.'

'It's correct he thought that, but it wasn't correct I was held captive. It's complicated. Look, I don't wish to discuss my personal relationships.'

'And you've certainly had your share!' Hanley said, his laugh tainted with contempt. 'Mr Allen up north, Mr Baker down here, and Mr Epstein who was down here, up there, and back down here again. And then there's this mystery windscreen-cracker with, what did you call it? "Boy stuff" issues about you. All those in the same week!' He stared at her, waiting for her response, but she simply held his gaze till he looked away. 'You're an odd one. I'm having difficulty in deciding who you are.'

'You don't decide who I am,' she said. 'I do.'

'Well, have you got any other boyfriends I should know about?'

'No,' she said, and then leaned towards the tape recorder. 'And I resent your insinuation.'

He regrouped his techniques.

'Not an insinuation, Miss Vaughan, it was a simple enough question. You'd have to agree you have had quite a few boyfriends in what? Less than a fortnight.'

She leaned back in the chair and got comfortable beneath his interrogation. 'It's not really any of your business what I regard as a few.' She saw his lips shape a reply but added: 'Or enough,' before he put sound to it.

He looked at the machine recording his battle tactics.

'I am simply asking if there are any other boyfriends tucked away who might have some grievance with Mr Baker.'

'Check your tape recorder and you'll discover I already answered "no" to that question. Look, am I free to go now?'

'You're not under arrest,' was all he could retaliate with, 'but we will require a sample of your fingerprints before you leave, in order to eliminate them from the crime scene.'

As he busied with the inkpad and file sheet, Amaranth asked, 'Can I collect some of my things from Gary's house?'

He looked surprised at the request. Forensics had finished there, but he explained that the house was all locked up.

'I have my own key,' she stated authoritatively.

'Then I can't stop you,' he conceded, handing her a wet-wipe for her fingertips. 'However, I caution you that the ex-Mrs Baker, a...' he checked the paper file in front of him, '...a Ms Katherine Harrison, is returning from overseas next Tuesday. She is his official next-of-kin, and any items removed that she deems...'

'I just want a change of clothes,' she interrupted. 'And my toothbrush.'

The taxi pulled up outside Gary's house, and Amaranth paid the fare, got out, and it drove away. She walked up the driveway past Gary's car. Like he was home. But she knew he wasn't.

Somewhere up the street, a motorbike engine switched off, but she didn't hear it; her attention was on finding the key in her bag and losing the memories in her mind.

She opened the door and stepped over the chalk outline on the hallway carpet. It chilled her, and she snapped the light on even though it was not yet fully dark outside. There was a matted brown stain around the chalked head shape, and her upper lip curled with repulsion.

She moved quickly to the bedroom and turned that light on too. She began to wonder if there really were any of her previous possessions that warranted suffering this ordeal. It had seemed such a simple task before she arrived.

She slid her suitcase from under the bed, and remembered her journal wedged under the mattress. She pulled it out and put it at the bottom of her suitcase, throwing those items of clothing she could still imagine herself wearing on top of it. She straightened up and quickly looked around the room. Then again, slowly this time. This room of his.

Outside, in the darkening evening, someone sneaked up Gary's path, opened the side door to the garage, and slipped in. Gloved hands silently rummaged amongst the tools, eventually selecting a short, hooked crowbar.

Amaranth walked out of the bedroom to the bathroom, where she collected her toothbrush and toiletries. She bent down to find her make-up case in the cabinet below the sink, but it was too dark inside so she stood up and turned the light on. She didn't notice a face duck down outside the window.

She was being watched.

She went back into the bedroom and collected her suitcase.

Outside, the gloved hands reached in through the unrepaired broken kitchen window, and unsnibbed it. Something that they'd done before.

Amaranth went into the lounge room with her things and set them in a neat pile on Gary's desk, with her make-up case balanced on top of the suitcase. She took her phone from her purse and dialled a taxi, giving her address and the airport destination. They told her it would be at least forty minutes before a cab could get to her, which she reluctantly accepted.

She ended the call and put her phone down on some strewn letters on the desk. She idly examined them to see if any were for her, and was surprised to see one was. It had her name handwritten on the envelope, but no address. Before she could open it, she heard a noise in the kitchen. She hovered between caution and curiosity, but then suddenly her mobile rang and she was startled into responding to it.

'Hello?' she asked, noting her voice was higher pitched than normal.

It was Daniel.

'Are you okay?' he asked.

'Yeah. Fine.'

'You sound a little shaky. It must be strange there for you.'

'How do you know where I am?' she asked.

'The police interviewed me this arvo. They mentioned you were coming down, I just guessed you'd be staying at Gary's.'

'I'm not staying here. I'm actually leaving in a few minutes.'

'Where are you going?'

'Back to Byron.'

'Why? You only went there to get away from Gary. There's no Gary anymore.'

'Gary has nothing to do with why I'm going back.'

Daniel was silent for a moment.

'Don't tell me you already got someone else.'

'That's nothing to do with it either.'

'There *is* someone! Who is it? Another pub-worker? Who?'

'I haven't met anyone new. I'm going back because that's where I want to be.'

Daniel took a deep breath.

'So what about us, then? Now there's no danger?'

'I need to have some time on my own, Daniel. I'm sorry,' she heard herself say.

'Are you?' he accused rather than asked. 'You don't sound sorry to me. You sound, I don't know, almost excited.'

'I'm just in a hurry. I've got a taxi coming. A plane to catch. I've really got to go.'

'No, wait. I'm not far away. Let me speak to you in person.'

'Maybe we should call each other in a few weeks,' she tried.

'Why the hurry? What are you afraid of? That I'll take you prisoner? Rough you up a little? Mmm? That what you miss?'

She heard another noise in the kitchen. A quiet noise, but not the noise a house makes alone.

'Is someone there?' she called out, hoping for no reply.

'Amma? What's going on?' Daniel shouted down the phone.

'I'm not sure. I thought I heard something.' She paused to listen, and heard her thoughts. 'Are you on your mobile?'

'Yes,' he said.

'Are you here? Is that you in the kitchen, Daniel? Is this some sick little game where you pretend to be the bad guy?'

'The police thought I was.'

'Daniel, they let you go. I saw the report. You were still up north when Gary was attacked.' She heard a noise in the kitchen again. 'That is you, isn't it? I'm coming in.'

She hung up the phone and stuffed it into her little shoulder bag along with the envelope with her name on, and turned toward the kitchen, but someone stepped out through the doorway and into the lounge room. He was wearing a tracksuit top with a hood over his head. A crowbar in his gloved hands.

'Daniel?'

'I've been waiting.'

It wasn't Daniel's voice. It was a voice she didn't recognise.

'Who is that?'

'I knew if I kept checking, you'd come back. All your things are still here.'

'Who are you?'

He carefully pulled off his hood. The front part of his head was shaven and there was a large, jagged, new scar that traced what looked almost like a trough. He saw that she didn't recognise him.

'I risked my life for you,' he said, 'and you don't know who I am, do you?'

She shook her head.

'Behind the station in Regents Park. I tried to stop him raping you. Remember?'

He kicked the door behind him, angrily, the slam coinciding with her realisation.

He isn't dead! Gary didn't kill him!

'Well, *I* remembered. I read you his name and his address, didn't I?' he spat. 'Didn't tell anyone I remembered. But I remembered.'

She looked at the crowbar, and saw the impending threat.

'You just sat there,' he said, continuing his outpouring tirade. 'You let him beat the crap out of me, and then you left me lying in the park and took up with the fucker. You didn't even have the decency to call me an ambulance.' His voice whispered a shout.

'We thought you were dead,' she explained.

'Did you check? Did you give me even one thought?'

'You were just lying there. You looked like you were dead.'

'So you go off and live with a bloke you think just killed someone? What are you?'

'I was scared,' she pleaded. 'I had to go with him.'

'Had to, my arse. You were still living with him when I got out of hospital. Do you get off on being raped? Is that it?'

'He didn't rape me,' she corrected, as though that made any difference to him.

'Too right he didn't, because I stuck my neck out for you.'

'Yes, you did. Thank you very…'

'Bit late now. What were you doing when I was lying there bleeding? Where the fuck were you then? Too far up your own arse to give anyone else a thought. But I was ten fucking days in hospital thinking about you. The pair of you.'

181

He moved towards her and she took a step backwards, nearly tripping over the suitcase that was waiting patiently. He smacked the crowbar against his gloved palm.

'I paid him back good and proper,' he threatened. 'But you: you are the real twisted one. You need something much worse. You need to suffer before…'

Reaching behind her, she seized her make-up case and hurled it at his intentions. It delayed him long enough for her to run to the front door and wrench it open, but he caught up to her and slammed it shut. Grabbing her hair, he flipped her back into the centre of the room. He leapt at her, gripping a clutch of her clothing with one hand, and raising the crowbar with the other.

She grappled the callous iron bar with her left hand, and she struck wildly at his head with her right hand. His scar hid a healing skull, and he grimaced painfully as her knuckles slammed directly into it. Inspired by the reprieve this gave her, she instinctively brought her knee up, hard, against his groin. He cried out, crumpled and fell, releasing the bar to her grip.

She turned towards him. She had the crowbar in her hand.

'Not so big now,' she said.

'My head. I had a massive blood clot removed there.'

'You killed Gary,' she accused.

'I gave him what he gave me, that's all.'

'He didn't kill you.'

'He thought he did.'

'By mistake,' she said.

'Well, I didn't mean to kill him either. Just wanted him to end up in hospital, same as me. Look, I need a doctor.'

'And what were you going to do to me?'

'I dunno. Scare you. Make you say "sorry".'

'With a crowbar?' she shouted.

He held his painful head with both hands now.

'I need to get to a doctor. I could be bleeding inside again.'

'What were you going to do with the crowbar?'

'I told you. Scare you, that's all.'

'And if it didn't scare me?'

'Nothing. Get me a fucking doctor!'

'You said I deserved something worse. What was that?'

'I dunno. Worse. You're worse. You're the whore that likes men fighting over you, you sick fuck. And then bashing you. You get off on that, don't you?'

'Oh, God! I'm so sick of hearing men say that crap to me.'

'Maybe you should listen then,' he cried.

She shook her head. 'Maybe you should think it might just be *your* fantasy.'

'Still don't get it, do you?'

'And you reckon you were going to give it to me? You? You're a kid. A kid with a banged-in head. You were going to scare me? How? With this?' She held up the crowbar. 'This scary thing? So, how scared are you?'

He fell silent. She turned the bar in her hand so it was no longer a bludgeon. It was a hook. With a chisel-sharp blade.

Suddenly, the front door burst open, and Daniel dived onto the youth, pinning him to the floor.

'Call the cops!' Daniel screamed to her.

She was rigid with adrenalin.

'Call the fucking cops, Amma!' Daniel repeated urgently.

Outside Gary's house, two uniformed police officers drove the youth away. A detective shook Daniel's hand firmly, then, raising his eyebrow towards Amaranth, he climbed into his car and followed.

Daniel strode over to where she sat on the front steps.

'Reckons I'm a hero,' he relayed the detective's praise. 'Solved the case, caught the murderer, and saved the girl.'

'You didn't save *me*, Daniel.' She looked down the street after the youth in the police car. 'You saved *him*!'

'So, who *is* going to save you, Amma?'

'From?'

'From you.'

A taxi pulled up and tooted its horn.

'See, it's comments like that make me glad I have to go,' she said.

Daniel sat there and watched her walk to the cab. She threw her cases on the back seat and climbed in beside them.

He sat there for a long time, even after the taxi turned the corner and disappeared.

Chapter 23.   Cochin

Amaranth's flight into Gold Coast Airport was eleven minutes early owing to a favourable tailwind, but it was after eleven-thirty by the time she got home to Byron. She dropped her suitcase by the door and looked at her bed.

It was empty.

She hurled herself onto it and then she did something she hadn't done for a very, very long time.

She wept.

Deep, sobbing wails. And each teardrop was like a miniature version of the snow-dome she'd been given one Christmas. Each scene torn from her book of pain. Her mother. Her father. Her Uncle Warren. Her cat, Misha. The Tree Gang girls. The endless sugarcane. Mal. Kirsten. Ms Howard. Gary. Poor, poor Gary. Gary, who was so much more damaged than she ever was. So much more fragile. Just like Daniel. Like Scott. Like all the guys she'd known, actually. Not counting Chris. He wasn't anything that she didn't like, except not there when she got home. But all the others — why had she been attracted to such weak men?

She stopped crying.

Wait a minute. She sniffed her thoughts through her litany of lovers. *I hadn't been attracted to them. They'd all been attracted to me, and my weakness had been to take what was offered. My weakness? I always thought that was my strength.*

She questioned how it could be weakness to bear what life had flung at her, without complaint, or protest, or even one single tear before now. No, that wasn't weakness. But it also wasn't strength. That was numbness. And her tears watered the return of feeling.

Her phone rang.

'Hello?'

'I had a late shift, baby, I'm so sorry,' Chris said. 'I thought I'd be out of here by the time you got home but we had a massive incident at work. I've just this second knocked off. I'll be at your place in ten minutes.'

It was almost noon when she woke up. She opened her eyes and saw him, still sleeping beside her. He was lying on his stomach, his head turned away from her. This dancer. This leaper-into-waves. This nudist runner. This man who wanted nothing from her, but what she wanted to give. She liked this man.

It was a glorious blue-sky morning and a warm sun called them out. They went to a little restaurant at the edge of the car park that overlooked the ocean opposite the Beach Hotel, and sat at a table while the waiter cracked pepper over their eggs and said he'd be back with their coffees.

She looked out over the sparkling sea, out to the pencil-line horizon that divided the familiar from the unknown.

She waited till their coffees arrived and they were unlikely to be interrupted, and then she told him about Sydney. About Gary. About the youth, the police, the fight.

He stared at her, as enthralled with the tale as he was with the teller.

'What do you reckon?' she asked. 'Enough for one day?'

'And then some,' he said. 'Seriously. I've never had a day like that.'

'So,' she said, 'what did you do yesterday?'

'Pales before yours, I mean there was a fight in the pub last night, but nothing life-threatening. Chairs, tables, broken glasses, that sort of thing. That's why I was late; we had to clean it all up. Stupid blokes who can't handle their piss. Oh, but I have some good news: I got the dive instructor job.'

'In Thailand?'

'Yeah. A touristy island called Koh Samui. Two months' work. They'll even arrange the visa and stuff, I just have to get there.'

'When?' She tried to sound joyous.

'Less than two weeks,' he said. 'Is that long enough?'

'For what?'

'For you to come with me.'

'With you?' She was genuinely astonished. 'Are you serious?' she asked..

'Absolutely,' he said.

'Serious?' she repeated.

He nodded, as she considered the idea.

'I've got more than three thousand left in savings,' she calculated. 'I could do it. Do you really want me to?'

'Of course, silly.'

'But what will I do while you're out diving?'

Chris ignored her objection.

'What are you going to do here? Besides, the job's only for two months. When it ends we could have a look at other islands. We've got plenty of time.'

'I'll need more than three thousand dollars, Chris.'

'Not over there, and I'll have my pay from the dive job.'

'Let's do this, right,' she said. 'Let's just head off, all over the world.'

'Well, "all over the world" might be asking a bit much from two months of Thai wages.'

'I wasn't thinking about wages, Chris. I was thinking about selling something.'

'Okay. What have you got to sell?' he asked.

She grabbed her shoulder bag and pulled out the envelope from Gary's desk.

'I've got a boat,' she said.

They arranged it so they were both flying from Brisbane Airport on the same day. Chris was flying to Bangkok, Amaranth was flying to Sydney. She would have two months to get her passport and to sell the yacht. They hugged goodbye in the departure lounge.

'Here,' Chris said, taking the little Buddha pendant from around his neck. 'Take this – it's my good-luck charm. Maybe it'll bring you good luck, too, and you'll sell the boat straight away without any hassles.'

'No, no,' she said. 'It's yours.'

'Yeah, that's right,' he said. 'You have to bring it back to me. Oh, that's my flight they're calling now.'

A long hug. A quick kiss. A hurried wrenching away. A goodbye flittering of fingers. Then: gone.

She fastened his necklace round her neck, picked up her bags, and went outside to catch the shuttle bus to the Domestic Terminal.

His good-luck charm had plenty to do, however. Before she could sell the yacht, she had to first contest a caveat Kate had rapidly placed on it. Kate's lawyers had argued that Amaranth had not yet registered the yacht in her name and, since it had been purchased with money Gary hadn't settled in the divorce at the time he'd bought it, it was part of their shared estate and thus Kate's property on his demise.

It cost Amaranth both time and money for a solicitor to verify the signed ownership papers that proved Gary had indeed given it to her, and eventually she had the authority to sell it. She placed it with a sales company that the marina manager recommended, and the salesman said he was confident it would sell quickly.

Chris had insisted that they only use texting so as to avoid the expensive roam charges for calling, so her fingers were excitedly tapping her news.

'They say I should get forty grand for it!' Amaranth typed. 'That's more money than I've ever had!'

'Fantastic! When r u coming ova? My contract ends in three weeks.'

'Perfect! I'll be there!'

The three weeks had almost passed and the yacht had still not sold. Amaranth's savings had all but gone on surviving in Sydney after paying the legal fees to secure the yacht. She explained to Chris that she only had just enough for the ticket over now, and he texted back that they could start somewhere easy and then head off to wilder, more exciting places. He had enough to cover for them till the money came through from the yacht, and he said she should fly to Bali on the same day he would, and they'd meet up at the airport there.

'Whatever!' she said. It was all exciting to her. Anywhere away was.

Departure Day arrived. She had never been overseas before, and she felt her heart start to thump. She looked around at the other passengers. They were all so calm, so matter-of-fact about getting into a lump of tin and hurtling thousands of kilometres through the sky for six and a half hours.

Nervous is just another word for excited, she convinced herself.

Chris had told her to just bring one carry-on bag and a purse big enough to hold her passport and stuff, so she went straight to the check-in counter queue. There was only one couple in front of her. A tall, fairly solid guy, mid forties with a thick mane of golden hair swept casually back from his suntanned face. Despite wheeling an expensive-looking, small black leather travel bag, he was only wearing shorts and a shirt, both with Indonesian patterns, and sandals on his feet, all of which announced he had been to Bali before. He was travelling with a woman who was standing just ahead of him in the queue. She was perhaps just a little younger, but her tanned face was grooved with time and experiences. Lean body. She looked like she was on an African safari, with her khaki shorts and an olive-green shirt. She had an SLR camera in a case slung around her neck and she pulled a medium-sized alluminium wheelie-case.

The man turned to Amaranth and smiled.

'And vair are you flying today?' He spoke in a presumptive English, even though he had a distinct foreign accent.

'Bali.'

'Ah, yes, Bali.'

German, she thought. *He sounds like the colonel in Hogan's Heroes on TV.*

'For holiday, or are you living zair?' he inquired.

'I'll live there for a while,' she said, eager to not sound like a tourist.

'Vee also are. Oh, zay are ready for us.' His companion was at the desk as he strode across to join her and present his ticket and passport. As they left, and Amaranth took their place, he threw her a smile that asked only for one in return.

Once through the security gate, she had enough time to meander in the shopping alley. Souvenirs of Australia for the visitors leaving, books to replace ones read by transitting passengers, an array of

189

foreign electrical plug adapters, and duty free perfumes. All of no interest to her, but it was entertaining to browse till her flight was announced. She took her final step away from Australia, off the loading ramp and into the plane.

'Vell, kvite a small verld, isn't it?' the German guy said, as Amaranth reached her designated seat and saw him sitting in the same row. He stood up and helped her place her bag in the overhead luggage compartment and remained standing to allow her to pass into the row. She shuffled past his companion who was in the middle seat and plonked herself down next to the window.

'I am Cochin. Zis is my sister, Nina.'

'Hi. I'm Amaranth.'

'Exotic name,' said Cochin. 'For an exotic girl.'

Amaranth never considered either herself or her name as exotic. 'Amma, for short,' she said. 'Cochin is more exotic. I mean, it doesn't exactly sound like an ordinary German name.'

'It voz given to me by my guru,' he said proudly.

'Cochin told me you said you are living in Bali,' Nina interupted their mutual name-praising. 'Where?'

'Oh, I don't know yet.'

'You haven't booked somewhere?'

'No,' Amaranth said, and immediately wondered if she probably should have.

'So, Kuta, Ubud, Sanur, where are you heading?' said Nina, establishing her knowledge of the island.

'Kuta, I think,' Amaranth said.

Nina screwed up her nose.

'Kuta is very unpleasant. It was touristy twenty years ago, it's hell now. Legian is going the same way. Kuta and Legian are pretty much the same place anyway. We live in Seminyak.'

Amaranth shook her head.

'Ze next beach after Legian,' Cochin explained, leaning into the conversation. 'Kuta, Legian, Seminyak, like so. Vee have a house, at ze norzern end.'

'The quiet end,' added Nina.

'If you are brother and sister, how come you don't have an accent, Nina?' Amaranth asked.

190

'Oh, thank you. Most people say I have a strong South African accent.'

'But your brother…'

Cochin took over again. 'My sister voz raised by our muzzer in Cape Town. I left viss my farzer venn I voz four, and he took me back to Germany. Vee lived in Hamburg.'

'And now we live together in Seminyak,' Nina explained, grabbing the conversation once more. 'Cochin has an export business and I do some photo-journalist work for a couple of international publications.'

'Cool,' said Amaranth. She didn't notice the pause they left for her to fill.

'So,' said Nina eventually, 'what do you do?'

'Oh, I.. right now… I'm living!' *Creatively evasive answer.*

Brother and sister looked at each other, then Nina turned back to her.

'We are all living, Amma. But what do you do to *earn* your living?'

Talking to someone who owns their own export business and someone who is a photo-journalist for international magazines makes it hard to say you haven't worked for the past three months, and before that you spent your time putting files in drawers and fetching coffees for an ungrateful boss.

'I've just sold my yacht,' she said, hoping for some equality.

Nina smiled. She wondered how this girl had had a yacht. Daddy? Divorce? Dealing? Who knows?

Nina flicked over the page of the inflight magazine on her lap.

'Oh dear,' she said, tapping a half-page picture of a child with a paper kite on a tropical beach. 'This is one of mine. I took it three years ago for Thai Air. Now how did it end up in a Garuda flight magazine?'

Cochin looked at it. 'It's probably zat bitch, Barbara, at Allied Pictures. She's selling your verk behind your back. You mustn't let her get away viss it, Nina.'

Amaranth sat back and prepared for take-off.

About twenty minutes before they landed in Denpasar, Nina went to the toilets. Cochin slipped across into her vacant seat.

'You know, vee have a very big house, viss a large svimming pool, and close to ziss beach viss no people. Just real locals. It's very special. Very private. Vee have six bedrooms. You are velcome to stay viss us for a veek or so. Living. Doing vot-ever you like.'

'I'm meeting my boyfriend in Denpasar.'

'Oh,' Cochin's surprise equalled his disappointment. 'You have a boyfriend living in Bali?'

'He doesn't live there. Not yet. He flies in from Thailand tonight. I haven't seen him for two months.'

'Two months? Okay. Vell zen, you must both stay viss us. It vill give me someone to talk viss venn Nina is chewing off your ear.'

Nina came back and sat in the empty aisle seat.

'Amma has a boyfriend zat she hasn't seen for some months. He is flying into Denpasar tonight.'

'You're meeting him?' Nina said.

Amaranth nodded. 'Midnight.'

'Midnight!' laughed Cochin. 'It's still morning. You surely are not going to vait at ze airport for tvelf hours? Zat gives you plenty of time to have a look at our house and decide.'

'Decide what?' Nina asked sharply.

'I offered one of our rooms to Amma.'

'But she has a boyfriend coming.'

'Not a problem, Nina. Vee vill see.' He turned to Amaranth. 'Vee have a Jimny – a small jeep – parked at ze airport. It's less than an hour to Seminyak. So you vill come, yes?'

Amaranth thought Chris would be very impressed if the house turned out to be as lovely as Cochin described, and besides, this was exactly the kind of wonderful thing she expected Life to offer.

Cochin got out of the Jimny and opened the tall, iron gates to the driveway of their house. He got back into the car and drove it to the front steps. Nina got out and jiggled her seat forward so Amaranth could get out from the back, while Cochin crunched back down the drive to close the gates again. And lock them.

The single-storey house stood on stilts in a half-acre garden at the end of a cul-de-sac. The first thing Amaranth noticed was how quiet it was, a secluded tropical paradise. Then she saw how large the house actually was. Obviously Cochin's business was booming.

As Amaranth followed Nina up the stairs, she looked at the detail of leaves and lizards that were hand-carved in the two-metre tall wooden pillars that the house stood on. The front door opened to a spacious room with three broad lounges, each strewn with an arrangement of brightly decorated cushions. On the walls there were enlarged and framed photographs – award-winning mementos à la Nina, no doubt. There was a cocktail bar in one corner and beside it, sliding doors opened onto a verandah overlooking the pool and out over the neighbouring roofs to the sea beyond.

Amaranth slipped the small document shoulder bag from around her neck and put it on top of her backpack by the door.

'What an opulent home you have,' she said to her hosts.

'It's a bitch to keep tidy,' Nina said, glancing at her guest's bag by the door. She held up her mobile and tapped it to show her brother coming in behind them that she was going to make a call, then she picked up her own bag and left the room.

Cochin dropped his bags beside Amaranth's at the door.

'So vot can I get you to drink, Amma?'

'Oh. I'm fine, thank you.'

'Come on, I'm pretty sure vee have everything.'

'I'm sure you do,' she said, clearly displaying how impressed she was.

He went to the bar and opened the fridge there. She heard ice cubes clunking into a glass. He poured something and whisked it with a long stainless steel spoon. He walked over to her and handed her one of the two glasses he was carrying.

'So, sit. Let's talk about zis boyfriend of yours. Vot does he do?'

They sat, each on their own couch.

She sipped the cool juice. 'He is a Dive Instructor.'

'In Thailand, you said? How come you didn't go viss him?'

'We only just met when he got the job, and anyway, I had to stay and sell my boat in Sydney.'

Nina came back in. She nodded to Cochin as she headed to the bar.

'Ah, yes,' she said, joining the conversation, 'tell us about your yacht.'

'It was just a little twenty-six-footer.'

'And why did you sell it? Aren't you going back to Sydney?'

'I really don't know where I'm heading,' Amaranth said, shrugging. 'And I sold it because I don't know how to sail.'

Nina looked up at her. 'You had a yacht, but you can't sail?'

'It was a gift,' Amaranth said. She was slipping into a conversation she didn't want to have.

'A rather expensive gift,' Nina pushed. 'Daddy?'

'No. A friend actually.'

'Pretty good friend,' Nina said, clearly incredulous.

'Yes, he was. He really helped me find myself.'

'And did you? Find yourself?'

'Yes.' Amaranth replied, trying to smile.

'And where were you hiding?'

Nina's tone was tainted with distain, and Amaranth didn't like it at all. She took another sip to mask that she was considering her answer.

'I wasn't "hiding",' she said as soon as she swallowed. 'I was just a little lost, that's all.'

'But vee have found you now, Amma,' Cochin said, cheerily breaking the harshness of the interview.

Nina wasn't finished. 'You said, "was a good friend". Why "was"? What happened? Did you argue?'

'He died, Nina.'

Cochin coughed. 'Sad,' he said insincerely. He waited to see if his sister had something to say, but she just raised her eyebrows. 'Okay zen, let's change the subject,' he said, with a burst of energy. 'Life is for ze living, yah? Tell me, do you like to party?'

'Oh,' Amaranth said as cheerfully as she could manage, 'you know.'

'No,' Nina said. 'We don't know.'

Amaranth was unsure where this was going.

'You mean like dancing?' she said.

'Dancing. Entertaining. Did you ever do zat professionally?' Cochin continued his research.

'No. Not for a living. I like dancing though. Is there somewhere around here…'

Nina cut her off. 'You can dance here, if you like.'

'No, I mean is there a bar?'

'Vee have a bar.'

Amaranth laughed. A silly little laugh that said she was feeling awkward. Uneasy. Vulnerable. Both of her hosts seemed comforted by that.

'I think Amma would probably like a swim after the plane,' Nina announced, rescuing her from the moment.

'No, I'm good, thanks.'

'I get you a towel,' Cochin said, his assumption pushing her further to acceptance whilst faking helpfulness.

'I think another drink first, Cochin,' Nina instructed. 'I think. Another drink.' She raised one eyebrow to him.

'Now?' Cochin said.

'Definitely,' his sister decreed.

Amaranth said she was okay. Not really thirsty.

'All right, just another juice then… Wow, what's in it? Is that alcohol?... It's a little too early in the day, don't you think?' She coughed. 'It's quite strong. What is it?'

'Mostly mango puree and coconut and pineapple juice,' said Nina.

'It's got a little bitter backtaste. Is that alcohol?'

'Just a dash,' said Cochin.

'Oh, what alcohol is it?' Amaranth exaggerated her drinks knowledge.

'Just a tiny dash of white rum, that's all. Same as the first one. To soften the sweetness and kill the bugs. Very refreshing. Drink up.'

Amaranth stepped down into the pool that felt like silent music. A space spilled open for her as cyan ripples slithered away. She floated on her back and stared up at the deep blue sky behind a canopy of glistening palm fronds. She loved this place. She loved this. She loved.

The water around her wobbled, and she let her legs slowly sink to the bottom of the pool till she was standing in chest-deep water. There was a man in the pool. She didn't remember there being a man there. He swam right up very close to her, and she seemed to be expecting that. He was from Java, he said. A business associate, he said. He asked if he could kiss her. She heard a girl's voice say "yes", and she wondered if it was hers until he kissed her and she thought it must have been her because that seemed the right thing to be doing.

What a strange dream, she thought.

Nina was standing at the edge of the pool, looking majestically beautiful. She was wearing a long, flowing lime-green kaftan, holding open a large white towel. She called to Amaranth.

'Come.'

Amaranth walked regally up the steps at the shallow end and turned so that her back nestled into the award of Nina's soft towel. She looked down at herself. Her wet body was naked, and somehow she was not surprised by that. The Javanese man clambered out beside her. He was wearing bright red skimpy Speedos. He nodded at Nina and politely took Amaranth by the shoulders, pulling her against him. Her nakednesses touched his bare chest. His leg pressed against hers. Cool. And slippery.

'We go,' he said, and led her inside to a room.

She sat on the bed. It was soft and smelled of jasmine. The man rolled down his bathers and kicked them off. He sat beside her on the bed and handed her some lotion. He turned his back to her and she saw a tattoo on his shoulder of an eagle with chains around its talons. He reached behind and placed her hands on it. She began massaging his shoulders.

He turned and lifted her chin with his forefinger so they were staring into each other's eyes. But she didn't notice that. He gently pushed her backwards and she surrendered to the sheet. He spread her legs and rolled a condom on himself. He tipped lotion onto his palm and slid a finger into her. Then he was lying on top of her, pounding against her groin. Thrusting hard, his face dripped sweat onto hers.

We must be having sex, she thought. *Oh, there's a gecko on the ceiling.*

196

Chapter 24.   Sean

Chris looked out of the plane's little window at the terminal lounge gliding slowly past as they taxied to a halt. The clatter of seatbelts, the crush of eagerness to disembark, the impatient waiting in line, the thump of a welcome stamp in his passport.

He looked for Amaranth among the faces waiting to greet the arrivals, but there were only taxi drivers there. He wondered if she had perhaps gone to the toilet at the last moment, or was she at a different exit? He unzipped his bumbag – the utilitarian but uncool holdall that first-time travellers use to keep their valuables in one place – and swapped his passport for his mobile. He switched it on and waited impatiently for it to crawl back from oblivion. It took a further minute or so to find a network, and yet more frustrating seconds before the voicemail and text messages finally kicked in.

Nothing.

He blew their tradition of avoiding the expensive roaming charges, and rang her.

She didn't answer.

He left a message so she could hear his confusion and disappointment, but five minutes later he reverted to texting to explain he was going to try to find somewhere to stay the night.

He checked his phone again for a text from her. Nothing. He scrolled back to her last message to him; the one that replied to his suggesting they meet in Bali. "Whatever" she'd said. That suddenly sounded quite different from how he'd taken it at first. Half an hour later, he realised she wasn't coming. Maybe a girl with forty-thousand travel dollars had found somewhere else to be.

Damn!

'Tek-si, mister? You want trrrransport? What your hotel?'

He didn't know. It was late. *What are the chances somewhere would still be open? Oh, everywhere. Good. What would the driver recommend? Oh, lucky. Thanks. Sounds perfect.*

He plonked his bag down on the blue-and-white-striped sheet draped over the double bed in his room and looked out of the open window down onto the street below. He was in the heart of Kuta. The paradiddle of motorbike engines and their incessant staccato of horns, coughing two-stroke into the sultry air to mingle with the fragrance of jasmine and fried rice. The fervent throng of tourists, shuffling through the weak DC lighting, desperately examining the colourful street stalls for something quintessential but not common to souvenir. So many faces, and none of them hers.

He checked his phone again. Still nothing. His mind churned the possibilities.

I should've gone to Sydney with her, he thought. *She could've come to Thailand with me, I had that hut completely to myself. She could've...* He stopped himself. *Should've, could've, would've: bullshit! If she'd wanted us to hook up again she'd have been here. Pretty fucking obvious she's cashed up and gone off on her own little adventure. Well, stuff it, I'm going on mine!*

The following morning he went for a walk to find some breakfast. And some direction. He'd only come to Bali for her, and without her, he just wanted to get out of there.

He just followed his feet and ended up meandering to the beach, plonking himself down on the sand under the shade of the trees above the high tide line. Within a minute he was fending off men selling wooden carvings and women offering him a shoulder massage. They were like those irritating flies that ruin a picnic. He stood up, brushed the sand and the sellers off his legs, and sauntered back towards his small hotel. At least there he could sleep this day away and think.

As he passed a group of three small shops at the end of a laneway, his eyes chanced on a curtain of beaded necklaces for sale. Without intending to, he focused on a small, wooden effigy of Buddha attached to a strand of plaited cottons. He needed that good luck charm again.

'How much?' he asked the young local guy with long dreaded hair that was sitting outside the shop.

'You want?'

'Maybe. How much?'

'Oh, very nice Buddha. I make cheap for you. Sunset price.'

'It's still morning,' Chris said.

'You pay what money?' the Rasta guy asked.

'US dollars,' Chris said. The dive centre paid him in US cash.

'Five US dollars, my friend.'

Chris pulled out a five.

The Rasta guy took the note and plunged it into a bumbag slung like a holster on his hip.

'You maybe want...?' he asked, tapping his lips with two fingers.

'Want what?' Chris said.

'Smoke? I have good stuff.'

'Oh. No. Not today, mate. But, hey, thank you for this.' He took the pendant, placed it around his neck, and left.

Further up the street, he passed by a tiny travel agency with a flurry of postcard-sized tour advertisements plastered over its window. Once again, his attention was drawn by his eyes which ceased panning across them, resting decisively on one particular card. It said "Borneo – for the REAL Asian adventure".

Direction!

No more of that sitting around, not having a clue what to do when your chick ups and offs on you. Stuff that, he thought, stroking his new necklace.

#

Amaranth woke up.

Where...? Oh, yeah. The house with that German guy and his sister. Shit! Is it morning? Did I sleep the night here? I was supposed to meet Chris last night. He'll be frantic! What am I wearing?

She looked at her gown. Long. Silk. Tied across her breasts with delicate laces.

I don't remember putting this on.

A thigh-high vent slitting one side of the skirt open.

Is that a bruise? How did I get that?

199

The door handle jiggled.

Was that locked? Was I locked in here? I don't remember even coming in here.

Nina opened the door.

'Ah, you are awake,' she said. She walked over to the window and snapped open the bamboo shutters with a rough jerk. Daylight jabbed Amaranth's eyes. 'You still feeling ill?'

'Ill?' Amaranth asked sleepily.

'You fainted. You were sweating heavily. I changed your clothes to make you more comfortable. I didn't call the doctor. It must be something you picked up on the plane. They're the best place to pick up all sorts of things.' She smirked at her own pointed meaning.

Amaranth was awake but her head was clogged, and Nina's voice was slightly echoey.

'What, like a virus or something? I've never passed out before. Never in my life. Not from a virus, not from shock. Oh, but once when I hadn't eaten, I did get sick from drinks. I remember drinks yesterday.'

'You had a fruit punch, same as me, same as Cochin, and we are fine, so it's not that,' Nina was quick to establish.

'I was supposed to meet Chris at the airport. Where'd I put my bag? I need to call him.'

'So, today, I think you should just take it easy,' Nina said, ignoring the question. 'Relax. Get well. We'll see how you are tonight.'

'Tonight?'

'Yes, we are having some guests over. You'll get to meet a few. So back to sleep with you if you're still tired, or get up and shower and I'll fix you some fruit for lunch.'

'Lunch? What time is it?'

'It's two.'

'Two o'clock? Shit, I slept hours! No, I've had enough sleep. I just need to wake up. Still a bit groggy.'

'Well,' Nina said as she turned to leave, 'take your time. Have a shower and I'll see you on the verandah. You'll be fine.'

'Yeah. Thanks.'

'Plenty of time. You don't have to be ready till seven tonight.'

'Ready? Ready for what?' Amaranth said, as Nina left the room and closed the door.

Amaranth felt better after she had showered. She looked around the bedroom for her bag with her phone and her clothes, but it wasn't there so she slipped on the gown Nina had given her.

She tried to remember when she had just blanked out the previous day, but she couldn't get hold of the event.

It's really strange. Could have been that drink, you know. Yeah, I remember Nina saying it had rum in it. Too much rum. I told them it was too strong. I knew it. They didn't get sick; they must be used to it. This is horrible. I wonder what Chris did last night? I've got to call him and explain all this. He'll be so worried about me.

She opened the bedroom door and wandered barefoot to the living room. Cochin was there at the bar. She thought he mustn't have moved since yesterday. There he was, still mixing a drink.

'Hair of ze dog,' he said, and handed her a tall glass.

It smelled of mango, banana, and coconut.

'Oh no,' she said, turning her head from the glass. 'I couldn't do another of those.'

'This will fix you. Fixes everything. Nice. Come, try.'

'No, seriously, Cochin. Even the smell makes me want to puke.'

'Well, I can't have you being sick again,' Cochin said, withdrawing the glass.

'Make her a spritzer,' Nina said. She was curled up in a chair that hung from one of the massive wooden beams that held up the roof. 'Spritzer is fizzy. Good for an upset tummy.'

'Yeah, okay,' Amaranth said. 'But no rum.'

'Just a dash of vine to kill ze bugs zen,' Cochin prescribed. 'So you're okay for tonight.'

Cochin put the fruit concoction into the bar fridge and set about making the spritzer.

'Tonight?' Amaranth began planning. 'I expect I'll hook up with my boyfriend. I'm not sure where we'll be tonight.'

'Well that's up to you,' Nina said quite coldly. 'We told you we have a spare room. It's yours if you want it.'

'That really is incredibly generous of you, Nina. Thank you. Where did you put my shoulder bag?' Amaranth said. 'I need to call him. My phone's in there.'

Her hosts both shook their heads.

'A brown bag with tassels? I left it on top of my pack. Where did you put my pack?'

Nina pointed to the front door. 'Where you left it. Behind the door there.'

Amaranth went over to the door. Her backpack was open, but there was no shoulder bag on top.

'Did someone open my pack? I never opened it. And my shoulder bag isn't there.'

They ignored her.

'I really have to find my shoulder bag. It's got my passport and my phone in it. I left my boyfriend waiting at the airport last night. He'll be very worried about me. He'll be turning Bali upside down, looking for me.'

Cochin came over with the spritzer.

'It's okay, Amma. I help you find your purse. First, drink zis. It vill calm you down and clear your mind so you can remember ze place you put it.'

'I put it right there,' she shouted. 'I know where I bloody put it!'

'But if it's not zair, Amma, and vee didn't touch it, you must have put it anuzzer place, yes? And zis vill help you remember. Drink.'

She took the glass.

#

Chris woke up in Kuching city at six a.m. to that same droning wail he'd heard the previous afternoon. Borneo is a Muslim country, and the mosques don't use church bells to call the faithful; the muezzin climbs up to the top of the minaret and sings the summons to pray, using a microphone and loudspeaker. He does it five times a day. Every day. And Chris's hotel window looked straight at the minaret across the street.

He ate a breakfast of fruit salad followed by banana pancakes and coffee. The city was bigger than he'd imagined. It straddled a broad river.

Where is there that's nice to go around here? he wondered. Some pamphlets on the hotel counter recommended Damai Beach, about a forty-minute bus ride away.

The small tourist bus, an old Nissan Starwagon with extra seats, rattled into Damai and unloaded the passengers in front of the resort there. Chris didn't go in. He turned and headed straight for the sand.

He looked at the South China Sea. The tide was still a fair way out. The beach was broad, the water flat.

Not nearly as pretty as the beaches in Thailand, he thought.

He walked away from the area directly in front of the resort. Too many people there. He didn't want to be around people. He wanted to swim, which would mean leaving his bumbag with his shirt and sandals on the sand, and he worried someone might steal it if they were close enough.

At the far end there was a small cliff with a flat, rocky foreshore at its foot. The high tide would cover these rocks later in the day and it looked like it was coming back in, so he decided to explore there first. He would be able to see round the point; perhaps there was a better, more private beach to get to.

His sandals were slipping on the wet rocks so he took them off and carried them, hopping dexterously from spot to spot. In the cracks and crevices, he could see that the ocean was still there, about a metre below. The tide didn't go right out, it merely shrank to expose the tops of these rocks.

Twenty minutes of stumbling and jumping, he eventually reached a point where he could see fully into the next bay – but it was just more rocks, and totally useless for swimming, so he turned and headed back.

The tide was indeed coming in. It was already splashing halfway back over the rocks, but he could see he still had enough time to get to the sand. As he jumped a crevice, he slipped and dropped a sandal. It fell between the rocks. He looked down at it. It was in the shallow water there, but when he reached down, he was still half a metre short.

Damn! Can't walk around barefoot in Kuching. No telling what I might stand in. He looked around, hoping to see a washed-up stick or something he could use to hook it. Nothing. He lay on the rock and reached down again, stretching his arm as much as he could. He was only a few centimetres short. He wriggled his torso further into the small hole. His fingertips brushed the sole of the upturned sandal. A little more wriggling in and he could flip it over and grab the strap. In he went, his lower body and legs flailing on the surface of the rocks.

He got it! His fingers triumphantly curled around their prize and he tried to pull his head back out of the miniature chasm. But he was too far in. The bulk of his body was in the hole, from his thighs to his extended hands which were over his upside-down head. There wasn't enough space for him to slither further in and turn around to climb out. He was alone – trapped in a handstand, his feet in the air, his head in the hole, and the tide promising to return behind him.

He panicked, he pushed, he shouted, he grunted, he heaved. His thighs were gashed by the rocky ledge. His hands and arms were scraped from the walls, but his eyes were on the water level in the bottom of the crevice. It was wrist deep when he had grabbed his sandal, it was past his elbows now. He had tried clawing up the walls, he tried using his arms to spring up, but to do that he had to bend them, and that brought him even further in the hole with more body weight to push back up. The top of his scalp was touching the water. Within ten minutes it would have risen past his eyes and be up to his chin. And he'd have drowned.

I'm fucked! I'm totally fucking fucked!

He went into a mad frenzy of panic and anger. Flexing and straightening his arms rapidly in his prison, his legs thrashing wildly in the outside free air.

What a complete fucking idiot I am! This: for a fucking sandal. I could buy a new pair for two fucking dollars.

'Help!' he screamed into the stone silence. 'Help, help, help, help! Ahhh!' He could hear his scream being smothered as soon as it left his throat. The crevice walls were effective soundproofing, and the incoming waves were splashing against the rocks, creating a masking distraction.

Why did I have to get away from where the other tourists were?

He kept on trying. He dug his nails into the cracks, only to feel the skin on his fingertips being grated away. The muscles in his arms ached. His legs were bruised and scraped. The water level was up to his ears now on his up-turned head, and ripples muted all sound. Salt water stung his vision; he closed his eyes. Thinking was seized by panic. The waterline licked over his nose and salted his lips. All his senses were gone now. He passed through the nightmare and entered the dream. He surrendered.

Something clamped onto his leg. A croc? A snake, dog, crab, what?

'Push up!' a muffled voice shouted to him through the gurgles.

He pushed. Arms circled his thighs and pulled him upwards. He walked his hands up the wall. His waist came out. His chest. And then, in the glaring sunlight of rescue, he was free of the dungeon.

He sprawled across the rocks and shaded his eyes with his rasped hand, which was still clutching the lost sandal. He looked up at the person who had saved him. A guy in his mid-thirties. Broad but not at all overweight. A cheery face beaming through a red stubbly beard. A leather cowboy hat. A tourist from the resort.

'Oh man, I was totally fucked there,' Chris said breathlessly, laughing a mixture of relief and embarrassment. 'Seriously, you saved my fucking life.'

His saviour grinned and said, with a distinct Irish brogue, 'And moight Oi arsk what you were doing exactly wit your head down dat hole?'

'I was getting this,' Chris said, holding his sandal up like it was the severed head of a gladiatorial rival.

'Oi tort you was fishin for crabs or sumtin,' the Irishman said. 'You looked a sorry soight, I can tell you dat. Moi name is Sean.'

'Chris.' They shook hands. 'Mate, Sean, seriously, thank you. Thank you so much. I would be dead if you hadn't come along. Can I at least buy you a beer?'

'A beer? And why not? A beer is always good. We best get cracking, the sea's going to be all over these rocks very soon now.'

As they sat at the resort, Sean told tales of up the Rejang River where head-hunters had roamed only a generation ago.

'You can only travel so far up da river,' the Irishman said. 'It's still pretty woild. But it's fuckin awesome. Tourism hasn't ruined the place. Yet. Not many spots left in the world dat a man can travel to and it's loike it was centuries ago. Although, come to tink of it,' he added raising his glass, 'dere's quite a few in Ireland.'

Chapter 25.   Dana

'Amma. Zis is Eric. I vant you to be extra nice viss Eric. Okay?'

'Okay,' Amaranth heard a sleepy voice like hers say.

Eric was very tall. Maybe the tallest man she had ever seen.

He should be wearing red-and-white-striped pants and be in the circus. She laughed.

'What's so funny?' Eric asked with an American accent.

'You're very tall,' she said.

'Only when I'm standing, little darlin',' he chortled, looking for and getting Cochin's camaraderic smirk. 'Come on, you can measure me lying down.'

Eric led her to the bedroom. He opened the door and pushed her inside.

'Lie on the bed,' he snapped. 'Face down.'

She found instructions were easy to follow.

'Young lady, you need to learn it's impolite to laugh at someone if they happen to be a little taller than you,' he said as he slid the leather belt from his trousers.

Dreams became wakings.

'Come on, get up,' Nina barked.

Amaranth stirred. She sat up slowly and rubbed her face.

'Come on. Out!' Nina pulled the bedcover off and flung it to the floor.

Amaranth was naked. She tried to remember if that was all right.

'Up!' shouted Nina. 'We don't have all day. I want you washed and tidy by three.' She looked at the watch on her wrist. 'It's quarter past one. Come on!'

'Quarter past one in the day?' Amaranth asked.

'Of course, the day. Look outside, brainiac. Does that look like night?'

'Only I just… I don't remember it being night yet.'

'Yes, well, don't worry about that. Worry that you won't get your bare arse into gear by three.'

My arse? There's something different there. Like sitting on a hot water bottle and it's finally stinging me. She ran her hand over it. It felt different. Like it needed ironing. Like it had creases. Creases: like welts from a leather belt.

Nina saw her registering the marks.

'By Christ, Amma, if you don't get a move on, I swear to God, I'll give you worse than those playful slaps. I mean it, girl. Three o'clock. You have an hour and a half.'

The shower cubicle was exactly how Amaranth felt. Clean, but fogged up. She stood under the pulsing water that was washing her, waking her.

She dried and found the robe Nina had left on the bed for her. She towelled her hair again, and then she looked in the mirror.

Jesus! Is that me? I look terrible. Look at my puffy eyes, and my skin!

She threw the towel over the ensuite door, finger-combed her hair, and left the room.

A girl with bright orange hair was walking towards her up the corridor, coming from the living room. She was mid-twenties, pasty white, and extremely thin. She was wearing a yellow bikini top and white shorts. She kept her eyes on the floor in front of her, completely ignoring Amaranth.

Nina was on the verandah. She was seated at the large wooden table there, eating a bowl of fruit salad as Amaranth joined her.

'If you want coffee, it's over there,' Nina said, pointing to a servery.

'Yeah. Coffee would be good,' Amaranth said, turning and traipsing towards the table. She lifted the percolator and poured herself a cup. 'Do you need a top-up?'

Nina shook her head. 'Just take some fruit salad. You need to eat. You haven't eaten much for two days now and you chucked up.'

Amaranth took a small bowl and spooned some fruit salad into it. There was a plate with toast on it and she grabbed a couple of slices, decorating the plate with three little single-serve packets of jam.

She sat opposite Nina and looked at the pool glistening behind the lush garden.

'It's nice here,' she said, sipping the coffee.

'Don't get too comfortable, Amma. It's getting late. You know the drill.'

The drill? Yes, something. It'll come to me.

'The girl with red hair,' she asked Nina. 'Does she live here too?'

'Oh, you've met Dana.'

'No. Not really. I saw her just now. In the hall. We didn't speak.'

'You won't get much conversation from her. She doesn't talk much, that one. And, like you, she doesn't eat. Come on, have your breakfast. You don't want to end up looking like that scrawny bitch.'

Amaranth ate some toast. She looked past Nina and could see into the kitchen. There were three local girls in there, fussing with food preparations.

Of course. They have staff to cook and clean.

Now she looked more thoroughly, she also saw the local man raking the path around the pool and picking fallen leaves from between the bushes.

Cochin came onto the verandah and tapped the back of his wrist.

'Nina,' he said.

'She's just eating something. She'll be ready,' Nina said, checking her own watch.

Amaranth ate her toast. She managed several pieces of the fruit salad too.

Nina took the bowl away.

'Good girl. Now go and brush your teeth before Cochin gives you your medicine.'

'What medicine?'

'To stop you feeling sick. Remember? You don't want to be sick again, do you? Go on. Off you go. There should be a new toothbrush in there. And a hairbrush, so you can do your hair while you're at it.'

Amaranth stood at the bathroom sink. There was a toothbrush still in its plastic wrapper in a glass there. She opened it, squeezed a bead of toothpaste onto it, and brushed her teeth.

I used to have my own toothbrush. What happened to my bag? Oh, yeah, where did I put that? I need my phone. Chris! I have to call Chris. Fuck, my hair does look like shit.

She spat into the sink, rinsed her mouth and wiped it on the hand towel. She found a hairbrush and forced a track through the jungle on her head.

Cochin knocked on the bedroom door and, without waiting for her reply, he opened it and came in. He handed her a glass.

'What is it?' she asked.

'Your medicine.'

'I need to find my bag,' she said, taking the drink from him.

He said nothing. He just stood there until she drained the glass, and then he left.

She went back to brushing her hair. Presently that feeling returned. That feeling like everything was packed in safety. That nothing could hurt her. Nothing could go wrong. That it was obvious what she should do. They would tell her. She liked this feeling. She wanted to remember it. She forgot everything else.

They sat her on a couch in the living room. Dana was seated on the opposite side of the large room, also on a couch. Both girls were wearing silk kaftans, but Dana was hunched so lifelessly that she looked like she was a yet-to-be dressed store mannequin with a dust cover wrapped around it for modesty.

There was talking at the door. Cochin came in with two Japanese men. They were older. Late fifties. They were wearing perfectly pressed clothes. And gold: watches, rings, necklaces. They smelled of bergamot and tobacco. They studied the two girls. There was talking. Cochin was pointing at Dana. The Japanese men were both shaking their heads. Cochin shrugged his shoulders. He gestured, lowering with his hands. One of the men gestured lower. Cochin agreed. The other man was grinning at Amaranth.

210

'Amma. Zis is Hiro. Hiro does not speak much English. You must be patient. Listen to vot he says and give him your best. You understand?'

'Yes. My best.'

My best what? Oh, he'll tell me. It's all right. Nothing to worry about.

The Japanese man gave a small nod and an even smaller smile. Then he held his hand forward in a gesture to guide her to her room, and she led him there.

Yes, the room. I go to my room. Must remember this.

He closed the door behind them and immediately grabbed her by her shoulders and kissed her face. He avoided the lips, but quickly kissed down her neck and onto her chest. He fumbled with the lace straps. She helped him by slipping them off each shoulder. She was naked. A statue. A doll. A toy.

He gave an excited giggle that made him seem more like a schoolboy than a businessman.

'Titties!' he said, rubbing her breasts.

Her instinct was to push his irritating hands off her, to preserve dominion of her intimate areas, but there was an over-riding compulsion to relax and allow whatever was happening. And she obeyed that.

He stepped back from her and undid his trousers. He slid them down to his ankles without removing his shoes. Then lifted his underwear over his arousal. He pointed at the bed and she drifted to it. She sat and watched as he hopped towards her.

Kangaroo, she thought. He tried to push himself into her but he failed. He said something in Japanese. She stared blankly at him. He mimed shaking a bottle into his empty hand and pointed at her. She reached over to the bedside table and took the massage lotion that was there.

How did I know it was there? She handed it to him, but he refused. He pointed to her and then to between her legs. She stroked the lotion onto herself and returned the bottle to the table. Then he flung himself onto her and into her. And then he was finished. He withdrew and he peeled off the condom.

I didn't see him putting a condom on. He pulled her up so she was sitting once more. He stood by the bed and lifted his limpness to her face. She just looked blankly at it. She could smell the slight fragrance of salty rubber.

What is he doing? This feels silly. He held his soft, small manhood between his finger and thumb and shook it a few centimetres from her eyes, as if it was waving goodbye to her.

'Genki desu,' he said. 'Good. End now. Arigato.'

She pulled the kaftan back over her head and followed Hiro out to the living room. Cochin was waiting in his familiar place at the bar. Ignoring Amaranth, he offered Hiro a drink. Whisky. Ice.

Amaranth sat on the couch like she was waiting at a bus stop. Hiro looked at her, then turned to Cochin and raised his glass.

'Good, she. Good,' he said.

His friend came out from Dana's room. Alone. He shook his head. He was not quite angry, but clearly displeased. Cochin spoke quietly to him but he wanted none of it. He raised his arms to refuse a drink. Hiro spoke rapidly to him. Both of the Japanese men looked at Amaranth, then at Cochin who nodded. The second Japanese guy walked over to her, pulled her up as though they were going to dance together, and led her back to Dana's room.

'What the fuck...?' Dana shouted as they came in. 'Not in here! She has her own room!'

She has an accent.

The Japanese guy pushed Amaranth towards Dana and wiggled a finger between them, indicating they should embrace.

'No way. I don't do it with girls,' Dana asserted. 'I don't do it with any fucking body!'

Was it German?

Nina rushed in. She had a glass of water and some pills.

'Dana. Dana. Calm down. You need your medicine.'

Amaranth looked at the glass.

Medicine? I take medicine. It stops me from feeling sick again.

'No more of your fucking drugs,' Dana shouted. 'That shit you mix just fucks me up. Give me the real stuff or give me nothing.'

The Japanese man was getting very upset. He didn't like the shouting. He didn't like Nina coming in. And he certainly didn't like Dana.

Nina gripped Amaranth's arm with one hand and ushered the Japanese client out with her.

'Okay,' she said to him as calmly as she could. 'You take this girl. No extra. No money. Free. You take.'

And with that, she pushed them into Amaranth's room and closed the door.

Outside they could hear Nina shushing Dana. Agreeing with her. Telling her everything would be all right. That it was all a big misunderstanding.

The Japanese guy looked at Amaranth. He just stood there and looked at her.

What's he waiting for me to do?

He calmed his anger and then he aroused his desire. He pointed to the shower.

'You wash,' he ordered.

She washed. He watched.

She dried. He undressed.

She lay on the bed. He put a condom on. It was the same as the man before.

Oh yes! I remember. I wanted to remember stuff. Now why was that, again?

She woke to shouting. It was a girl's voice. A girl with an accent like Cochin's, but different.

It's the red-headed girl.

Amaranth slid out of bed and put on the kaftan. She turned the handle of her bedroom door but the door didn't open. She tried it the other way. Nothing. It was locked. She rattled it, partly in protest, partly to alert someone that she wanted to come out.

She heard Nina say, 'Christ, now the other one's awake.'

Dana shouted, 'You can't make me! I didn't take your precious fucking medicine. Yeah. Different now.'

Amaranth heard footsteps pattering up the hall.

213

Nina shouted through Amaranth's door for her to go back to bed. That there was nothing going on.

Amaranth climbed back into bed and sat with her knees up. She swept the cover around her and rocked herself into comfort. She heard Cochin's voice, at first attempting to instil calmness, but rising with frustration at his failure to do so. Then there was another voice. A man's voice. A voice she had never heard before and yet it was somehow familiar.

'Geez, settle the fuck down, will ya?' the voice shouted. 'There's no need to get revved.'

It was familiar because it was Australian, and it was followed by a slap, a scream, a scuffle, another shout, a door slamming, muffled screams and furniture being budged around. It sounded like furniture.

And then there was the most frightening scream she had ever heard. It shattered through her door and slammed into her fear. Her mouth froze as open as her eyes. Her neck stiffened. Then she heard coughing. And groaning. And pleading. A voice she didn't recognise, just whining. *Was that Dana's voice? What's going on? Is this right?*

Sometime later, she couldn't be sure how long, she heard keys unlocking her door. Nina came in and closed the door behind her.

'Did you hear all that, before?' she asked Amaranth.

'Who was shouting?'

'It was that fucking orang-utan. It's all okay now.'

'Orang-utan?' Amaranth knew she meant the red-head, but she also knew Nina was being insultive, and she wondered why.

'That orange-haired skank, Dana,' Nina said dismissively. 'Don't worry about it.'

Orange. Yes, not really red is it? Must remember that.

'She's all right?'

'Yes, yes. She just gets hysterical when she forgets to take her medicine. She's okay now. She's left.'

'Where has she gone?' Amaranth asked.

You can leave?

'I don't fucking know, Amma. Back to Holland, China, Timbuktu, what's it matter where? She's gone, and we are well rid of her. She was nothing but trouble, that one.'

'Trouble?' Amaranth asked.

'Wouldn't do what she was asked to. Wouldn't take her medicine. Wasn't nice to our visitors.'

As Nina spoke, she was preparing something in her hands. She raised the thing up to the light and tapped it. It was a syringe.

'What's that?' Amaranth asked.

'Same as you've been having, but better this way. Give me your arm.'

Something, Amaranth didn't know what, something wasn't right about that. She needed to think.

'Your arm. I'm not going to have the same crap from you, am I?' Nina barked.

'No,' Amaranth said, straightening her arm and offering it up. 'I don't want to be any trouble and I don't want to feel sick, do I?'

Amaranth watched her arm as Nina pushed a thin belt up over the elbow, tightening it so that her veins throbbed larger. She didn't feel the needle going in, but she felt a dull sensation as Nina pulled the plunger out slightly, filling the chamber with a tiny swirling red cloud.

Blood! My blood! I thought she was giving me something, not taking... Nina pushed the plunger back in, emptied the chamber, withdrew the needle, released the belt.

Oh yes. I know this feeling. N-i-c-e. There's nothing to worry about. There's nothing and I'm just here, in the centre of it. The world is moulded around me. I can't fall.

There was a man. There was sex. There was something else. There was something she wanted to remember.

What was that?

Again: daylight. Bright. Clear. She slid off the bed and looked out through the window. She could see some garden, but the pool was way over on the other side of the house. Her view was just trees, but then a bright orange kite floated above the tree tops.

Who is flying that?

She glared through the foliage and could just make out some roof tops. Other houses!

Of course. There are people out there. Someone's flying a kite. So orange. Orange? The Dutch girl! That's what I was trying to remember. What happened to her? Did she go? They said that she'd left. That's right, so, I could go.

She went over to her door but, as usual, it was locked. She went back to her window and looked down. It was almost three metres to the ground, but to the right there was the end of the verandah that wrapped around from the front of the house, and right below that there was a rainwater tank. If she could get onto there she could easily slide down to the garden.

Amaranth had a limited history of escaping. Mostly, she had avoided rather than escaped. There had been so many situations in her life that she had had the impulse to walk away from, and she had Gary to thank for forcing her to learn to act on that impulse. This time was different, however: this time her impulse was to run.

She quietly climbed out of her window and lowered herself till she was just holding on to the window ledge. She swung her torso like a pendulum, and her left leg hit the verandah post. She swung back and then repeated it, hooking her foot in-between two rails.

Now what? She was spread-eagled from window to rail. She pushed all her body weight onto the hooked-in leg and, like a spider, she padded her hands across the wall, her nails in one of the grooves of clinker-boards. And then she was on the verandah.

As quietly as she could, she stepped down onto the tin covering the water tank, and then lowered herself down into the garden. She pushed aside some huge plant leaves, and made her way from the house. She came to a wire fence. She followed it away from the driveway, and presently came to a section that was curling up with just enough room for her to wriggle under.

She was out!

She was in some neighbour's little garden, and she stepped carefully over the vegetables growing there. Some chickens squawked and that awoke a dog who joined in the complaint which, in turn, alerted some men who were playing cards in their kitchen. They came out and saw her. They chattered to each other rapidly and with a degree of agitation.

One of them, the oldest there, came to her.

216

'You from big house, yes?' he said authoritatively.

'Yes.'

'You not be here. Not good. Must go back, yes?'

'Okay,' she heard herself say. 'I'll go back.'

Why did I say that? Wasn't I going away?

'I walk you back now, okay?'

'Yes.'

She followed him out of his house and up the lane to Cochin's gates. The man rattled them and shouted, and eventually the gardener came and, after some talking, took Amaranth inside.

Cochin came down the front steps.

'Amma? How did you get here? Where were you?'

'Neighbour brought,' said the gardener. 'Say she in his garden and he bring you.'

'Is the neighbour still there?' Cochin asked. 'Give him this,' he took some notes from his wallet, 'and tell him "thank you".'

He turned and walked back up the stairs without checking she was obediently following. She was.

'She got out of the vindow,' Cochin explained to Nina as they went inside. 'A regular acrobat.'

'Get them to put a lock on the window,' Nina said. She looked at Amaranth. 'What the fuck do you think you were doing? I thought you weren't going to give us any shit. I've been very nice to you, Amma, and this is the crap you pull. Go back to your room, I can't bear looking at you.'

As Amaranth walked off down the hallway she heard Nina say, 'That scrawny bitch started this. We can't ever take a junkie again, Cochin. They're more trouble than they're worth.'

Cochin said, 'And zay aren't worth very much anyway.'

Amaranth slowed her steps so she could linger to hear a little more.

'Oh, we still could have got three for her even so,' Nina said, matter-of-factly. 'Douglas always seems to find someone desperate enough to bid for a skank like her.'

Amaranth looked at Dana's door. It was slightly open. She pushed it wider and peeped in. The room showed signs of last night's struggle; there was still broken glass on the floor and an upturned chair, but Amaranth's gaze fell on the bed and froze there.

The bare mattress had an enormous stain on it. Still damp. A stain that glistened with dark maroon. The sheet was bunched and discarded on the floor. Like it had been used to mop something up. It was once white but now was also stained, and the colour was more obvious on it than on the patterned blue mattress. The colour was an old red.

Blood.

Amaranth stared and remembered images of yestertime. Dana shouting. Screaming.

Oh, that scream! And Nina, and footsteps, and noises. An Australian man saying, 'Settle the fuck down. No need to get revved.' And she remembered the silence.

Amaranth felt fear.

'Vot are you looking at?' Cochin said behind her.

Amaranth raised one finger to point at the mattress.

'Get her away from there, Cochin,' Nina shouted from the living room.

Amaranth fixed her eyes on the bloodstain.

'Where's Dana? Where's Dana? Where's Dana?' she shouted.

'Get her away!' Nina rushed up the corridor. 'Amma, go back to your own room.'

'Where's Dana?'

'We told you. She left.'

'What's the blood?'

'Vee didn't hurt her. Of course vee didn't,' Cochin asserted.

'The blood! What's the blood?'

Nina grabbed her and she jumped.

'Hey, hey calm down. You're panicking. That trash just... that trash just had her period, that's all. Leaked all over the mattress. Ruined it. That's why we told her to go. She was dirty, that one. I never liked her. I'm glad she's gone. Gone for good. There? See? All explained. Nothing to get excited about is there? So, just go back to your room. I'll bring you something to help you sleep – something to settle you. You'll be okay, Amma. We aren't going to hurt you.'

Chapter 26.   Dinh

Chris got up and looked outside his Kuching hotel window at a lemon sunrise. He could smell the wafts from a small fire burning cinders on a street vendor's cart parked at the edge of the courtyard. Behind that simple kitchen, a furore of impetuous traffic was dashing people to the left from the right, to the right from the left. Chris's attention ignored the motors and there, in the tree, he heard a small bird singing. Not the mournful drone from the mosque, but a sweet, pretty melody that promised a good day. *A good day to go!*

A brief viewing of tourist brochures showed him that to journey right up the Rejang River he must first make his way to Sibu, a town about five hours by boat from Kuching. After that, it would be a couple more days of long river riding before he would be in the wilds to find the adventure that Sean, his Irish saviour, had suggested.

The boat ramp was a bouncing wooden plank, slippery with the run-off from the constant rain that was drenching the start of this adventure. Chris was sandwiched in a conga-line of passengers as they shuffled to board. Every fifteen seconds, the captain revved the motor to steer the boat back to the wharf because the soggy rope that tethered it's prow was too long. The propeller churned the muddy brown water and the air blackened with diesel fumes.

Grateful to be finally onboard, Chris put his feet on his backpack and hunched his knees into forming a table to rest the paperback he'd bought from the hotel book exchange that morning. He glanced once more at the grey drape of rain smearing the windows, opened his book and began reading.

He had finished it when they arrived in Sibu just after one that afternoon.

The rain had eased, but there was still a depressing garland of mist lurking in the forest at the muddy river's edge. He decided to take the very next boat heading upriver that afternoon. Hanging around would have felt like having to roll a six in order to start a game of Snakes and Ladders, and he was keen to begin.

Three hours later, the public jet boat pulled into Kapit, the first town upriver, and he shuffled with the line of passengers getting off there. He walked up the ramp to search for a restaurant and somewhere to sleep that night.

As he turned left into the street, a dark-skinned local man, with wide-open eyes rolling in a pantomimical crazy, ran up to him and thrust his face a centimetre from Chris's surprise.

'Ha ha, white man! My grandfather ate your grandfather.' That said, he grinned playfully, and jaunted off down the street.

Chris recalled that he was in territory which, within living memory, was once peopled by cannibals. He looked around him. This was neither Kuta nor Koh Samui. He was on the threshold where tourists cease and travellers begin. He counted the Europeans he could see. A young couple with a map across the street. A woman talking to a shopkeeper further along. Three teenage girls with small, bright red Canadian Flags sewn to their packs, busy heading somewhere. And him. All the other people were locals.

He wandered into what he assumed was a shop, but was more like a museum. On display, there were old photographs, carvings, weapons, and genuine shrunken human heads! Real heads, but a quarter-size and with shrivelled skin and strands of bedraggled hair unexpectedly decorated with dull beads.

The girls with the Canadian flags came in and giggled and gasped at the displays.

'G'day,' Chris said, offering his nationality.

'Hey,' one of them replied. 'Are you staying at the Rejang Inn?'

'Haven't decided yet,' Chris said. 'Is that a good place?'

'The guidebook says it's the closest to the wharf and we don't want to hump these packs too far,' she said. 'I thought you might know where it is.'

'Doesn't your guidebook say?' Chris asked.

'It's got a map of the streets and everything, but we can't work it out.'

Chris looked at the guidebook she was opening for him. He ran his finger along from where there was a picture of the boat ramp, up the street and along to where they were.

'So, it's… just around the corner there,' he said. 'Come on, let's find it.'

He led the three girls out and up the street like he was a regular tour guide.

'Where in Canada are you guys from?' he asked, more to fill in the short journey than from any real interest.

'We're from L.A. in the United States,' the talkative one said. 'We put the flags on because there's a lot of anti-American stuff in the world.'

I should have known, Chris thought. *They were way too loud to be real Canadians.*

He scored a small room with a single bed, and a table with a fan on it. The lighting was dim and the room was lined with laquered two-ply, which further dulled the experience. Down a squeaky lino corridor there was a cold water shower, which tended to rouse him rather than rest him just before he turned in for the night. He lay there, imagining tomorrow but the effort of dragging his thoughts from wondering what Amaranth was doing right now eventually tired his mind, and he fell asleep; the droning fan, twisting back and forwards in time with his breathing.

In the morning, over breakfast in the hotel dining area, he saw the Americans again.

'So, what are you girls up to today?' he asked, simply to make conversation while waiting for his breakfast order to arrive.

They told him their guidebook said this was as far as it was worth going, so they were heading back down river. They were pretty unimpressed with Borneo.

Depends what you were looking for, he thought, but chose to leave their observation unchallenged.

'Are you heading back on the eleven o'clock boat?' one of them asked him.

'No, too soon to turn back for me,' he said. 'I think I'll have a look upriver from here.'

The girls looked at each other. 'Why?' one asked him. They clearly weren't at all inspired by his plan. Rather than thinking he was bold to be heading further on, they wondered how desperate he must be if he wasn't going to give this the flick. They soon fell into excited expectations about one of the hot spots featured in their guidebook and hardly spoke to him again over breakfast. Chris didn't mind; he had further to go. And as soon as he'd finished eating, he went.

After another six hours on the river, and in a considerably smaller boat, he arrived in remote Belaga. Here, he was at the end of the run. No public boats went further upriver past this place.

He looked around for somewhere to stay the night and discovered there was a small guesthouse close to the shambling wooden wharf. Perhaps there were more further back or signed for locals only, but the one he found was just fine anyway. It was a sweet little building comprising a reception area and four rooms. The guy running it spoke English in short, practised sentences, all relative to renting his rooms, but he did have a local map pinned to the wall beside his desk. Chris studied it.

It doesn't make sense to have to go back the way I just came, he thought. He traced his finger across the page to Bintulu on the northern coast. *It's not that far. And that looks like a road there, just a way up from here.*

Using broken words and rudimentary signs, he asked the man at the reception desk about using that route.

The hotel manager shook his head and said, 'No can.'

'But is that a road?' Chris pushed.

'No for tourist.'

'Why?'

'Too much dangerous.'

Fuck it. That sounds like a road I want to go on.

'You ask police,' the manager said. He pointed to the police station three buildings along. 'Must get paper.'

The next morning, the police made Chris sign a form that relinquished them from all responsibility for his safety. Further upriver was Penan territory. They were still a mysterious people. They were the last tribe to be tamed. They had very little to do with the other locals there. Trade with them was merely leaving items in a jungle clearing, and the following day collecting what they exchanged them for. It was always a fair trade for anything they considered of value or use – other items were still there the following morning. The Penan took nothing that they didn't want, and paid for what they took with generous supplies of forest foods.

Clutching his police permit document, Chris went to the wooden wharf. However, there were no public boats going further upriver, and none of the locals working around the wharf spoke any English. He waved to get their attention and pointed upriver, pointed to their canoes, and then pointed to himself. They simply turned back to their chores and ignored him.

He sat on an empty oil drum and watched his chance of a ride fade into the afternoon. Just then a young lad, maybe sixteen, steered his canoe to the wharf and shut off his outboard motor. He opened a canvas bag he had slung around his shoulder, counted out some money to pay the man in a blue singlet, and proceeded to hand pump fuel into two tanks on his boat from one of the large drums standing along the wharf. The front of his canoe had a name painted on it. *Proud Mary*. In English!

Chris knew that song. 'Big wheels keep on turnin'…' he sang as loud as he could. 'Proud Mary keeps on burnin'. Rollin', rollin'…'

The lad looked up at him and beamed a smile as he broke into singing along. 'Rollin' on da ribba!' He beckoned Chris down to his boat. 'Hello, my friend, you know my boat's song!'

'Sure do. Where you going?'

The lad pointed upriver.

'How far?'

'Long way. My home.'

'I want to get to the road to Bintulu. Can you get me close?'

'Bintulu? No, sorry, my home not close. No road.'

Chris was crestfallen.

223

'But I can take you to road that go over mountain. Other river. Boat there take you to Bintulu.'

'Really? Man, that'd be great.'

'Get in, I go soon. What you name?'

'Chris. You?'

'Oh, Kris, like knife,' he made a wavey gesture with his finger to draw the blade. 'I am Dinh. Okay, Kris please sit, now we go.'

The Rejang River was broad, even this far up, and fast flowing against them. Because it had been raining recently the river was muddy and swollen. Dinh steered first up beside the left bank, then zipped across to the right to avoid the rapids he knew so well. For over an hour the motor whined like an angry bee and the little wooden canoe bounced perilously against the current. On each side, an almost endless wall of jungle zipped past them, broken only by an occasional clearing revealing a longhouse with some women washing clothes at the river's edge.

How'd they come out clean from such muddy water?

A large bird. Some wild pigs. More jungle. And then there was a little bay with a broad flat riverbank of trampled mud.

Dinh turned the canoe towards it and the boat skimmed to the mooring made from sticks. Chris leapt ashore from the front to hold it on the bank as Dinh hopped out to tie the prow to a tree stump. Some children ran down to the canoe and stared at Chris, asking many excited questions in a language he couldn't understand at all.

Their home was appropriately named a longhouse. It stood on three-metre-high stilts, and was much longer than it was wide. longhouses are divided in half lengthways, with a row of rooms on one side, each housing different families, and the other side becomes a covered communal verandah: like a small village street. Children were the responsibility of the whole house, not necessarily the parents. Food supplies were shared by everyone, but meals were cooked separately in their rooms.

Dinh led Chris to his door. He kicked off his thongs, and Chris copied by taking off his boots and socks. Inside, the room was a wooden kitchen bench in front of a plaited bamboo screen. On the bench were two pots and some semi-prepared food. The floor was bare wooden boards except for a small mat of woven straw. And that was it, apart from a blue guitar propped in the corner.

Dinh got the guitar and held it out to Chris.

'No, no, I can't really play,' Chris said, though he remembered learning 'Time Of Your Life', 'Blister In The Sun', and some twelve-bar blues tune.

'Guitar not right,' Dinh said, pointing to the strings and then his ear.

'Oh,' Chris said, taking the guitar in his hands and sitting on the floor with it. 'Tune it?' That he could do with a tuner, but it was much harder by ear alone, though he had learned how to do that. He put a finger at the fifth fret on the biggest string and plucked it. He then struck the second biggest string and turned its key, listening as it whined into agreement, before moving further across the fretboard.

Dinh heard him settle the final string into place.

'Very good, Kris. You moo-sishun! Play Proud Mary!'

And Chris tried to. A crowd of relatives soon assembled at the door, listening to the concert and grinning great approval.

A young woman brought some baskets to show him. Chris looked at their intricate beadwork.

'Lovely. Very nice,' he smiled returning them to her.

She pushed one back to him.

Shit, do I have to buy one from her? And how much, anyway?

He took the basket and rubbed his fingers against his thumb to ask the price. She shook her head. It was a gift.

He thanked her, and opened his bag to put it in there. To make room for it, he had to take out a pair of jeans. There was a slight, but noticeable stirring from the onlookers. Chris threw the jeans to Dinh.

'They should fit you okay,' he said, and then dug into his bag again, pulling out his stainless steel water bottle. He held it up towards the basket woman.

'You like it?' he asked.

She beamed a thank you.

Dinh came over and sat beside Chris.

'That one my sister number two. Name Puteri. She have daughter, name Suri. Must sell basket Bintulu.'

'Oh, great. She going to Bintulu soon?' said Chris.

225

'Husband die. Killed logging road. China driver, very fast, very danger. No can go now.'

'Why?'

'No man to go with. No safe.'

How perfect was this?

'I can go with her,' Chris said, without considering this was what Dinh had intended all along.

The announcement was made and the whole longhouse came down and gathered around. They were all very happy, and began getting their requests in for things Puteri could bring back. Dinh explained that they had a cousin in Bintulu who would escort her home again, but they had no way of contacting him unless someone made the journey there. This was a busy hunting and gathering season, and no one had the time to spare to undertake the three-or-four-day round trip, so they were very glad Chris had come along.

Dinh showed him the bathing area; it was a part of the kitchen screened off by that flimsy wall of platted palm leaves. A hose carried water to a tap in there from a plastic drum in the ceiling, which was fed from the rainwater tank only slightly higher, so the water pressure was almost a mere trickle. There was a hole in the floor for a toilet, and four black and white pigs grunted below the house, eager to sample what was deposited there. Chris wasn't sure he felt sorrier for the pigs having to suffer such indignation and diet, or for the family who would eventually be eating meat that had been nourished that way. He was glad the evening meal they shared with him was a bowl of rice and forest fern.

Later, Dinh tilted his head to one side and placed a hand against it, indicating it was time to sleep. Chris looked around and realised the mat was Dinh's bed, so he rummaged in his pack and pulled out a spare shirt which he bunched into a pillow, and stretched out on the floorboards where he was sitting. Dinh blew the glow from the wick in the kerosene lamp and then settled himself about two metres from his guest.

The night was hot and the jungle was vibrating with the electric zing of cicadas. An occasional and welcome breeze wafted in through the open hatch on the outer wall. It was carrying faint fragrances of ginger, papaya, ylang-ylang, all mixed with the must of the forest

226

floor. Chris lay there listening. His eyes, open to let the night ooze in, slowly slid closed and a deep sleep came and claimed him.

The sounds of Dinh splashing in his washroom woke Chris at sunrise the following morning. He stretched and looked outside. It was another grey day that threatened to rain again, but no one seemed worried about that. The jungle is called "rainforest" for a reason, and only the really heavy rains of a monsoon interfered with activities.

Time to head off.

Puteri's daughter, Suri, was about eleven or twelve. She was alert and pleasant. She carried a backpack filled with baskets, which was larger than it was heavy. Puteri had a smaller bag which held the more solid items and she brandished a machete. Chris was at the rear, though he looked more like he was leading the group of children that was following them all up the hill.

Where the track that led from the clearing into the forest began, the children stopped. Chris felt like the celebrity that he was as he shook hands with each of his adoring fans. He looked over his shoulder in time to see the determined Puteri way ahead of him. She was leading Suri into the jungle, her machete slashing off the fronds that had encroached across the barely defined path, so Chris slung his pack on his shoulder and scrambled after them.

An hour or so later, they paused for a rest near a trickle of water dribbling over a huge mossy rock. Suri cupped a handful and drank.

Chris dropped his pack to the ground, intending to sit on it till he remembered it contained the basket he'd been given so he opted for squatting beside it. He listened to the water. And the cicadas. An occasional bird call. Then a shrill chatter.

'Monkey,' Suri said in English.

Refreshed, they began their hike again but shortly after, it began to rain. At first it was little more than a mist, but when it intensified to raindrops, Suri broke off two large leaves from a giant elephant ear plant beside the track and handed one to Chris to use as an umbrella. It worked surprisingly well.

How cool is this? I'm a part of a forest-dwelling tribe. Part of nature. A regular Jungle Jim. Phantom – Ghost Who Walks.

He skidded in the slippery undergrowth on the muddy trail and fell flat on his backside. He got back up, only to slip again like a novice ice skater. Or jungle hiker. His pants were covered in wet mud; he'd dropped his umbrella leaf and the rain was streaming down inside his shirt collar. He was twenty metres behind the others, he was tired, he was wet, he was cold. And he felt great.

The rain seemed to ease right when the track opened out onto a wide bush road, but it may have stopped earlier and just been dripping from the jungle trees. The road was a graded, brown dirt with tyre tracks. *Tyre tracks!* Sure enough, from behind them they could hear the groan of an engine as a vehicle ploughed its way up the hill towards them.

Puteri waved it down, and it skidded wildly in the mud to come to rest about thirty metres ahead of them. It was a government requirement that all logging company vehicles must stop for locals. Convenience was the currency used to trade for trees.

Puteri ran to the ute and climbed onto the back tray. She reached down and took the baskets from her daughter, and no sooner were they all seated than the driver took off again. They huddled behind the cab to shelter from the driving rain and wind as the LandCruiser sped along. Corners were a sliding fairground ride. The run-off from the high bank on the right was forming small streams across the road where it dipped. The vehicle bounced into the runnels and zigzagged out of them as the driver accelerated hard to get up the slippery incline beyond them. He was one of the Chinese hired to drive, and he was rewarded for how many trips a day he made so, of course, he drove as fast as he could. Crazy driving. Chris looked at Puteri.

Must be all right if she's okay about it. She wouldn't risk her daughter if she thought it really was dangerous, he reassured himself. Then he remembered this was exactly how her husband was killed.

Down a very, very steep hill, around a very, very sharp bend and there was the camp. A scattering of small cabins and vehicles littering the dirty brown mud that replaced the greenness. Beside the river was a mountainous pile of sawn logs. Logs that were huge trees but a few days before. Trees that used be a forest. Now waiting to be floated downstream for butchering in the sawmills.

'Bloody hell,' Chris mumbled out loud. 'Looks like a war zone.'

Profitable forestry was the Malaysian description of any Orang-Ulu land, and clear-felling meant large tracts could be opened for development. The reward for the locals was supposedly the infrastructure – the forest roads that would allow them to access further and quicker from village to town. Of course, it was costing them their traditional land and the bounty of food it offered them to survive on, but the government argued that they could buy all their needs from the towns once the roads were open. That, of course, would mean they would need to have money, and to earn that they could work for the very logging companies that had destroyed their land. The standard scheme of Progress.

The LandCruiser skidded to a halt and Puteri jumped from it without a word to the driver. She helped her daughter down and they grabbed their packs as Chris jumped onto the mud to join them. The three trudged away from the industry by the river and followed a small path to some residential cabins.

Puteri had a cousin working there. She knew his cabin from previous trips and they sat at his door, waiting till his shift finished that evening.

The men returned and were glad to see two women at their door. They would eat a good meal tonight. While Puteri and Suri cooked, the men played dominoes and drank tea. After dinner, they all simply curled up on the floor and slept.

Around two in the morning, Chris was wakened by someone roughly rubbing his shoulder. He opened his eyes. One of the men was shining a dim torch and beckoning him. Puteri and Suri were already by the door and ready to go.

Following the inconspicuous beacon of the single torch, the party tromped off into the forest. It took them twenty minutes to reach the river they were aiming for. It was smaller than the one the logs were being dumped into, but still as wide as a city street. It flowed down the other side of the mountain. To Bintulu.

They squatted there and waited. Half an hour in the dark. Silence. Then a faint sound of a motor. A bright searchlight on the water. Louder motor. The man with them jumped up and flashed his torch-gleam on and off and waved it over his head. The vigilant searchlight swung to shine on them, and the boat veered to the shore.

It was a longboat with a single cabin that ran almost its length. Inside were two rows of seats facing each other and a crowd of more than forty locals with bags, baskets, pigs, chickens, kids, vegetables, and so on, all sitting in the dark.

Puteri and Suri stepped down into the dungeon, but Chris hesitated.

It's like a creepy tomb in there, he thought.

A crewman asked him for his fare, fifty ringgits, about fifteen Ozzie, and he gestured that Chris could sit outside if he wanted. He wanted.

The boat took off once more, with Chris seated at the prow like some kind of figurehead to ward off evil spirits – or perhaps to act as a buffer if they crashed into a fallen tree trunk.

The wind was cold and he huddled his pack to his chest for shelter. The scene before him was an endlessly opening curtain of grey, misty chiffon that the yellow spotlight tried in vain to penetrate. Gradually, the night thinned and little by imperceptible little, the day crept through. It was now light enough to see the thick stands of trees, right on the water's edge, festooned with a tangle of creepers. Birds, alarmed by the noisy animal that was roaring down the river, clattered to the safety of the sky. The dark green forest eventually thinned, and then there was a garden. A hut. A clutch of huts. A house. And finally, a whole town.

Chris said his farewells to Puteri and Suri. They seemed disproportionately grateful for his supposed protection getting them there – but who knows what dangers he'd shielded them from, merely by being with them and being male? They walked off towards the market and Chris faced the town.

There were banks, municipal buildings, post offices, stores, hotels: everything. He had only been away from a large town for a few days, but the infrastructure suddenly appeared wondrous again. He was Robinson Crusoe getting off the rescue ship and stepping back in civilisation. He felt shabby from his jungle trek. His clothes were dank and muddy, his face stubbled with neglect. His first need was a place to throw his bag down and head to a bathroom.

Cleansed and dressed, he headed out to the streets again. Exploring them meant discovering where they went. Around a corner, beside a river, behind a station, and out of town.

What's out there? he wondered.

The tourist office recommended a visit to explore the Bat Caves at Niah, so off he went. He hiked the trail through the forest till he stood in awe at the entrance of the caves. They were as high as a cathedral, and almost as reverend. As he wandered further in, the darkness welcomed him to share their secret world. Dripping, rusty stone walls. Mosses. Cockroaches by the million. And small mountains of guano bat-droppings. There was a fusty smell of damp sulphur, which he managed to get used to.

When he ended up back in Kuching the day before his flight out of Borneo, his confidence in joining in conversations at backpacker breakfasts had grown exponentially now he had some traveller's tales of his own to tell, and it was during such an encounter that he heard tips of where else to go in Malaysia.

A couple from Belgium told him there was a beautiful island called Langkawi, near Penang. A French guy said Penang was the best place to see the amazing old opium dens. A young German guy said from Penang it was only thirty dollars to fly to Medan in Sumatra and that was where there were hardly any tourists. And loads more adventures.

Once you begin travelling, Chris thought, *there needn't be an end to your journey, only a series of lingerings here and there.*

When he'd flown to Kuching from Bali, the plane had stopped over in Malaysia's capital, Kuala Lumpur. That meant he could get out there on his return leg for a side trip to this Langkawi Island and then have a look at Penang. Sumatra sounded tempting too.

See how things turn out, he thought, ritually stroking his lucky necklace. *It all just sort of happens.*

He counted the nights he'd slept since he'd left Thailand. Seven. Just one week. It seemed so much longer than that. Australia was even further away in his mind. Perhaps one day it would be far enough so he couldn't hear the crashing of tyres flattening a pile of sheet iron. Or the sound of Amaranth's excited scream as she jumped into the wave with him.

Chapter 27.   Col and Ron

Amaranth's "medicine" was increased in an attempt to calm her hysteria about finding the bloodied mattress. She fell in and out of the delirium where she held on to fragments of moments but failed to string them into coherence.

She heard Nina say something to Cochin about how she was getting to be as much of a problem as Dana. She saw Nina's face. Angry. Shouting. Worried.

There was a bald man, she thought. *There was sex. No, that was with that man who had mean little eyes. No, it was him. Well, someone. There was music. Dancing. Was that me? Nina said I was a good dancer. There was blood on Dana's mattress. I had a bag when I arrived.*

The drugs were so effective that Nina stopped locking Amaranth's door at the end of each night and they didn't bother getting someone to install a window bolt. She was guaranteed to sleep till ten each morning, and was zombie enough to be content with just hanging around till she had to get to work again with the evening's guests.

Her clients came and went, but they all recognised she was so out of it that she was like a blow-up doll, and many complained because they had paid for a living girl. Nina haggled the price down to placate their complaints, but she began to see that Amaranth was hardly worth keeping.

'She's costing us more than she earns,' Nina said one late afternoon whilst Amaranth sat across the room. They could speak freely in front of her, confident that in her dormant state she was not registering a word of what they said. 'I could up her onto scag – we've got a whole bag of Dana's fucking stuff still.'

Dana. Must remember Dana.

'No,' Cochin said. 'I keep zat. Maybe I sell it to ze Greek. Or Douglas? He could probably find a buyer for it.'

'I don't want us selling fucking heroin, Cochin. It's bad enough we bought it, but selling it is far riskier.'

Heroin.

'Vell, vee can't just throw it in ze river. It voz expensive.'

'I wasn't suggesting throwing it away. I want to use it on this other piece of shit. I don't like us keeping a swag of smack in the house.'

'It's safe. No one touches ze Buddha in my room.'

'But there's no point having it if we don't use it. It's not a fucking souvenir, Cochin. If we get her on it, we might be able to get her to work with at least some semblance of being conscious.'

'But zen if she makes trouble about Dana for us, and vee are in shit for zat. I like her. On your medicine.'

He looked at the submissive doll that Amaranth had become – merely sitting there, waiting for his instruction.

'You like her?' Nina picked up on that. 'What do you mean?'

'I vood like to keep her. I like ze look of her. Is zat so bad?'

'For you, you mean? So now you want to risk having her as a toy for yourself? And then you'll go and get all hung up on her, just like you did with Lisa, and she won't earn a cent for us.'

Toy?

'These girls are products, Cochin. They're products. We invested in them, we need to make a return. We keep them separate from our personal lives. You know that.'

'Vell, I don't like seeing her becoming... I don't know.'

'So what do you suggest? You want to get rid of her too? We are so out of pocket on this. That Dana business just cost us over ten grand.'

'Okay, fuck it zen. Vee sell her.'

I can be sold? Am I dreaming this? I am, aren't I?

#

Chris walked onto the patio of the hut he had just hired by the sea on Langkawi Island. The broad beach was fairly busy – beauty is usually popular – but only an hour ago he had been pushing through the scrabbling crowds in Kuala Lumpur so he thought of it as a shared isolation.

To the left the beach curved into a long bay. Huts, little restaurants, one hotel, and palm trees. Small, brightly painted, local fishing boats with their steadying outriggers boppled on the ocean. There were also three yachts, each moored about two hundred metres from the shore, two down the far end and one closer to where he was. To the right, it was only a short stroll along the beach to a knoll that ended the bay.

He stepped back into his room and opened his pack. He changed into his boardies, slung his bumbag across his chest like a Mexican bullet belt, and went down to the sand.

Although it was rainy season, the sky was blue, the sun was hot, the water inviting.

Should have left the bumbag in a safe or something, he thought. *What am I going to do with it here? Can't just leave it on the sand. I should've brought a towel, at least I could've stashed it under that.*

He waded along the shoreline of the warm sea. The waves were no more than large ripples. He could see the top of the knoll clearly from where he was. There was a café or something perched up there and a zigzag staircase winding up to it. He decided that if he wasn't going to swim, he might as well check out the top of the knoll.

The view should be pretty good from up there, and I might be able to grab a bite at the café.

The view *was* pretty good from up there, and there was plenty to choose from to eat. He ordered a banana pancake and a coffee, and sat at a table made from three planks of rough-sawn timber. He gazed down at the beach. The sixty or seventy people on it seemed a much smaller crowd from his new vantage point because he could see that the bay was long and the beach was wide.

At the table beside him, a young French couple stood up to leave.

'It ees beautiful, no?' the girl said to him.

'Yeah.'

They left, and two middle-aged men, who had been sitting at the bar on tall bamboo stools, came over and took their table. One of them cleared the empty plates into a pile for the waiter. He nodded to Chris.

'Where you from, mate?' he asked.

The first thing Chris noticed was the familiar accent. *Ozzies!*

'Born Sydney,' he replied. 'But living in Northern New South Wales before coming here. You?'

'Tassies, mate.'

His friend leaned across. 'Identical twins,' he said with a cheeky grin. 'Born eight years apart!'

'To different mothers,' the first guy added, raising his half-empty beer bottle and draining most of it.

Tasmanians sometimes like to get that kind of humour out of the way.

'So, what's a Sydneysider doing in these waters?'

'Just having a look around before I head back home,' Chris said. 'You?'

'Home?' the plumper guy replied. 'See that yacht there?' He pointed to the one in the bay just below them. 'That's home, right there,' he said, as he skulled the last of his beer. 'In that little beauty, you can head home, leave home, and stay home all at the same time!'

His mate reached for his own bottle.

'I'll drink to that, skip,' and he did.

The plump one stood up and gathered his empty.

'Same again, Ron?'

'Same as always, Col. Same as always.'

Col turned to Chris. 'Wanna beer, mate?'

'I'm good. Just ordered a coffee.'

'Suit yourself.'

He left to get the round in.

'Name's Ron, as you probably heard. That mutton head is Col. He's a good bloke, bloody good sailor too. So what's your name?'

'Chris.'

They shook hands to clinch the deal of being friends.

Col came back with the beers and handed one to his mate. They chinked bottles and each took a long swill, as though it was the first bottle of the day when in fact it was already the sixth. Almost together, they each let out a relieving burp followed by an out-breath as they closed their mouths.

'Better out than in,' Col explained by way of offering an apology. 'Bad case of the winds there.'

'Any wind is a good wind to a sailor, mate,' Ron said. It was a routine they frequently performed, as much for themselves as for anyone in their audience.

The man behind the bar came over with Chris's pancake and coffee and cleared away the plates from the Tasmanians' table.

'Very sorry. Very messy.'

'No wuckers, mate,' said Col.

Chris looked down at the sea below.

'Good spot, this,' he said as he tucked into his pancake.

'Yeah,' Ron said. 'We come back here every four years.'

'Yeah, ' his mate confirmed. 'It's a memorial thing.'

Chris sensed they meant it had something to do with a death of a relative or friend. He was uncomfortable probing further, but Col clearly wanted to explain.

'We was sitting here finishing a couple of beers off. The lads were on board our yacht,' Col went on. 'My missus…'

'Who was my sister,' added Ron.

'S'right. My missus, his sister, was on board with my two lads…'

'Alan and Adrian,' added Ron.

'S'right,' Col continued, 'Alan and Adrian with Desley…'

'His missus.'

'S'right. They was on board there. We could see them plain as day. See their faces, even from up here. And then we noticed the tide was going out pretty damn quick.'

'We even said, didn't we, Col? We said the tide was going out too fast.'

'S'right. mate, we did.'

Chris grinned and sipped his coffee. The beers were finally catching up with these two sailors.

'Tide just swept back. Real quick like.'

'Too quick,' added Ron.

'And then,' Col said, suddenly getting solemn, 'that's when we knew what was happening.'

They both looked at Chris, expecting him to know too, but he shrugged and took another sip of coffee.

'Tsunami,' Ron said.

Chris stopped sipping, removed the cup just a centimetre from his lips and held it there.

'Tide rushes away from the shore and then comes crashing back,' Col explained.

'Twenty foot high,' added Ron.

'Boat bottomed out. Stuck in the mud, two hundred metres from the sand on the beach.'

'Thick mud,' Ron said. 'Couldn't walk in it.'

'So we just watched them. Nothing we could do. Boat bottomed out in the mud.'

'Des and the boys looked back at the horizon. They saw it coming at them,' said Ron. 'They knew.'

'They knew all right,' Col continued. 'Des looked right up at me. Even from up here I could see what she was thinking. Then she held the boys to her and that bastard wave came walloping down on them.'

'Nothing we could do, as you said, Col. Not a thing.'

They took a moment to swig their beers. A moment to remember that day. It was why they were on the knoll – to sustain the memory, and to drown it.

'There was people on the beach,' Col said, 'about as many as today. They knew it was coming. They saw the tide going out fast, and they ran. Some of them ran up here where we was, then we huddled like sheep in a pen. Some of them ran inland a bit.'

'Not fast enough, and not far enough,' Ron added.

'There was only the one wave. The screaming and yelling stopped, and then there was this bloody horrible silence.'

'The ocean was all over the land for hours, wasn't it, Col? Up here was like we was on one of them little islands you seen drawn in cartoons. A whole bunch of us and hardly a person said a word. Everyone just watching.'

'And then,' Col went on, 'slowly, the sea just sort of shrank back. The knoll here joined the land again, but it weren't the same. All down there, that was homes and businesses just a few hours before – nothing but mud and wreckage.'

Chris realised his mouth was gaping. He snapped it shut and put his cup down beside his plate. His breakfast was as cold and abandoned as that beach must have seemed.

'What happened to your yacht?' he asked.

'Oh, it was smashed to smithereens. Des, Alan, and Adrian: gone. Never seen 'em again.'

'Never found their bodies even,' added Ron. 'Lost my sister and my two young nephews. His missus and kids. Gone, like that!' He attempted to snap his fingers but they were wet from the beer bottle and only made a pathetic flopping sound.

'We slept the night up here. About fifty people. On the tables, under the tables.'

'On the roof even, remember, Col?'

'S'right, on the roof. Anywhere. No one slept much anyhow. Thinking about what we'd seen. What we'd lost.'

'And whether a bigger one was forming in the night. Come and sweep us all away,' added Ron.

'Next morning was beautiful, but. Blue sky, calm sea. Weird. The land though, well it was pretty bashed around.'

'Looked like a huge muddy rubbish tip, didn't it, Col?'

'Pretty much, mate, yeah. Bits of smashed-up houses, upturned cars, dead fish, dead dogs, dead people. Oh, there was bodies just lying there in the sun. Looked for Des and the boys, but never found 'em. They was gone, somewhere way out to sea.'

Ron raised his beer. 'The ocean claims its own,' he said.

'Everything was as still as a picture,' Ron ignored the toast. 'As clear today as it was back then. I remember thinking as I looked down that first morning before the boats came to rescue us, what if we hadn't come up here for a beer?'

'Yeah,' Chris said. 'You'd have drowned too.'

'Nah, that's not what I mean,' Col confessed. 'If we hadn't hung around having them beers, we'd have set sail an hour earlier, and Des and the boys and us would've all been out at sea where that fucker was just a ripple. But the Good Lord had different plans, I guess. It's not like we knew there was a danger coming. We did what we did and hey: shit happens!' He chugged a mouthful of beer to drown his guilt.

Chris replayed his own what-ifs. What if he hadn't swerved back in Sydney that day? What if those kids hadn't been playing in the tin? Whose fault was it? Whose responsibility? A tsunami killed thousands more than he had. It's the lottery of living. The chance. Simply how it was. It was no one's fault that the tsunami came. Or the kids were in there when the brakes failed.

He recalled the ashen-faced man running towards him on that building site.

'Oh, God, you ran right over them!' he was screaming.

'Oh, GOD,' he was shouting, *'YOU ran right over them!'*

Chapter 28.   Mamasan

There were three strangers – two European men and a Japanese woman – standing side-by-side, looking at Amaranth in the living room.

'She's wasted,' said one man with a distinctive Cockney accent. 'I can't take someone that smashed on a fucking aeroplane.'

Cochin reassured him that she would dry out easily.

'By zis time tomorrow, she vill be straight. She had a very busy night last night. But she is clean and vell behaved. Vee give you some medicine viss her to keep her calm.'

'And what's this "medicine" of yours do, apart from get me busted at the fucking airport? Nah, mate. Stuff it. I ain't taking the risk, which is a pity cause she's a nice piece of arse.'

The other man was a German, like Cochin, but he spoke only English as a courtesy to the others there. He said he could use her. He had a club in Jogjakarta. He held up two fingers like a peace sign.

Cochin shook his head. 'She's vorth fifteen, at least, Heinrich, and you know zat as vell as I do.'

Heinrich remained firm and revolved his hand playfully so his fingers relayed an additional meaning.

'Ach,' Cochin said contemptuously, 'and you are using too many fingers. Viss an offer like zat it should be just zis one!" He thrust his middle finger up at Heinrich's face.

'Three,' the Japanese woman said.

'Three and a half, Cochin,' said Heinrich, 'and it's my final offer, and only because I like her more than I like you, you thief.'

Amaranth began to realise some sense of what was happening. The fog floated in and out, sometimes it was clear, sometimes not. She was being sold, and the German guy looked ruthlessly mean. She pulled her eyes across to the short Japanese woman. Heavily powdered face. Thin painted eyebrows. Bright red lips dabbed onto a tiny corrugated mouth. Almost satirical, but deadly serious. About fifty or even older. Or just looking older.

I hope she buys me. She looks kind. She'll help me get away from all this. That's right, I don't want to be doing this, do I? Hah, I forgot that. How could I have forgotten that? And now I remember that I already knew that, so it was still in my mind. Somewhere. Where do things go when they are forgotten? What are we doing?

'Vot are vee doing?' Cochin said. He looked at the Japanese woman.

'Five,' she said.

'Okay, I go five and a half,' the German said.

'Ten.' The Japanese woman said sharply.

'Ten US?' Cochin said. 'Cash? Now?'

She nodded and tapped her purse.

'I didn't come for games,' she said.

Heinrich shook his head. 'I hope you get vot you pay for.'

'Oh, I think I will,' she said. 'You have her passport?'

Cochin nodded. 'You're getting a good deal at ten. She's worth double that. I'm practically giving her away.'

'I'll take her now.'

She opened her purse and counted some notes inside it. 'There you are: one hundred, one-hundreds.'

'That's a lot of cash for a lady to be carrying alone,' Heinrich said.

'Oh, I'm not alone.'

The two men looked around and out through the window.

'I don't see anyone,' said Heinrich.

'But he sees you,' she said, taking Amaranth by the hand and pulling her to her. 'Now, the girl's passport, please. She fly Japan tomorrow.'

The dream slipped away overnight as Amaranth slept in one of the hotel twin beds, with the Japanese woman in the other.

In the morning she was vague, but it was all beginning to make some sort of sense to her.

She asked what was going on and the Japanese woman explained that she had rescued her from some people who were drugging her and using her for prostitution.

Prostitution? Amaranth looked at the woman and tried to appear neither comfortable nor ashamed with that revelation. *Drugged? Yes, they drugged me. That medicine shit.*

'I remember something about...'

'All in time. How do I say your name? In your passport?'

'Amaranth Vaughan. A-mar-anth Vor-an.'

The Japanese woman repeated it as best she could, settling on "A-ma-ra Vor-an", and then said, 'You can just call me Mamasan. Ma-ma-san. Got it? All the girls call me that.'

'Yes. Thank you, Mamasan. You saved me from hell back there.'

'Do you have money?'

'A little. With my passport in my purse. Did they give you my stuff? I had a bag.'

'They gave me only your passport. So, I will buy your ticket today for you. In Japan I will get you some new clothes and some money. You will be all right. My brother is in next room. Always ten steps away. Watching.'

'Oh, I can't tell you how much I appreciate what you are doing for me. But Japan? I really just want to get home to Australia. I can get a new bankcard there. I think there should be some money waiting for me in Australia by now. Oh, if you have a phone I could use, there's someone I can call in Bali.'

'Family?'

'Boyfriend. An Australian. He'll get me home, I'm sure. If I can just call him.'

'He has ten thousand dollars?'

'I don't know. Probably not, but he'll help me get it, I know he will.'

'No call. I no have phone. You come Japan.'

'I can use the phone downstairs.'

'I tell you no phone!'

'Why not?'

'You come Japan. I have your passport. You pay me back for what I pay to get you free. Not fair I pay and you fly Australia. Maybe never see my money again. Ten thousand American dollar. You give back now or come Japan and I find you work.'

Bloody hell. Was it ten grand? That would take months to pay back. Surely the yacht must have sold by now. I have to call the bank and have my card stopped and get a new one issued, but then how friggin long is that going to take? So we'll go to Japan then. I'll call Chris from there. Maybe he has enough to cover it. Or maybe Dad, if he'll even speak to me. Anyway, one way or another I'll get this woman the money and put the whole mess behind me. What a nightmare!

The plane to Japan stopped over in Manila. All the passengers had to get off and wait in the terminal concourse while the cabin was cleaned. A squat Japanese man followed them off the plane and sat close by without saying a word. Mamasan's ever-watching brother.

Amaranth asked Mamasan if it was all right if she used the toilet, and she went in alone. There was a slim black woman fixing her lipstick at the washroom mirror.

'Excuse me,' Amaranth said. 'Do you speak English?'

'American.'

'Oh, great. Do you have a mobile phone on you?'

The woman looked at her, assessing any threat.

'A cell phone you mean?' she asked with a thick Southern accent. 'Why?'

'I really have to call someone. It's a matter of life and death.'

'This your boyfriend, sugar?'

Amaranth nodded.

The woman raised a sympathetic eyebrow and fossicked in her bag to produce a phone. 'It works jes fine. I jes used it myself, honey. Keep it short, though, it ain't cheap from here.'

Amaranth managed a smile of gratitude as she took the phone and stared hard at it.

'Don't think about what to say, hon,' the woman sympathised. 'Jes tell the boy what's in your heart.'

'I'm trying to remember his number,' Amaranth said.

243

She closed her eyes and then there it was: written on a blank page in her memory. She dialled. It went to his voicemail. She cupped the mouthpiece to be sure her words would fall in to it.

'Chris. I was kidnapped and I've been drugged for a week and terrible things have happened to me. I think another girl was murdered. Some woman came and saved me and is taking me to Tokyo. I'm borrowing this phone from a very kind stranger – I lost mine and my money and everything. I really need your help, Chris. I'll call you from Tokyo. Please…'

The message timed out.

With a smile and a thank you, she handed the phone back to the American woman, whose mouth was wide open; a slight but distinct smear of red lipstick smudged from the corner of it and onto the edge of one cheek.

The plane landed at Narita Airport. Mamasan accompanied Amaranth through Customs, creating some reason why she herself was in the foreigner queue to the officer so she could keep possession of Amaranth's passport.

The taxi pulled up in a small street in Nishi Azabu, a northern suburb of Tokyo, and Amaranth and her two escorts got out. Mamasan led her into a house which was attached to a restaurant. At the rear of the house there were three very small rooms. She opened one door and directed Amaranth in.

'This your room. Work restaurant. One hour, ten dollar.'

'I need to call someone,' Amaranth said. 'To get you the money.'

'You work. You get money.'

'Ten dollars an hour? It'll take me months.'

'You have months. Can't work in that dress. I get you dress. What size? American six, yes?'

'But if there's a phone…' Amaranth continued.

'No phone till you pay me.'

'Why? If I can phone I can get the ten thousand dollars.'

'Not ten thousand dollars,' Mamasan said.

'Oh, thank goodness. How much then?'

'You also owe for air ticket, four hundred dollar, and visa, and hotel, and this room three hundred dollar one week. You want food?

You need dress? I lend you money, but you must pay back. That's fair. Already you owe me twenty thousand American dollar.'

Amaranth shrugged as she was processing that she was trapped. The chemical handcuffs had been replaced by financial ones. Mamasan had her passport. She had no money whatsoever. And now she was heavily in debt. But ten hours a day, assuming that it was even available, would only yield her a hundred dollars. If she managed five days of that each week, she might just have enough to pay her food and rent. It was impossible to repay twenty thousand dollars like that. She just needed time till she could contact Chris.

'I don't give you phone so you call boyfriend come make trouble. You go, no pay – very bad for me.'

'I will pay you. Every cent. I just need the phone.'

'You pay me twenty thousand American? Cash?'

'Yes.'

'Okay,' Mamasan said, calculating she had almost doubled her investment. 'One phone call.' She handed Amaranth her little pink mobile phone. Amaranth dialled Chris's number. Again, it went to his voicemail.

'Chris. I'm in Japan now. I owe this woman money. A lot of money. I really need you to help me. Please call this mobile and ask for me. As soon as you get this. Please.'

At seven that evening, Mamasan knocked on Amaranth's door.

'Yes?'

'Your boyfriend not ring you. You must work. I cannot give you more money. Okay?'

Amaranth nodded.

Just till he calls. He will call. He must be angry I wasn't there to meet him at the airport, but surely if he's heard the messages, he knows something huge happened. He'll call.

She slipped on the plain black dress Mamasan offered her and followed her to the restaurant.

'You don't speak Japanese,' Mamasan said. 'Job difficult. Can not take customer order. Come.'

Mamasan led her out of the restaurant area and into a small room that was attached. She slid the door across and the clamour faded.

'This room for special guest,' she explained. 'Businessman who need quiet. Maybe someone pour a sake. Someone listen to them tell about bad day. Maybe rub their head like this,' she said, rubbing her own temples slowly. 'You can do this?'

'Yeah.'

'Okay. Easy job.'

She sat Amaranth on the couch and left the room. She returned with a small man in a suit. She sat him beside Amaranth and spoke to him in Japanese. She took Amaranth's hand and placed it on the man's forehead.

'Satchosan has headache. You fix.'

Amaranth began massaging his head. He relaxed, and took off his spectacles to invite her to continue as Mamasan quietly left the room.

Amaranth rubbed his temples, then his scalp. She gently pulled at his wispy hair. He closed his eyes and dropped his head forward. She rubbed his neck and worked the top of his shoulders. Twenty minutes. Hard massage. He straightened and cleared his throat.

'Arigato. Genki desu.' He stood up and bowed to her. She nodded a reply and he left the room.

What now? Do I sit here and wait till someone else has a headache? What?

Mamasan came back in.

'Was that okay?' Amaranth asked. 'Did he say he felt better?'

'Yes. He is pleased. You earn fifteen dollars tonight. Not enough for you. Not enough for me. You need more massage, but no have customer with headache. Tell me,' she said, her tone changing to a more serious one, 'what you were doing in Bali? At that house?'

Amaranth looked to the rug on the floor. She was hoping for sympathy, but she got none.

'They didn't pay you?'

'No!'

'Here. You will get paid. One man. One hundred dollars.'

'No way. I don't do that.'

'You did that,' Mamasan reminded her.

'I was drugged.'

'And now you are desperate. One man: one hundred US. I don't run charity house for you. I am businesswoman. You pay me what

246

you owe me, or you work enough to pay me. You owe twenty thousand dollars. You earn fifteen dollars. You eat more than that today! I cannot afford to keep you.'

'Then let me go,' Amaranth shouted.

'You go when you pay or I tell Inagawa-kai. They not allow dishonour.'

'Who is "Ina-go-whatever"?'

'Inagawa-kai is family. Big family. I have Kenji, remember. He always watching. Make sure everything okay for me. He won't let you not pay.'

'I'm going to pay. I want to pay. Just not by doing that.'

'What else you do?'

'I don't know. I just need time to…'

'You don't have time. Time now. Inagawa-kai here tonight.'

'So? What's it matter if he's here or not?' Amaranth said, as though that mattered.

'You not know Inagawa-kai?'

'I don't know anyone in Japan except you.'

'You may know them by other name.'

'Which is?'

'Yakuza.'

Amaranth certainly knew them by that other name. The Yakuza was famous. And frightening.

'Tonight, Miss Amara. I bring you Kenjisan. If he likes you, you can work upstairs. Pay you one hundred dollars.'

She was trapped. The horror wasn't over at all. This was Bali continued. She was afraid and she was desperate. She slapped the sides of her head rapidly, hoping it would knock a solution from a shelf in there. But there was none. Other than the one Mamasan proposed.

Kenji was waiting upstairs. It was a small room lit by three scented candles that floated in a saucer of water on a side table. There was a chair and Kenji had his clothes draped on it. He was lying naked on his stomach on a futon mat on the floor – it was a little wider than a single mattress. His body was tattooed from neck to knee with ornate flowers and reptiles.

Perhaps he only wants a body massage, she hoped. She saw a bottle of lubricant lotion and oiled her hands. *No worse than massaging Scott.* She began working on his shoulders, but he was irritated and flicked her hands off. He rolled over. *Oh,* she thought, *here we go.* She recoiled into feeling dirty and scared.

Kenji handed her a packet. A condom. It was nothing like Bali because this time she was fully conscious. She had agreed to it, yet she was unwilling to be willing. This was rape without violence – and she was both victim and self-perpetrator.

She tore the packet open and pulled out the slippery condom. She involutarily curled her lip up in anticipation of the experience as he helped her put it on his arousal. She smeared the lotion on her hands in-between her legs to ease what was about to happen. She waited for him to move over so she could lie beside him and he could roll on top of her. But he didn't move. He just lay on his back. And beckoned her to climb on him. If she'd been under him, she could've switched off her mind and convinced herself she wasn't participating, but with her on top, she would have to deliver a performance. He was deliberately humiliating her, like breaking a horse in, establishing dominance. It almost made him smile.

It almost made her vomit.

She knelt over him and and then he eased her buttocks into position. She felt him slide inside her as she sat straddling him. Then he pushed her shoulder roughly, and gestured for her to move up and down on him.

Oh God, please, this isn't happening.

She studied the plaster on the wall behind the bed in an attempt to alienate herself from what she was making her body do, but she knew all too well. She had to make the moves, control the rhythm, deliver the pleasure. She hated it, but she knew the better she did it, the quicker she'd be done with it. He just lay back with his arms behind his head. He stared at her face the whole time, but he was expressionless until he suddenly squinted his eyes closed and opened his mouth. He pushed his lower jaw forward in a breathy whistle, and then his lips relaxed into a thin but satisfied grimace.

248

She lifted herself away from him and he peeled the condom off. He sat upright and looked at her face carefully. He decided she needed yet more indignity, and handed her the tiny filled bag.

And she took it. She was surprised how dutifully she took it, she was seething with such loathing and shame.

Kenji stood up and dressed. He turned to face her. She felt disgraced. She was still holding the used condom and he glared at her. He pointed at the rubbish pail and she walked to it and deposited the little sack there. Kenji nodded and left the room.

'One man not enough,' Mamasan said. 'Take too many months. You need five men to pay one week's food and rent. You must twenty-five men, one week – pay me two thousand back. Ten weeks like that. Okay? Better for you, better for me.'

Chris! Call me, for Christ's sake. Fucking call me! I can't do that. I won't do that. I'm not going to do that!

Chapter 29.   Nurlani

Amaranth opened her bedroom door to go to bed for the night. The door next to hers opened and a dark Asian face peered out. A girl, younger than Amaranth, with wet and red eyes.

'You okay?' Amaranth asked.

The girl put her finger across her lips and beckoned Amaranth into her room.

Once they were both inside, she peeped out to the corridor and then closed her door. She ushered Amaranth away from it and over to the open window.

'Car noise good,' she whispered. 'You working here?'

Amaranth nodded.

'My name Nurlani. I am from Laos. The womans here lie to me. In my village she tell I can work in restaurant in Japan and earn more money in one day than one month in Laos. She pay my passport and visa and plane and give me clothes and room, but now I must be with a man to pay her back because restaurant not pay enough.'

'Yes, they caught me with the same lie, I know what you mean,' Amaranth whispered back. 'What was your name again?'

'Nurlani. You?'

'Amma.'

'Oh, Amma is holy name,' Nurlani said. 'You are good person.'

'I try,' Amaranth said.

Nurlani almost smiled, but soured herself.

'I hate what I must do here. Been here more than one week,' Nurlani continued. 'I am married. My husband sick. I wanted work restaurant for money to pay to doctor in Luang Prabang – my home. But now already one week and I still not pay what I owe womans.'

'Same for me, Nurlani. It's a trick. We'll be here, doing this disgusting stuff, for months.'

'I want to leave, but I am afraid of man with tattoo. He gangster.'

'Yeah. He's a gangster. They all are.'

Nurlani pulled her closer. 'And she have my passport. I cannot leave without it. Police will arrest me. Big trouble.'

We're trapped.

'Tonight,' Nurlani said, 'was the most bad. Customer man wanted me to…' she couldn't say, but rounded her lips and mimed a finger being pushed in and out of her mouth. 'I couldn't do that. I not even with my husband. But man angry. Tell Mamasan. She angry. Tell me no pay if not do.' She looked down, still carrying the shame she felt. 'So I did.'

'Yuk! What a bitch!'

'Then she tell all the mens I do that for free to all tonight. She say that to hurt me because I first say no. So she make me… with eight mens.' She angrily wiped her mouth. 'I want die.' Tears poured from her eyes, but she refused to cry out loud in case she howled louder than the background traffic noise.

Amaranth put her arms around her new friend and held her close.

'You have to get away from here,' she whispered right into her ear. 'We both do.'

'Cannot without passport.'

'Then we'll have to find out where she keeps them,' Amaranth said.

'I know this. She keeps them in office. She has safe in bottom drawer of desk,' Nurlani whispered. 'But key is together with other keys around her neck.'

'Well, she can't sleep with a bunch of them around her neck,' Amaranth said as quietly as she could, 'so all we have to do is get the keys from her room when she's sleeping.'

'She's sleeping now, isn't she?'

'She's in there, but she won't be asleep yet.' Amaranth looked at her watch. 'I'll go in at three.'

'You not afraid?'

'No.' Amaranth looked fiercely at her new friend. 'I'm angry.'

The two conspirators sat in silence as time crawled through the dark towards three a.m.

Amaranth stood up to leave.

251

'Wait,' Nurlani said. 'I have torch.' She went to her pillow, pulled out a tiny teddy bear and handed it to Amaranth. 'It has light if you press head. Helps me find toilet in dark.'

Amaranth pressed the head of the bear and a discreet LED light lit up their excited faces.

'Perfect,' she said with a grin.

'Not get caught,' Nurlani said. 'I'll wait at the door, see no one come.'

Staying awake till three would have been the hardest part but Amaranth had been too excited to feel even remotely tired.

Excited is another word for nervous, Amaranth noted the reversal of her usual mantra as she twisted the handle to Mamasan's room.

It opened.

Nurlani lingered in the doorway as Amaranth stepped inside. The aircon was chugging away quite loudly, which covered the slight sound of her movements. She walked to the bed and looked at Mamasan's sleeping face. *Deep asleep.* She looked at the bedside table. No keys on it, just a radio alarm clock and a half-empty glass of water. But the table had a small drawer. She drew it open, centimetre by silent centimetre, and shone the teddy light into it.

No keys.

Nurlani came in to join her. Amaranth pressed a finger against her lips as though her friend needed that advice. They looked around the room, following the soft beam. There was a table by the window with a marble statue of Pu-Tai, the fat, seated Buddha on it. On the floor was a plastic rubbish bin with some used tissues in it. A chair with a handbag hanging on its shoulder seemed the most promising. Amaranth went to it and pried the bag open. No, not in there. In the shoes? No.

She shone the torch to the small table by the window. Nurlani crept across the room to it and carefully picked up the statue to see if there was anything under it. It was only about twenty centimetres tall, but it was quite a heavy marble to lift. Nothing.

Amaranth re-examined the sleeping Mamasan. Surely the keys weren't still around her neck? No, but remembering where Nurlani had kept her teddy torch, Amaranth looked closely at the pillow. There it was: the tail of the chain poking out from a corner.

Amaranth reached slowly down and pinched the end of the chain. She tugged it softly, but the weight of the sleeping head was pinning it under the pillow. Amaranth started to lose her nerve. She looked at Mamasan's face again. Still asleep. She worried that she would wake simply because someone was staring at her, so she directed her eyes to the chain once more.

Mamasan moved. She rolled to the side. Amaranth froze and snapped her torch off. The aircon lulled, but it did not disturb Mamasan. The two girls froze like ninjas in the dim shadow. They waited a long time. Just standing still, and motionless. Then Amaranth stealthily touched the chain again and pulled it.

It moved.

She pulled it a tiny bit harder. It began to slide towards her hand. Then she could see the keys coming out from under the pillow. Then: they were there on the sheet. Just waiting to be picked up. She reached her hand slowly down to them.

And Mamasan opened her eyes.

'What you do?' she shouted, her voice croaking like an old witch. She raised herself onto her elbows and saw the keys in Amaranth's hand.

Suddenly, Nurlani pushed past and there was an awful thumping sound – like a melon falling from a shopping trolley and splattering on the ground.

But it wasn't a melon.

Nurlani was holding the Buddha statue in her hands, its white marble smeared with blood from the head of the woman sprawled on the bed.

'Must get passport before she wake again,' Nurlani shouted in a whisper.

Amaranth stared at Mamasan. Her body was twisted awkwardly, her mouth gaped, her eyes were locked open. Already there was just so much blood. She wasn't going to ever wake up again. This wasn't like the boy on the bike. This time, she was quite clearly dead.

'Come on!' Nurlani hissed.

Amaranth snapped back to action, and they ran to the office. It was locked, of course. She fumbled the keys into some sort of order and tried first one, then another till the lock clicked open. They slipped into the room. Amaranth squatted behind the desk and pushed a key into the keyhole on the safe. It opened and she pulled out a pile of documents and flung them on the desk. They sifted through them, panicking to find their passports. Nurlani found hers, Amaranth's wasn't there. Nurlani looked back in the safe. She stood up slowly. In her hands she had Amaranth's passport, but it was hidden by a thick handful of dollars.

'This will for taxi to Embassy,' she said. 'Here, before womans wake up.' She handed Amaranth her passport.

They scurried out to the corridor. Amaranth glanced into Mamasan's room. The dead woman was exactly as she'd been, her face toward the door. Mouth gaping. Eyes jammed open with shock.

Amaranth quietly closed the door. An extra dose of fear rushed through her veins. Getting caught now would mean far more than being scolded or fined. These gangsters would certainly kill them, but they'd want to torture them first.

They stood still and listened. Had the ruckus wakened anyone else? Where was the supposedly ever-present Kenji? Were the Yakuza still in the front?

The girls crept to the passage door. It opened with the cracking of parting varnishes. They waited, and then pushed the door further open. They peeped into the restaurant. It was empty. At the far end was the front door. They could see flashes of light as cars passed by. They sneaked over to the door. It was locked.

Amaranth still had the keys in her panicked hands. She fumbled one into the lock, and they stepped into the street.

Leaving the door open, they ran across the road and around the corner. There was a taxi. *Thank God there was a taxi!* They flagged it down.

'Australian Embassy,' Amaranth shouted to the driver. 'You know Australian Embassy?'

The driver just stared at them.

'Laos Embassy!' Nurlani screamed.

The driver was blank.

'Okay, airport! Airport!' Amaranth shouted, and mimed a jet plane taking off.

'Oh!' the driver registered. 'Okay!'

'Wait,' Nurlani said. 'What we do at airport? Have passport but not money for plane.'

'They speak English there and there'll be someone who can call the embassies for us. Just go. Just go,' Amaranth urged the driver, with a flurry of small hand gestures.

The driver took off and the girls collapsed together in the back.

'Is there enough for the taxi?' Amaranth asked.

'American money all look the same. I will see how much,' Nurlani said, as she began counting the notes.

'Well,' Amaranth said urgently. 'Is there? I don't want any hassles with this guy.'

But Nurlani was silent. She had stopped counting the hundred dollar bills when she got to forty of them.

'Shit' Amaranth said, when she saw their haul. 'We can just fly straight out!'

The taxi stopped at the airport and they jumped from it. They gave him one of the bills. He refused. Said he needed yen, that he didn't know what dollars were worth.

'This same as ten thousand yen: ichiman en,' Nurlani said. 'You keep. You take all.'

He nodded agreement, took the note, and drove off.

They checked the flight board. There was a plane to Laos at nine that morning and Nurlani managed to book a seat on it. Amaranth wasn't sure whether to go back to Bali to try to find Chris, or to get safely to Australia, so she delayed buying her ticket. She bought a mobile phone and a sim card at the souvenir shop. There was a flight to Bali that afternoon, and two to Australia in the evening. She had time to decide, so she tried calling Chris again.

She got his voicemail.

'Chris, where the hell are you? Did you get my message? Well, don't worry, I'm free now. I got away. Something terrible happened, but I'm okay. When you get this message please call me right back on this number. I'm at Narita Airport in Tokyo. I really need to hear from you. It's Amma, by the way.' She laughed and hung up.

Where the hell is he? How come he hasn't texted back? God, I hope he's all right. What if he got eaten by a shark, diving in Thailand? What if he's just pissed off I wasn't at the airport and he's gone back to Oz? Sulking. Or surfing. I'll give him an hour or so before I buy a ticket home, just in case he's still in Bali. What's the time? Shit, it's almost six. Sun'll be up soon, won't be long before someone will find Mamasan.

The girls had nothing to do now but wait. The fluster, the drama, the danger, all now seemed gone, and with each hour closer to Nurlani's flight, the more convinced they were that they had escaped.

They ate breakfast together, discreetly dividing the money between them. There was over nine thousand dollars. Nurlani would be home with way more than she needed to help her husband. Amaranth had enough to fly back to Australia and to live on until she got a new bank card and the money from the yacht. It was all working out okay.

Until the police were called to a robbery at the restaurant.

Thieves had killed the owner during the night and stolen a large quantity of cash. They were described as two "gaijins", aged in their thirties. One Asian – Thai or Vietnamese, and one Westerner – English or American.

Police procedure was to contact all the taxis working in that area in case they had seen them.

Chapter 30.   Kenji

At eight-fifteen, Amaranth hugged Nurlani goodbye and watched as she entered the departure lounge for her flight back to the safety of Laos. She still hadn't heard from Chris and was pretty sure she wasn't going to now, but she realised that Bali was two hours behind Japan time. She'd give him till it was noon in Narita. If he was still in Bali, he'd surely be awake by then.

At nine, she saw the plane to Laos take off. She felt relieved for Nurlani.

She made her way to the bookshop, hoping to find something to shrink the waiting time. There was a kerfuffle at the airport doors. A small army of uniformed police was swarming into the terminal.

What's going on? Bomb threat? Or... are they looking for me? She picked up a magazine and pretended to be reading it as she hid her face and peered over its ridge at the activities. The police were stopping only Western travellers. Only women.

Shit, they ARE looking for me!

With the police concentrating on passengers actually boarding, Amaranth managed to slip into the ladies toilets.

Now what?

Her phone rang.

'Hey, it's me,' Chris said. 'Are you okay?'

'Shit Chris, where have you been? I've been calling you and calling you. I'm in serious trouble.'

'I'm so sorry, Amma, I was in Borneo so I didn't get any of your messages till I got back to Bali. What the hell is happening?'

'Borneo? Shit, I don't know where to start. I've been to hell and escaped, but now I'm in even more danger. I'm hiding in a toilet at Narita Airport and the cops are outside looking for me.'

'Cops?'

'It's a mix-up. I'll explain when I see you. If I see you. So you're in Bali?'

'No, I left there last night.'

'Shit. I was hoping to catch you before you left.'

The washroom door opened and a male voice shouted in Japanese. Then it pushed wider and two policemen came in.

'Too late,' Amaranth said. 'I'm fucked!' She clicked the phone off and faced the uniforms.

One of the policemen stayed at the door. The other approached her.

'Passport.'

She held it out to him.

'Where flying?'

'Australia,' she said.

'You how long Japan?'

'A few days. If you look at my entry visa there.'

'Why come? Business or holiday?'

'Holiday.'

'What hotel?'

'What?' *Shit! What's the name of a hotel in Japan?*

'Name of hotel you stay for holiday?'

'I stayed with a friend. My Japanese boyfriend.'

'What his name?'

Shit, shit, shit. A Japanese name. 'Kenji. Kenji Inagawa-kai.'

The policeman blanched. 'Inagawa-kai?'

Amaranth still didn't realise Inagawa-kai wasn't a surname. It was the name of the Tokyo sect of the Yakuza, but she saw his reaction. He knew that name.

She nodded very slowly.

Yeah, you don't want to mess with a Yakuza girl.

'Okay,' he said, returning her passport. 'Very sorry to have disturbed you. We looking for girl look a little like you. She with Thailand girl. You have seen them?'

Amaranth shook her head.

'We go. Very sorry. Thank you.' And they bungled back out to the concourse.

She waited a few moments and then she opened the door. She could still see police were checking female Western passengers. They were walking up and down the hall, they were running into the departure lounge and walking back out. They had no idea what to do. No accurate description of the girls. No real clue on their nationalities and hence their likely destinations. They were just swarming there, hoping to stumble on something.

Amaranth felt confident she could go and buy her ticket now. The police had let her go, and if any other of them harassed her, she would use the Inagawa-kai name thing again.

She headed across the concourse to the escalator that led to the ticket sales office upstairs. About halfway across, a policeman approached her, but just as he was about to speak to her one of the officers from the washroom called him away.

She stood on the escalator and looked back as it carried her up. The hall had perhaps three hundred people milling around. Passengers arriving, passengers leaving, people saying goodbye, ground crew, cleaners, police, but her eyes met only one person.

Kenji.

He was there looking for her too. He had been giving his statement to the police at the restaurant when the call came in that the taxi driver had been located, so Kenji had followed them to the airport.

Fear rushed up her spine like a scurrying centipede. She saw that he recognised her. He was standing right beside three uniformed police, but he didn't point her out to them. He didn't want the police to find her. Not alive, anyway.

He moved quickly, but not so quick as to attract attention to his activity.

Amaranth turned and ran up the escalator. Her only chance was to lose him somehow. She reached the top and looked back to see him barging through the people at the bottom behind her.

Got to find a place to hide? Where? Think! She started to run, whilst glancing back to see if Kenji had arrived on her level yet, and bumped into someone pushing an airport trolley.

'Get on the trolley!' a voice said. A voice she recognised.

'Chris?'

'Get on and I'll cover you up,' he said. 'Quick!'

She bunched herself into a ball on the trolley and he flung his jacket and his bag over her just as Kenji reached the top of the escalator.

Chris pushed his "luggage" right past the gangster and headed for the rear of the upper hall. He stopped by a window overlooking the runway and leaned on the trolley handles as though he were resting there.

'So who's chasing you?'

'How did you get here?' his luggage asked in a muffled voice. 'You said you'd gone back to Oz?'

'No, I said I'd left Bali. I got your weird message and came straight here. I was standing just along there, looking down to the ground floor when we were speaking. I saw the cops dashing in. Then I spotted you running up here. Who's chasing you?'

She remained hidden in the trolley as she told him about Cochin and Nina.

'They drugged me and sold me to a Japanese woman and I had to work in a club in Tokyo to pay her back. She had my passport and she wouldn't let me call anyone apart from one call to you. I was trapped. She forced young girls into prostitution and one from Laos bashed her with this little statue thing – she killed her, Chris! That's how we escaped. Now I've got the police and some guy from the bloody Yakuza chasing me. She's dead, Chris. I know she's dead. She's dead because I woke her up getting the keys. It's my fault. Mine.'

'She got exactly what she deserved,' Chris said. 'Don't give her a second thought.'

He told her to stay hidden in the trolley while he pushed it into the male washroom. He opened a cubicle door and handed her his backpack.

'There's a cap in that, and bung on the trackie daks and a hoodie,' he said, closing the cubicle door behind her.

She tucked her hair away into the cap and with the hood over it, she disappeared into being a teenage boy. Her shoes were a little effeminate, but at least she wasn't wearing heels. She opened the cubicle door and stepped out. There was a man using the urinal and she felt very out of place despite her convincing disguise. She scurried out of the washroom, resisting the urge to wash her hands first.

Chris followed her out and abandoned the trolley in the concourse. Slipping his jacket through the straps of his backpack he cocked his head signalling her to follow him into the airline ticketing office.

They went strtaight to an empty counter.

'Can we get two one-way tickets to Australia, please?' Chris asked the girl behind it.

'Wait, wait, wait,' Amaranth said, seizing his arm as he pulled out his wallet. 'No, not Australia. Not yet. I need to go to Bali first.'

'Bali? Why the hell would you want to go there?'

'I have to do something there,' she said solemnly.

'Like what?'

'Make sure that German couple can't ever do this to anyone else,' she said.

The flight was long enough for rest and recollection. After those around them had settled into sleep or headphones, Amaranth pulled his ear close to her lips.

'They had me on some weird drug, Chris,' she whispered. 'It was in the drinks they gave me. They said it was a medicine to stop sickness. It made me, I don't know, just sort of docile. I kind of knew what was happening but somehow it all seemed okay, like it was supposed to be happening, and then there were huge chunks of time when I just totally blanked out. They got me to do all sorts of things.'

'Like what?' he asked as softly as he could.

'I was drugged, Chris,' she said. 'I don't know. I can hardly remember.' She paused and pulled her face away far enough to look him in the eyes. 'They brought men to me.'

'Okay,' he said, feigning the acceptance he knew he ought to have. 'So then what happened in Japan?' He was trying to move over the awkwardness for her. And for him. He was as hesitant to hear her story as she was to tell it.

'I was a prisoner. Some Japanese woman bought me in a slave auction. She had my passport, I had no money. She told me I owed the Yakuza twenty thousand dollars.'

261

'So they got you to do the same thing there? They brought men to you?'

He hoped she would say "No", but she said nothing.

'Go on,' he pushed.

'She said it would be waitressing at first, but then she told me I owed her twenty grand all together. Shit, I couldn't earn enough to even pay her for my room and food doing waitressing. That was her little scheme. Then there was this one Yakuza guy – the one who was at the airport looking for me – she made me go with him. And she said there'd be more. Lots more. But I wasn't going to do that, so I had to escape. It wouldn't have happened if you'd answered your phone. I tried to contact you so many times. I rang you and rang you.'

'What are you saying?' he said. 'That it's my fault?'

'No. Just that it's not mine either.'

He calmed. 'No, of course it wasn't. I'm sorry. And I was off doing my own thing.'

She looked at him sternly.

'Didn't you ever wonder where I was and what was happening to me?' she asked. 'How come you weren't worried when I didn't show at the airport? Shit, I would have torn Bali apart looking for you.'

She had tears in her eyes, but she wouldn't cry. She lowered her voice to the faintest of whispers.

'I can still hear the thud as the statue… shit, Chris, I am now, in all innocence, guilty of murder.'

'No, you're not. Firstly, you said it wasn't you that hit her.' He paused as someone trudged up the aisle past their row. 'And secondly, like I said: she deserved it anyway.'

She escaped further examination by looking out of the window at the cloudbank.

Chris thought for a few moments, and let the quiet soften her tension.

'I'm so sorry. I thought, when you weren't at the airport, that you must've got the boat money and just gone off by yourself or something.'

'How could you think that?'

'I don't know. I'm stupid, I guess. I suppose I thought if you had all that travel money, what would you need me for?'

'It wasn't about "need", Chris. Not then.'

'I fucked up,' he said. 'I've fucked up heaps in my life. I seem to have a habit of making wrong choices.'

'You and me, both,' she said, 'but at least yours don't get someone killed.'

This was that time to tell her.

'I met a couple of old sailors in Malaysia. They saw their family get taken by that big tsunami a while back. It killed thousands. Death,' he said, 'is just a part of a living fluke.'

He took a deep breath and told her about driving his truck into the pile of tin.

'My God, Chris!' she said, clutching his arm.

After all they had each gone through, this was the incident that most impacted on her. She recognised that it contained something quite unique in their litany of horrendous experiences. This one included the opportunity for soul-destroying self-condemnation.

'You couldn't have known there'd be kids in there, Chris. No one would've thought that.'

'Maybe,' he said. 'Except it was my decision that killed them, and I carried a whole lot of shit about that. But hearing the story of the tsunami, or even this Japanese woman...' He paused and drew a breath. '...I can see now that it was just how things go. We aren't to blame if Life places us somewhere in its story. We do what we do, and that does what it does. I am so sorry for those kids, for the Ozzie sailors' family and all the others on that island, but it's no one's fault. Just the way it goes sometimes.'

She nodded. That explanation helped her conscience too.

They sat in silence for a few relieving seconds.

'So,' he eventually said, 'how are you going to prove it to the cops?'

'Prove what?'

'That those Germans drug and sell girls,' Chris whispered.

'The cops won't do anything, even if they believed me.'

'So what's your plan?'

'I haven't got a "plan", Chris. Yet. But it won't involve the Bali cops, they aren't interested in anything except drugs.'

'The Germans have drugs, don't they?' said Chris. 'They drugged you, didn't they?'

'Yes, but I don't know if their drugs are prescription or what. They might not have illegal ones.'

'Then I'll have to sell them some,' Chris whispered.

'Oh, yeah, and you've got some to sell,' Amaranth said sarcastically.

'Not yet,' he replied with a smile, 'but I know where to buy some.'

Chapter 31.   The Free Ride

The police gave up their search in Narita Airport.

But Kenji didn't.

Mamasan was his family. Yakuza. He had her little pink mobile. There was a new voicemail message on it. When Chris had got all Amaranth's messages the previous day, the first one he'd heard was the one she sent from Mamasan's phone telling him to call back to that phone and ask for her. Before he heard her latest message and rang her new phone at the airport, he had rung Mamasan. As instructed, he left a voicemail for Amaranth Vaughan, saying he was at Denpasar but would fly to Narita immediately.

Kenji had a name now. He also had an associate at the airport who could access passenger lists for that morning and tell him exactly where this Amaranth Vaughan was travelling to that day. He could then either fly to wherever she was going and try to pick up her trail or he could call the Tokyo police. They could call the police at her destination. They could arrest her as she landed and extradite her back to Japan. But there would be questions about how she knew his sister, how they had met, and what she had been doing at the restaurant. The backroom business would be officially identified. His family preferred the shadows. Better that he track her down himself. And besides, although Japan has the death penalty, it is reluctant to impose it on foreigners.

Unlike the Yakuza.

#

Chris and Amaranth's flight landed at Denpasar Airport and they proceeded to Immigration.

'Passport!' the Customs officer said.

They handed them across to him and he examined their previous destinations.

'Thailand?' he said, seeing Chris's stamp. 'You have been Bali before and then out and back in. Why?'

'I went to meet my girlfriend,' Chris said.

The officer looked at them both. Her hoodie, their travellings, prompted a comment. 'You know the penalty for trafficking marijuana in Bali?'

They shrugged.

'Life,' he said dramatically.

'Yeah, well,' Chris said, offering an innocent chuckle, 'we're certainy not...'

'You know the penalty for heroin?' the officer continued, ignoring their nonchalance.

They shook their heads.

'No life!' he said, wiping a finger across his throat with a malicious grin, and handed them their passports.

They had no checked bags so they were amongst the first to step onto the footpath outside the Arrivals area. An airport official approached them.

'This you name?' he said, showing them a clipboard with her name on it.

'Why?' Amaranth asked.

'You very lucky. You number one million customer fly. Here – this taxi free, no money, take you your hotel.'

He handed the driver some money and gabbled something in Behasa to him.

'Cool,' Chris said, opening the taxi door. 'So, it's official: you're a girl in a million, hey?'

'What hotel you stay?' the driver asked, as the lucky travellers shuffled on to the rear seat of his cab.

Chris gave the name of the place he'd stayed the one night in Kuta, and they set off into the late afternoon glare.

'Good score,' Chris chortled to Amaranth. 'Lucky, hey?'

'That reminds me,' she said, hauling his little pendant from under her hoodie. 'I brought your good luck charm back.'

'Nah, you keep it,' he said. 'The good luck isn't in the necklace anymore than courage is in a medal or love is in a wedding ring. They're all just tokens of what you already have, and I've got another one anyway,' he said, holding up his wooden Buddha.

'Well, thank you,' she said, slipping it back in the hoodie and giving it a reaffirming pat. 'It sure seemed to bring me good luck.'

'I wouldn't call what you've been through "good luck",' he said.

'It's not what I went through, but where I got to.' She smiled.

Amaranth stepped out from the shower and wrapped a towel around her body. Chris was sitting on the bed when she came into the room.

'I need to buy something else to wear, Chris. I'm tired of being a boy.'

'Okay then, I just need to find an ATM first,' he said.

'No need,' she said. 'I grabbed a heap of cash from that woman.'

'All right then, let's go shopping,' he said. 'We are so cashed up.'

There's that "we" thing again. I like that, they each thought.

They shopped for her clothes, and she opted to keep one new dress on as they wandered on to find a warung to eat in. From where they sat, they looked straight into Legian Road, Kuta's main tourist street. They each had a long, cool fruit shake and a large serve of fried rice.

He put his hand across the table and took hers.

'Hey, you,' he said softly.

'Hey, you,' she answered.

The smile flung them back to when they first met. It's like that moment when you suddenly get a joke or crack a riddle. Click! On!

'Let's go back to our room,' he said.

'I'm already on my way,' she said.

They ambled, arm in arm, along the street thronging with eager tourists, peddlers, money changers, and food sellers. They turned into the forecourt of their small hotel and headed towards the front desk. There was a man in a suit talking to the desk clerk at the check-in. He had his back to them.

But: a suit? Amaranth thought. *Who comes to Bali in a suit? Shit!*

She squeezed Chris's arm and spun him around. He knew something was very wrong, and surrendered to her scurrying them back into the crowded street.

267

'What is it?' he said when they were safely away.

'That was Kenji – the guy who was chasing me at Narita. He's Yakuza. We are so in the shit, Chris. We really have to go to the police now.'

'And tell them what? That some Japanese guy is chasing you because you killed a madam of a brothel you were working in?'

Brothel? Working in? Her reaction to those words was overtaken by her reaction to his judgment.

'I didn't kill anyone, Chris.'

'But someone did, and you ran away with that someone, and you stole a clutch of the dead woman's money. They'll call that "accomplice to murder" or something, with robbery the motive. That's a pretty serious crime.'

'Yeah, okay, all right: no cops. How did Kenji find us here?' she puzzled.

'Free taxi, my arse!' Chris said. 'We should have sussed it. Millionth passenger: so simple. Well, we can't go back to that room. There's a pack full of my things gone! Thank Christ for the ever-present bumbag. Okay, let's keep moving and find somewhere else to stay.'

'And let's be as discreet as possible,' she added. 'In case he asks every desk if there's a girl and a guy just checked in. You book a room by yourself, and I'll slip in once you have.'

It would have been exciting if it hadn't been scary.

They turned down into Poppies Lane, past the souvenir stalls, and tour-booking offices. A short distance after a couple of rowdy bars, they found an accommodation place that had bungalows in a garden setting. He booked one while she lingered across the lane in a shop that sold pirate CDs, and then he beckoned her over. They locked the door and Chris pushed the heavy timber table across it as extra security.

The ceiling fan hurriedly chopped the air into cooler chunks. The sheets were crisp and clean and waiting.

He lay beside her and pulled her gently to him. Their legs tangled but they just held each other. Tightly. She felt secure, not captured. He softly kissed her mouth, but she turned her face away ever so slightly, just enough to let him know it was too soon for her. Images of different bodies pressing against her, their selfish urgencies, their breath stinking of alcohol and spiced seafood. But Chris wasn't a stranger. His body just seemed to fit the shape of emptiness around her.

She turned her face back to his. And kissed his lips. A lingering kiss. No tongues, just breaths.

Something stirred in her, something she hadn't encountered since their last time together in Australia, and it smothered all the murky dreams she'd been having.

#

Someone was scratching the leaves from the path outside with a broom made of twigs. Kenji woke with a start. He was at the hotel the taxi driver had taken Chris and Amaranth to. He had slipped into a sleep while sitting behind the door inside their room, waiting, waiting, waiting. His frustration had been eased away by the Yakuza code that whispered in his mind: the serpent moves slowly, but strikes quickly.

That they didn't come back last night meant that they were either much craftier than he gave them credit for, or else they had somehow discovered he was there.

He considered his options. Inagawa-kai are resourceful. Failure is not an option. He would find them.

#

'I don't think we should stay here again tonight either,' Amaranth said. 'In fact, I think we should get out of Bali quick as.'

'First,' Chris said, commandeering her suggestion, 'we have to sell some dope to the Germans so we can tell the cops they have drugs there.'

'Two things, Chris. One: the cops may not find the drugs you've sold him. Shit, Cochin won't just leave it lying around on the table or anything. And who's to say they won't arrest you as you're buying it? And secondly…'

'You already said two things,' Chris interrupted.

269

'What?'

He counted on his fingers. 'Cops may not find any. Might bust me.'

'Chris. Two things, three things, what's the difference?'

He controlled the urge to say "One".

'The OTHER thing is I don't know how to get to where their place is.'

'What? You leave it till now to tell me that?'

'I didn't think about it till now.'

'But you remember roughly where it is? You know what suburb? What the street's called or, at the very least, what it looks like? Yeah?'

She nodded. 'It's in Seminyak. Next beach north of Legian. There's a motorbike shop on the corner with big blue doors. The house is down a lane beside that. A big house with huge iron gates. Big garden with a pool. About two or maybe three streets back from the beach there.'

'Good. Well remembered.'

'Oh, and there's a hole in the fence we can get in through a neighbour's yard.'

'Perfect,' said Chris. 'Anything else?'

'No, I think that's it.'

'So tomorrow, we'll have a crack at finding them. Okay?'

When he was in Australia, Chris had vowed he'd never drive again, but you don't drive a motorbike. You *ride* one. The next morning he hired a 90cc Honda Sepeda. They strapped on helmets, and wobbled off shakily down the lane that joined the busy road to Legian.

Busy, of course, meant slow. Chris rode with both his feet off the pedals and poised just above the ground like human training wheels. It was difficult maintaining balance as they crept along, bumper to bumper at first, but soon enough the main shopping area was behind them. The traffic eased in volume and increased its speed so he lifted his cautious toes onto the bike footrests.

Seminyak was a longer beach than he had guessed, but Amaranth remembered Cochin had said they lived at the far northern end. Chris steered them along one street back from the beach, then back along the second one. Up a hill and along the third one, back along the fourth. Along the fifth – and there was the motorcycle shop with the big blue doors.

He slowed the bike.

'No,' she said, gripping his shoulder, 'don't stop. Go on.'

He accelerated and they continued down the street past the lane. When they were almost a kilometre away, he pulled over onto the dirt shoulder.

'I'm sorry, I can't do it, Chris,' she said. 'I can't go there.'

'You don't need to,' he said. 'I know the house now: the big one at the end of that lane. I'll come back alone after dark and sneak the dope in.'

He checked behind them for traffic, and with a wobbly revving he rode them away.

Instead of returning south to Kuta, they rode further north. They passed through a couple of villages and then the road opened out into a postcard of terraced rice paddies. Wide green steps with trickles of rivulets. People in conical straw hats, planting rice into the muddy pastures. A kid flying a kite. A bullock pulling a small cart laden with bananas. This was a world away from the stress they'd been under.

The sun was behind a grey cloudy veil but it wasn't raining and didn't look like it would. Chris veered to the left and they headed down a dusty track towards the sea. He stopped at the edge of a beach. There was no one there but them. They left their helmets on the bike and wandered onto the sand. A little way along there was a simple structure – basically a platform made of sticks and a roof of thatched palm leaves. They sat there and relaxed in its obscurity.

'What are we doing, Chris? Maybe it's madness to be trying to get those guys. And I've got the Japanese Yakuza after me too. I was wrong to drag you into this. Maybe we should just let it go and get out of here.'

He said nothing.

'The money from my yacht will be through by now. We could have an amazing holiday back in Oz. Or Fiji. Or wherever.'

'Is that what you want? A holiday?' he said.

'Well, what do you want then?' she asked.

271

'Same as you wanted: retribution,' he said determinedly. 'But you go. You don't need to be here now. I know the house. He's German. She's South African. There's a hole in the neighbour's fence. The Japanese guy doesn't have a clue who I am. Easy. You go.'

She stared at the determination in his eyes. 'So what's your plan, again?' she said.

'Okay,' he said excitedly. 'I'm going to buy some dope then I'm going to sneak in to the big house and stash it – somewhere easy to find. Then I'm going to call the cops and tell them exactly where it is. That's it. That's all. A deal of dope is a very serious offence here. They'd probably cop five years in prison. That'd do, wouldn't it?'

'That, of course,' she said, 'is the same as you'll get if you get caught with it on you before you've stashed it. And even if you don't, there's still the dogs barking when you try to get through the fence. And then there's Cochin to deal with.'

'Deal with!' Chris sat up straight, a new idea visibly registering on his face. 'Oh, Amma, that's it! I'll sell him a whole deal! He doesn't know me. I'll sell him an incredibly good deal, say, half a kilo for way less than we buy it, a deal he can't possibly refuse, and then dob him in. That way, I won't have to smuggle it into his house or nothing, just sell it and report it. Half a kilo is dealing, Amma. Remember what that guy at the airport said about dealing dope? Life in jail. Life! Rotting away in an Indonesian hellhole.'

'And where will you get this incredibly good half-kilo deal?'

Chapter 32.   Blade

They returned the bike and walked around the corner to Kuta Beach. There was the now-familiar gamut of wares being sold along the strip. A mix of voices called out to them.

'Hello, Mister, where you from? Very cheap for you. Sunset price. I no business. You want sarong? Plait you hair? You want massage? Teksi?'

At last, they reached the lane with the shop on the corner. There were three local guys, mid-twenties, sitting outside. As it became obvious that Chris and Amaranth were heading into their shop, they each stood up.

'Yes, yes, come, come. Looking. Looking. What you like?' one of them shouted. The other two were subdued but curious. They watched as the two tourists approached.

Chris stopped just outside. 'I'm looking for the guy with the dreads. Is he here?'

They hunched their shoulders.

'Yes, mister, you looking for T-shirt?'

'The guy that sits here. With long hair.' He twisted his own hair into approximate braids. 'Rasta guy.'

'Ooooo! Rasta?' one of them said. 'You know Rasta?'

Thinking that must be his nickname, Chris nodded.

'You know Haile Selassie?' the guy said, and his mates laughed out loud.

Must be his actual name, Chris thought, and nodded again.

'You know Bob Marley?' the guy continued.

'Of course I do.' Chris broke out into song, 'One Love.'

They liked that. The tall, quiet one entered the shop and, with a tilt of his head, he beckoned them to follow.

Inside, the shop was festooned with sarongs and T-shirts. All Jamaican colours, with motifs of marijuana leaves and quotations. There was a table laden with bongs, pipes, and a couple of hookahs. Hardly subtle, and considering the harsh penalties for the drug, the shop was blatantly advertising products that supported its use.

A curtain at the back of the shop parted and there he was. The young guy with the dreads.

'Hey, my friend,' he said. 'You have pretty girlfriend now. You want Buddha necklace for her too?'

'Hey, man,' Chris said, fondling his necklace. 'Is it cool to talk in here?'

The guy looked around his shop. 'What you think?' he said.

'You had some stuff the other day. Can you still get some?' Chris cut straight to the chase.

'Ah!' the Rasta guy said. He walked to the front of his shop and looked at the lane. He said a couple of sentences to the others and they returned to their seats outside.

'You want to get high, man, eh?' he beamed an esoteric grin.

'Yes,' Chris said.

The Rasta guy pulled a rolled plastic bag from inside the top of his jeans. 'This number one. Smell.'

Chris took the offered bag, opened it, and drew a deep breath through his nose. 'Sweet. How much?'

The guy looked at him. 'It's number one. Good smoke. You want to try first?'

'Yeah. Sure.'

The young guy wondered about Chris. He was not sure about him. Something wasn't quite right. Dealing is always a potential danger. Either he could be an informant, or just stupid enough to attract the attention of the police.

'Not here,' he said, rolling the bag closed and hiding it in his pants again. 'We'll go to the beach.'

He left the shop and they followed. He walked briskly to the road and crossed between a bus, a car and eight motorbikes. It took Chris and Amaranth thirty seconds longer, but they caught up to him on the sand.

'Why the beach? What's going on?' Chris puffed.

'Can see everyone coming. No one knows what we are doing.'

He sat when they reached a part that was theirs alone. The nearest other people were fifty metres away. He spread his legs and took the bag out, pushing it in the sand in front of him.

'What money are you using?'

'US dollars,' Amaranth said.

'Ah, you are the banker!' the Rasta guy said.

'It's one hundred US. Very good smoke.'

'It would want to be for a hundred dollars,' Amaranth said, feigning experience.

Chris took over. 'Can you get more?' he asked.

'Of course.'

'How quickly?' Amaranth pushed.

'How much more?'

'Can you get us half a kilo?'

'Half a kilo? A pound? You mean an ounce, don't you? A kilo is...'

'I know what a kilo is,' Chris said. 'We want half a kilo. Five hundred grams of good smoke, and we want it tomorrow. The question is: can you get it?'

The dreaded guy sat very still and thought. Half a kilo of premium grade was a huge transaction for him to handle. His profit would be a fortnight's worth of risky dealing bag by bag to tourists.

He nodded. 'Yes, I can get. But it will cost you three thousand. You have that much?'

'Three?' Chris spluttered. 'We don't want Ozzie skunk. Just good quality local weed. Sumatra or Aceh stuff.' He was displaying some of the education he had acquired during the couple of months he had spent in Thailand chatting with the other Ozzie instructors there.

'Aceh smoke expensive.' Rasta shook his head.

'Two. I'll have two grand in US dollars tomorrow. That's no sunset price; it's way more than we ought to be paying, but good luck for you. Half a kilo, two grand. But only the good stuff, okay?'

The Rasta guy looked hard at them both, weighing his trust and their determination.

'I will need money first. I can't buy unless I have the money.'

'No way!' said Chris.

'So how can we do this?'

'It's easy,' Chris said. 'You take me with you when you buy it and I pay when I have it.'

'Not possible. I take you to where I buy and they shoot us both, man.'

'Then take me,' Amaranth said.

'I can't take anyone there. But, you know where my shop is. You know...'

'Man, do you want this deal or not?' Chris said. 'We can't just hand over two thousand dollars and sit around waiting to see if you turn up with the hooch, can we? You, however, could go to wherever it is you go and explain you'll be back with their money later the same day or else you'll bring them their dope back. They know who you are and where your shop is. They know that you know what they'll do if you rip them off, so they'll be okay with that.'

'You come to meet me here, this spot on the beach, tomorrow morning at nine,' the Rasta guy said. 'Exactly at nine o'clock. Don't be later. I try tonight, see what they say.'

'Okay,' Amaranth said.

Rasta tapped the little bag in the sand. 'This seventy for all.'

'Half a kilo,' Amaranth said, 'that's all we want.'

'How I know you come tomorrow?' Rasta said. 'Maybe you not here. Come on. Sixty for you because you pretty lady. Special. I have no business.'

Amaranth fumbled in her purse and pulled out fifty dollars, which she then handed to Rasta. 'Keep your little bag. This is for your time, to show you we aren't mucking around. We'll have two grand here tomorrow. For half a kilo.'

'Okay, business lady,' he said with a broad smile. 'Because I like you. Nine o'clock tomorrow morning, with two thousand American, here. Okay?'

'Okay.'

He rolled up the bag and pressed it back into the top of his pants as he stood up. They waited a few moments and watched him go, then they strolled off down the shoreline, only leaving the beach when they were near the strip with all the warungs.

They chose one, and sat at a rear table to watch the parade of people wander past.

'So, two thousand dollars,' he said. 'How much of that are you prepared to lose?'

'Lose?' she asked.

'I'm going to sell it to him cheap to make sure he'll buy it. Say, two-fifty. That's crazy cheap, but you'll lose seventeen-fifty in the deal.'

'I won't lose anything, it's not my money,' she said. 'It's from that woman and I don't want a cent of it and besides, I'd spend twice that to get those scummy people.'

Chris nodded that he understood. He'd never met Cochin and Nina, but he already depised them.

It was getting dark quite quickly when they finished eating. The street was hung with strings of lights and shops glowed their invitations.

'Wanna have a look around?' Chris suggested.

'Sure. What do you feel like doing?'

'I don't know. One of those fruit shakes with ice? A bar or something? Just not shopping.'

The obvious spots were crammed full of rowdy and already drunk tourists. Mostly Australians, interlaced with a few British guys, all looking to score an easy lay. The smaller places were better, they still offered some degree of Bali-ness while serving local beers at only twice local prices.

Away from the main area, they found time to appreciate the feel of the warm tropical evening. They ceased to be visiting there, and began to feel they were living there, that they weren't merely watching the scene, they were *in* the scene. To anyone walking past the little bar that they were sitting in, they would just seem like part of the picture.

But Kenji wasn't just anyone.

He was scouring all the nightspots, looking for exactly who he saw there. His obvious suit gone, in shorts and shirt, his Asian face blended well enough to lend him invisibility to the young couple, but still he slunk into the shadows on the far side of the lane to make sure. All round eyes looked alike to him, but he was pretty sure she was his target. He pulled out his sister's mobile phone and brought up Chris's message.

Then he pressed call, and waited for his proof.

Chris's phone rang. And then stopped before he answered it.

'Weird,' he said to Amaranth, 'but then it's Bali!' He slid the phone back in his moneybag.

Kenji watched them very carefully. The boyfriend looked like he wouldn't present much trouble. The Yakuza punisher now need only wait for the right place and time. The serpent code.

'Chris!' Amaranth whispered urgently. 'Don't look now, but across the lane. Oh my God, I don't believe it!'

Chris was burning to turn and look, but he resisted the urge.

'What?' he said.

'Sitting in the restaurant. Second table from the right. The guy with the yellow shirt facing us. Turn and look very slowly.'

Chris looked firstly to the left, as though trying to catch the waiter's attention, then to the right, and he glanced across the lane.

'I see him.'

'That's Cochin, the German guy,' she said. 'I don't know the guy with him. Most likely a customer, if he already has other girls at the house.'

Chris took another look.

'Stop staring!' she whispered. 'If we can see them, they can see us.'

She slipped across to Chris's side of the table and sat with her back to the lane.

'What're the chances of him being there? You wouldn't believe it. There's hundreds of bars in Kuta, dozens of lanes. And he lives in Seminyak. What's he doing here?'

In a tourist spot like Kuta, the throng is restless. It's constantly moving: bar to bar, street to street. Faceless and frantic eyes pass eyes and occasionally recognise a shirt or a haircut, something vaguely familiar. "There's that guy with the big red moustache," or "Isn't that the American girl from the bus in Ubud?" sort of thing. Faces glimpsed and perhaps recalled, but unknown. With such a churning in the crowd, it is entirely likely that if you sit still in one spot long enough, you will encounter everyone – including the ones you were hiding from. What Amaranth didn't know was that the chances there would be both Cochin and Kenji in the same place at that same time were far more unlikely. And yet there they both were – one at a table in a restaurant, one in the shadows outside. One unaware he was being watched. One watching the watchers.

'We have to slip out of here, Chris. He mustn't see us.'

'Or,' said Chris, 'we could sneak into the shadows in front of the restaurant, and see if we could hear what he's talking about.'

'If he sees us, we'll never be able to sell the deal to him,' Amaranth said.

'Yeah, but he doesn't know me at all. I could waltz over and sit right beside the fucker. He doesn't have a clue who I am. Wait here. Keep your back to the lane.'

Before she could protest, he stood up and went outside. Kenji pressed himself back against the wall, his hand fondling the handle of the knife he'd bought that morning.

Chris stepped into the restaurant. A waiter came to him.

'Table just for you?'

'Yes please.'

'This way', the waiter said, heading towards the tables at the front.

'No. Over there,' Chris nodded.

He sat at a table close to Cochin and appeared to be reading the menu, but his attention was all ears.

'Zis is always vot you get from zem,' Cochin chuckled as he finished his drink. 'I gave up trying to import anything to zis fucking country. Zay hold it in Customs for seven veeks and zen charge me for zat!'

'Too right,' said the man with red hair sitting opposite him, 'you're not wrong, chief.' He had a broad Australian accent, and Chris looked at him. Aged mid-thirties. Short cropped hair. Maybe ex-army. Certainly ex-sports type, his body still holding the muscles you only get from vigorous training.

Cochin glanced up at Chris. 'Good evening,' he called. 'Can I help you?'

'Sorry,' said Chris. 'Haven't heard an Ozzie accent for quite a while now. Where're you from, mate?'

'Fremantle,' the redhead replied.

Cochin was puzzled. 'You haven't heard an Australian accent? Vair have you been? Timbuktu? Zair are more Australians here zan Balinese!'

'Nah. I've been in Borneo. Stayed in a longhouse with a family and had to escort a mother and her daughter across the mountains.'

'How come you had to?' the Australian asked.

'I was the only male not busy chopping trees down,' Chris said.

'Fucking lucky, mate. Hard yakka them trees. Have a beer?'

'Thanks, mate,' said Chris, exaggerating his nationality as much as possible as he dragged his chair over to their table.

The redhead signalled the waiter over and ordered a round of beers for them all.

'So,' Cochin said, 'how long since you vere in Borneo?'

'Couple of days. It's…'

Cochin's face stiffened. 'Shit!' he said. He was looking past Chris. 'Vot's going on in ze lane?'

Kenji had walked into the bar and sat beside Amaranth almost as soon as Chris left. His code insisted he find both the girls who killed his sister, and Amaranth was the only way he'd be able to locate Nurlani too. He was not going to kill Amaranth. Yet.

She had visibly jumped when he sat down. He'd grabbed her arm and then surreptitiously showed her the knife handle poking out above his belt. He'd told her if she made a scene she would have a dead boyfriend with a cut throat, but if she came quietly with him, no one would have to get hurt. He just wanted to talk to her about the Thai girl's whereabouts.

Amaranth's fear had stretched to include Chris. If he got involved in a scuffle, he would surely get stabbed. If she had the chance to talk to Kenji maybe he would let her go if she could explain it was Nurlani who had hit Mamasan. She could protect Nurlani by agreeing she was from Thailand, not Laos. He'd be looking in the wrong country while she would be safe in her homeland. Maybe that was all she need say.

'Why can't we talk here?' she'd asked Kenji.

'Boyfriend may return. Boyfriend always trouble.'

280

She'd agreed to walk up the lane with him. They stepped out of the restaurant and she suddenly thought she could get away if she ran, but Kenji had literally leaped on her, seizing her arm forcefully.

That's when Cochin looked into the lane and saw them.

'I know zis girl,' he said. 'Vot's zat Chinese guy doing viss her?'

The Australian and Chris both looked to see what Cochin was glaring at.

'Yeah, there's some shit going down there, all right,' said the redhead.

Chris was already on his feet. Even in the flurry of the moment, he knew the assailant wasn't Chinese – it was that Yakuza guy from Narita, and Amaranth was really in trouble.

The two Ozzies and Cochin all ran outside. The waiter shouted about the bill for the drinks and that got the barman across the lane shouting about Amaranth's drink tab. Kenji looked at the three men rushing at him. Too many. Have to strike fast. Strike now. His hand disappeared under the hem of his shirt.

'Look out!' Amaranth shouted. 'He's got a knife!'

The redhead picked up a flowerpot from outside the restaurant and flung it at Kenji. It hit his face and shattered. As his hands instinctively wiped the soil and blood from his eyes, he dropped his knife. The Ozzie slammed into him, knocking him down to the ground. But Chris picked up the knife. That was all he remembered doing till Cochin pulled him by his shoulder.

'Come on,' Cochin shouted. 'Let's go!'

Chris stood up and looked at the Japanese guy lying at his feet. A face all smudged with mud, and a shoulder oozing blood around the wooden handle of the knife protruding from it.

The strange company ran down the lane, led by Cochin.

'Through here!' he shouted, as they passed a tiny lane between two older buildings. He knew where he was, and where he was heading. His Jimny was parked at the far end of the lane, and soon they were all in it and he was speeding them away.

Once they were far enough from the scene, Cochin laughed.

'I haven't run so much for many years.'

'Did I stab him?' Chris said. 'It all happened so fast.'

'You stabbed him all right, mate,' said the redhead from the passenger seat beside Cochin. 'You probably killed the cunt.'

'Oh my God,' Chris uttered. 'I'm so sorry, I just sort of panicked.'

'It was his knife,' the Ozzie said. 'He pulled the blade, mate. He was asking for it.'

'Zat's right,' Cochin added. 'It vos his knife.'

'I had him, but,' the redhead bragged. 'Did you see the pot smack him? Right in the face from fully five metres. I still got it!'

He turned to Amaranth in the backseat.

'What was he doing with you, love, anyway?'

Amaranth shook her head. 'He just grabbed me.'

'Oh, you an Ozzie too, are ya?'

'Fuck me, you Nazi bastard. You said this place is full of us,' the Australian said.

Cochin pulled the car over to the side of the road and turned to speak to the group.

'I think vee need to get to know each uzzer a little better now vee are involved in zis unpleasantness. I know ze young lady. Amma, yah?'

She nodded.

'How ya goin'?' said the redhead. 'I'm Simmo.'

Cochin looked at Chris. 'I'm Cochin.'

Did Amaranth ever mention to Cochin that she had a boyfriend? Did he know the name Chris? Better make one up, just in case.

'I'm Ken,' he said, recalling Kenji's name.

'You don't look like a Ken,' said Simmo.

'What's a Ken look like?' Chris rushed to defend his new name.

'Like a fucking Barbie doll,' Simmo said, and laughed. 'Mate, I'm gonna call you "Dagger". No, hang about, you'll cop "Dag" for short.' He spluttered a laugh and looked back to Chris to make sure he was in on the humour. 'We'll call you "Blade" then,' he said.

Blade? Again with the knife thing, Chris-called-Kris thought.

'Lucky for you we was all there, love,' Simmo said to Amaranth. 'So where are we going, Cochin?'

'Vee go to my place. Who knows? Maybe vee have a little party.'

'No thanks,' said Amaranth firmly. 'I've been to one of your parties.'

282

'Now, Amma. Please. Vee just saved your life. I reckon a little gratitude vill be in order. Don't you?'

Chris cut in. 'Yes, Amma. Let's go and have a little party.'

Chapter 33.   Rasta

The tall iron gates were opened by the gardener who was sitting just inside until Cochin returned that night. He pushed them closed behind the car as it crunched up the drive to the front steps.

It was another balmy evening, but Amaranth shivered. She had clear recollections of doing this before, but she also had clear recollections that she had hardly any recollections of what happened after she went inside the house.

And she was doing it again.

All her confidence rested on Chris, and she knew he was making it up as he went. Simmo was an unknown factor. He was an Ozzie and had rushed to her aid in the lane, but how was he associated with Cochin, and what did he expect of her at this "party"?

Nina came to the door as they climbed the stairs.

She looked straight at Amaranth.

'Well, well, look what the cat's dragged in. I'm surprised to see you here, I thought you flew to Japan.'

'I did. And then I flew back here.'

Amaranth forgot her dread as she faced Nina. This time she wasn't drugged. This time she was angry.

'Didn't someone help you to get there?' Nina played. 'Help with your finances?'

'Yes. And I paid her back in full.'

'How very resourceful of you,' Nina said almost sarcastically. 'Or was it from the sale of that yacht of yours?'

'Something like that,' Amaranth said.

'And so now you're just visiting your old friends Nina and Cochin?' Nina continued.

'Something like that.' Amaranth was finding it hard to conceal the hatred that seethed in her.

Nina squinted. 'I don't quite get it,' she said suspiciously. She eyed Chris. 'This the boyfriend?'

'No, zis is Blade. Simmo and I met him earlier,' Cochin explained. 'Zen vee saw Amma being attacked by some drunk Chinese guy in Kuta.'

'So I chucked a flamin' flowerpot right on the Chink's head and we ran off,' Simmo said, avoiding mentioning a knife. 'Funny as.'

'And what was our Amma doing in Kuta at night?' Nina asked.

Amaranth shrugged. 'Just celebrating being unemployed.'

'It doesn't add up to me,' Nina said. 'You left Japan and came back to Bali? Why?'

'I want my bag: my make-up stuff, Medicare card, some clothes, and a diary that means a lot to me. Besides, I kind of missed seeing Bali last time I was here,' Amaranth said. 'But most of all, I'm still looking for my boyfriend.'

Cochin butted in. 'You've plenty of time to find zis mystery man of yours. But first, tonight, vee are celebrating your lucky escape.'

Amaranth blanched. 'What do you mean?'

'From that crazy Chinese guy,' Cochin said, walking inside the house.

'Frying pan to fire, it sounds like to me,' Nina threatened, looking straight at Amaranth before turning her back and following her brother inside. Everyone tagged along.

'Right then,' shouted Simmo, when they got inside the living room, 'you got anything to drink around here?'

Amaranth squinted and screwed her brow up to signal to Chris to avoid drinking anything. She turned to Nina and asked, 'So, Nina, my backpack. Do you have it?'

'I'll check the back room, that's where the housekeepers throw everything. Cochin, get our guests something to drink.'

Chris sat in the swinging chair. 'You got a great house.'

'Yah, it's pretty good. Can I get you a drink, Blade?'

'Don't drink much. Could go a smoke though.'

Cochin pointed to a wooden box on the bar.

'Should be some American Marlborough in there. But please, not in ze house. Vee have a verandah.'

'I got rollies,' Simmo offered.

'Nah,' Chris said. 'Wasn't talking about tobacco.'

'Ah, yes!' said Simmo, rubbing his hands together like he was warming them over a fire. 'Now you're talking. Cochin, have you got any hooch here?'

'No, I'm afraid not,' Cochin said. 'It's actually a lot harder to find zan you vood imagine.'

'I can get it easy enough, but I'd have to wait till tomorrow,' Chris said.

'Good for you,' said Cochin. 'Zen you can get some tomorrow. I don't smoke. Not tobacco, not marijuana.'

'Is that dinkum you can score tomorrow?' asked Simmo. 'Christ, I haven't had a bong in ages.'

'Yeah?' Chris said. 'I can fix that easy for you. How about you, Cochin? You want me to score some for you too?'

'No, I told you. I don't smoke.'

Cochin brought out some beers and handed a bottle to each of them. *Safe enough.* They all took one, except Amaranth. She took the backpack Nina brought in for her and opened it. She fished inside and retrieved the small brown shoulder bag with tassels. She opened it and found her Medicare and bank cards. In the rear sleeve of her pack was her birthday journal. She slid it into her shoulder bag with the other precious documents.

'Everything there?' said Nina.

'Everything except my sanity,' Amaranth replied.

'Oh, your sanity pads,' Simmo laughed, 'that time of the month, is it?'

Chris faked appreciating the humour by raising his bottle to the red-headed Ozzie.

'So, Blade, this smoke tomorrow – how much?' Simmo asked.

'I can get you as much as you like.'

'No, I mean how much?' Simmo rubbed his fingers, indicating cost.

'Didn't you just arrive from Borneo or someplace?' Cochin said.

'That's right,' said Chris.

'And you already know vair to buy some local loco? Zat's a pretty bit fast isn't it?'

'Old friends. I've got them all over the world,' Chris said with a shifty confidence.

Cochin was intrigued. Here was a young guy, so well connected he reckons he can put his hands on any quantity of dope.

'How much for a stick of the good gear?' Simmo persisted, calling the young guy's bravado.

'Can't get a stick, only by the kilo,' said Chris. 'And only the good gear. Five hundred a key.'

'Zat's a ridiculous price. Must be shit,' Cochin laughed contemptuously.

'No, it's actually very good,' Chris played. 'I'm splitting a kilo with a mate, picking up my half tomorrow morning at nine. You boys can try it, you don't like it – no deal. You like it – you can have it for what I paid for it: two-fifty US. I can always get more. What you got to lose, eh?'

Simmo looked at Cochin. 'I'm only in Bali another three days, even I can't smoke half a fucking kilo in three days. Why don't you buy it, Cochin? You could flog it to one of your mates, and make a quid in the process. I mean: two fifty a half key would have to be worth giving it a go, wouldn't it?'

'You don't like it, I'll keep it myself,' Chris pushed. 'Cost you nothing to try.'

'What's in it for you?' Cochin asked.

'Nothing, Cochin. You guys saved me from that Chinese guy, it's the least I can do to let you in on my deal.'

'Vell zen,' Cochin's business mind began some calculations, 'if it's as good as you say, and as cheap as you say, perhaps I take it.'

The rest of the night tumbled into conversations about the Chinese guy's face when the plant pot hit him, how Amaranth shouldn't have been in the lane alone like that, and what it was like in Borneo.

Nina gave up first and said she was going to bed. She threw some large sarongs onto the couch nearest the window and said for everyone to crash over in the living room. She reminded Amaranth that there was a spare room for her, if she wanted.

Amaranth didn't want. She remembered locked doors and thought the isolation from Chris would make her too vulnerable to an uninvited visit in the middle of the night there.

Cochin wanted to offer her to share his bed, but he recognised even slightly over-pushing would likely scare her off.

Plenty of time, he thought, *and tonight zair is too much people here. Maybe tomorrow, after a little smoke, maybe a svim, zen when some of zem go, she might like to stay. I alvays liked her.*

So he played it cool, and left the three Australians to fall asleep, scattered like cushions on the lounges in the living room.

The early morning light lifted their eyelids and peeped in. The previous night's drama lingered in everyone's waking, but no one seemed upset about witnessing an Asian guy getting stabbed. It actually seemed to create a bond between them. Like they had been through a war or something together. For Amaranth, it was one more assurance of her liberty.

When Chris was ready to leave for town, she realised she was going to be left alone in the house with her two nemeses and their male associate, which obviously made her nervous, but she had faith in their plan and she wouldn't be accepting any drinks. Chris knew where she was, she knew he'd return. It would all be okay.

'I drive you back into Kuta, Blade,' said Cochin.

Chris refused. 'I just want to take a taxi,' he said.

'Oh, yes. Of course you vant to protect your source. I respect zat. So, vot time vill you get back viss ze gear?'

'An hour tops should do it,' Chris said.

'Okay,' Cochin said. 'I drive you to ze main street here in Seminyak. You can take a taxi zair. I meet you again in one hour. No taxis please coming to ze house and you carrying a bag zat smells of marijuana.'

Nina took Cochin aside and said she wasn't at all happy about him getting that much dope. She had her supplier of benzodiazepine and some other sedatives. She believed she could always prove those were for her migraines or anxiety or some such. The chemicals were relatively legal individually, but when combined they produced the effective cocktail that she used to control her victims. But half a kilo of dope would make them vulnerable to getting busted.

It would, of course, also make them ten times their investment if cut up into deals. Trouble was, she reminded Cochin, they'd have to be sold as deals, and each sale carried the risk of a bust.

Cochin placated her fears though.

'Vee don't do zat,' he said. 'If it's any good, I sell ze whole deal to Douglas. He'll be happy to take it for say: twelve, maybe fifteen hundred. He can move it at his hostel. All I have to do is get it from Blade, sell it to Douglas, and vee make at least a grand in ten minutes. Easy.'

Nina's right eyebrow raised. 'What if we bought a whole kilo of it, Cochin, and we did that every week? We need to find out where he buys it.'

Chris had two grand cash in US hundreds from Amaranth's remaining Japanese stash. He arrived at the Rasta lane just before nine. Nothing was open. Bali businesses sleep late. He walked across the road to the beach. Cleaners were dragging their rakes through the sand, gathering cigarette butts and juice bottles as they hoped for earrings and coins. Chris walked to the prearranged spot.

The Rasta guy wasn't there.

Hadn't thought of that. What if he's a no-show? What if he turns up with half a dozen mates and rolls me for the two grand he knows I've got? Or what if he does show, sells me the gear and then dobs me in to the cops? Everyone in Thailand reckoned that's what they do here.

Then he saw him. He was walking along the shoreline. Alone. He had a small batik backpack on one shoulder. Chris walked towards him, but as he got close Rasta guy said to keep walking up the beach and stop where there was a rainwater gulley that crossed the sand like a small river.

They sat about two metres apart.

'You have the money, my friend?'

'You have the dope?'

He patted the backpack and placed it between them. Chris slipped out the wad of dollars from inside his shirt. 'Two kay American.'

Rasta guy said he'd need to count it first.

'You understand, yes? It's business. Just put it in the sand where you are and then stand up and look at the water or something.'

Chris did as he was told, and Rasta guy stretched out on his back, grabbing the money as he did. He sat up again and discreetly did a count and inspection to be sure they were all actual dollars.

'How do I know there's a half a key in the bag?' Chris said when he sat down next to it.

'You'll weigh it at your place. I know you know where my shop is. I'm not looking for problem. It's half a kilo.'

'Okay, man. Thanks.'

'Walk along the shoreline with it,' Rasta guy said. 'That way you can see who's coming and you can always swim out with it. Break it up in the water. Policeman can't bust you if you don't have anything on you.' He laughed. 'But it's cool, man. It's really cool.'

Chapter 34.   The Accidental Buddhist

Cochin went back to Seminyak Centre, but it was over fifteen minutes before he finally saw Chris get out of a taxi, clutching the little backpack. Amaranth thought it had been the longest hour she had ever experienced, and not just because it had been almost an hour and a half. Time stretches when you have the time to watch it, but eventually the Jimny came back through Cochin's iron gates, which he'd left open when he'd left.

Chris's task now was to get Amaranth out and get the cops in.

But what do I do? Just ring them? Shit, I don't even know what this lane is called. Does anything have a name around here? What if the dope is hidden when they arrive? And I want to get that Ozzie guy away too. Bit ockerish, but he seems okay. No sense getting him caught up in all this.

They were all out on the verandah. As Chris walked in, he threw the bag back to Cochin.

'Is it there?' Simmo asked.

Nina stood up and went to take her morning shower as Cochin opened the bag and examined the weed. He took a small handful and smelled it, pouting his lips and making a small nod of approval. He broke off a pinch and handed that to Simmo who pulled out two Tally-Ho papers and carefully rolled the sample joint. He smoothed it to a perfect presentation and lit it. Three drags later, he gave his verdict.

'Yeah,' he said. 'Yeah, it's definitely okay. Well done, Bladey-boy.'

Chris sat at the table and grabbed some slices of sweet pineapple.

Simmo stood up and walked around to sit beside him.

'So what our host needs now, mate,' he said in a mock-pleasant voice, 'is to know who you get this from.'

'I can't reveal…'

291

Simmo leaned closer. 'See, he wants to buy this regularly. And in larger quantities. So where do you buy the weed?'

'I told you,' Chris said, 'it's not cool to…'

'See, there you go again,' Simmo said. 'Let me explain the situation to you. How should I say this? Oh yeah: you probably fucking offed some Chinese guy. I seen you do it. Cochin seen you do it. The lovely Amma seen you do it. But we're all friends here. Wouldn't want to have a falling out now, would we? We might accidently tell who-knows-who about what you did. Big problem for you that, old son. So why don't you stop fuck-arsing around and tell us what we want to know?'

'You see, Blade, vee need several more of zeez kilos.'

'And I'll get you more, Cochin. You just let me know when you want some and I'll get it for you and you'll get it at five hundred a key. That's what I pay for it, you can have it at the same price. I won't make anything on the deal.'

'That's not the point,' Simmo chimed in. 'You being such an international jet-setter and everything, flitting in and out of Malaysia and goodness knows where else, we reckon we need to be able to buy this stuff when you might not be around. See?'

Chris wouldn't see.

Simmo put an arm around him in a mock-friendly way.

'Why do you reckon we don't give a rat's about you stabbing that Chink in Kuta last night?'

Chris opened his hands and shrugged.

'I was SAS. Know what that means? I've gutted many a bloke. Iraq. Afghanistan. PNG.' He pulled Chris roughly closer. 'Now a nod from Mr Germany there, and I would be happy to…what should I say?.. Encourage you to tell us.'

Chris was trapped. He banged his hands on the table in frustration, the forks rattling on the plates emphasising his tantrum.

'I can't tell you!' he screamed.

'Yeah, all right, settle the fuck down!' Simmo said. 'There's no need to get all revved up.'

Settle the fuck down. No need to get revved up! That expression and that accent. Amaranth knew it was the voice she had heard in Dana's room on the night she disappeared. The night her mattress was

292

drenched in blood. This situation was far more deadly than she had thought.

Chris's brain was also busy. *Holy fuck!* he thought. *What a mess. If I tell him where I buy it, they might go there before I've had time to get the cops to come here. If they're expecting to pay five hundred a key, when Rasta tells them I paid four times that for a half, they'll know I'm up to something. This guy will probably beat the hell out of me. And then what's going to happen to Amma? She was right. Shit, shit, shit. We shouldn't have come here.*

Amaranth walked to the servery and took a cup of coffee. She could see Chris needed the distraction to have a moment to think. But the moment wasn't going to be anywhere near long enough. She beckoned Cochin over to her and led him back inside the lounge room.

'You are going about this all wrong, you know,' she said softly to Cochin's eager ear. 'It will only make an enemy of a friend.'

Simmo came inside to hear their conspiracy of whispers.

'What's up?' he said.

'She reckons vee do zis wrong. Go on, Amma.'

'We shouldn't be threatening him,' she continued. 'Instead of pushing him away, we should be getting closer. If you cut me in for twenty per cent, I bet Blade'll tell me where he got his big bag from.'

Cochin's tongue played with his front teeth.

'You learned a trick or two in your travels, didn't you? Okay, if you get ze source I give you ten per cent,' he said. 'Of our first sale only.'

Simmo sneered. 'And just how do you reckon on getting him to tell you?'

'I just need a few moments alone with him. To get closer.'

'Oh shit!' said Simmo. He eyed her up and down. 'Well, I'm up for getting closer too, sweetheart. Or do you fancy that little shit, do you?'

'Not particularly, and don't you worry, soldier-boy. I've got enough to go round. But first, give me a shot with him.'

Simmo gave her his go-ahead by thrusting up both of his thumbs, like an excited child in front of a laden Christmas tree.

'Well then, you go for it, love!' he chortled.

Chris scraped his chair as he turned it to face into the lounge room.

'What's going on?' he shouted from outside. 'We were all friends last night. What happened since then?'

Simmo belched. 'We found out you don't share with your friends, Blade.'

Amaranth walked out to Chris and put her arm around him.

'We share everything here, honey. That's only fair, isn't it? Come on, I'll show you.'

She stood up, grabbed her shoulder bag, and walked Chris back inside, towards her old room.

'Are there sheets on the bed?' she asked Cochin as she passed him.

Simmo hooted like he was at a footie game, and he pumped the air crudely with his forearm.

Cochin reckoned this was how she must have paid her debt to Mamasan so quickly. She certainly seemed at ease with her offering.

'Yah' he said. 'Zare are sheets. Vee see vot happens.'

Amaranth ushered Chris into her bedroom and closed the door.

'Come on,' she said quietly but urgently. 'The hole in the fence!'

She opened the window and climbed out. Chris followed.

They dropped to the ground and ran to the fence. She led him along it to the place where it still curled up. The dogs complained again that there were uninvited people in the garden. A woman saw them, but ran back in her house. They trampled though the vegetable patch, opened a gate and ran down the lane.

Chris ran into the motorcycle shop.

'How much? How much?' he shouted, pointing to a bike.

'No for rent,' the startled mechanic said.

'I buy. How much?' Chris babbled.

'No for sale.'

Chris pointed to another, but the guy shook his head. Chris pulled out all his remaining cash.

'Give me all you've got left, Amm,' he shouted. She handed him all the dollars she had left and he fanned it out with his and slapped the lot in the guy's hands. 'Sepeda! Bike, bike! Now,' he said.

'Okay, okay,' the shopkeeper said, flicking through the bunch of notes. 'This bike, you take. You have insurance?'

They pushed the bike to the street and Chris got on. He turned the key and started the motor. He looked ahead at the street. A taxi approached.

'Shit, we could've just grabbed that if we'd known it was coming,' Chris said.

The taxi only had one passenger in the back. It passed them and turned into the lane. About ten metres down, it stopped suddenly.

And Kenji burst out of the rear door.

What? He'd been watching over Mamasan the night she bought Amaranth. The keen-eyed Kenji had been to the big house before, and he'd recognised Cochin as one of the rescuers who would have killed him had the knife been two centimetres lower.

Despite the patched-up wounds on his forehead and in his upper chest, he was agile. And he was furious. Before she could climb on the bike, he caught Amaranth by her shoulder bag, jerking her backwards with such force that she sprawled to the ground. He grabbed Chris and yanked him off the bike, which fell spluttering on its side between them.

Chris stood and faced Kenji, but the Yakuza man reached over and hauled him across the fallen bike. Chris stumbled and fell to the ground and Kenji leapt on him, kneeling on his chest and thumping at his head with clenched fists.

Chris could do nothing but try to protect his face with his hands, but through spread fingers he saw Amaranth standing behind the assailant.

No, babe! Run! He'll see you!

But that's what she wanted. She wanted Kenji to see her because to see her he had to be facing her. To be facing her, he had to expose his shoulder, where blood was already oozing from the ruptured knife wound. She remembered what had happened when she punched the bandaged boy who'd attacked her at Gary's. A hard blow on an already painful wound was so effective. His knees still pinning Chris, Kenji twisted his torso towards her for a moment – the moment she needed to strike him with a small, clenched fist as hard as she could right in the redness on his shirt. Right at the centre of the pain. It was as if he'd been stabbed a second time.

Chris seized the wincing distraction to wriggle free, and with both his legs he slammed Kenji headfirst into the wall. Chris stood the bike up, which was still sputtering beside them, and straddled it. Amaranth leaped on behind him. He throttled it so hard that the front wheel raised a little, even with both of them on it. The motor screamed through a haze of blue smoke, and they hurtled away.

Kenji leapt to his feet and smeared the blood from his forehead where it had smashed into the wall. He ran back to the taxi and wrenched open the front door. He dragged the stupefied driver out and flung him to the gutter, got in, and reversed back onto the street in a wild skid.

Chris and Amaranth were thirty metres ahead. They zipped into a lane and came out on the next street over, but Kenji had predicted the exit and had hurtled down a side street to be almost on top of the bike as it emerged. The taxi tried to ram them but Chris saw an opening between it and a street vendor's stall. He revved the bike and aimed for the gap. His front wheel hit the kerb and twisted his trajectory to the right. The bike sped up the footpath with a loud whine, but he heard the taxi swerve behind him as it spun around to follow on the road.

Chris turned down into an unsealed lane. Dust billowing behind him, he tore along it, hoping it would lead them to an escape route. But there, right in front of them, the lane ended with a small fence all the way across it. It was only made of sticks and string, the bike could easily have smashed through it.

But what if there were children playing on the other side?

He skidded the bike to a stop, dropped it on its side, and grabbed Amaranth by the arm, springing to the wall as the taxi thundered through the blinding dust cloud they had made. It ran over the front wheel of the fallen bike, braked and slid, and then smashed right through the frail fence.

The frail fence that ran along the edge of the thirty-metre drop to the vacant lot below.

There was a tremendous crash. A pall of dust and oily smoke billowed right up to the level of the lane and then slowly, like a sad cloud from a finished firework show, it settled back down. Down,

down onto the smashed wreckage of the taxi and the battered body that used to be Kenji.

Chris hugged Amaranth. Tightly. They held each other till their flustered adrenalin dissipated and the relief that they had survived calmed their blood.

They walked to the hole in the fence and peered down at the wreckage below. Some locals came out and stood beside them. They could all see the dead man lying still on the ground beside the ruptured car. People were gathering around down there. Someone was phoning.

'Police come,' a man beside Amaranth said. 'You come there. We go down. Tell police.'

Chris and Amaranth walked with the man down the steep side street, and turned into the vacant lot where the wreckage was. By the time they got there, they had only to wait a few brief minutes before two policemen arrived in their car. The one who'd been driving spoke good English.

An ambulance came shortly after and stretchered Kenji's dead body away as Chris was giving his statement as a witness. He said they were just riding along when the crazy driver in the taxi came zooming past them and smashed through the fence at the end of the lane above the vacant lot. He reckoned the driver must have been high on drugs or something.

The policeman asked the pair for their passports, and noted down their names. He handed them back, his eyes wandering to the wooden necklace Chris had round his neck.

'Why do you wear this?' he asked. 'Are you Buddhist?'

'Maybe,' Chris shrugged.

'You know Siddartha Gautama?'

'Who?' Chris asked.

The policeman sniffed a contemptuous laugh.

'If you're going to wear such a symbol as fashion, at least know what it means.' He undid the top button of his uniform and dragged on a chain around his neck. Hanging from it was a small silver effigy of Buddha, similar to the one Amaranth still had round her neck.

The policeman shook his head. 'This,' he said, holding up his own pendant with a mixture of pride and scorn, 'is Lord Siddartha

Gautama Buddha. Not fashion, not jewellery. I do not wear Western religious cross or a Jewish star. I do not like how Buddha's sacred image is used as an ornament by Westerners. So, tell me again, how are you a Buddhist?'

Chris paused for a moment before he answered. His mind flicked over the children in the cubby and the fence he'd just refused to smash through.

'I'm a Buddhist by accident,' he said.

Amaranth thought about the statue in Mamasan's room.

'Same for me,' she said, hauling the little silver Buddha out from under her T-shirt.

The policeman's contempt for these two desecrators was interupted when the taxi driver appeared. His face was beaming red from running here, and with his bright green shirt it made him look like a parrot. He clutched his head when he saw the wreckage of his taxi and squawked excitedly to the police officer, pointing up towards Cochin's house.

The policeman slowly nodded and turned to Chris.

'This man is the taxi driver. He says his car was stolen by the Japanese man who was going to the big house at the end of the lane where the motorbike shop is. Japanese man was very angry with you. Why?'

'He just jumped out of the taxi and started hitting me. We got away but then he stole the taxi and tried to run us over. Sounds like drugs to me,' said Chris. 'There were lots of people going in to that house and coming out all crazy and stuff while we were buying the bike. You think maybe you should go talk to whoever lives there? Check out if they have any drugs they're selling?'

'We do not need to be told how to do our job,' the policeman said. The second policeman mumbled something to him and he retorted sharply, as though his duties were a burden that he had to attend to. Reverting to English, he told the two young tourists they should contact the police station in a couple of days to get the details for making a claim for their damaged bike against the deceased driver's insurance, if they could determine it. He closed his notebook with a definitive snapping, got back in his car, and then the whole cabaret ended without bow or encore, leaving Amaranth and Chris standing alone in the dusty lot.

'How much cash have you got left?' he asked her.

'Nothing. I gave it all to you.'

'Let's take the bike back to that shop and see if we can at least get enough for the price of a cab to town,' Chris said. 'I can withdraw the last of my savings if I can get to a bank in Kuta.'

'And I've got my bankcard back,' Amaranth said, tapping her tassled bag. 'The boat money'll be in my account by now.'

They walked back up the hill to the street above, and along the lane again to where their bike was. Chris stood it up. The rear wheel was undamaged but the front forks were twisted and the gas tank was lying separate from the frame. He gripped the front wheel between his knees and wrenched the handlebars to roughly straighten it. It was difficult to steer, but he managed to push it to the shop.

As they arrived there, they could see the police car down the lane, in the driveway of the big house. They knew that Cochin had left the gates open in his haste.

'Vots zis about?' Cochin nervously demanded, as he met the police at his door.

'It was about a visitor in a taxi, but now it's about that,' the policeman said, pointing into the house. The half kilo was visible on the table.

He snapped an instruction to his fellow officer, who then went straight over to the table where Nina and Simmo were standing.

'Nothing to do with me,' Simmo said, raising his hands in mock surrender. 'I don't live here.'

Nina looked at Cochin angrily. She wanted to shout at him and tell him this was exactly what she was afraid might happen, and that she'd told him not to get the dope, but chastising her brother would have to wait. First she had to find them a way out of the mess.

'That's not ours,' she announced. 'It belongs to our guests.' Her voice was steady. Her accusation was definite. She had, as usual, taken command of the situation. The police needed a culprit, and she had one in the spare room ready to throw at their feet. In fact, they could have two.

'Him and his girlfriend brought that here,' she said. 'We told them both to take it away. We don't want anything to do with it.'

'Your guests?' the cop beside Cochin said.

'Yes,' Cochin babbled. 'Zay are in ze bedroom. Come.'

He led the officer to the spare room where he expected to find Amma and Blade in bed, but the room was empty.

'Zay ver here a moment ago,' he tried.

The cop crossed the corridor and opened Dana's old room.

'Perhaps they are in here. Whose room is this?' he asked.

'No, zay ver in here. Zat's just anuzzer guest room. No one,' Cochin replied.

The cop closed the door again. He walked up the hall to Cochin's room and opened the door.

'Your mystery guests are not in here either,' he said.

'No, zay voodn't be. Zis is my room.'

The cop went to close the door but he saw the Buddha statue.

'You are Buddhist?' he asked.

'Zat? No, no. Just a statue. Furniture decoration,' Cochin said dismissively.

The irritated cop walked over to it and picked it up.

'I don't like how Westerners…' he began his complaint, but he stopped to examine the small plastic bag of white powder that fell onto the table from the base of the statue. 'Your room, you said?'

#

Safely back in the mingle of tourists in Kuta, Amaranth checked her bankcard balance.

'Thirty-seven thousand dollars,' she squealed excitedly. 'We can fly anywhere in the world!'

They chose Australia. To get sorted. To make a plan. To relax and feel safe. To start over.

The seatbelt sign pinged on and a soft voice announced they were about to land at Brisbane Airport. Instructions were given for the stowing of tray tables, the opening of window blinds, the fastening of seatbelts, and the returning of seats to upright positions. The cabaret of cabin crew emerged to do their final walk up the aisles, politely checking compliance and gathering rented earphones.

Chris nudged Amaranth's sleeping head from his shoulder.

'We're here,' he said. 'Seatbelt.'

She straightened up in her seat, clicked her belt on, and rubbed her face awake.

The sun glinted in through the portholes on the left as the plane banked steeply. The ocean appeared where there had been sky a moment before. Then there was the broken green coastline with islands and the sparkle of a river. The plane drifted down. Down over a suburban patchwork of roofs and swimming pools.

A flight attendant fastened the cabin dividers back before she took her own seat to prepare for touchdown.

The sun was on the right side now, so Amaranth could watch the runway coming closer and closer. The engines seemed to completely shut off, the plane was merely floating on the air, wafting like a falling leaf in autumn. The tyres grazed the tarmac with a small skid, then a thump, and the engines roared as they strained to hold the plane back, rattling the overhead lockers into applause.

And then: it was over.

With a paparazzi clatter of seatbelts, the other passengers rose to hover impatiently in the aisles.

But Chris urged Amaranth to remain sitting.

'They haven't even opened the doors yet,' he said.

She picked up her shoulder bag from below her seat and settled it onto her lap.

'What's the book?' he asked, pointing to the top of her journal poking out.

'A sort of diary thing,' she said, fingering the top edge protectively. 'I write these little notes to my mum. I've done it ever since she died.'

'That's either really sweet or really creepy,' he said. 'Shit, you've got stacks to write about this last couple of weeks.'

'Yeah, too much. I usually only scribble a couple of sentences to her, once a year on my birthday. Ha: might have to give it a miss this year, but.'

'Why's that?' he asked.

'What's the date, today?'

He looked at his boarding pass. 'Fourteenth.'

'Yep. It was my birthday yesterday,' she said.

'No way,' he said excitedly. 'Well, we have to do something – a fancy dinner or see a band. What are you up for?'

She smiled. 'Oh, I know exactly what I want.'

'Okay,' he probed. 'And what's that?'

'A surprise,' she said. 'I want a whole life of surprises. I really like not knowing what's next.'

~ ### ~

Lightning Source UK Ltd.
Milton Keynes UK
UKHW020750030619
343780UK00012B/1418/P